OSREALACH

BOOK ONE OF THE OSREALACH CHRONICLES

ADRIENNE HIATT

Copyright ©2023 Line By Lion Publications
www.pixelandpen.studio
ISBN 978-1-948807-59-3

Cover Design by Thomas Lamkin Jr.
Editing by Dani J. Caile

LINE BY LION
PUBLICATIONS

To the world we dream of and the world that made us,
And this one here and now.

And to you, dear reader.
Remember, you are the main character in your own story

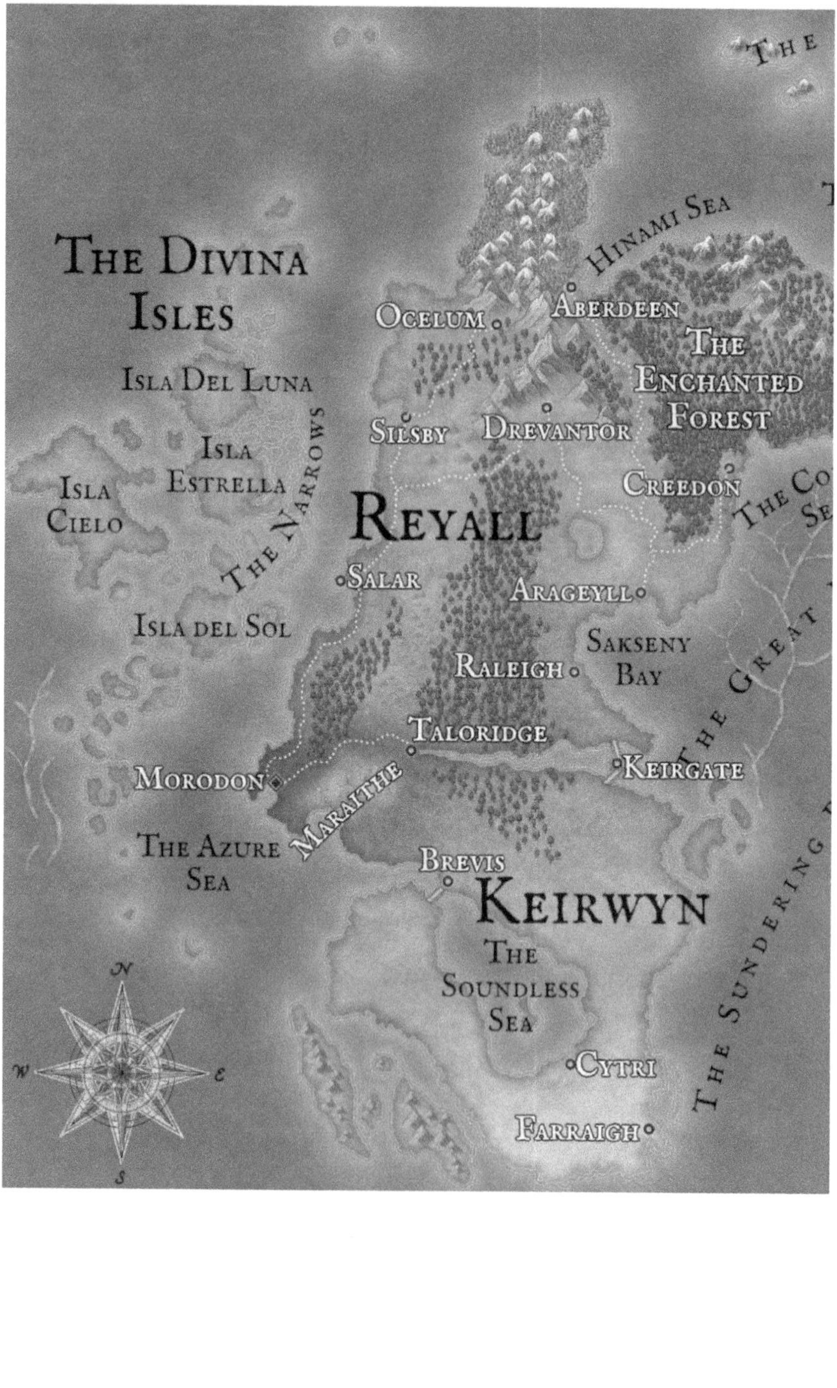
The Divina Isles
Isla Del Luna
Isla Estrella
Isla Cielo
The Narrows
Isla del Sol
Morodon
The Azure Sea
Maraithe
Ocelum
Aberdeen
Hinami Sea
The Enchanted Forest
Silsby
Drevantor
Creedon
Reyall
Salar
Arageyll
Sakseny Bay
Raleigh
Taloridge
Keirgate
Brevis
Keirwyn
The Soundless Sea
Cytri
Farraigh
The Sundering
N
S
W
E

DRAGON ISLES

INBHIR

THE BITTER EXPANSE

FHVIRNEIS

KAILUA SEA

CINNTIRE

DHEIRFUR MHOR

ERE VASAN

BEAG SIUR

COBALT
SEA

REEF

OSREALACH

IRIA

THOIRA

BLUE

TRAIGH MHOR

AZAR
BARAK

CHANTARA'S
TRIBUTE

BHEAR NARAIGH

CEATHAIR ISLES

CHAPTER 1

"IT'S time for bed, love," he said, as he poked his head into his daughter's room.

"But I'm not sleepy, Daddy!" Alice said through a yawn as she sat playing with her toys on the floor.

He smiled and shook his head. "Not sleepy… hmmm... is that right? Well then, I guess you won't be wanting a bedtime story." He feigned leaving.

"No, wait! Tell me a story. Tell me a story! Please, Daddy, please?"

"Only if you promise to go straight to bed after." He crossed the room and sat on the edge of her bed.

"I promise!" She jumped to her feet and hurriedly put away her things and climbed up to sit next to him.

"Oh, all right. Come cuddle close." He pulled up her blankets to cover her and arranged her pillows around them. He leaned back against the wall at the head of her bed. "Have I ever told you the story of Sir Alex and Bucephalus?"

"That one's my favorite!" She snuggled deeper next to him and rested her head on his side. He wrapped his arm around her shoulders as he began.

"Once upon a time, because that's how all the best stories begin…"

XXX

"Bucephalus!" Sir Alex yelled as he raced towards his horse

standing regally in the meadow, wind rustling through his mane. For a moment, the black war charger flicked his ears forward and back, then cantered toward him.

Vaulting himself into the saddle, Alex turned to face the treeline and cued his mount to stop. His heart raced as he took gasping breaths, out of breath from his sprint through the trees.

A massive reptilian creature snapped and snarled as it broke through the last of the underbrush of the forest. Its hide, covered in rough green and brown scales, glistened like snakeskin in the sunlight. Dark, beady eyes, deep-set above a long, narrow snout full of jagged, yellow teeth, locked on horse and rider.

The dragon charged toward them on all fours. Its razor-sharp teeth gleamed in the morning light as its long, forked tongue flicked out, tasting the air. Alex held Bucephalus steady, waiting for the right moment. Letting out a snarl, the monster lunged and slashed at them with its claws. Bucephalus dodged and pivoted out of its reach, just like they had practiced.

Alex pulled out his spear, readying himself for the dragon's next charge. He felt Bucepahlus shift slightly under him as he angled the spear at the monster before them. Alex counted under his breath as he assessed the dragon's speed. He needed to time his attack perfectly.

Alex aimed between its ribs where dark brown and green scales met lighter green and white skin. On a previous encounter, through sheer luck on his part, he discovered dragons have a tough hide, but soft underbellies. Striking their underside, however, was no easy feat.

Previously, Alex had fought several dragons alongside other knights. When he was summoned to fight this dragon, he rushed out without backup, praying this was a small one. He had tracked it to its den in the forest and found this one stood over a meter tall at its muscular shoulder and well over three meters long.

The dragon charged again but swerved at the last moment, making it impossible for Alex to hit his intended mark from this angle. His mind raced as he calculated tactics. They needed to wheel around to the dragon's side. If Bucephalus turned too soon, the dragon would simply pivot with them. If he turned too late, they would be within reach of its claws or teeth, a mistake that would prove deadly.

Bucephalus backed up a few steps and let the dragon close the distance between them. With practiced ease, he wheeled away and lunged toward the dragon's side, sliding to a stop. At the same moment, Alex loosed the spear with their combined strength and momentum and struck the beast in the ribs with a thud.

The dragon roared, toppling to the ground from the impact. Its tail thrashed as it clawed at the offending weapon stuck in its side. The spear shaft shattered. Alex had missed his mark, and the dragon was only wounded.

Alex blew out a breath of frustration and patted his horse's shoulder. "Well, here goes nothing," he murmured and unclipped his battle axes from the saddle. He flung himself off his horse, hitting the ground at a sprint.

Bucephalus cantered forward with his tail raised high like a banner trailing in the wind, drawing the dragon's attention. Blind with rage, the dragon snapped and lashed out at him, giving chase.

Adrenaline racing through his system, Alex fought to

control his breathing. He ran as quietly as possible through the tall grass while trying to stay in its blind spot and dodging its long tail. His steps faltered. For a moment, Alex doubted himself. His thoughts raced with worry for Bucephalus before he forced them away and redoubled his focus. *I can do this.*

Bucephalus turned to face the dragon and reared, kicking out his front hooves in defiance. The dragon roared in reply and crouched to attack, but the attack never came. With a heave of his axe, Alex drove the broken shaft, still stuck in the dragon's side, into its heart. With a grunt, the dragon collapsed to the ground, mere inches from Bucephalus' hooves.

Bucephalus snorted in indignation. Alex's heart raced wildly as he fought to control his breathing. "I know, I know. That was a close one," he gasped, out of breath. Alex wiped the sweat from his face with his tunic hem and pulled his collar up over his nose and mouth. The stench wafting off the dragon made his eyes water. He felt a surge of pride and triumph at their accomplishment as he assessed the lifeless form before him.

Rather than dragging the whole dragon back to town, he retrieved his axe and cleaved off its head. He would need to show the townspeople of Arageyll it was dead and arrange for them to dispose of its body, or whatever they do with it. If left here to decompose, it would blight the entire area.

He ran through what he knew of dragons in his mind. Dragons were mindless killers, only focused on their next meal. They did not discriminate between humans and livestock and could eat a whole cow at a time. Thank the Twins, they were not known to wander far from the forests during daylight unless provoked. If someone was caught out after dark, though, they might not live through the encounter... or so the tales went, anyway. He was pretty sure parents used these stories to ensure their children came home before dark, because most people had never actually seen a dragon.

He shuddered to think about what would have happened if it had wandered into town. After cleaning and stowing his axes, he leaned against Bucephalus' shoulder and let out a deep sigh of relief. "We did it. We actually slayed a dragon on our own." Alex patted Bucephalus' sweaty neck absentmindedly.

He moved to collect the broken pieces of his spear. "I'll never hear the end of this from Bronach." He sighed as he looked at the shattered shaft. This was his fifth broken weapon in so many days. Bucephalus snorted, seemingly in agreement.

Bronach, the local blacksmith from Alex's hometown Creedon, had gifted Bucephalus to Alex when he started knight's training. "I think yer good for each other."

Having ridden his entire life, Alex felt confident as he tried to saddle and bridle Bucephalus for the first time. "Come on, now!" Alex cried in frustration as Bucephalus dumped the saddle on the ground, shook himself, snorted, and walked away.

"Listen here…" Alex protested as he approached him again, but Bucephalus just turned away.

After Alex bribed him with sweet oatcakes and apples for a few days, Bucephalus finally stood still for Alex to put the saddle on him. Every time Alex tried to bridle him, though, Bucephalus simply trotted away.

"Why don't ye try riding him without it?" Bronach asked, coming up behind Alex. He laid a hand on Bucephalus' muscular shoulder. "I never needed one."

Unsure but willing to give it a try, Alex mounted up and

adjusted his stirrups. He squeezed with his heels, asking the horse to move forward, but instead of a gentle walk or trot, Bucephalus exploded into a flat-out gallop, sending Alex tumbling off his back.

Alex felt appalled and a bit embarrassed with himself. "You say he's been ridden before?" he asked as he stood up and dusted himself off. Bucephalus bucked and kicked his heels up as he raced around the paddock.

"Aye, he's just messin' with ye," Bronach chuckled. "Call him over and try tellin' him what ye want this time."

Feeling a little silly, Alex called Bucephalus over. "Alright you mischievous rascal, our mutual friend tells me to chat you up, so let's try again, shall we?" Mounting up once more, Alex felt a little bruised from where he had landed before. "Let's try a nice walk around the perimeter of the paddock... Please?" he added as an afterthought.

As if nothing had happened, Bucephalus set out at an even gait around the field.

"Try a gentle nudge with yer knee or shifting yer weight to give him directions. Ye won't always be able to talk to him," Bronach advised.

Alex did as instructed and nudged Bucephalus with his right knee. Bucephalus promptly spun in a circle, almost unseating him. Alex had to grab a handful of mane to stay on.

"Both of ye might take a bit of practice to learn what the other needs and wants," Bronach laughed, "but I think yer a good match for each other."

That was five years ago. Since then, Alex and Bucephalus had become inseparable. "Alright, let's get back to town and get some lunch." Alex shook himself from his memories. He mounted up and Bucephalus broke into a smooth trot away from the meadow.

CHAPTER 2

ALEX hummed off-key as they trotted along the packed-dirt road toward Arageyll. He couldn't wait to get back to town. He was imagining a long soak in a hot bath when Bucephalus pricked his ears at a sound in the distance.

"What was that?" Alex looked around for signs of the source. He knew of an old farm nearby, but no one had lived there in years. "It's probably nothing, just the old house finally collapsing," he said dismissively, but Bucephalus moved toward the sound, despite Alex's cues otherwise.

"Hey, c'mon. I'm starving. Don't you want food too?" he pleaded. Bucephalus trotted on as if he didn't hear Alex. "You know, if someone heard me talking to you like I do, they would probably think I was crazy." He laughed to himself.

"Stubborn horse." Alex shook his head and sighed. *Fine, what could be the harm in it?* "Alright, you win. Let's go check it out." Bucephalus broke into an easy ground-eating canter.

The old farm was in ruins, just as Alex expected. It must have been many seasons ago the house collapsed. The chimney, covered in overgrown ivy, remained like a lone sentinel marking what once had been. Patches of long grass and brush grew between sun-bleached boards. The barn's roof had long since caved in, and several sections of the walls had rotted away. Clearly, this farm had not been inhabited in a long time.

"See, there's nothing here. Can we go now?" he asked Bucephalus. Bucephalus snorted and continued to pick his way through the tall grass.

There it was again. The sound came from beyond the house. Halfway to the barn, the remnants of a well lay crumbled and strewn about a hole in the ground, half-covered in overgrown grasses. Alex dismounted to get a better look.

"Hello? Is someone down there?" Alex called skeptically. It was probably just birds or field mice causing more of the stones to crumble. He was about to turn away when he heard a voice.

"Help me, I'm stuck!" A woman's voice called back. He recognized wariness layered with the desperation and hope in her tone.

He stepped back in surprise. There really was someone down there. *Why am I standing here gaping?* He scolded himself. *Someone is stuck in a well, and they need my help.*

"If I toss a rope down to you, do you think you can climb out?"

"Yes, I believe so," she replied weakly.

Alex quickly retrieved the rope from his saddlebags, tied it to his saddle, and threw the other end into the well. When the rope pulled tautly, he asked Bucephalus to back up to help pull her out of the old well.

The woman's head and shoulders, caked in mud and slime, appeared over the edge of the well. Dead leaves clung to her hair. The reek of rotting leaves and stagnant water made Alex cough and his eyes water. She scrambled for purchase on the grass with one hand while clinging to the rope with the other. Her hands were shackled together with heavy chains.

Alex reached out to help her up, but the edge of the well crumbled out from under her and she slid backward. He lunged to grab her arm, but his hand slipped on the mud. His fingers snagged the chain between her wrists, but he lost his balance and toppled forward into the widening hole.

He grunted as he caught hold of the rope still tied to his saddle with his other hand. His legs and torso slammed into the side of the rock.

"Bucephalus, back!" he cried, as he slid further into the opening of the well as more ground gave way under his weight. Alex hung from his left hand, clenched around the rope above him. His arm and shoulder protested at the sudden strain. His right hand gripped the chain between her wrists. He grit his teeth and hoped his mud-slick hands would hold on to the chain long enough for Bucephalus to pull them out. The woman dangled below him by her wrists; pain written on her muddy features.

Bucephalus snorted and dug in. His hooves made deep tracks in the ground, soft from the recent rains. Slowly, Alex and the woman slid out of the well. This wasn't the first time Alex was thankful Bucephalus was every inch of his 18-hands, destrier frame. He was powerful, yet agile, proving his versatility repeatedly over the years. Alex would make sure Bucephalus received extra grain tonight as a reward.

"That's it. Good boy. Keep going," he encouraged. When Bucephalus had pulled them far enough away from the well that they would not chance falling in again, Alex climbed to his feet and helped the woman to her feet as well.

"Are you injured? How did you get down there?" he asked her. His heart raced from the excitement.

"I am fine." She wiped her hands on her dress. "I was abducted by bandits and they abandoned me down there when the land dragon attacked their camp. We should go. If it did not kill them, they will most likely be back."

She stood a hand shorter than Alex. Her long, tangled

hair was matted with leaves and twigs. She wore a simple, torn and muddy dress that hung off her lean frame like it was meant for a much larger person. She carried herself with poise that contradicted her appearance and her fiery, turquoise eyes were unlike any he had seen. They reminded him of the sea at midday, in his favorite cove near his hometown. Alex looked at her shackles, noting caked blood mixed with the dirt coating her wrists.

"Those monsters. How dare they treat anyone this way! Hold on. I have something I can use to cut the bolts." He rifled through his saddlebags and pulled out Bronach's pincers, which he had borrowed. They were primarily used to trim Bucephalus' unshod feet when they got chewed up on the road. He cut through the bolts, and they dropped to the ground with a metallic thud.

"Here. Let me treat your wounds, or at least take you as far as Arageyll." Alex stepped toward his saddlebags to retrieve his supplies.

"No. I will find my own way," She said resolutely. She turned to rest her hand on Bucephalus' neck. "How can I thank you? I owe you a life debt."

Alex repacked his rope and pincers, then gave a slight bow. "No thanks needed, M'lady. We were happy to help." He mounted up and rested his hands on the pommel. "If we may not have the honor of escorting you, then I will leave you with a traveler's blessing from my village: May your road be kind and your troubles few. May the storm clouds part, and your skies be blue." He waved farewell and cued Bucephalus into a trot toward the road.

As he trotted away, she whispered into the wind, "May

your waters be calm, and your sight be true, 'til your journey's end and destiny finds you."

CHAPTER 3

HE watched Alice sleep and listened to his daughter's slow, even breaths as she lay, curled up next to him. He stayed a few moments longer, stroking her hair, simply enjoying her presence.

> *"May your road be kind and your troubles few,*
> *May your storm clouds part and your skies be blue,*
> *May your burdens be light and your sight be true,*
> *May your waters be calm and your strength renew,*
> *May your hopes be realized and your dreams come true...*
> *But, 'til your journey's end, adventure awaits you."*

He smiled fondly at their nightly routine. After his declaration of bedtime, she'd respond she wasn't tired, begging for more adventures of Sir Alex and Bucephalus or occasionally of Sir Thomas and the Mouse. He would oblige, and she would drift asleep to the sound of his voice.

Not wanting to wake her, he slowly extricated himself from her tangle of limbs and slid off the bed. "I love you, little one. Sweet dreams," he whispered. Kissing her hair affectionately, he tucked her in and padded quietly to the door.

The next morning, Alice came bounding in as he prepared breakfast. "Will you tell me more of the story with Alex and Bucephalus over breakfast, please?" she asked, looking up at him with a hopeful expression. "I promise to help clean up and do the dishes," she added.

"And brush your teeth?" he asked, watching her from the corner of his eye as he continued to wash and cut the array of colorful fruit in front of him.

"Yes, I'll brush my teeth too, I promise!" She grinned as she took a seat on a tall stool across from him. She rested her chin in her hands and looked up at him expectantly.

Chuckling under his breath, he cleared his throat and began where he had left off the night before.

✗✗✗

"Get that disgusting thing out of my sight at once!" Garlow shrieked.

Alex stood awkwardly in the middle of the town hall, holding the dragon's head, uncertain of what to do with it. One of the house servants appeared at his side with a sack to put it in and then quickly disappeared with it. Garlow was the nobleman currently charged with overseeing the daily affairs of Arageyll. He was short and thin, with wispy hair, a sharp nose, and bulging eyes that were too big for his face. Alex had just reported his encounter, finishing by holding up the dragon's head. "Why would you think to bring it in here?" Garlow demanded, his face red and splotchy with outrage.

"The gate guard instructed me to present it to you to get paid for slaying it," Alex replied with confusion.

"You slew it? You mean to say you slew a dragon all by yourself and have not even a scratch on you? I find that hard to believe." Garlow sneered incredulously, looking Alex up and down.

"Yes, Nobleman, I did. I have the broken pieces of my spear to prove it, too." Alex said, trying to contain his frustration.

"We sent a group of thirty men to fight that dragon. Those that came back were severely wounded! You will not swindle me or the good townsfolk of Arageyll with your tall tales." Garlow practically spat at him.

Alex tried to protest further, but Garlow cut him off. "I will not pay you for what you didn't do! Now get out!" Garlow's voice had risen to shrill levels.

Alex stormed out of the hall, furious. *The nerve, calling me a liar! How dare he?* Alex was outraged, but if he were being honest with himself, he was not actually surprised. Of course, they couldn't believe he could single-handedly slay a giant monster plaguing the surrounding area. That would be crazy, right? Except he had done it.

He sighed and stalked through town, lost in his thoughts. Almost running into the corner of a building, Alex found the Pot & Kettle Inn. The large double-level building was made of roughhewn beams latticed so they fit tightly together and the cracks filled in with a mud putty meant to keep the warmth in and the damp cold out. He was hungry, but didn't know how he was going to pay for food, let alone the stable fare, since Nobleman Garlow had refused to pay him.

As he walked in, he saw a few townsfolk and several other knights sitting around tables in groups or alone. The smell of hearty stew and fresh bread made his mouth water and his stomach grumble.

"Barkeep, another round!" one of the knights yelled, holding his mug in the air.

"Leave yer weapons at the door, sit where ye like, and I'll be right with ye," the balding man in an apron behind the counter said to Alex. Setting his bag down on the floor, Alex took a seat at the bar. After pouring another round for the knights, he lumbered over to Alex. "What'll ye have then?" The bartender asked as he dried his hands on his apron.

"Whatever it is that smells so good and some bread,

please," Alex answered. "Oh, and some hot cider; if you have any," he added.

"Aye. Will ye be staying the night as well?" the bartender asked.

"No, thank you. I'll sleep in the stable with my horse," Alex said. The bartender shook his head.

"To each his own, I guess. The name's Brodney. And ye are?" he asked.

"Alex. It's a pleasure to make your acquaintance, Brodney." Alex nodded to him.

Brodney grunted and left through the doorway into the kitchen, muttering to himself, "At least this one seems to have manners."

Alex took a moment to survey the other patrons in the inn. There was a group of four knights sitting at a table in the middle of the room, engaged in an intense conversation. Alex recognized two of their faces from Summits in Aberdeen, but didn't know their names. There were two men against the far wall quietly eating their stew. Down the bar from Alex sat a few scattered individuals, intent on their meal and ignoring everything going on around them. In the corner, a lone, hooded figure hunched over a steaming mug. This struck Alex as odd, since the room was quite warm. The stranger had to be sweltering under that thick cloak.

Before Alex could puzzle further, Brodney returned with a steaming bowl of stew, a large roll, and a mug so full it was spilling over the rim. He set them in front of Alex and as if on cue, Alex's stomach growled loudly.

"Thank you, Brodney." He tore the roll in two and dipped it in the dark broth. The mushrooms and potatoes had been simmered in the broth for many hours and had soaked up its rich flavor. The meat was tender and melted in his mouth, needing very little chewing. It was simply delicious. Alex tried savoring it as he ate, but in a few minutes, it was gone.

"I would think ye haven't seen a proper meal in a week by the way ye devour yer food." Brodney chuckled as Alex finished wiping his bowl with the last of his roll. "What are ye in town fer? Just passing through, or are ye here to join those crazy knights in their hunt fer the menace of a dragon?" he asked Alex.

Alex frowned, still bitter over his conversation with the nobleman. "Just passing through," he finally answered. "I... already killed it," he added, barely above a whisper.

Brodney stopped and looked at him with a startled expression. He studied Alex's face, deciding whether or not to believe him. "You killed a dragon.. All by yourself?" he asked incredulously.

"This lad? Fight a dragon?" One of the knights laughed cruelly. "Did you hear that, Cole?" He yelled over the din in the room.

Alex was startled; he had not noticed the knight come up behind him.

"Aye, Fintan," Cole replied noncommittally to his comrade.

"So you think you are good enough to fight with us? We'll let you tag along and show you how it's done." Sir Fintan smirked and sauntered back to his seat.

"No thank you, I'll pass," Alex replied after a moment, taking another sip from his mug.

"What? Is our profession not good enough for you?"

Fintan sneered.

"No, I personally enjoy hunting dragons, but I'd probably prefer their company to yours," Alex quipped. As the words came out of his mouth, he knew he should have held his tongue, but it was too late now.

"Who are you to come in here saying you can kill a dragon single-handedly?" Fintan bellowed as he rose from his chair, sending it crashing over backward.

The other three knights remained seated, but were no longer lounging. They watched the conversation unfolding intently. The rest of the room went silent.

"Well, if you must know, my name is Sir Alexander of Creedon," Alex said.

"Oh, so you are *that* knight. From what I hear, you're not a knight at all. Just because you paid or threatened someone to say you are a knight, doesn't make you one." Fintan spat at him.

Alex bristled at the insinuation, but knew better than to respond. Fighting back would only provoke him further.

"Why don't you go back home to your little backwater town and leave the real protecting to actual knights." Fintan continued.

"When I find one, I'll ask him," the hooded stranger in the corner interrupted with a smooth, masculine voice. He rose from his table in the corner, chair legs scraping against the floor. "All I have seen you do is swagger around, ordering people to do your bidding and disrespecting anyone you believe to be less important than yourself. You are a disgrace to your order," the stranger continued.

Fintan sputtered incoherently. Suddenly, Fintan moved towards the weapons rack, but before making it halfway, the stranger appeared behind him with a knife to his throat.

"I wouldn't do that if I were you," the stranger said in a low voice. "We wouldn't want to embarrass you in front of your companions, so I'd advise you to go sit down and finish your meal."

Fintan turned to punch the hooded figure, but his opponent caught his arm and twisted it behind his back before flipping him over his head and throwing him to the floor. The stranger knelt on Fintan's chest with a boot, pinning his other hand to the floor; his knife still to the man's neck. The room went silent, waiting with bated breath for what would happen next.

"I think it is time for us to leave," Cole said, rising from his chair. "I apologize for my companion's bad manners and conduct. He will be reprimanded accordingly," he said to Brodney and the rest of the room. "Fintan, on your feet. Let's go." He strode to the door.

The stranger stood and prowled to the bar, never turning his back to Fintan or the other knights. Fintan made a show of getting up and dusting himself off. The other two knights dropped coins on the table to pay for their meal. They kept their heads down as they collected their weapons and left without another word. Fintan glared at Alex and the stranger in the hood. "This isn't over!" he growled, before slamming the door behind him.

The stranger quietly spoke with Brodney for a few moments, paid him, and then left without another word.

"That was interesting," Brodney said to Alex as he watched the stranger leave.

"I'm sorry for the trouble I caused you," Alex started. Brodney cut him off with a shake of his head.

"Nah, yer fine. No harm done," Brodney said. "Would ye like another bowl of stew and mug of cider? It seems we have ye to thank fer exterminating the monster that's been killing our livestock recently," he continued. "It's the least I can do. And no, before I hear talk about paying fer yer meal, it's already been settled up," he added.

Alex was shocked. "Thank you, I would like that," he said finally. Brodney nodded, disappearing for a moment, before reappearing with another bowl and mug. After finishing his meal, he thanked Brodney again, gathered his bag, and headed toward the stable.

He felt better now that he had eaten, but the accusations of both Garlow and Fintan still stung. He stalked through the stable and kicked an empty bucket harder than he intended. The bucket rattled down the walkway and into the wall with a clunk.

Several startled horses stuck their heads out of their stalls at the noise. He stroked one of them absently. "I don't understand. Why is it so hard for them to believe that I am capable of slaying a dragon on my own? It's not like it hasn't been done before, has it?"

The horse lipped his hand, looking for treats. When it realized he didn't have any, it returned to munching on its hay. Alex retrieved his saddle and a cleaning cloth. He sat heavily on a stool and proceeded to take out his frustration on the dirt and grime. He was almost done when he noticed he had an audience.

A small face peeked around the stable door, watching him clean and stow his tack and weapons. Letting out a sigh, he beckoned them to come in. A young girl, maybe seven or eight, shyly shuffled toward him. "What's your name?" he asked her softly. He crouched to her eye-level, trying not to scare her.

"Genevieve, sir," she replied with wide eyes.

"Hello, Genevieve. I'm Alexander, but everyone calls me Alex." He smiled warmly.

"Are you a knight? Like, an actual knight?" she asked in awe, admiring his newly cleaned armor.

"Yes ma'am," he said with a bow of his head. "At your service."

She giggled into her hands at that. "Can I see your horse? Is he mean? Mother says knights' horses can be mean. She would know because she sees a lot of horses that stay here on their travels. The last knight that came, his horse was mean. Or so I was told. I didn't get to see it, but the other kids did and they said it was mean. They said it tried to bite and kick everyone, even the knight. They also said the knight was mean and a drunk. Are you a drunk?" she rambled without taking a breath.

Alex held up his hands and laughed. "No, I'm not a drunk. No, Bucephalus isn't mean. So your parents run the stables? I'd like to think I'm not mean either, but you can be the judge of that, I suppose," he answered. "Oh, and yes, you can see Bucephalus." He pointed to the stall across from him. Genevieve walked over to the door but was too short to see in.

"Do you think I can go in?" she asked.

"I don't see why not." He rose and unlatched the half door. Bucephalus dozed in the corner, but blinked at them when they opened the squeaky door. "You have a visitor. Genevieve, meet Bucephalus. Bucephalus, meet the Lady Genevieve," he said with a flourish.

"I'm not a lady. I'm just Genevieve," she giggled.

"Yes, M'lady." He winked. Bucephalus lowered his head and snuffled her hair and pockets, making her giggle even more.

"That tickles!" she said as she produced an oat and honey

cake from her pocket and fed it to him. Bucephalus held very still as she rubbed his cheek and petted his nose. "Do you think he would let me hug him?" she asked.

"Why don't you ask him?" Alex replied.

"Mr. Bucephalus, would you mind if I give you a hug?" she asked timidly. Bucephalus let out a snort.

"I think that means yes," Alex said.

Slowly, she wrapped her arms around his head and squeezed gently. As she let go, she whispered something in his ear.

"Are you telling my horse secrets?" Alex asked with a smile.

"I'll never tell." She giggled. "Just kidding. I told him I wanted to be a knight just like you when I grow up," she said seriously. "Thank you, Sir Alex, for letting me see your horse. I better get back to my chores before I'm missed." With that, she dashed off.

Smiling and shaking his head, Alex made sure Bucephalus had plenty of water before bedding down for the night in the next stall over. Sleep eluded him, though. No matter how much Alex wanted to pretend Fintan's insults did not affect him, they did. *I should be used to it by now, should I not?* He wondered.

CHAPTER 4

"WAIT a minute, Daddy," Alice interrupted, wiping sweat from her face with her sleeve. They were in the barn cleaning and sweeping out the stalls. "Why do the other knights not like him?" she asked.

"Well, you see, unlike the rest of the knights, he didn't grow up being a page, then a squire. He jumped straight to his knight's training. Other knights spent years serving as errand boys, watching and learning from the knights, dreaming of the day they would catch a knight's eye and be accepted as their squire. Then they would spend many more years learning and training under their knight, all the while serving them in whatever capacity they deemed necessary," he instructed his daughter.

"You mean the squires do their chores for them? I want someone to do my chores for me too, Daddy. Can I have a squire?" she asked, looking around at the piles of shavings around her.

He chuckled and ruffled her hair. "Chores build character, sweet one," he said. She harrumphed at his comment.

"Then, if the squires pass all their trials, they *might* be initiated as a knight trainee and be assigned a mentor knight. If and when their mentor deems them fit for knighthood, the trainee will spend a full day and night in silent solitude, after which their mentor charges them with a quest they are to undertake alone. If they come back alive and *if* they succeed in their quest, they are knighted and accepted into the Knight's Order," he continued.

"I think Sir Alex was sent to go save a princess in a tower guarded by a monster, but when he got there, the monster had already been slain and she was rebuilding the castle surrounding the tower and didn't need him." She tapped a finger on her chin thoughtfully. "Or he was sent to chase off trolls who were preventing people from crossing a bridge, you know, like a big bridge that everyone has to use all the time, and making them pay a toll to cross or get eaten for supper," she grinned mischievously.

"Trolls, huh?"

"Uh huh!"

"Who is telling the story?" he asked playfully. "Since you seem to know, what happened next? hmmm?"

"They lived happily ever after?" she asked.

"Oh, okay. They lived happily ever after with the trolls on the bridge. The End."

"No, that's not what happened. It's not the end yet!" she objected hastily.

He laughed. "Maybe I like your version better."

"No, you tell it, Daddy," she conceded. She giggled as he ruffled her hair again.

xxx

"To be a page, you had to be of a certain social standing. Your family had to have titles and land and usually wrote a letter of request to the King or Count. Every once in a while, someone would perform an act of valor so brave and selfless that he would be granted the privilege of becoming a knight trainee. Alex was one such person.

All his life, Alex had been shunned and looked down on, so he learned to keep to himself. He was the product of a forbidden love affair. His mother, Rose, was the daughter of a wealthy, retired general and his father was a merc. Mercenaries, while still considered freemen, were not looked upon favorably by the nobles, since they didn't have any particular loyalties and fought for the highest wage, sometimes on opposing sides.

When Rose's father found out she had fallen in love with a merc, he forbade her from marrying him, threatening to disinherit her. As his only child, her father wanted her to marry another noble and have children to carry on the family legacy. She was young and in love with this rogue, who regaled her with exciting tales of his adventures, so she disregarded her father's wishes.

The night they planned to run away together, however, her lover never came. Heartbroken, she blamed her father. A little less than a month later, she found she was with child. She overheard her father making plans to give away her baby, so she fled to a little town, not much more than a fishing village, on the edge of the kingdom to raise her child on her own. The townspeople were suspicious of outsiders, so for many years, they simply ignored the woman and her child with no family and a mysterious history.

Alex remembered the day when everything changed for him."

XXX

Early one morning five years ago, Alex gathered his spearfishing gear. He was just about to head out when the ground rumbled with hoofbeats. He poked his head around the corner of the boat shed to see what all the commotion was about. *Who could possibly have business in the tiny fishing village of Creedon?*

Sunlight glinted off weapons and shields bearing the crests of the Knight's Order. Alex shook his head, disgusted. *What could they possibly want here? Were they lost?* Nothing good would come from this surprise visit; he could feel it in his bones.

"Hey! You there, come tend my horse. C'mon, be quick about it. I don't have all day!" One of the knights yelled at Seamus, one of the fisherman's younger boys.

The boy gawked for a moment longer, then sprang into action. The knights dismounted and stood expectantly, as if they assumed they would be greeted warmly and waited on hand and foot.

"We require several of your best boats," another knight said, walking toward the shore.

Alex had heard enough. He was *not* getting stuck babysitting knights on the water. He sneaked over to his boat, thankfully out of view from the knights. He tossed his gear in the small boat and shoved off quickly and quietly.

After a few minutes of paddling, he stopped not far off the reef. This was usually the best spot to find the bigger fish. The biggest fish lived on the other side of the reef and occasionally swam or were washed onto this side.

He took a deep breath of the salty morning air. He loved being out on the water. It was quiet and peaceful... any day except today it seemed. Judging by all the noise and splashing, the knights had succeeded in convincing someone to take them out.

Ignoring them, Alex stood balanced on the prow of his boat with his spear in hand. He searched the cerulean waters for anything. "Seems the knights excel at scaring away all the fish," Alex grumbled under his breath. He saw a flash of scales in the water. He aimed his spear, waiting for the right moment.

The knights shouted, startling Alex and causing the fish he was aiming for to dive away. He looked up. They had managed to hook a swordfish.

The Knights were busy congratulating themselves and left only one of them to reel it in. Alex watched in amusement. These knights had no idea the fish was toying with them and was about to make a run for it. He grinned as he saw the line go taut, knocking the man off his feet.

"Here we go," Alex mused to himself. This would be entertaining after all.

The other knights piled on top of the one with the pole to keep him from being pulled overboard. Instead, the fish pulled the boat into the deep water beyond the reef. They should have let go, but Alex guessed they did not hear the fisherman's warning to not stray past the reef.

The water began to bubble and froth around the boat. The other fishing boats headed back to shore as fast as they could. They knew what was coming. The sea monsters had come to protect their territory.

An enormous shadow emerged from the deep, much larger than any fish. Suddenly, the knight holding the line was yanked overboard. Several moments went by, but he never resurfaced. The knights retreated toward shore, paddling as fast as they could. The shadow appeared again, headed for them. In their desperate attempt to flee, they capsized the boat, dumping everyone into the water.

Alex sighed as he paddled towards them and pulled a

knight into his little boat. "Make for the reef, you idiot," he instructed the sputtering man. He secured his knife, then dove into the water with his spear. He intended to fend off the threat for as long as he could, to give them as much time as possible.

Taking a deep breath, Alex dove underwater to locate the sea monster. There it was! A massive, blue-green smudge chased after the knights still in the water. It seemed to be toying with them. It let them stay just out of reach but closed on them if they slowed down. Alex surfaced to get another breath of air and check on the knight in his boat.

Good, he had made it back across the reef and was halfway to shore, he thought. With long, powerful strokes, Alex swam towards the flailing knights still in the water. They were doing more splashing than swimming, he observed.

He added that to the already lengthy list of activities knights were useless for. They did not know how to track, fish, build a fire in the woods, or even catch their own food. As far as he could figure, knights were loud, obnoxious, full of themselves, and useless for anything practical.

Suddenly, he realized he could no longer see the smudge in the water. He scolded himself for getting distracted and losing focus on the danger at hand. He turned. His heart stopped as he came face to face with a creature many times larger than a great white shark.

He had heard the tales shared by the old fishermen over the campfire. Stories of people disappearing after they foolishly crossed the reef to chase the fish. Merchants anchored their vessels outside the reef only to find their boats missing or in pieces. Alex had always assumed they were exaggerating.

To call it ginormous would be greatly understating its size. Its head was twice his height and triple his width, with a mouthful of intimidating, sharp teeth and a long, snake-like neck. Most notable were its dark, intelligent eyes gazing back at him.

It circled him, causing large swells in the water. He tread water as he studied it, attempting to keep his head above the waves this massive creature was creating.

Alex hoped it was simply curious. Having grown up next to the sea, he was a strong swimmer, but despite his prowess among humans, he was hopelessly outmatched against this great sea predator. His heart pounded as he waited to see what it would do. He refused to attack something simply because he didn't understand it.

The creature turned and watched the rest of the swimmers as they neared shore. *That is fortuitous.* Alex smirked humorlessly to himself.

Abruptly, it launched itself out of the water in a majestic display of power. It had six massive flippers and a long, powerful tail. It dove back into the water, creating an overpowering undertow, pulling Alex deep underwater.

Surprised and disoriented, his lungs burned from lack of air and the crushing weight of the deep as he was dragged deeper.

He was in trouble.

The churning water made it impossible for him to guess which way was up. His lungs seized, and he involuntarily breathed in the water. Helplessness and desperation shuddered through him as darkness closed in around him.

XXX

Alex felt his body breach the surface and gulped in the sweet air.

He coughed and gasped, his body desperate to rid itself of the burning salt water in his lungs. He was alive. But how? How he had resurfaced and washed up on this mound of sea debris? Shaking with exhaustion and shivering, he collapsed face up staring at the sky, letting the afternoon sun warm him. He laid there until he was mostly dry and his shaking had subsided. His mind refused to acknowledge what had just happened, and he had almost drowned.

Wasn't it just morning? How is it afternoon already?

Finally, Alex pushed himself up onto his knees and looked around to get his bearings. He shook his head and wiped his eyes. He must still be disoriented, because where there should have been a familiar, rocky shore, there was only water. Puzzled, he looked in the opposite direction and saw an unfamiliar densely forested shoreline where there should have been open ocean.

Legends told of an enchanted land across the sea, but they were just stories. Bedtime stories parents told their children. Weren't they? Lush green and dark brown trees grew so close together it was a wonder anyone could walk through them without getting snagged.

His floating island of debris shifted. He found himself staring at his reflection in a giant black eye.

He froze.

Questions whirled in Alex's mind. Foremost among them, *How am I alive?*

The creature remained still. Smooth, iridescent blue and green scales shimmered, changing with the reflection of the sun. Alex realized he was kneeling on its back. It tilted and turned its head. Two nostrils, not much more than slits on the end of its face, opened wide and sniffed him.

It hasn't eaten me yet, Alex thought with a shrug. He felt drawn to it somehow. He moved his hand to touch its face but it recoiled abruptly, almost sending Alex into the surf.

"I'm sorry. I didn't mean to startle you." He yanked his hand back. "What are you?" he breathed with surprised reverence.

He did not know why he was talking to this sea predator or why he assumed it could understand him, but it felt right. "Bronach says the horses understand us, so why wouldn't something as magnificent as you be able to as well?"

He recognized he was rambling, but couldn't seem to help himself. It made him feel better, at any rate. The creature tilted its head and opened and shut its mouth once. It had double rows of impressive, sharp-looking teeth that would put a shark's teeth to shame.

"Are you trying to talk to me?" Alex asked incredulously.

It tilted its head again.

"Would you mind if I touched your nose?" He slowly reached out his hand. Better sense clanged a warning in the back of his mind, but he ignored it. Instead, he held very still with his hand outstretched, waiting to see what it would do.

Slowly, its head advanced until it was less than a hand's width from his fingers. Its nostrils flared in and out. After what felt like minutes, it crossed the final distance to his hand and his fingers barely grazed its smooth scales.

Shock zinged up his arm and made his whole body tingle. The sea creature shivered, knocking Alex over in the process. It nudged him gently, asking to be pet again.

"Where did you come from? Do you have a name?" He

slowly stroked its nose. He marveled at the smooth, almost velvety feel.

"Well, you saved my life, so it's only fitting I give you a name. How about Eirach? It means magnificent."

Eirach nodded.

"So you can understand me!" Alex exclaimed. "Where are we? Do you know the way back to my village?"

The sea creature nodded again.

"Can you take me there?"

Eirach nodded a third time, then turned his head to face forward. With powerful strokes, they flew through the waves. Alex knelt on Eirach's back, marveling as they covered a great distance in a very short time. Alex wondered briefly if they had actually left the water altogether and were in fact flying.

A short time later, they neared a cove north of his village. Eirach deposited him in the shallow waters. Trees and brush surrounded the cove; its pebbled beach strewn with sun-bleached driftwood. A lone falcon perched on a high branch overlooking the cove.

"Thank you for saving my life and sparing theirs. I hope to meet you again someday, Eirach," Alex said.

Eirach bumped Alex's chest with his nose one last time before he submerged, disappearing into the depths. Relieved and surprisingly sad, he watched the dark shape recede. He was relieved to be back on solid ground and alive, but also sad to be parted from his new friend so soon. He stood staring out across the horizon and listened to the surf a little longer before turning to walk back to his village.

CHAPTER 5

DARKNESS had fallen as Alex neared Creedon. Shouts cried out as a throng of villagers rushed toward him, surrounding him, talking over each other. The entire village must have been out here.

"Step aside! Make way! Coming through!" a voice rang out over the crowd.

"Fin!" Alex yelled as a familiar figure pushed her way to him. Seraphina, "Fin", was broad-shouldered, with a strong and curvy build from years of working the fishing nets with her father. Her rich, honey-brown eyes caught the sunset, glimmering like they were on fire. Her long, black curly hair, normally tied back out of the way, hung free over her shoulders and down her back to her waist.

Alex felt his breath catch as she hugged him. *When did she become so beautiful?* He thought with a start.

She pulled back from their embrace. "Don't you dare scare me like that ever again, Alexander!" she scolded. "You made me so worried. I got the whole town out looking for you. What were you thinking?" she demanded, smacking his arm lightly.

Alex ducked his head and mumbled, "I'm sorry, I didn't think."

She had always just been Fin, his best friend since they were little. They had built little boats and took turns pretending they were the finest captain of the seas. They raced each other to see who could gather the most oysters or clams. They pretended they were explorers of wild new lands. They were inseparable, but when anyone insinuated that they were more than just friends they just laughed before running off to play.

One day, Fin's father decided she was old enough to learn the family trade, running the fishing supply and trade for Creedon. Their wild adventures together were at an end. From then on, the only time they saw each other was from a distance. She would wave at him from across the village gatherings or he would greet her when he ran errands to get supplies for Bronach or one of the fishermen.

"Is it true there was a sea monster?" one of the villagers asked, breaking Alex out of his thoughts.

"How did you survive?" another asked at the same time.

"Did you see it up close?"

"Did you scare it off?"

"Did you injure it?"

"Where have you been all day?"

"Tell us what happened!" Everyone talked over each other, making it impossible for Alex to get a word in edgewise.

"Let's get you to the hall so you can dry off and eat," Fin said in his ear, looping her arm around his shoulders and steering him through the crowd.

"Is my mother here?" he asked Fin as they walked.

Fin shook her head. "She went to the market in Arageyll. We sent someone to fetch her when you didn't come back, but they won't be back until tomorrow."

Alex was partly relieved she had not been here, but felt guilty she would rush home with worry. They approached the largest structure in Creedon.

Made of rough-hewn wood and stone, the gathering hall was not much more than a large room with a cookstove at one end and a large fireplace at the other. Someone dragged a stool near the fireplace for him, and someone else brought him a bowl of fish broth soup.

As he ate, the room filled with more of the villagers eager to hear the story. Alex told them about how he saw the shadow and dove in to help. He recounted how it dove under, and how he washed up on the sea debris, then floated on the current until he could swim to shore.

He chose to leave out the strange shoreline, as well as Eirach, because no one would believe him anyway. As he finished, five knights dressed in blue and gray tunics and tall riding boots strode into the hall.

"Everyone out!" one knight shouted. "Except you." He pointed at Alex.

Fin squeezed his shoulder and gave him a sympathetic look, then exited with the others. While everyone else filed out of the hall, Alex studied the knight before him. The leader was tall, broad-shouldered, and had long, curly, salt-and-pepper hair. His tanned face was leathery and sun-weathered, with laugh lines around his sharp, steel-gray eyes.

Two of the knights took up posts on either side of the entryway, and the other two stood at the opposite door. Alex didn't bother telling them that the door had not opened in many seasons, due to sea wash buildup.

"It seems I am now in your debt for saving my men." He took a seat opposite Alex in front of the fire. He gave off a stern disposition, like someone who does not tolerate argument or lack of discipline. "I am McCannon, Knight Commander of the Knight's Order."

"Alex." Alex coughed on his last bite of bread.

"It is in my power to grant a great many things, Alex. Make your request," he said in a low, gruff voice.

Alex stared at him. *Was this a joke?* "I don't... understand," he stammered finally. "I saw them in danger, so I tried to help. I only did what anyone would have done."

McCannon snorted. "No one in their right mind would risk their own life and dive into monster-infested waters; not to save their family and definitely not to save strangers... the world simply doesn't work like that, boy," he said, shaking his head. "Silver? A plot of land? Both so you can wed that bonny lass you fancy?" he asked.

Alex turned to stare at the fire as he replayed the events of the day in his head. It felt like a dream. It was true, he had acted without thinking and, by all rights, should be dead, but he had made a friend and seen a land he would not have otherwise. He wanted to see more. He couldn't explain it, but it called to him. When he looked back at McCannon, he had made up his mind.

"I don't need any of that. I only did what needed to be done. Your thanks is enough," he said. He was going to try to find that mysterious land. Maybe Eirach would help.

McCannon briefly raised his eyebrows, then nodded. "Well then, may I make a request of my own?" he asked after a moment. "I would like to train you to become a knight." Alex started to protest, but McCannon cut him off.

"We need more people like you, lad. You have the character I desire in a knight. I can train you in everything else.Weapons and combat mastery will be required of you. You'll be expected to learn diplomacy and arbitration, as well as social etiquette for many differing circumstances. You would be called upon to perform numerous tasks and quests that are dangerous and potentially deadly, but also monotonous ones as well." He paused and held up his hand to keep Alex from interrupting.

"Contrary to what you might think, a knight's life is not all fame and glory. You will be admired by some and despised by others. It will be grueling and thankless at times but rewarding like nothing else. And you would be a part of something much greater than yourself. Can you say as much about your life here?" he finished.

Alex mulled it over. *I would finally get to leave Creedon. I could be more than just a fisherman from a tiny fishing village at the edge of the kingdom. Maybe I can even make my mother and the rest of the villagers proud of me. But a knight? Do I want to become something I grew up making fun of? I could be different...? I will be different,* he vowed to himself.

"Alright, I'll do it," he said at last.

McCannon nodded and grasped Alex's forearm. "It's settled, then. We leave in two days."

CHAPTER 6

LAYING in the hay adjacent to Bucephalus' stall in Arageyll, Alex finally drifted off to sleep, lost in his memories.

He ran down a long, dark corridor, lit with low burning torches every few paces. Desperately looking for something as something chased him, and he needed to hurry. He stumbled into a room, tripping on the uneven floor, which sent him sprawling into a large stone basin filled with water. When he touched the surface of the water, it started to shimmer and glow with a strange blue light. "What do you seek, Little Defender?" echoed around him. Alex opened his mouth to answer, but he did not know. He felt he should, and he was running out of time. What did *he want?*

The next morning, Alex woke to a tickling sensation on his face. He opened his eyes to Bucephalus standing over him in the stall, tossing bits of hay all over him.

"All right, all right. I'm up! How did you even get in here?" He asked as he stood up and brushed himself off. To his dismay, hay covered in horse slobber stuck to his face and chest.

"You'll get your breakfast soon," he grumbled as he picked off strands of hay one by one.

The feelings from his dreams lingered, so he shook his head to clear his mind and went to get Bucephalus's breakfast of sweet oats. While Bucephalus ate, Alex hummed an old sea shanty and packed his gear for the long ride home.

"Are you the one to speak with about the headless dragon in the meadow?" A man asked as he walked with a slight limp into the stable.

He was slim and wiry, dressed in a maroon and russet patchwork shirt tucked into dark brown pants with a matching dark brown vest trimmed in yellow embroidery. Alex could see the hilt of a dagger just above his right hip, poking out of a crimson sash tied around his waist. He wondered how many more weapons this man had hidden on him.

The stranger wore his long black hair in a single braid down his back. His high cheekbones highlighted an old scar in his bronze skin from his left temple to his jaw. He wore an ornate gold cuff on his right ear and a couple of rings on each hand. Everything about this man said he was a merchant from Keirwyn, the southern kingdom.

"Sure, I guess. What do you want with it?" Alex asked.

"I'm a trader of sorts. I specialize in hard-to-attain items: dragonhide, claws, teeth, and the like," he replied. "I'd like to buy the remains. I'll pay you forty silver for it, seventy if you have the head too."

Alex coughed. "What?"

"Is it not enough?" the man asked. "I'm afraid that is all I can offer."

"No, that's fine. You can have it," Alex replied quickly. He pointed to the sack in the corner where Nobleman Garlow's servant had dumped it the night before. "The head is there."

"Excellent!" He clasped his hands, looking pleased. "I'll be back momentarily," he said as he strode out of the stable.

"That was odd. Well, at least we can pay for the night and some supplies now," Alex said to Bucephalus as he finished tacking up and tied on his saddlebags.

The trader returned a few moments later with a small pouch. He handed it to Alex. "It's all there. You can count it, if you like," he said to Alex as he picked up the large sack in the corner.

Alex opened the pouch and saw it was full of silver drops. He did not bother counting it, guessing by weight it was probably close. This was more than he'd made in several seasons combined. The merchant nodded, hefted the sack over his shoulder, and left.

XXX

Alex paid for the night in the stable and purchased some needed supplies, then headed home towards Creedon. Not long outside of town, he ran into the other knights returning with a covered cart. Fintan scowled up at him from his blood bay but said nothing. Bucephalus pinned his ears. Alex looked away, not wanting to start anything, but didn't reprimand Bucephalus either.

Cole stopped next to him and whistled. "McCannon was right about you," he said with a tone of admiration. "You have a knack for this. Oh, I believe this is yours." He reached around and pulled out the spearhead Alex had left lodged inside the dragon.

"Thanks," Alex said warily, as he tied it to the back of his saddle. "I sold the dragon remains to a merchant in town. Didn't catch his name though." He shrugged and gave a description of the merchant.

"I have a few questions if you would spare me the time," Cole said. Alex nodded. "Go on ahead. I'll catch up with you later," he said to the other knights.

Fintan frowned and narrowed his eyes, but did not break his silence. The other two knights nodded and continued on toward Arageyll with the cart. Alex watched them go before turning back to Cole.

Cole had dismounted and picketed his horse to graze. He'd taken a seat on a mossy rock nearby. Alex slid down from Bucephalus, but instead of picketing him with Cole's bay, he just let him wander.

"I noticed you don't have a bridle on him or tie him up," Cole began. "Your horse master must be very skilled indeed."

"Bronach? No, he's just the blacksmith," Alex replied, taking a seat next to Cole. "But he does have a way with horses I can't explain."

Cole studied him, his face unreadable. "I have to know, how *did* you kill the beast? I spoke with Nobleman Garlow before we left. He said they sent two score townsfolk after it, and they couldn't even get close."

"You believe me, then?" Alex asked skeptically.

"Sure. I have the proof before my eyes. No matter how unlikely," Cole said. "We followed the carrion birds and found the remains where it had been reported. So, how did you do it? There is not a scratch on you or your horse," he continued, gesturing to Bucephalus.

"I entered the woods on foot and tracked the dragon to its den. I threw rocks and sticks at it until I made it mad enough to chase me, then ran for my life to the clearing. I used my spear, but even with a mounted throw, I didn't quite hit the right spot," Alex said with growing enthusiasm. "I ended up using my axe to drive the shaft into its heart."

"How do you know where to strike it?" Cole asked seriously. "Their hide is too thick for ranged weapons, as you well know… and on your own, you can't get close enough for swords or axes to be effective without getting bitten or clawed."

"Well, just behind their front leg, about the size of your fist, there's a spot that is not as armored as the rest of their body." Alex held up his fist to illustrate. "Honestly, it was a bit of luck when I found it." He shrugged.

Cole looked thoughtful. "I'd like to come with you on the next one, if you don't mind. After the Summit, that is. I'll be tied up with other duties 'til then."

Alex looked at him warily. He wanted to believe Cole was genuine, but having been on the receiving end of endless ridicule and cruel jokes at the hands of other knights, he hesitated.

"Well, you don't have to make a decision right now," Cole said as he stood and walked to his picketed horse. "Think about it and give me an answer by the end of the Summit." As an afterthought, he said, "And I'd like to meet this blacksmith of yours. Seems I could learn a thing or two from him about horse training."

"Next time you are in town, I'll introduce you. Or if he will be traveling, I will send word." Alex rose as Bucephalus trotted towards him. He couldn't resist showing off a little. Alex jogged to meet him, grabbed the saddle, and let his momentum carry him up onto Bucephalus' back.

Cole chuckled behind him. "Until the Summit then," Cole said, grinning.

"Til then." Alex nodded down at him and saluted respectfully.

XXX

It was well past nightfall when Alex and Bucephalus trotted into the sleepy little fishing village they called home. The torches outside the main hall burned brightly, like twin beacons leading them home.

He nodded politely to several of the villagers he knew in passing, but they ignored him. He wasn't actually surprised, since he was generally ignored unless they wanted something from him. Most of the time, he preferred it that way, but every once in a while he imagined the whole town rallying to welcome him home or see him off on his next journey.

"That'll be the day, eh boy? The day they welcome us home like heroes and acknowledge our accomplishments in keeping the kingdom safe." He chuckled under his breath, reached down and patted Bucephalus' shoulder. They stopped outside Bronach's blacksmith shop and he slid to the ground.

His horse nickered and bobbed his head. Alex assumed it was because he was impatient for the warm oats waiting inside, but he liked to imagine Bucepahlus actually responded to his monologues. It kept the loneliness at bay most of the time.

He sighed and leaned his forehead against his steed's warm shoulder. "I know. But I can dream right? Truth is, I wouldn't know what to do with all that, anyway. So maybe it is for the best."

Alex led Bucephalus into his empty stall at the back of the shop. Bronach looked up from his stool where he sat cleaning his tools by the light of his forge.

"Alex, yer back. How was the journey? Did ye find it? Was it a wee one like you'd hoped?" He set aside his rag and tools and rose to help Alex untack.

Bucephalus stood perfectly still as always, munching on oats while they removed the weapons, saddlebags, and the saddle.

"No, it was huge! I wish you could have seen it. It was this tall." He held his hand up to show how tall the dragon was. "And longer than this stall is wide. But we did it." He blew out a breath as he spoke, half expecting Bronach not to believe him. "We slew the dragon on our own. I say 'we' because I couldn't have done it without our boy here. I'd be dead if it weren't for him." He stroked Bucephalus' shoulder absentmindedly.

Bucephalus chose that moment to snort in between mouthfuls of his sweet oats. Bronach remained silent, so Alex paused before looking at him to see his reaction. When he did, Bronach smiled and looked him in the eye. "I knew ye could, lad." His baritone voice rumbled with pride.

Alex let out a deep sigh, feeling the tension leave him for the first time since he had set out. He grabbed his grooming brushes and brushed Bucephalus until his coat shone. Exchanging his brushes for a comb, he methodically worked out any tangles in his mane and tail.

Bronach inspected all of his weapons, only raising a bushy eyebrow at the pile of broken spearheads. "Right then, what'll ye be needin' for yer next one? And how long have I got?"

Alex put away the comb and came to stand next to Bronach's giant, muscular frame. "I don't actually know. I have the knights' Summit in Aberdeen in a fortnight, but otherwise..." He shrugged.

He put away his saddle and started to get out his sharpening stones when Bronach laid a hand on his shoulder.

"I've got it from here, lad. Go see your mother. She'll be wanting to know you are back."

"Are you sure? I can just..."

Bronach chuckled, "Off you go." His tone saying he wouldn't take "no" for an answer.

Alex huffed and put away the rest of his things. He passed through the doorway when Bronach called to him. "Oh, Alex." Alex turned back. "Welcome home and well done." He winked at Alex and made shooing motions.

"Thanks." Warmth spread through his chest.

He heard Bronach talking to Bucephalus as he walked away. "Thanks for bringing him back to us..."

Alex smiled as he headed home, his boots crunching on the gravel path.

CHAPTER 7

ALEX rode north to Aberdeen in the dreary cold. The steady drizzle made travel miserable and did nothing to lift his sullen mood. He had been summoned to the annual Summit of the Knight's Order, but did not particularly like going. Every year, he spent six days enduring the other knights' condescension and thinly veiled contempt. He particularly hated parading around for the pompous nobility who were more concerned with what they were wearing than the governance and wellness of the people of Reyall.

They rode along the path at the edge of the Enchanted Forest. The wood jutted between Creedon and Aberdeen, such that to go around took an extra day of travel; a day he did not have to spare. He sighed in resignation. He was going to be late, furthering their low opinion of him.

He dared not go through the Enchanted Forest. Most who attempted to traverse the thick woodland were never heard from again. The few who did return appeared many seasons later, spouting nonsense of being held captive by fairies or monsters and other wild tales.

Alex groaned as it began to downpour. The hood of his cloak barely kept the rain out of his eyes. Visibility was poor, and Bucephalus was slipping dangerously in the mud.

"Should we take shelter, boy?" he asked, signaling to him to halt. Bucephalus snorted. He bobbed his head, sending a spray of water into Alex's face. "Alright, let's do it, but we'll only go in as far as we have to 'til the storm ends," he said, wiping his face with his already damp sleeve.

They took shelter under a large tree on the edge of the forest to wait out the storm. Piece by piece, he took off his soaked cloak and leather armor and hung them on nearby limbs to dry. His damp clothes stuck to his skin in places, but his cloak seemed to have kept him mostly dry.

He gathered the least wet sticks and dead grass he could find to build a fire. It took longer than he expected, but he finally got it to light. Once the fire was burning steadily, he removed his bags and saddle from Bucephalus.

Steam rose from the horse's drenched back. He used his hands to scrape as much water off Bucephalus as he could, wishing he had something to help dry off his steed. He considered his mostly dry tunic and debated for a moment before pulling it over his head. It was not very thick, but it was better than nothing.

When his tunic was soaked through, and Bucephalus was as dry as Alex could make him, he hung his now horsehair covered tunic alongside his cloak and armor.

"Don't wander too far," he said. Bucephalus nickered as he looked for a spot to graze.

Alex took some dried meat from his saddlebags and sat down next to the fire. He sighed with exhaustion. He wondered if it was more to do with his apprehension and stress about the upcoming Summit than the journey so far.

The rain wasn't going to let up any time soon. He leaned back against the tree and let his eyes drift closed. The steady rhythm of the rain soothed his tired mind. *I'll only rest for a few minutes.*

XXX

What felt like a short time later, he heard children's laughter drifting through the trees. He groaned. His body felt stiff and his neck ached. The rain continued to pour as steady as ever. *I should check on Bucephalus and see if the gear is dry.*

He rubbed his tired eyes and opened them. His fire had gone out and the sun had set. *How did it get to be so late?* He rose and brushed the pine needles clinging to his pants, shivering in the cool air. He reached for his tunic, but it was still wet, so he left it hanging on the branch. He fished out one of his older tunics he wore for training out of his bag. It was also damp and smelled of sweet oats and grain.

He couldn't show up to Aberdeen wearing this. The gate guards would never let him in, and when they did, the other knights would never let him live it down. He clenched his fist in frustration, then sighed. He was already late. What was a few more hours? They couldn't go back out in this until the weather let up anyway.

Alex strapped on his weapons and was about to gather more firewood when he noticed Bucephalus was nowhere in sight.

"Bucephalus!" he called. "Bucephalus, where are you?" The forest was eerily silent, except for the rain and wind rustling the leaves on the trees. He looked out through the storm across the fields, but hoped Bucephalus would not have gone out there.

Laughter sounded again, louder this time. Not knowing what else to do, he followed it to a clearing with a huge bonfire in the center. The hair on the back of his neck rose, and he felt frozen in place. He realized his blunder. The voices did not belong to children. They were fairies. Very real and very dangerous.

Panic rose in his chest. His heart pounded as cold sweat broke out on his skin. The legends were true. He never should have stepped foot into the Enchanted Forest. Fairies were rumored to be mischievous and even cruel.

Slowly and quietly, he backed away, trying to remain hidden. No sooner had he turned his back on the clearing, they found him. Before him stood two slender figures dressed in dark green tunics and black pants that seemed to absorb the firelight.

"Oh! It seems we have an uninvited guest," one fairy said to the other. He had angular cheekbones, a sharp jawline, and long pointed ears poking out of his short, messy hair.

"Yes! Will this one, too, say he was lost?" the second fairy said with feigned amusement. She had similar features, except she wore her hair long and twisted in a single braid over her right shoulder. Alex thought she had wings like a butterfly, flickering in the firelight, but when he blinked, they were gone. Could he trust his own eyes?

"I'm sorry. I didn't mean to intrude. My horse is missing. If you don't mind, I'll be on my way," Alex's voice came out strained, betraying his fear and panic.

"If we don't mind?" The first fairy narrowed his eyes. "We do mind, don't we?" he sneered.

Struggling with his shock, Alex strained to recall the campfire tales he had heard as a child. Which stories were true? One such tale said fairies could twist words to entrap the unwary.

"What should we do with him?" the second fairy asked the first. She looked at him critically, tilting her head and arching her eyebrow.

"Let's have a bit of fun!" he replied with an impish grin.

They nodded to each other in agreement and turned to face Alex. "If you can make it back to the edge of the forest, we'll let you live," he said, with a mischievous glint in his eyes. "But... If we catch you, you must do whatever we tell you. We'll even give you a head start."

What have I gotten myself into? Alex thought to himself. "And if I don't agree to your contest?" he asked, looking for a way out.

"Then we make you do whatever we tell you," the first fairy answered, grinning at his own cleverness.

"Or we'll kill you on the spot. Your choice," the second fairy quipped.

Alex's crestfallen face betrayed his fear and anxiety. He did not know how to fight a fairy. Was this his only way out? He hoped Bucephalus was nearby and might hear the commotion and come to his rescue, but that was a long shot at best. "Alright, deal. When do we start?"

"NOW!" they shouted in unison.

He sprinted toward his campsite. *I know the way back. I didn't come that far, right?* As he rounded a large tree, light flickered up ahead. *Almost there! I'm going to make it!*

As if they could hear his thoughts, laughter sounded behind him. Redoubling his effort, he raced toward the light. His heart pounding, and his breathing labored, he broke through the trees... Only to find he was back at the clearing with the fairies' campfire.

He must have gotten turned around in the dark. Not stopping to wonder, he raced back the way he had come. *Faster, faster! I have to make it out of these trees.*

His lungs burned. His legs ached. He could hear the fairies to his left as he caught a glimpse of something up ahead. He emerged from the trees again and staggered to his knees, panting.

"What is this!?" Alex exclaimed, exasperated. Again, he was back at the clearing where he started. He felt a tap on his shoulder.

"Gotcha," one of the fairies whispered in his ear. It dawned on him what had happened.

"You cheated. You used magic." he gasped, trying to catch his breath.

"So what if we did?" one asked.

"Those weren't the rules," Alex panted.

"We didn't cheat. You never said no magic," said the first. "We won fair and square. You belong to us now."

Before Alex could say another word, the second fairy snapped her fingers, and a vine snaked around his wrists in front of him. The vines glowed faintly. They pulled a hood over his head and removed his sword and knife from their sheaths on his hip and his dagger from his boot.

"Come along," the first fairy said as he pulled Alex to his feet. Alex tried to resist, but the fairy was deceivingly strong for his small stature. His feet were propelled forward, seemingly of their own volition.

"What is this?" Alex cried out. Fear hammered in his chest as he tried, and failed, to fight it. *I don't understand this magic! "To defeat this new threat, you need to know your enemies' abilities."* He could hear McCannon's voice in his head. Neither fairy answered.

"Where are you taking me?" he demanded. Still no answer. "How did you do that?" He tried a different approach.

"What are your names? You aren't a very chatty couple, are you?" he said to no one in particular.

"We are *not* a couple, and it's none of your business," she said matter-of-factly. "You'll see when we get there. Now be quiet!" she snapped.

Left alone to his own thoughts, he let his mind wander as he listened to the night sounds of the forest. He tried to keep track of their progress, but after a while, he gave up. *Where is Bucephalus? I hope he is okay. He's a smart horse. He'll find his way back to town. At least they haven't let me trip over roots or hit me in the face with branches. What do they plan to do with me? What use could fairies have with a human?*

Admittedly, he didn't know much about magic or fairies. *I can't keep calling them "him" and "her," so if they won't tell me their names, I'll just have to give them names myself. Lilly is a nice name, and he seems like a Fitz.*

XXXX

What seemed like hours later, he heard rushing water up ahead. It sounded like a large waterfall, judging by the cascade. But, without being able to see, it was hard to tell. He could feel mist on his hands, so they must be close.

"What if he can't swim?" Fitz asked Lilly.

"What do you mean? I thought all humans can swim."

"I guess we will find out," Fitz snickered.

Shoved from behind, Alex pitched forward. He threw his bound hands in front of him to catch himself, but was met with a face full of water. Sputtering, he gathered his legs under him to stand. Although his hands were still bound, he could wade well enough in the chest-deep water. Still unable to see, he wondered where they were going.

The spray of water increased against the hood over his face, and a thunderous deluge of water poured on his head. *We are going under the waterfall?* He lost his balance as his feet slipped out from under him. Completely submerged, the water pulled and tugged at him from all directions as he struggled to right himself. Disoriented, he felt the scrape of rocks and submerged tree limbs against his side.

He wrestled the hood off his head, but all he saw was water. His lungs burned. He couldn't hold his breath for much longer. He needed to find his way to the surface soon. *Wasn't this water only chest-deep a minute ago? Why can't I seem to stand up?*

An aqua light flashed in the water, and suddenly, he found his footing. Sputtering, he breached the surface and gasped the sweet air.

"No!" Lilly shouted.

"I win! He figured it out. You have to do a week of my watch duty," Fitz taunted.

Alex wiped the water from his eyes and surveyed his surroundings. They stood in a rough-hewn tunnel carved out of the rock behind the waterfall. The walls glowed faintly from invisible sources.

Lilly scowled down at him with her arms crossed. Fitz grinned and danced a happy little jig. Alex wasn't sure which was scarier, Lilly's scowl or Fitz's grin. Either way, they had tried to drown him in their little "game."

They continued to argue about what the bet had been, and who owed who what. *I have to find a way out. They are going to kill me if they keep this up.*

Lilly and Fitz seemed distracted by their banter. Alex spied a small opening in the tunnel wall, behind him to the right. The main tunnel continued to the left with a narrow path running along either side of the water channel.

If he could just make it out of sight, he might have a chance to get away. The fighting duo stood between him and the waterfall. He couldn't go back the way he had come. He wasn't sure he wanted to anyway, given they had just tried to kill him.

Slowly and quietly, he submerged himself until only his nose and eyes were above water. He backed one step at a time towards the opening on his right, keeping an eye on the pair. As he approached, he saw it was perfectly sized for the small fairies, but he would have difficulty squeezing through the narrow opening. The path looked well-worn from use. Maybe it was not his best choice.

Another thought occurred to him. This might be where they intended to take him anyway. There was also the matter of getting out of the water without drawing their attention. He decided to stay in the water around the bend, and then figure how to get out once out of sight. His hands were still bound, but if they discovered his attempt to flee, he could still swim with his legs. He needed to find something to cut the rope.

How far does this tunnel go? He backed slowly around the bend and out of sight, their banter echoing through the tunnel. They hadn't noticed his absence yet, but it was only a matter of time before they came looking for him. The channel narrowed as he went until it was only his shoulder-width apart and knee-deep. The water disappeared through a stone grate in the wall. A dead end.

Frustration fueled by fear threatened to overwhelm him. He took deep, calming breaths until his racing heart began to slow. He cleared his mind and resolved to handle one problem at a time. Free his hands first, then deal with the sadistic fairies.

Fitz had relieved him of his knife and dagger, and with his hands still bound, he could not reach the blade hidden in the small of his back. He needed to rethink where he kept that one, or add another somewhere he could reach if he found himself in this kind of situation again. But first, he needed to get himself out of *this* situation.

Alex grimaced and looked around to see if there were any rocks or sharp edges he could use to cut his bindings. He felt along the bottom, under the dark water, until his hands found something with an edge. *This might work.* He pulled a pyramid-shaped stone the size of his palm out of the water. If worse came to worst, it would make for a good bludgeoning weapon.

Not wasting any time, he sat on the ledge and held the rock between his knees. He rubbed his restraints against the edge of the stone until the vines frayed, then snapped. He climbed out of the water, careful to make as little splashing sounds as he could. A breeze blew through the tunnel and caressed his face. He hadn't realized how warm the water had been until he shivered from the cool air.

With the rock in one hand and his small blade in the other, he slowly made his way back toward the tunnel entrance. If they tried to kill him, he would fight. His footsteps squished loudly to his ears. He neared the bend. It was quiet, too quiet.

His heart pounded in his chest in anticipation for the coming fight. He pressed his back to the wall, listening intently… or he would have, except the wall was no longer there. He tumbled backward into blackness.

CHAPTER 8

ALEX held tightly to his weapon in his disoriented tumble, but the stone slipped from his grasp and clattered away. He rolled to a stop. It was eerily quiet without the rush of the waterfall.

His pounding heartbeat echoed loudly in his ears. He wished for a torch or light, anything to light the surrounding area. As if on command, a faint glow appeared next to him. Clusters of blue crystals were embedded along the base of the smooth walls. He attempted to pry one out with his knife, but it held fast.

The light illuminated three dark passageways branching out before him. A glimmer on the floor caught his eye. He picked it up to inspect it. The rock he had used to cut himself free earlier was no longer rough and jagged; it was a polished dark gray with smooth sides and clean-cut edges. Inscribed on the bottom in silver, it read:

"What you wish will be reflected.

What you are will be revealed.

The pure of heart hold the key

To that which has been sealed."

A riddle? A poem? What does it mean? Who built these tunnels? Do Lilly and Fitz know about them? He worried at any moment they would come through the wall. He needed to pick a way and try it. *What could possibly be waiting for me in these super secret tunnels - with an invisible entrance branching off from other secret tunnels, all hidden behind a waterfall?* He thought sarcastically.

As he approached the split, a green crystal began to glow down the center passage. *That seems like as good a choice as any.* As he neared the green crystal, piles of gems, jewels, and gold mounded up along the wall of the path, forking off to the right. He had never seen such wealth before. He glanced down the left tunnel; sacks and crates overflowed with fruit, nuts, cheese, and bread. *What sort of place is this?*

As tempting as the gems were, it had been a while since he had eaten, and if he was going to be stuck in here, all the riches in the world wouldn't do him any good if he died of starvation. As if on cue, his stomach grumbled loudly. Choosing left, he filled his pockets with as much food as he could, munching as he went. There was sweet bread, savory rolls, more fruits than he could name, and countless cheeses he'd never tasted before.

He continued down the tunnel and came to a round room with 4 doors. Upon each door was mounted a glowing crystal. One with purple, one with yellow, one with white, and one with pink. A door behind him slammed shut.

The only other light source shone down from a little hole in the ceiling. On further inspection, there were no handles or latches. He pushed on a door, but to no avail. One by one, he tested the others, but they also would not open. As he crossed over to try the last door, a flash of light caught his attention. He whirled around to see where it came from, but it had vanished. He started back toward where he came in, and again, he saw the flash. This time he turned slowly and saw that it turned with him. *But where did it come from?*

A light beam pierced the darkness from the ceiling. He looked down and saw the sides of the stone in his hands had turned into a mirror. "This is no ordinary rock," he mused aloud.

He would ponder it further later.

On a hunch, he caught the light from the ceiling with the rock and aimed it at the door with the pink crystal. Pink smoke seeped out from around the door. Alex coughed as the smoke burned his lungs. *Nope! That's not it!* He quickly removed the rock from the light.

The smoke continued to billow into the room and already covered the floor, ankle-deep. In a panic, he randomly picked a different door. This door had a white crystal. At first, it seemed like nothing happened, but then suddenly the floor dropped out from under him.

He hit something further down. It tilted steeply, causing him to lose his footing. He slid uncontrollably toward the wall. A hole opened beneath his feet, and he continued his slide into blackness. He reached out to both sides but found nothing to grab hold of.

There, a light! Abruptly, his descent came to a halt as he exited the blackness of the tunnel, landing in a brightly lit room full of sand. *It's warm! How is that even possible this far underground?*

Marveling, Alex let a handful of the warm sand slide through his fingers. Flames burned in sconces, set at close intervals, illuminating a flowing, ornate script scrawled around the cornerless room. Wanting a closer look, he wandered around, occasionally stumbling in the thick sand. He was not familiar with the language, but it was beautiful, like the gods had written it with their own hands.

What did it say? Who wrote it? Why is it here? Where is here? How do I get out? Questions swirled around in his head; it seemed like the sand was swirling outside his head as well. *Wait a minute, the sand really is swirling around my head, or the entire room actually.* He thought. It seemed random at first, but it began to take shape. In moments, a massive sand golem stood before him, staring down at him.

Seconds felt like hours as Alex and the sand golem stood, locked in each other's gaze, neither moving nor breaking eye contact. *If you can call staring into the abyss, eye contact,* he thought in a moment of wry humor. He felt completely naked, as if this impossible creature saw right through him and knew everything about him.

Its voice rumbled like thunder echoing throughout the space. "Little Defender, it... is time."

⚔ 200 years earlier ⚔

Zeit tapped his foot impatiently. For a master of time magic, he was not known for his patience. *Where was she? She's always running late!* He thought. *What is the point of having an assistant if they are never where you need them to be?*

Earlier that day, the meeting of the masters had not gone his way, so he needed to hurry if he didn't want to get caught. In his opinion, they were a bunch of shortsighted, lackadaisical, unimaginative fossils. At only 100 years old, he was the youngest to have achieved master status. All the others were in their 300s. They think that just because they are older than *me,* they know more than *I do.* Well, *I'll* show them.

For the last 1,000 years, fae and humans had been at war, but it hadn't always been that way. There was a time, long ago, when humans and fae coexisted peacefully. As master of time and ancient histories magic, he had access to all the Fae's history. He and the other historians, as their peers called them, were tasked with recalling events to help enlighten and instruct.

He knew it was possible to be at peace again. Cathal, the war and strategy master, didn't think so and seemed bent on convincing the rest of the council. If they had peace, would they even need a master of war or military? In any case, the other five masters wanted to table the discussion of peace talks with the humans until the following solstice.

Cathal's main point was since the humans had fractured into warring tribes, making peace with them was impossible. He also believed they were deceitful and power-hungry and were not capable of change. Zeit believed differently, and if they would not take him seriously, he would have to show them. He had brokered a peace child swap with Bronwyn, the leader of the strongest human clan. In an effort to promote understanding and harmony between fae and humans, they would trade a child, raise them as their own for twenty years, and then swap back. It could only be twenty years because the human lifespan is so much shorter than fae.

Kadupul, the Fae leader, was inclined to hear him out at least. But not today. Tonight was The Revealing Ceremony, and she needed to rest before the festivities. She might be old and nearing the end of her time, but she was still very sharp, with a keen sense of leadership. Zeit hoped she would be proud of him for taking initiative.

Aryan, Zeit's assistant, was already supposed to be here with the child. He had left it up to her to talk one of the families into this scheme and to keep them quiet about it 'til later. He was supposed to meet Bronwyn very soon to make the swap. He would just have to go without Aryan and the child, and they would catch up. On his way to the passage, he also needed to return the guardian crystal to the control room. Distracted by his frustration after the council meeting, he had forgotten it was in his pocket. He could not wait any longer. He had to go, or he would be late.

As he neared the exit, "Zeit, there you are! I was wondering if I could have a word with you?" Kadupul's soft voice froze him in place. "Did I catch you at a bad time?" she asked.

"Oh, hey, Kad. I was just going to watch the sunset through the waterfall. What can I help you with? I thought you would be resting before tonight." Over Kadupul's shoulder, he caught sight of Aryan with the baby. Discreetly, he waved her away. They had planned for this possibility. She would go a different way and meet him on the other side.

"Oh, in that case, I would love to accompany you," she replied. "Shall we go? I'd hate for you to miss it."

As they walked through the passageway in silence, Zeit mulled over how to excuse himself without betraying his plan. Just as they reached the backside of the waterfall, Kad gently touched his arm. Startled, he looked down into her eyes and saw a knowing look. Pulling him down to speak into his ear so she could be heard over the din of the water, she said, "I know your true intentions for coming out here today. I want you to know it is not your fault."

As he was about to ask her meaning, she stiffened and fell into the water, an arrow protruding from her back. Speechless with horror, he watched as the water around her instantly turned red. He jumped in after her, but she was being pulled under the waterfall by the current. Diving under to try to reach her, he wished for the first time in his life that he had water magic.

CHAPTER 9

THE sand golem had a low, smooth voice; not at all how Alex would have guessed... if he guessed that a being made entirely out of air and sand could speak, that is. Feeling overwhelmed and a little snarky, he muttered, "Time is what you make of it."

"That...is one way to look at it, Little Defender," the sand golem replied slowly. "But it is not incorrect. You have a gentle strength about you. You doubt yourself, and you desire to be accepted." He continued.

"You will need your courage and your wits for what lies ahead. You will also need this." As he spoke, the sand parted around the pyramid-shaped rock. He must have dropped in his slide down the chute.

"What is it?" Alex asked.

"It is a key and not a key," the sand golem said. "It is a guide and not. It is what you need it to be, but... not."

"I don't understand! What does that mean? Why do you call me 'Little Defender'? What do you mean 'it is time'? What is this place? How do I get out?" The questions tumbled out one after another as he tried to make sense of everything.

"Is that not your name? Do your peers and family not call you Alexander?" the golem inquired softly. "I have been waiting for you for a long time. Come and see. When you have seen everything I have to show you, and if you still wish to leave, I will show you the way."

When he finished speaking, the sand churned like waves on the ocean. At the center of the room, an onyx pyramid the height of three men rose from the sandy floor. When the room had settled, the golem was nowhere in sight.

Unsure of what to do, Alex approached the nearest side. Nothing happened. Not sure what he was expecting would happen, he let out a sigh. He had more questions and was no closer to answers. How in the world was he going to find Bucephalus? His suppressed concern bubbled up to the surface before he stuffed it back down again. There was no time to worry about that right now.

"Focus, Alex. Focus!" he said to himself. It had been one puzzle after another since he encountered Fitz and Lilly in the enchanted forest. Maybe he had to find a way to get in, in order to get out. What was it the golem had said? The "not rock" was a key... but not? Not having any better ideas, he held it up and touched the base of it to the wall. Silently, the stone dissolved like sand and revealed an opening. Taking a deep breath, he stepped inside.

All at once, images of people and events flashed all around him. It was overwhelming. Two armies readied for battle. Winged warriors collided above the clashing armies. Fire ravaged across forests and fields. A lady found a baby in a tree nook and took it home to raise as her own. A fairy shot in the back with an arrow fell into a river that looked a lot like the waterfall passage. There was that same fairy, only much younger, in a ceremony next to an ornate flaming brazier.

Wait, he recognized one of the symbols engraved on the side. *Why was the crest on my father's ring also on the side of the fairy fire bowl?* he thought. More images flashed by, but he was no longer paying attention. His thoughts raced as he tried to process what he had seen. He had seen enough. It was time to leave. He was going to ask the golem to show him the way out.

As he turned to leave, a familiar figure caught his eye. It was the lady from the well, standing next to the brazier. Exiting the pyramid, he called out to the golem, hoping he could hear him. "Who is she? What does all this have to do with me? I don't understand! Please help me!"

"The answer you seek is found with the lady of the lake," the golem's voice echoed around him.

As quickly as it had risen, the pyramid disappeared, leaving no trace it had been there at all. On the far wall, a doorway opened up where there had been a solid wall before. The sand golem had been true to his word.

"Thank you!" he called, not expecting an answer. As he started into the passageway, it collapsed on him and the floor gave out beneath him. *Not again!* He thought as he plummeted. Shutting his eyes against the swirling sand, he tensed for impact... only to find himself laying on a cool grassy bank by a river with no sand in sight. *Am I dreaming?* He was unsure what his senses were telling him anymore.

XXX

"Go faster, Daddy. Go faster. Giddy-up horsey." Alice giggled.

He pretended to snort and stamp like a horse, then trotted around the yard with his daughter on his back. "Oh, look up ahead. What is that?" He pretended to shy away from an invisible monster.

Alice shrieked and giggled as he nearly unseated her. "Onward, mighty steed. Have no fear. I will vanquish any threat!" she declared, dropping her voice as low as she could in her best imitation of a knight. She pointed forward over his shoulder. "Go that way!"

He complied and imitated cantering in a figure-eight. "Clip clop. Clip clop. Over the bridge." He made sound effects for their maneuvers.

"Look. It's only a baby dragon. Do you think it wants snacks?" She paused. "What do dragons eat, Papa?"

"I don't know, sweet knight. Why don't you ask it?" He chuckled as he trotted forward and continued his horse-like antics.

"Can I have a snack? I'm hungry. All these heroics have really worked up an appetite." She said dramatically.

He laughed, "Of course, my love."

"What happens next?" She asked as he trotted them toward the kitchen.

"Well, after the sand golem helped him out of the labyrinth, Alex found himself on the bank of a river."

CHAPTER 10

"**OH!** Hello! My, my, my! Can it be...? It is!" an energetic baritone voice broke into Alex's thoughts. "I can't believe I get to finally meet one! Oh, this is splendid, simply splendid!" he continued as he clapped his hands together.

Before Alex strode the oddest creature he had ever beheld. Standing on two hoofed feet, it had the head of a bull and a torso and arms of a man. He wore a jade green sleeveless vest over an orange sash tied around his waist and loose black pants to the knee. *What else do you call it... a hock?* Alex mused. Rabbit fur bracers, an ornate leather satchel slung across his body with papers and scrolls poking out from the ends, and what appeared to be reading glasses on the bridge of his nose accented his bizarre ensemble. Tucked under his arm, the man-bull held a book larger than Alex's head. The surreal compilation of sight and sound before him further added to Alex's dream theory.

"You are human, yes?" The creature nodded to himself as if answering his own question. "How did you get here? Are you considered average for your race?" he said, as it took out a book and a charcoal stick and began taking notes. "You see, I have never actually met one, so, as you can imagine, I have lots of questions. I was about to put on some tea. Would you like to come have tea with me? Do humans drink tea?" He paused for a moment before continuing, not allowing Alex to respond. "Come, let us have tea and we can discuss everything. My home is just over there." He pointed away from the river bank.

Alex's mind raced with questions of his own. Without waiting for a response, the creature turned and strode away in the direction it had indicated. Not wanting to be left behind, Alex had to run to catch up.

"Here we are." He paused near the base of an enormous tree.

Alex did not see anything resembling a house. "Wait!" He finally found his voice. "So far in the last day, I have been chased, tied up, almost drowned, lost in some underground tunnels, almost poisoned, dropped into a sandpit, and then dumped here. I don't know where I am, who or what you are, or what you intend to do with me. All I want is to know how I can find my horse and go home!" Exasperation and desperation laced his words.

"If you will oblige me a small indulgence, I believe I can illuminate at least a few of your inquiries and perhaps even assist you," the creature rumbled. "Ah, where are my manners! My name is Mahkai. I am a minotaur of the Makanui clan." He pounded a fist to his heart.

"I am Alex of Creedon," Alex said with a slight bow.

"Come, Alex, welcome to my humble home," Mahkai said with a smile. He made another note in his book and mumbled under his breath, "Humans bow, like fairies, to show respect. Hmm, interesting." He snapped the book closed and tucked it under his arm before leading the way.

As Alex rounded the tree base, stairs growing out of the side of the tree spiraled around the massive trunk up to the canopy. Mahkai nimbly ascended the natural steps, pausing long enough to ensure that Alex followed. Near the top, Alex halted to look out at the surrounding forest. He wondered where he was, since this did not look anything like Reyall. "Wait until you see the view from up here," Mahkai's voice interrupted Alex's musings from above.

Ascending the final few steps, Alex climbed through an open hatch. He stood on a balcony wrapped all the way around the perimeter of the room in the center. The view before him was breathtaking. They were above most of the rest of the forest. Rolling hills of open fields, rich green forests, sparkling blue rivers, and mountains rising out of the trees. Alex had been all over Reyall with McCannon, and while each area boasted its own unique beauty, none of it came close to rivaling the wild, magnificent landscape stretching out before him. Even the air smelled different here.

"Tea is ready. I hope you will pardon my forward assumption for flavor selection. It is my own special blend of honeysuckle tea. Do you prefer sugar, honey, or my personal favorite, alfalfa sprigs?" Mahkai called through the open doorway.

Moving inside, Alex found a large overstuffed leather chair, flanked by ornate matching side tables. He spied a hammock hanging off to one side next to a large cactus with a hole cut out of it. A tiny pygmy owl peeked out and blinked at him. A large map covered the entirety of one wall. An elegant tea kettle and cups sat on a ledge above the fireplace. A large table in the middle of the room was hidden under piles of papers, maps, and drawings. Every other inch of the room was lined with books, papers, and scrolls. There were even cubbies in the rafters in the ceiling.

Mahkai handed Alex a mug of hot, sweet-smelling liquid that reminded him of a meadow after a summer shower. "Please, sit." Mahkai indicated the only chair in the room, as he folded his long legs and sat on a cushion on the floor.

The oddity of a half man, half bull sitting cross-legged on the floor, sipping tea, in a tree surrounded by books, combined with the stress from the last day or so - *has it only been a day?* Alex marveled. He couldn't keep his shoulders from shaking with laughter. Not the sort to take offense easily, and buoyed by Alex's laughter, Mahkai snorted a laugh, spraying tea out his nose. Soon, without truly knowing why, they both shook with laughter, wiping tears from their eyes.

Feeling better, Alex decided to ask Mahkai some of his burning questions. "So where are we exactly?"

"How do you not know? We are in Osrealach, of course... the kingdom of the Fae." Mahkai responded incredulously.

"Kingdom of the Fae? I've never heard of such a place." Alex asked.

"Fairies, minotaur, dwarves, puka... you really don't know, do you?" Mahkai responded.

"I'm familiar with fairies. Two of them tried to kill me earlier," Alex grumbled.

"Oh, that sounds like a story best told over more tea. And maybe some scones." Mahkai rose to refill their empty cups. He settled back down on the floor and looked at Alex expectantly, chewing on a mouthful of scone.

Taking a deep breath, Alex retold his adventures since he entered the clearing, and the deal he struck with Lilly and Fitz. "And then I was on the riverbank and met you," Alex finished.

"We call your Enchanted Forest 'Cinntire' and the waterfall you refer to is called Ere Vasan," Mahkai chimed in.

"That is quite an adventure! A sand golem, you say? How big was it? What did it sound like? What did it smell like? What did it feel like? Did it have a name?" Mahkai peppered Alex with questions as he took notes feverishly. "Did it look more like this, or this?" he asked, holding up two sketches for Alex to look over.

"The head of this one and the body of that one. It's close, but not quite," Alex replied, pointing to Mahkai's drawings.

Pausing from his sketching, Mahkai looked up with large, soft brown eyes. "Oh! I have always wondered this; when you strike down your enemies, do you eat their hearts raw or do you cook them first?" he asked innocently.

Alex coughed, choking on the mouthful of tea he had just sipped. "What? No!" he croaked finally.

"I was told that humans eat the hearts of their enemies. By your reaction, they must have been mistaken." Mahkai scribbled in yet another book.

They continued talking about a variety of subjects long into the evening. Mahkai showed Alex where they were on the map, and Alex helped him fill in missing details about Reyall. "Mahkai, help me understand. There are four kinds of magic? Is magic not all the same?" Alex asked.

"There are five actually. Some argue about a sixth, but that is widely debated," Mahkai answered. "You have water, earth, fire, air, and time. Or as some call it, histories, since you can't actually manipulate time, only view it."

Alex gaped at the minotaur for a moment. "So Lilly would have had earth magic, since she seemed to control the vines used to bind me?"

Mahkai nodded. "She is an Arboreal, yes."

"That is incredible. Is it a family trait or do you get to choose?"

"No one knows what they will be born with or what strength, since it is random, as best we know, so everyone goes through a variety of training until they turn thirty," Mahkai instructed. "At sundown of the summer solstice, we have a Revealing Ceremony. The Fae fire in this giant brazier changes color to reflect what their magical affinity is, and they choose what specialty they want to pursue," he continued.

"So someone who wields earth magic is an Arboreal? What are the others called?" Alex rubbed his thumb over the designs on his father's ring as he committed the words to memory.

"Someone with fire magic is called Ardere. Water is Aqualyte. I am an Aerophyte, because in theory I should be able to manipulate wind. And finally, those who can see and project past events are called historians."

Alex's mind spun with all the names.

"But enough about that. The golem said you need to find the lady of the lake. I think he means Althenaea, as she is the water master and lives by the lake. If he did not, maybe she would know who this lady of the lake is. Tomorrow is council and she will be in attendance, so we will head out at first light. I hear it will be quite the council because a notorious war criminal was caught breaking their banishment," Mahkai babbled.

Alex nodded in agreement, stifling a yawn. His mind reeled with everything he'd learned, but he was exhausted and not sure he could keep his head up any longer. He would ask more questions tomorrow when he could focus better.

Hopefully, Mahkai was right, and this Althenaea could help him.

Mahkai offered his hammock to Alex, but Alex declined. He preferred to sleep in the chair instead, not feeling comfortable so far above the ground yet. He drifted off almost instantly, thinking about Bucephalus.

✗✗✗

The next morning, Alex woke to little clawed feet hopping on his chest. He waved it off as he wiped the sleep from his eyes. Mahkai was already up. For such a large being, he moved rather lightly and silently. After tea and breakfast, they left at first light, taking a pack of food and water and two bags stuffed full of books, with the owl peeking out of the flap of one of them.

"Do you need all those?" Alex asked Mahkai, pointing to his bags.

Mahkai grinned. "You can never have too many books to go adventuring! You never know what you might need." He turned to follow the path near the base of his tree house.

They arrived just as it was beginning. Before going in, Mahkai told Alex to put his hood up so no one would realize he wasn't fae. Council was held in a large, oval room made of tree branches and vines woven together intricately to make solid walls. The canopy overhead was also intricately woven to let in light but keep the rain off.

Mahkai indicated the council members seated at the far end of the lower level. The room was so packed with fae that Alex had trouble seeing anything beyond his immediate surroundings. Eventually, they found a space where they could see, with their backs to the wall so as not to draw attention to themselves.

"The iron ring down there is meant to keep the accused from using their skills or magic during sentencing. It's quite fascinating, don't you think?" Mahkai said a little too loudly. The fae around them glared and shushed them.

Alex tried not to stare. There were fierce-looking minotaur, like Mahkai, dressed in leather sleeveless vests with tools and weapons strapped to their back and hanging off their hips. He made a mental note to not get on their bad side, if he could help it.

Small fairies like Fitz and Lilly, as well as winged, human-sized fairies hovered above the open center of the room. Birds flew in and landed on the railing, only to turn into human-looking fae. Alex almost gasped out loud. Giants gathered around the lower level. They must have been at least twenty-one hands tall. Alex felt very out of place. He looked around the room in awe.

"Giants?" Alex whispered to Mahkai.

"No silly, those are dwarves," he replied. Mahkai was almost vibrating with excitement as he took notes. Of what? Alex was unsure. They were shushed again, but Mahkai only shrugged and shook his head.

"Bring out the accused!" a voice rang out over the noise of the room.

Instantly, the room became silent as a figure, flanked by two towering dwarves, entered the lower level. His clothes were rumpled and dirty, but looked like something Alex would wear. His ragged, jet-black hair fell over his face. He walked with a slight limp, head bowed and shoulders slumped. He was led into the ring in the center, which they closed behind him, and stepped back a few paces.

Alex had trouble believing this was a hardened war criminal. He had attended his fair share of disciplinary courts with McCannon during his knight's training. Those criminals looked ferocious, like they were happy to kill and intended to do it again. This man did not have any of that malice, hate, or anger. He had the look of a man utterly defeated with no fight in him.

"Let it be known to all, the crimes for which he has been exiled," the voice boomed again. "Ronin, formerly Captain Ronin of the Protectorate, blatantly disobeyed a direct order resulting in gross injury and loss of life of his direct subordinates. He was stripped of his rank and sentenced to thirty years of exile for his flagrant actions. Under penalty of death, he was not permitted entrance to Osrealach until such a time as his exile concluded," the voice continued.

The room rumbled as the audience whispered and grumbled to each other. "He was found and captured across our borders, while still under exile, which is punishable by death," the speaker finished. "How do you plead?"

Ronin did not lift his head or respond.

"Do you have nothing to say for your actions? You had plenty to say last time, if memory serves," someone else taunted.

"Enough, Corsen!" another voice cut in. "Ronin, do you have an explanation for your return?" she asked. "You knew the law, and yet you came anyway. Why?" she pressed. "Last I saw you..."

"No! Don't!" Ronin interrupted her, finally looking up.

"But why?"

Something was nagging at Alex's memory, but he could not figure out what. He stepped forward to get a better view of the speaker. "I know that voice!" Alex whispered to Mahkai. She was clean and dressed differently, but Alex was sure it was her.

"How do you know Althenaea? You said you hadn't been here before," Mahkai said, forgetting to whisper. The fae around him started to grumble loudly, causing the council members to look their way, interrupting the proceedings. Mahkai tried to pull Alex back from the rail by his cloak, but accidentally pulled off his hood in the process. Suddenly, the entire room was looking at Alex and Mahkai.

"A human! Here?" Cries went up all over the room as they all got a better look at Alex and recognized he was not fae.

Everyone around Alex drew back as far as they could, as if touching him would burn them. Before he could react, vines wrapped tightly around his arms, legs, and throat, pinning him to the wall. He could barely breathe.

This was the second time Alex found himself in need of his knife, yet it was out of reach. He scolded himself for forgetting to address that issue yet again. He struggled against his restraints, but they held fast. "What is the meaning of this?" one of the council members asked Mahkai. "Is he with you? How dare you bring your human slave here?" they demanded.

"Oh my. He is not my slave, but the focus of my most recent research. Begging your pardon, I didn't realize it would be problematic," Mahkai stammered. Air currents swirled around them haphazardly, gaining momentum the more agitated Mahkai became.

"Mahkai! You will calm down and cease your magical outburst immediately!" A lady dwarf commanded. Alex remembered Mahkai had called her Fiacra, the aerophyte master. Mahkai shrank back. The eddies and gusts diminished. Two minotaur appeared on either side of Mahkai and clamped iron cuffs on his wrists. "We will deal with you later," she said sternly. They started to lead him away.

"No, leave him alone! He did nothing wrong!" Alex yelled. "I made him bring me here. If you need to punish someone, punish me, but please let him go. He did nothing wrong." Alex struggled as hard as he could, but his restraints held tight. Voices all around the room started shouting as everyone expressed their outrage at the events unfolding before them.

"There *will* be silence!" Althenaea's voice cut through the din as she made her way over to Alex. "We will take some time to deliberate. For now, Council is dismissed," Althenaea announced to the rest of the room. Everyone except the Council members, Mahkai, Alex, Ronin, and a handful of guards left the room slowly, talking among themselves as they left. When they were finally alone, Althenaea had Ronin escorted over and Mahkai released.

"I see now," she said cryptically, to no one in particular as she looked from Alex to Ronin. "Does he know?" she asked Ronin. Ronin met Alex's eyes and a look of recognition followed by relief crossed his face.

"No, he doesn't," Ronin replied to her, his eyes never leaving Alex. "How did you...?" Ronin started, but shook his head. "I knew the penalty when I entered our realm, but he was brought here against his will. I accept the consequences of my actions, but please let him go and return him to his home." His voice was low yet pleading.

"You will most certainly die! And so will he," Corsen cut in, coming to stand face-to-face with Alex. Corsen was just a little shorter than Alex. He had long, dark brown hair, a lithe build, pointed ears, and four translucent wings that looked like a dragonfly's. "Humans can't be trusted. They are violent, uncivilized, back-stabbing barbarians. The only good human is a dead human," he spat as the vines tightened. Alex gasped for air. His vision blurred, going black along the edges. He heard Ronin yelling, but could not make it out when Althenaea stepped in.

"That is not how we do things," she said with clear authority. "You cannot let your personal feelings intervene here. Release him!"

Corsen grumbled indistinguishably. The vines loosened their hold on Alex's neck. He coughed as he tried to catch his breath. *I really need to keep a tally of how many times these fae try to kill me.*

"What do you know that we do not, Althenaea?" Fiacra asked as she sat on a nearby chair.

"Oh, I see it now." A male voice interjected. "May I?" he asked the group.

"This is Amsah, our master of histories," Althenaea introduced him to Alex. "And yes, please proceed."

Amsah's hands glowed, and images appeared between them like on the walls in the golem's pyramid. It showed Alex and Buchephalus pulling Althenaea from the well, and then Alex being chased and captured by Fitz and Lilly with Ronin following them. Ronin let out a low growl.

Alex watched as he made his escape in the tunnel, and Ronin came through the waterfall and was captured. *So that was why they didn't come after me!* Then it showed Alex appearing in front of Mahkai. "So you see, they saved my life from the well and the slavers." Althenaea said when the images faded. "Ronin only broke exile when he thought Alex's life was in danger, but the law is the law. What do we want to do?" she asked the council.

"What is so special about this human that you would forfeit your life for his, Son?" Amsah peered at Ronin.

"Wait, what? Son?" Alex blurted out, looking between father and son. Now that he looked closer, Alex did see the family resemblance. They had the same eyes and build, only Ronin was a hand taller and broader than his father. "Why would you allow your own son to be exiled? Let alone condemn him to death?" Alex asked Amsah.

"He saved my life," Ronin said to his father.

"I did? When?" Alex asked Ronin. "What did you mean by *they*?" Alex asked Althenaea. He was asking a lot of questions, but no one was answering him.

She laughed and looked at Mahkai. "Did you teach him about Puka?"

Alex looked from one face to another, feeling left out of an inside joke. Ronin just studied the floor as if he suddenly found it very interesting.

"Oh! You mean Ronin is... Bucephalus?" Mahkai exclaimed, clapping his hands with delight. He took out a notebook and started writing. "That explains quite nicely."

Stunned speechless, Alex leaned against the wall and slid to the floor, staring at the opposite wall. His mind refused to make sense of this.

"Puka are shape changers," Mahkai said gently to Alex. "Each person can shift into a few animals, which are specific to them. I find learning through experience easier than abstract. Ronin, would you demonstrate, please?" Mahkai asked, looking to the council for approval.

"No! He's a human! This is not our way!" Corsen protested.

"Oh, but he's going to die anyway, right?" Althenaea replied sarcastically. She signaled for the guards to release Ronin.

Ronin nodded and shifted into a black falcon and flew to land on the floor below. He shifted to a huge black panther, then an even bigger black dire wolf. Lastly, he shifted into a beautiful black stallion—Bucephalus. Alex could not believe his eyes. Ronin shifted into his falcon form, flew up to the landing, and shifted back to his fae form. Alex continued to stare at the floor, not saying a word.

"Back to the matter at hand," Corsen interjected with a wave of his hand. "Are we ready to execute them?"

"I have another matter to address first," Althenaea responded.

"What could possibly be more important than this?" Corsen demanded.

Althenaea did not answer him. "Let's reconvene in three days' time," she said, looking at the rest of the council. They nodded.

"And what exactly do we do with them for three days?" Corsen said, gesturing to Alex and Ronin.

"Ah-hem," Mahkai cleared his throat. "They may stay with me, if you are agreeable."

"No, you have done enough," Fiacra chimed in. "Althenaea, you will take responsibility for these two. You owe them your life, after all. It's only fitting that their lives be in your hands now."

Althenaea nodded once. "Amsah, may I speak with you?" she asked, as the other four exited. She dismissed the guards and waited until Alex, Ronin, Mahkai, and Amsah were the only ones present. "Will you accompany us on our journey?" she asked.

Amsah's eyes flicked from Ronin to Alex, and back to Althenaea. "What do you have in mind?" he asked thoughtfully.

"Just a theory. I want to see how it plays out," she said cryptically.

At this, Alex's head snapped up in alarm. "Journey? Where are you taking me?" he asked, rising to his feet.

Amsah nodded. "Let me gather some supplies and I will meet back with you shortly," he said, striding to the exit.

Alex tensed, ready to run, but hesitated when he glanced at Ronin. Ronin looked back at him like he was burning with questions. Alex had many of his own questions still unanswered, so he relaxed a little, hoping he would find an opportunity to escape in the next three days.

"Now, for you." Althenaea looked at Mahkai. "I would like you to accompany us as well."

Mahkai looked shocked. "Me? It would be my pleasure!" he said excitedly.

"Are you hungry?" Althenaea asked the three of them. "I could do with some lunch. Follow me." She glided toward the closest exit, power and confidence exuding every step.

As they walked through the trees, Alex whispered to Ronin. "Why did you…"

"Not here!" Ronin cut him off in a low, urgent voice. He looked around warily as if someone were watching them.

XxXxX

They arrived at a small house built entirely out of driftwood on the edge of a small lake. The walls were made of large, sun-bleached logs, while the roof was made of darker, smaller branches. The door, if you could call it a door, rippled like the surface of the lake. Althenaea walked straight through it without pausing to open it. Mahkai paused to shove the edges of his books and papers further into his bags before following her through.

Alex hesitantly reached out to touch the surface. Remembering the waterfall trick, and how he had almost drowned, he withdrew his hand quickly. "It won't bite you, you know," Ronin teased. "You can just walk through it."

Alex looked up at him sharply and shook his head. He let out a sigh. "I… the waterfall," he faltered, not sure what else to say.

"Ah," Ronin simply responded. "Wait here." He walked through the water, and, a moment later, the water parted like curtains. He poked his head out, grabbed Alex's arm, and dragged him inside. The water curtain closed behind them.

Inside, the house was larger than it seemed on the outside. A large spiral staircase formed out of pebbles and sand led down to a second floor. The upper floor consisted of an alcove of books with a hammock chair hanging in the corner on one side and a bed on the opposite side. The walls were made of sand inlaid with glass shards and seashells as decoration. Alex had never seen anything like it. At the center of the lower level, a fire burned brightly in a ring of stones dug out of the sandy floor. Seated on cushions around the fire, Mahkai and Althenaea chatted over steaming bowls of something that smelled delicious. They beckoned him to join them.

As he followed Ronin down the stairs, he saw a small cooking area against one wall and another water door leading out the back. Ronin dished two bowls, handed one to Alex, and sat down next to Althenaea. He tasted the delicious noodles, fish, and seaweed in a savory broth in his bowl. Alex closed his eyes as he reveled in the delectable fare.

When they finished, Althenaea stared at Alex and Ronin expectantly.

"It is safe to talk here," she said as she poured tea into mugs.

Alex lifted his mug and blew gently across the surface to help it cool as he struggled to collect his racing thoughts. "I don't know where to begin," he said, looking from Althenaea to Ronin to Mahkai. "I have so many questions."

"Maybe tell them what you told me last night?" Mahkai suggested.

Alex retold all of the events from the time he was separated from Ronin in the Enchanted Forest, to when he showed up on Mahkai's doorstep, leaving out the parts with the "not rock." "The sand golem said my answers lay with the Lady of the Lake. Mahkai thought you might be her, or at least know who she is and how to find her."

Althenaea looked lost in thought and did not respond right away. She finally looked up at him. "You spoke with Kynthelic? He showed himself to you?"

The awe and fondness laced in her words surprised Alex. He blinked at her before taking a sip of his tea, unsure how to respond.

"We are going to the Revealing when Amsah joins us. I won't know for sure until we perform the ceremony, but I believe you have fae ancestry."

Alex looked at her sharply and coughed on his tea. "I what?" He set down his mug and began pacing. "I mean, why wouldn't I? I just found out fairies and magical creatures are real, and my horse isn't a horse, so why wouldn't I be?" he ranted.

"He's not tall enough to be a dwarf, and he's definitely no minotaur. He could be a fairy or puka," Mahkai said thoughtfully, taking notes. "Tell me, Alex, have you ever felt the urge to become an animal?"

"He's not a puka," Althenaea said. "But, yes, maybe fairy. Have you had any manifestations of your magical abilities yet?" she wondered aloud.

"He's Ardra," Ronin said in a low voice.

"But that's… impossible," Mahkai said. "Are you sure?"

"I'm sure," Ronin said, staring at Alex steadily across the fire.

"How do you know?" Althenaea asked

"Show her your father's ring," Ronin urged Alex.

Alex looked questioningly at Ronin, but pulled the ring, hanging on a chain around his neck, from under his tunic, and held it out to Althenaea. She took his ring and studied it for a long moment before handing it back.

"The first time I saw Alex, he was washing up on shore from swimming with a sea dragon," Ronin said.

"A sea dragon!" Mahkai exclaimed. "You didn't tell me about that!" He pulled out yet another of his notebooks to take notes. "You have to tell me everything! What it looked like, what it sounded like, how it acted…"

"The day I saved the knights? How do you know about that? I was the only one… oh," Alex said, realization dawning on him mid-sentence. "You were the falcon in the tree."

Ronin nodded. "Sea dragons do not socialize with humans. They eat them or drag them to the bottom of the sea to drown them. They don't interact with fae either, except the Ardra. So I figured you had to be special for it to not eat you, let alone to bring you back to shore."

"When I inquired about you to Bronach, he said he was still piecing it together himself and suggested I keep an eye on you. He knew I needed something to keep me out of trouble until my exile was finished, and you needed someone to look out for you. He would have done it himself, but no one brings their blacksmith along during knight's training." Ronin chuckled.

"You were a soldier before your exile. That's how you picked up on all the maneuvers so quickly?" Alex asked. "Wait, that day on the bank of the river… that was you? You pulled me out when I was caught on a branch and drowning. Why didn't you show yourself to me all this time? We've been together five years, and you didn't once think to say or do anything? Why? Why should I trust you?" Alex finally took a breath, having released many of his pent-up questions.

Ronin rose and stood directly in front of Alex, forcing him to stop pacing or run into him. Ronin was a little taller than

Alex. He held Alex's glare unflinchingly. His dark eyes glinted in the firelight. "I could not. It was part of my exile. Bronach knew me from before, but he was the only one. As you know, to be different in your kingdom means to be hunted and killed." His voice was bitter and raw with emotion.

They stood motionless, staring into each other's eyes as if trying to read the other's soul. Alex's other questions went unvoiced. A storm raged in him. He had spent the last five years telling Bucephalus, Ronin, everything... what he thought, how he felt, his frustrations and fears, his bad jokes, everything. He felt betrayed, but also something else.

Ronin could have left at any time, but he stayed. He'd even broken his exile to try to save him from Lilly and Fitz. Alex knew almost nothing of this man standing before him, but Ronin knew everything about him. If they lived through the next three days, did he want to continue traveling with Ronin? Would Ronin want to stay with him? He shook his head. One thing at a time.

Ronin remained still, simply staring at him with eyes full of unspoken words. Alex was grateful. His warring thoughts and feelings were most likely written all over his face anyway.

A snap brought their attention back to the others in the room. Mahkai had broken his writing utensil and was rummaging around in his bag for another. "So about the sea dragon...?" he asked.

Amsah chose that moment to appear in the doorway upstairs. "Alright, are we ready?" he asked.

Althenaea nodded and held her hand out to the fire. Water rose from the sand, dousing the flames with a hiss, then disappeared. Ronin laid his hand on Alex's shoulder for a moment before turning to climb the stairs to join his father. Mahkai replaced his notebooks in his bags and followed Ronin up the stairs. Althenaea approached Alex.

"Outside, do not speak of this again until I say it is safe. Do not trust anyone besides the four of us. Your life depends on it. There is more at work here than you know, but I cannot tell you more. What I can tell you is that Ronin is worthy of your loyalty. Trust him. And keep your ring hidden until we reach Thoria," she said, her voice barely above a whisper.

She handed him a knapsack and put on one of her own. Without another word, she gestured for him to join the others. This time, Alex did not hesitate passing through the water door after the others. His ears popped as if he had just swum up from deep water. Amsah looked from Ronin to Alex, noticing the change in their demeanor from earlier.

"What did I miss?" he asked.

"Nothing." Ronin shook his head.

"Nothing? You call that nothing? It was..." Mahkai exclaimed.

"That's enough, Mahkai," Althenaea interrupted.

"Oh my! I do apologize. I seem to have forgotten myself in the excitement," Mahkai said.

Amsah "hmmed", then turned to walk regally next to Althenaea. Alex and Ronin trailed behind Mahkai who was busy humming and writing in one of his notebooks again. He was prone to walk into trees as he was not watching where he was going, so they would steer him the right way if he got too far off the path.

As they walked, Althenaea and Amsah chatted but were too far ahead for Alex to hear what they were saying. After a few hours of walking, with only his thoughts for company, he broke the silence.

"Thank you," he said quietly to Ronin. "For saving my life countless times."

"You are welcome. If given the choice, I'd do it again. I hope you know that," Ronin replied earnestly. "You saved my life too, you know. That night in the snowstorm when you found me in the barn with the gash in my side. You stayed up all night making sure I didn't freeze while my wounds healed."

"You healed incredibly fast. I was so amazed. I should have seen the signs, looking back on it all," Alex replied.

"You saw what you expected to see," Ronin said. "A horse. An exceptional horse maybe, but still a horse."

"Why did you stay?" Alex asked. "You could have left at any time."

"For your singing." Ronin grinned teasingly, nudging him in the shoulder. "No, but seriously, I did leave. All the time. While you were sleeping or out training or in meetings, I would sneak off and go hunting or watch you or explore. If you aren't aware, standing in a stall eating hay is not exactly exciting," he said sarcastically.

"You nearly caught me a couple of times, though." He laughed sheepishly, rubbing a hand on the back of his neck. His mood darkened. "I got lazy. I was out hunting when you woke up in Cinntire and ran into those two despicable fairies. If I ever get my hands on them..." He trailed off. His eyes turned bright amber and took on feline qualities. He shook his head to clear his thoughts, and his eyes went back to normal.

Fascinated, Alex watched him, but did not know what to say. Up ahead, Althenaea stopped at the river bank. She waited for the rest to catch up before creating a boat out of water. "Our journey will be faster this way," she said. The boat was little, with room for only three or four.

"I don't believe we will all fit," Alex pointed out.

"We don't have to," Ronin said, handing Alex his knapsack.

Ronin shifted into a falcon and launched himself into the sky, swooping low and flipping several times before flying high again. Amsah shifted into a sparrow and took off after Ronin.

"They'll follow us above," Althenaea said as an explanation. "Come, let us not waste time." She stepped into her water boat and stood at the bow.

Mahkai held his breath and tentatively stepped in after her. He looked like he thought he would sink at any moment. "Oh!" he said when he sat down, letting his breath out.

As Alex sat down, they started moving. He could see through the bottom as they sped through the water upstream. The trees flashed by at incredible speeds, faster than a horse and rider could keep up. Up ahead, mountains loomed, steadily getting closer. He looked up to see Ronin's shadow far overhead, but Amsah was nowhere in sight.

Alex felt his eyes drifting closed. Lulled by the swish of water, he was unable to keep them open any longer.

CHAPTER 11

ALEX sensed them slowing down. He straightened and wiped his eyes. Judging from the angle of the sun, he guessed they had been traveling for several hours. Mahkai had not moved and was still reading, the same as before Alex fell asleep. Althenaea had not moved either. Alex wondered how taxing it was to do what she was doing, whatever that was.

"Mahkai, how does magic work?" Alex asked, not wanting to bother Althenaea. "Mahkai?" No response. "Mahkai!" He practically shouted.

"Yes? There is no need to yell," Mahkai said, looking up from his book.

Alex blinked at him but chose not to comment. "How does magic work?" he asked finally.

"I…" Mahkai paused. "I believe I am not who you should ask to teach you about that." he said, barely above a whisper. He looked embarrassed.

"I don't understand. You know so much about everything," Alex asked perplexed.

"Ah, um… It's not that I do not know, I just cannot control mine very well. I've never been very good with my magic, you see. Like I mentioned last night, I am an Aerophyte, but I am not proficient. When I concentrate, to use magic on purpose, nothing happens. You saw the extent of my abilities earlier," he said. "I accidentally create wind currents and eddies haphazardly, when I get really flustered." He hung his head and looked at his hands.

"I understand. There's nothing to be ashamed of, though. You have other skills you are great at. Magic isn't everything," Alex said gently.

Mahkai shook his head. "That is very kind, but here in Osrealach, magic is everything. The apprenticeships or positions open to you, your social status, and even finding a partner are all dependent on your abilities."

"But why? You don't get to decide what you are born with. Why should that determine your worth or future?" Alex asked. "In Reyall, it is all about what family you are born into. I hate it," he said bitterly. "It shouldn't be that way."

Mahkai nodded.

"Then change it," Althenaea said tiredly, turning towards them.

Startled, Alex and Mahkai looked up. They had come to a stop next to a pebbled bank, and the boat was slowly losing shape. They gathered their bags and quickly jumped out just as the boat completely dissolved. Just beyond where they stopped, the river narrowed to little more than a shallow stream, flanked by densely packed trees and shrubs. The sunlight filtering through the trees showed it was late afternoon.

Without another word, Althenaea shouldered her knapsack and strode with purpose down the trail along the river bank. They walked along the trail for a few hours, each lost in their own thoughts.

Alex replayed all the events from the last five years that led him here. He wondered about his father and his ancestry. If Ronin was right, and Alex was fae - whatever Ardra was, then it had to be from his father's side.

His mother hadn't spoken of his father often, but when she did, she seemed heartbroken. Alex stopped asking about him after she cried herself to sleep several nights in a row. He touched the ring hanging on its chain around his neck through his tunic.

He needed something else to keep his hands busy, so he put his hands in his pockets. He felt the "not rock," but also something else. Surprised, he pulled out the objects to investigate them. He stopped so suddenly Mahkai ran into him.

"Oh! Pardon me," Mahkai apologized, looking down at Alex. "Oh, that is lovely! Where did you get it?"

In Alex's hand rested a small, uninteresting bread roll and an orange topaz-colored gemstone the size of an apricot. "The tunnels? I put fruit in my pockets for later." He checked his other pockets for the fruit he had stashed there and found they had all turned into gemstones. "I don't understand," he said, bewildered.

"I do not know either," Mahkai admitted. "That is not something I have heard of being done before." He pulled out one of his notebooks and sketched a quick drawing and took a few notes before replacing his notebook back into his bag.

Alex put the gems back in his pockets and resumed walking. They jogged to catch up with Althenaea. He broke the roll in two, offering half to Mahkai.

Mahkai shook his head. "I must decline, but my deepest gratitude."

Alex looked up at the tops of the trees, trying to see Bucephalus, or Ronin rather. He always seemed hungry. As if reading his mind, Ronin swooped down next to Alex, shifting just before he touched the ground.

"Someone mentioned food?" Ronin asked, grinning at Alex.

Alex laughed and handed him the other half of his roll. "I would offer you fruit too, but it seems they have turned to stone," he said, pulling out one of the fruit-sized gems to show Ronin.

Ronin looked at Alex as they walked. "That's different," he shrugged, before taking a bite of the roll.

"How can you eat that? You don't know where it's been," Mahkai asked. "No offense intended, Alex," he added hastily.

"I know exactly where it's been… in his pocket," Ronin said. "Do you happen to have any of those sweet oatcakes in one of your pockets too?" he asked Alex hopefully.

Alex smiled and shook his head. "No, they are all in my saddle bags under the tree in the forest, sorry."

Ronin's hopeful expression faded. "No worries. Well, I better get back up there." He ran a couple paces, then launched himself into the air, shifting as he jumped. He flew circles above them until he reached the treetops, then vanished.

Alex let out a deep sigh. He was still trying to process everything and didn't know how he felt about this shifting thing. He wondered if he had gained the friend he had always wished for.

As the sunlight faded on the horizon, Alex assumed they would stop for the night. He wished he had his cloak and was kicking himself for not grabbing it before running off to look for Bucephalus.

They continued on through dusk until it was almost completely dark. He wished he had a lamp or torch when he stumbled over a root for what felt like the thousandth time. He considered pulling out the "not rock" to see if it would glow for him, but was not ready to show it to anyone yet.

On a hunch, he pulled out one of the gems, but no such luck. It did not glow. He put it back in his pocket just as he caught sight of a light up ahead. It was fully dark now, and he could barely see Althenaea's silhouette two paces in front of him.

As they approached the light, a large door appeared on the side of the sheer rock face. *When did we get so close to the mountains?* Alex thought. He felt a warm breath on the back of his neck and turned to look over his shoulder. "Mahkai, what are you..." Alex stopped mid-sentence.

Alex was a handbreadth away from the jaws of a giant snow leopard. A deep growl rumbled in its chest. It bared its teeth.

Alex's mind raced as his training kicked in. He jumped back and into a crouch. His left hand went to his hip to find his axe or knife, but came up empty. That's right, Fitz had taken them. His right hand gripped his hidden blade, but he kept it hidden behind his back.

The leopard crouched, waiting, watching him intently. At any moment, it would pounce. One foot at a time, Alex inched backward toward the door. He had no idea what he was going to do when he got there. Maybe he could pound on it, and someone might let him in. *Where are Mahkai and Althenaea?* He didn't dare take his eyes off the leopard before him. *Maybe it's a shapeshifter like Ronin.*

"I don't want to hurt you!" he said, trying a different approach. "If this is your territory, I'm sorry. I didn't mean to intrude."

The snow leopard did not respond.

What if I'm wrong and this is a real snow leopard? Alex's heel grazed the cliff face behind him. He had run out of space and time.

I'm in trouble.

The leopard leapt at him with claws out and jaws open. Alex dove to the ground and rolled to his feet, narrowly missing the claws aimed at his head. The leopard rebounded off the rock and launched itself at Alex again. This time, he spun to his right, pulled out his blade, and backhand-slashed at its face.

It snarled viciously, and he knew his attack had connected. When it turned to face him, blood dripped from a shallow cut over its left eye.

He was breathing fast, and his heart was pounding with adrenaline, but a part of him knew it was only a matter of time before he made a mistake or was not fast enough. His knife was too short to keep this up for long, but he would not go down without a fight.

They crouched in a standoff. He truly did not want to have to kill it, but he would if it gave him no choice. The whoosh of wings from above caught his attention. He looked before he realized his mistake. The leopard used his distraction to knock him to the ground. Its claws dug into his left shoulder and right arm, pinning him.

He cried out as pain lanced through him. He tried to kick at it with his legs, but it was too heavy to get the right leverage. He stared defiantly into its eyes. It stared back at him, as if it wanted him to know it could kill him any moment it chose. It was toying with him. Unexpectedly, it jumped off him and retreated.

Alex tried to stand, but the best he could manage was kneeling with his right arm, holding his knife out in front of him. Blood ran freely down both arms. The pain in his shoulder made him hiss when he moved. The edges of his vision went fuzzy and his focus drifted. His left side burned. He looked down but could not see the source. Maybe his mind was playing tricks on him.

"Use it, Young One!" a voice called in his head. *Use what?* Alex asked the voice. *What? Use what?* He thought desperately. *Please help me!*

"It is a key and not a key. It is a guide,
and not. It is what you need it to be,
but... not."

The memory surfaced as he felt his strength leave him. He collapsed on the ground. Struggling against the pain and spreading numbness creeping down his arm, he dug his hand into his pocket and grabbed hold of the "not rock." It was hot to his touch, and he almost dropped it, pulling it out.

He cradled it in both hands and drew his knees to his chest. The heat from the "not rock" spread up his arms, into his chest, and down his torso and legs. His whole body burned from the inside.

Gradually, the heat faded and with it, the pain and numbness. He felt exhausted, as if he had gone through the knight's trials without sleeping for a week. *I am alive at any rate. That has to count for something, right?*

He flexed his arms and legs, groaning from the effort. He would be sore for days. He opened his eyes. Four scarlet and obsidian scaled legs the size of tree trunks stood over him. It smelled of campfire and forge. The scales looked as if they were lit from the inside, with firelight dancing and swirling in each one. The armored legs connected to wicked-looking clawed feet. His body refused to cooperate as he attempted to retreat. He looked around wildly. He was under it, whatever it was.

"Stay put. Let your body regain its strength," the voice from his head instructed, only now it came from above him.

He tried again to get up, but it was too great an effort, so he just lay there looking at the "not rock" in wonder. *"How am I alive? I thought I died,"* he asked the voice.

"You almost did, young one. Though, you need not yell. We all heard you," she replied.

"We? Who are you?" He asked.

"We have many names, but you know us as dragons. I am a fire dragon, to be precise. You may call me Saoirse," she said in his mind. *"You would do well to put the Guardian stone away before anyone sees it. Kynthelic entrusted it to you. It is your duty to guard it… at all costs."*

"The guardian stone? Oh, the 'not rock?' You said, 'we all heard you.' What did you mean?" he slipped it back into his pocket.

"When you engaged the young puka, you relayed your peril. As you touched the mountains, they amplified your distress to all of my kin. You should have been trained better when you were younger. It was very rude," she admonished.

"I am so very sorry. I didn't know."

He tried moving again and found he could push himself up to his knees, though his muscles screamed at him for it. Saoirse moved as he sat up. He was lightheaded, and his vision swam, but he managed to look around. The snow leopard was fifty paces off, still watching him. Behind it appeared two glowing eyes in a massive black shadow.

"Tell your friend he can come out now. The young puka will not interfere with you while I'm here," Saoirse said.

"Ronin? Can he not hear you as I can?"

"He could, but I choose not to speak to whom I do not wish. It is our way."

"Why do you choose to speak to me?"

"Because I choose to," she replied cryptically.

Alex was pretty sure that was not an explanation, but did not want to be rude again. "Ronin?" he called out.

The black shadow emerged into the light. Ronin's massive direwolf snapped at the snow leopard, narrowly missing him as he walked by. Startled, the snow leopard jumped sideways and retreated.

"Alex, are you alright?" Ronin asked after he shifted to his fae form, keeping his distance from Alex and Saoirse.

"I have a splitting headache and am sore all over, but otherwise, I'm fine. Where have you been? You missed all the fun," he joked.

"Quinn, I should have known you would be behind this," Ronin growled at the leopard.

The leopard shifted gradually, a fair bit slower than Ronin, Alex noticed. Quinn had short, black curly hair, ebony skin, and strong, broad shoulders. He wore a white sleeveless tunic with asymmetrical lines over white pants that stopped just below his knees. Notably, he was also barefoot, which struck Alex as odd.

"Ronin," Quinn growled. "Last I heard, you were exiled. I've been sent to bring you back to the council," he threatened. "How is this one alive?" he gestured with his chin in Alex's direction. He looked at the dragon standing between himself and Alex. "Also, while you are explaining things, explain why she would get involved with this... *human*, let alone protect it." He spat like the word 'human' left a foul taste in his mouth.

Alex felt uneasy, but surprisingly not because of the dragon.

Ronin shook his head and shrugged. "I don't know. Why don't you ask her," he said sarcastically.

"You know full well she would not speak to either of us," Quinn accused.

They stood awkwardly silent for a while. Alex's head pounded, and he still felt unsteady, but he attempted to stand.

"*I would not do that yet, Young One,*" Saoirse said to Alex.

He barely made it to his feet before his legs gave out, and he crashed back to the ground. Ronin took a step towards him, but stopped. He flashed a look of concern, but stayed where he was.

I don't understand. What is wrong with me? Alex asked her with his mind. Wait, *can you hear my thoughts?*

"*No, I cannot hear your thoughts unless you direct them at me. To answer your first question: you were dying, and you used magic you are not trained to handle, so it took its toll on your body,*" she instructed slowly, as if speaking to a child.

"*There is a balance which is directly influenced by your strength and will. The stronger your mind and body, the greater the feats you can do. It takes no small measure of practice, concentration, and discipline, which you will soon become more familiar with,*" she continued. "*You should have already been taught all of this by your clan. Who are they? I will direct one of the elders to address it,*" she finished indignantly.

I don't know my clan. I only found out I was possibly fae earlier today. Ronin thinks I am Ardra. What is Ardra anyway? Alex asked her.

He was starting to feel more steady, so he attempted to stand again. He stumbled a little and caught himself on her side. Instantly, sparks shot out from their point of contact. He gasped and pulled his hand away like he'd touched hot coals. His hand tingled.

Saoirse whipped her head around and glared at him with one of her large amber eyes. *"In addition to being able to speak to dragons, Ardra can wield all types of magic,"* she snapped. *"You are very fortunate to have the guardian stone, Young One, or you would be dead. In the future, you might endeavor to avoid touching a dragon if you wish to survive,"* she warned. At that, she leaped high into the air, unfurled her wings, and disappeared into the night sky.

Ronin and Quinn froze in stunned silence.

CHAPTER 12

ALEX gazed at his hand, flexing repeatedly, as he mulled over the most recent development. He glanced up at the starry sky as he fidgeted with his family ring, still hanging on its chain around his neck.

He was relieved he had not lost it in the fight, though he couldn't say as much for his tunic, which hung in bloody tatters from his shoulders. Silvery scars streaked down his arm, the only evidence of his near-death experience. He heard footsteps approaching behind him and turned to see Althenaea striding swiftly toward him.

"Alexander, I see that you are alive."

Alex glanced down at his arm and shoulder and back up at her. "Yes."

His tumultuous thoughts warred in his mind. He was afraid if he said anything more, he might say the wrong thing. *Where was she while I was fighting Quinn? Why didn't she intervene? I thought she didn't want me to die, was I wrong? Can I trust her?*

She studied him with her other-wordly cerulean gaze. Alex shifted uncomfortably under her intense scrutiny and looked down at his feet. *Did I do something wrong?*

He spied the hilt of his knife sticking out of the grass and knelt to pick it up. The tip had broken off at some point during the fight. He was weaponless. Again. He let out a frustrated sigh and put the hilt in his pocket. Althenaea gestured to Ronin and Quinn to join them.

Quinn looked intently at Ronin and probed. "Will you answer honestly if I ask you something?"

Ronin narrowed his eyes and looked at Quinn with a guarded expression.

"Corsen ordered me to capture and retrieve a rogue minotaur and its human cohort, but this seems much more complicated than that. What is going on here?" Quinn asked, perplexed.

"Captain Quinn," Althenaea said, coming to stand next to Ronin.

"My lady!" Quinn exclaimed, standing a little straighter. "I had no idea you were here. I was instructed to retrieve the exiled and the human." He looked at Alex quizzically.

"Corsen... I should have guessed he would interfere. That won't be necessary, Captain. Would you please release the minotaur? Your service is no longer required," Althenaea said.

"Respectfully, my lady, I cannot return without the human," Quinn said, though his face betrayed his conflicting thoughts.

"Then you will simply have to accompany us on our journey. We will return in two days," she said matter-of-factly.

Quinn opened his mouth to protest, but thought better of it and conceded. "Yes M'lady.". He whistled. Five hulking figures emerged from the tree line and stepped into the torchlight.

"Release him," he said to the minotaur holding Mahkai.

While Mahkai stood a head taller than Alex, this minotaur was another head taller than Mahkai. It was also broader and significantly more muscular. Its well-defined arms were adorned with studded leather bracers. It wore a sleeveless, sculpted-leather chest plate with a massive double-headed axe strapped to its back, and a collection of throwing knives on a bandolier across its chest. An impressive war hammer hung from one hip. It was a warrior among warriors, especially next to Mahkai's scholarly build. The minotaur removed Mahkai's restraints and Quinn dismissed them, promising to meet back with them in a couple of days.

Mahkai opened his mouth to say something, but Althenaea cut him off saying, "We need to get moving. We don't have time to waste." Not waiting for a reply, she strode towards the torchlit open door.

Once everyone was inside, an unseen force slammed the door behind them. Crystals embedded in the ceiling glowed along the corridor, lighting their way with warm, orange tones, giving the ambiance of firelight. Periodically, they came across other tunnels branching out from the one they were on, but they remained unlit. Alex wondered where they led, but couldn't see more than a couple of paces beyond the divergence.

Their footsteps echoed on the stone floor, making their group sound bigger than it was. It made stealth almost impossible. He wondered if there was some intentionality behind the design or if it occurred naturally. They emerged into a mammoth, brightly lit cavern and were greeted by two identical giants. *Dwarves,* Alex reminded himself.

The two dwarves were a head taller than Mahkai. They wore thick leather aprons and had broad, heavily muscled shoulders and chests, as you would expect of someone who spent most of their time at a forge. They wore their long, blonde hair half pulled back and their beards long but trimmed and well-groomed with metal and glass beads braided into them.

The cavern was massive. A large chandelier hung from the center of the cavern, lit with more of the same orange and yellow crystals that had been lining the tunnel. Against the far wall, an enormous forge loomed, glowing bright white, surrounded by a workspace piled with projects at various stages of completion.

"This is Gremlore and Bailor. Also known as the 'Fire Dwarf Twins,'" Althenaea introduced them to the rest of the group. "I require your assistance," she said to the twins.

The one called Gremlore wore an ornate torc made of a silvery blue metal Alex had never seen before. He wore a tan tunic with the sleeves rolled up to reveal corded, tattooed forearms under a worn, scarred, and singed leather apron that had seen a fair bit of use.

Bailor dressed similarly. He also had silvery blue beads braided into his long, curly, dark hair.

"What happened to ye, lad?" Gremlore asked, looking at Alex.

"A misunderstanding," Quinn said abruptly, cutting Ronin and Alex off.

"Hmmm, interesting," Bailor said, but did not comment further.

"You are already familiar with Captain Quinn. This is Alex, Mahkai, and Ronin." Althenaea introduced each of them to the dwarves.

"Isn't that...?" Gremlore asked his brother.

"Mmmm." Bailor nodded.

"Isn't he...?"

"I'd imagine so,"

"Well, it's good to see ye, Althenaea. To what do we owe the pleasure of yer fine company?" Gremlore asked. "Do ye wish to commission a new weapon or finally let us make that armor for ye?" he continued.

"No. I require your skill in other matters, but we can discuss that at a later time. How are things here? Please fill me in." Althenaea said.

"Absolutely, m'lady!" Bailor said. "Let us move to somewhere more comfortable."

Alex was very interested in their conversations, but his mind refused to focus. Exhaustion dragged at his mind and body, tired from his fight with Quinn and the events leading up to it. He sat on a stack of crates and tried to fight it, but as his mind wandered, his eyes drifted closed.

XXX

Next thing he knew, he woke up on a pallet next to the forge.

"Ah, yer awake!" Gremlore said cheerfully as he put several metal rods into the forge to heat up. "There's some water to wash up over there," he indicated with his head to a basin to his right. "And some food here for ye if yer hungry." He nodded to a plate sitting on a ledge.

Alex sat up and a blanket fell off his shoulders to his lap. Someone had removed what was left of his torn tunic while he slept. Alex blinked in surprise.

He wasn't sure what surprised him more, the hospitality or the familiarity someone felt to remove his tunic. After washing his face and arms, he inspected his scars again.

"Those are some pretty nasty scars ye got there," Gremlore commented, not looking up from his tools. "How did ye get them?" he asked.

"I had a disagreement with a snow leopard earlier," Alex said as he traced his finger along the longest scar on his forearm.

"Earlier? As in recently?" Gremlore asked incredulously. He looked over at Alex briefly.

"Right before we came here. We fought, I started to pass out, I felt like I was burning from the inside out, and when I woke up, there was a dragon," Alex said.

"That's quite the story, lad," Gremlore said as he took out the glowing rods from the fire with his tongs. "How might ye be acquainted with Saoirse?"

Alex looked up at him sharply. Gremlore's rhythmic hammering echoed through the cavern.

"The comings and goings of dragons are according to their counsel and cannot be explained by mere mortals," Gremlore said by way of an explanation, as he put the somewhat flattened rod back into the fire.

Alex nodded. "That seems an apt explanation."

He picked up the plate and took a bite of the delicious-looking scone covered in cream and berries. While he ate, he watched silently as Gremlore repeated his pattern, heating the metal in the forge and pounding it with his hammer.

Surrounded by the familiar smell of hot metal, Alex felt himself relax for the first time since he'd left Creedon. He closed his eyes and could almost hear Bronach's rich baritone voice singing in time with his hammer.

Bronach stood with his back to Alex, singing as he pounded his hammer on the glowing metal bar that would become a horseshoe. Surrounded by the sweet smell of hay, horses, and the forge, Alex let out a deep breath. He could relax here, he was safe. His heart pounded in his chest. He was out of breath from his escape from the village bullies. Bronach either did not notice his presence or chose not to acknowledge him. This was the third time this week Alex had hidden behind the woodpile next to the forge. The other children wouldn't bother him here.

Bronach put the horseshoe in the hot coals and wiped the sweat running down the side of his face with a cloth tucked in his belt. It was always peaceful here. As Alex watched, trying to calm his breathing, Bronach walked over to stand at the horse's head, stroking its neck, talking softly as if it could understand him. The fire popped and one of the horses stamped and snorted.

Alex took a deep breath and let out a sigh. He rolled his shoulders, willing them to release their tension. For a fleeting moment, he truly felt at home again. He glanced up to find Gremlore watching him with an odd expression on his face.

"Ye seem to know yer way around a forge," Gremlore said, more as a statement than a question as he turned back to the forge.

Alex did not know whether he should comment or stay quiet and was still debating with himself when Gremlore asked him to hold the tongs as he took another rod out of the fire. He twisted the hot metal in a spiral around the one Alex was holding, then asked him to put it back in the forge.

Alex did as he was instructed. As he was turning away, something on the edge of the fire caught his attention. Teardrop-shaped disks, blackened on the edges and the same color as the flames in the center, rimmed the forge.

"Gremlore, are those dragon scales in the flames?" Alex asked.

"Aye, lad. It's how we keep the fire hot enough to work the metals." Gremlore took one of the disks out of the fire and plunged it into a bucket of water before handing it to Alex to examine.

"Normal flames wouldn't be adequate. It takes a dragon to light and dragon scales to insulate it so the forge doesn't crack or melt."

Alex inspected the scale, turning it over in his hands. The firelight reflected through it as if it were lit from the inside. It was still warm to the touch, and he wondered if it ever truly lost its heat.

"Is this one of Saoirse's?" It looked familiar. "Do dragons shed scales?" Alex asked.

Gremlore nodded. "Dragons shed scales occasionally, and if they're in a generous mood, they give 'em to us to use in the forge. We have long suspected that it's not the only use for scales, but dragons aren't known for their generosity; so I don't have any to spare to test with. We use a special blend of metals we call Piridios, which must be heated well beyond normal means," Gremlore continued.

"Piridios? I've never heard of it," Alex said, curiously.

Gremlore chuckled, "No, ye wouldn't have in Reyall, I'd expect. Bailor and I alone, know how to make it. Well… and our half-brother, but he doesn't have access to a fire dragon or the metals, so it does him no good. You might, perchance, have met him. You were hummin' his favorite song just before," he said.

"How do you know I'm from Reyall? I was? When?" Alex asked, confused.

Gremlore sang the Traveler's Blessing Alex thought was just a thing his village did. "When ye looked lost in thought."

"How do you...?" Alex trailed off as he realized what Gremlore was implying. "Bronach is your half brother?"

"Aye," Gremlore said as he pulled the rods out of the fire again.

Alex started to ask more, but was distracted as Ronin walked over with a bundle in his arms. He handed it to Alex.

"I thought you might want these, since there was almost nothing left of your tunic," Ronin said with a shrug.

"Thanks. Did you know Bronach is their half-brother?" Alex asked Ronin, as he pulled the new black tunic over his head. It was a little big, but would be fine once he could belt it.

"Mmhmm," Ronin nodded. "Gremlore told me where to find him 15 years ago, right before I was exiled."

"But you didn't show up as Bucephalus until right before McCannon did," Alex pointed out.

Ronin sighed and sat down on the pallet with his back against the wall, and drew his knees up to his chest. He stared at the floor gravely for a few minutes as emotions played across his face.

"It took almost ten years before I could reach out to anyone," he said somberly. "I wanted them to execute me... it's what I deserved."

"You don't have to tell me if you don't want to, but what happened? Why did they exile you?" Alex asked as he sat down next to him.

They sat in silence for a long time, while Gremlore continued working at the forge. Alex was about to get up and offer to help again when Ronin began to speak.

"It might surprise you, but not so long ago, the fae were divided. The leader had been assassinated, the histories master went missing and was accused of orchestrating it, and the rest of the council fractured."

"The fairies wanted to take control of everything, the Ardra withdrew and went into hiding; the minotaur, refusing to be ruled by the fairies, fought back. The puka worked things out with the fairies, so when the minotaur took up arms, we were drawn into the fight. All my life, I had heard about the monstrous minotaur who only wanted violence and wouldn't make peace. So after my revealing, I requested to join the military."

"To say my parents were disappointed would be an understatement. I rose in the ranks quickly and was tasked with holding a strategic point against a particularly elite band of minotaur. I was to hold it until told otherwise, but when they began to storm the point, we had no choice but to meet them head-on."

"We routed the band of minotaur but at the cost of my entire team. Immediately after, I got word that they had negotiated a peace treaty. We were to stand down." Ronin's voice broke.

"I had gotten my people killed unnecessarily." His voice was coarse and gravelly as he continued. "If I had only waited… If I had never given that command… If it weren't for me, they'd still be alive. It was all my fault… my pride and impatience got them and a lot of minotaur killed," Ronin said bitterly. He fiddled with the hem of his tunic as he clenched and unclenched his jaw.

Alex did not know what to say. He couldn't even imagine what that would be like, so he waited silently next to Ronin, letting him work through whatever was going on in his head. Gremlore glanced over at them and nodded with a small smile before returning to grind whatever he was working on.

Alex nudged Ronin's shoulder with his. "For what it's worth, I'm glad they didn't execute you. I owe you my life a hundred times over, and as crazy as this sounds, I see you as a friend."

Ronin studied him for a long moment and gave him a half smile. How many times over the last few years, as he sat alone at the campfire, did Alex wish he had a friend? How many times, as he rode across Reyall, did he wish Bucephalus actually understood him and could talk back? Ronin, as Bucephalus, had gotten him out of many deadly situations and probably many more he didn't know about.

Steam rose and water hissed as Gremlore dunked the blade into the bucket beside his anvil. He inspected his work closely before he took it over to the grinder to sharpen its edges. When it was finished, Gremlore handed it to Alex.

"It's beautiful." Alex admired the weapon. The blade shimmered white, with ribbons of blue and silver running through it. It felt lighter than any blade he'd held before. Perfectly balanced, it felt like an extension of his arm as opposed to something he wielded. The pommel fit his hand like it was a part of him.

"It's time to go," Althenaea's voice echoed from across the cavern.

Mahkai, Quinn, and Bailor stood waiting with their packs by the other entrance. Mahkai muttered to himself as he packed and repacked his bags with his books, scrolls, and papers. His little owl perched on his shoulder and preened its feathers, unphased by his blustering.

Alex attempted to hand the blade back to Gremlore, but the dwarf held his hands up and said, "No, that is for you. Saoirse said ye lost yers."

Alex looked at him incredulously. "I can't accept this," he protested.

Gremlore shook his head and put his hands over Alex's. "Take it. It is meant for you," he said quietly.

Ronin watched with wide eyes but offered no comment before turning to gather his and Alex's packs. He tossed Alex a belt and his pack and made his way over to where the others had gathered. Alex looked around one last time, savoring the unexpected feeling of home before he joined the rest of the group.

By the time Alex was ready to go, Gremlore had changed into a different, more ornate tunic and joined their little group.

They followed Bailor through a series of tunnels out of the mountain and emerged into a bustling village built along the side of the mountain and down a winding path into the valley. Most took no notice of their odd group traveling along the main path to the valley floor, but a few recognized Althenaea or the twins and called out to them or smiled and waved.

Alex wondered if all of Osrealach was like this. There were some who watched curiously, but none came forward to impede their travel. As they descended further down the path, they saw fewer fae crossing their path. As they passed the last few outlying houses, they entered a wood filled with tall, stately oaks, pines, and redwoods stretching up to the brilliant blue sky.

Alex stared in awe, drinking in his surroundings. He had never seen trees so tall. The forest felt old and well maintained, yet wild and vibrant. The air around him thrummed with life. Black crows, colorful songbirds, and even tiny hummingbirds flew above and around them. Alex heard more in the surrounding trees as well as squirrels and other animals. They seemed to watch the party pass by with an air of anticipation. Alex realized he was being left behind, so he jogged to catch up, the leaves crunching beneath his feet.

A large group of fae gathered up ahead. As Alex reached the crowd, the hum of dozens of conversations filled the air as they waited to be given entrance inside the amphitheatre. The structure jutted out of the valley floor like a solitary monument surrounded by open grassy fields. The pillars were wrapped with vines and flowers growing along the walkway leading up to the large stone doors. As they entered, he saw a ring of stone pillars standing around an enormous bronze basin. The viewing area was covered with a ceiling of interwoven vines and branches, but the center over the basin remained open.

Amsah greeted them and led Alex to the ring of stone pillars. In the center was a massive bronze bowl inscribed with insignias. The same ornate writing he had seen in the room of sand with Kynthelic scrawled around the rim.

"Place your hands on the bowl," Amsah instructed. As he tentatively stepped forward, Althenaea, Amsah, Ronin, Quinn, and Bailor began a slow, captivating chant in a language Alex did not understand.

A light emanated out of Althenaea, bathing her in ethereal blue hues before rising to create a translucent ceiling across the open amphitheatre. At the same time, emerald light emerged from Ronin, golden light from Amsah, ruby light from Bailor, and white light from Quinn. Warmth and light spread from Alex's fingertips, up his arms, and throughout his body, as the words and symbols began to glow. After a moment, the center of the bowl erupted with fire. Its flames swirled red, blue, green, yellow, and white. He was entranced and could not look away.

Alex stared into the spiral of flames in front of him. He felt paralyzed. He heard gasps from the fae gathered around. The sound of rushing wind drowned out everything else.

He blinked and found he was alone in the amphitheatre. He looked down at the brazier, but instead of flames, he saw the world he knew and loved. Osrealach and Reyall looked like a raised map, but the closer he looked, the more he thought he could see waves crashing on the shore and birds flying. *Maps don't do that*.

"Welcome, Little Defender. We have waited a long time for this moment." He heard a low, smooth female voice echoing around him.

A water golem appeared before him. "You have many questions. That is alright," the voice continued.

Alex could not speak.

"Some will be answered in time. While we could answer them for you now, it would rob you of your journey and growth from discovering the answers for yourself," a gravely male voice rumbled to Alex's left.

Alex turned to look at the voice and found a lava golem rising from the ground next to a familiar sand golem. His mind reeled. *There are more than just Kynthelic? How are they here? Where is 'here'?*

"Calm your mind and focus," Kynthelic said gently. "Ask your question."

Alex tried to sort out which of his questions he wanted to ask. *Who am I? What am I? What does all this mean? Why me? What am I expected to do? Who are they?* It seemed like everyone wanted something different from him or for him. But what did he want for himself? That... was his question. *What do I want?*

"Ah, there it is. Well done, Little Defender," Kynthelic commended him. "Sometimes it is not about the answer, but asking the right question."

"They need you, but if you will not, there will be others. Choose your path wisely," the water golem's voice chimed in.

"Trust the wanderer and the counselor," the lava golem interjected.

"I believe there are a few who would like to congratulate you," Kynthelic said.

Alex heard a chorus of voices welcoming him as he saw images of different dragons flash briefly in his mind. Saoirse's voice sounded smug, yet proud. It was overwhelming, but he felt strangely at peace, and something else he couldn't name.

All at once, the rushing wind came back, then died down, and with it, the flames in the center of the brazier until they were both completely gone. Alex blinked a few times to clear his vision. He could finally look away. He felt strange, exhausted, yet very alive.

No one in the amphitheatre moved. As he looked around, shock registered on everyone's faces, except Ronin. Ronin wore the biggest grin Alex had seen. Mahkai leaned against a pillar, writing feverishly in one of his notebooks again. Ronin looked to Althenaea, who nodded before he stepped off the platform he was standing on. He clapped Alex on the back and slung his arm around Alex's shoulders.

"I knew it!" Ronin said triumphantly.

Alex stiffened in surprise. "I don't understand. What just happened?" he asked.

"The flames confirmed you are Ardra, of course," Ronin said smugly.

"Why... is everyone staring?" Alex asked as he nervously looked around.

"Since all the other Ardra were either killed during the wars or went into hiding, you are the first Ardra Kokiri at a revealing ceremony in over a hundred years," Ronin replied.

Alex relaxed a fraction. He was the only one who had seen Kynthelic and the other golems. Before he could ask what a Kokiri was, Gremlore walked up to them carrying a long pack slung over his shoulder.

"That did ma heart a lot of good to see, lad," he said to Alex.

"What does a normal ceremony look like?" Alex asked.

"Normally the revealing festivities occur over three days leading up to the summer solstice, with the actual ceremony taking place on the evening of the third day," Gremlore said.

"For anyone not Ardra, that wasn't normal. For one, all the rest of us only get a single-colored flame. It burned so high and hot, it's a good thing there is no roof over the center, otherwise, it would have burned clean through it," he continued.

"It was always my favorite three days of the year. Everyone comes together from all over to have games and competitions, lots of great food..." Ronin interjected excitedly.

"You and food," Alex teased Ronin, shaking his head.

Ronin grinned, not contradicting him.

Gremlore chuckled. "Aye, the food is amazing."

"What's a Kokiri?" Alex asked.

"On the third evening, the Kokiri, those participating in the ceremony, don special robes and promenade to music and fanfare into the amphitheatre. One by one, they place their hands, as ye did, on the brazier."

"The fire in the center indicates the strength and type of their magic based on what color and how big the flames are. Afterwards, they're given the opportunity to talk with various members of the community to choose or be chosen for an apprenticeship or profession," Gremlore instructed.

"Wait, you are saying I can use all five types of magic? How?" Alex asked incredulously.

"Gremlore and I will teach you," Althenaea said as she joined them. "And I expect Ronin will as well." Ronin nodded in agreement.

"Oh, yes! Splendid!" Mahkai interjected. "This is very fascinating! Tell me, what did it feel like? What did you hear? What did you see?" He held his notebook, ready for Alex's answers.

Alex felt uneasy about answering, not wanting to talk about what had happened just yet. "But what about the trial?" he asked Althenaea, avoiding Mahkai's questions. "There is no point in teaching me magic if the rest of the council are just going to execute me."

"Let me handle that," Althenaea said dismissively, waving her hand. "Now that we know for certain you are fae, you have a lot to catch up on."

"Wait, how is this even possible? I don't understand," Alex asked her, but she had already crossed the room to address a group of children watching shyly from the doorway.

Mahkai watched expectantly for a moment, then realized Alex had no intention of answering his questions. His shoulders slumped as he closed his notebook and tucked it back into his satchel before wandering off dejectedly.

Alex felt terrible, but didn't know what to say.

Ronin walked over to the bronze basin, circled it slowly, then beckoned him over. As Alex approached, Ronin pointed out a symbol. "I think you will recognize this one," he said.

Alex was torn between wanting to go after Mahkai and curious about what Ronin wanted to show him. He could talk with Mahkai later, so he walked towards what Ronin was pointing to.

He took in a sharp breath and pulled out his father's ring, hanging on a chain around his neck. He held it up to the brazier to compare. They were identical.

"So my father is at least part fae? Did my mother know? Why didn't she tell me? What happened to him?" Alex mused aloud.

He had more questions than answers, but with this new insight into his origins, some of his feelings from childhood were falling into place. He never felt like he belonged, and the rest of the village children either tormented or excluded him for it.

Alex rubbed his fingers over the raised design on the top of his ring out of habit, borne from years of looking at it wondering what secrets it held. He felt he had a piece to the puzzle but was no closer to figuring out the mystery of his absent father. He made a mental note to ask Mahkai about the history of this symbol. Maybe he could provide more insight.

Alex put the chain back around his neck, tucked the ring back under his collar, and looked up to see Ronin watching him closely. Ronin's piercing gaze seemed to study Alex as if looking for something, but then his face relaxed and returned to normal.

Althenaea watched them for a moment from the door. "Come, we have many things to show you and discuss," she called before exiting the amphitheatre.

Quinn appeared out of the shadow of a pillar and exited directly after her. Alex debated whether to ask Ronin what he seemed to be looking for, but before he could ask, Ronin spoke up.

"It's just an idea, so don't worry about it right now, though," Ronin offered by way of explanation, as if he guessed what Alex was wondering.

Ronin and Alex followed Althenaea, who practically floated back up the path toward the mountain forge, the picture of grace and power in perfect control. A few individuals approached Alex to congratulate him, but many others watched warily from a distance. Some people smiled and waved, but many more frowned or turned away.

Alex was a bit perplexed by their reactions. His head spun trying to process everything. Word had spread ahead of them, not only about what had happened at the ceremony, but also that he was rumored to be human. Ronin also got his fair share of glances and glares, but seemed unfazed by it.

Glancing over his shoulder, he saw Mahkai trailing behind, looking a bit downcast with his hands clasped behind his back, and his head and shoulders slumped.

Alex noticed Amsah was no longer with their group and mentioned it to Ronin. Ronin just shrugged, but Alex saw a flash of bitterness and resentment on his face. Alex realized he did not know anything about Ronin's family, or what that must have been like to be exiled by your own father. He did not have much experience in father-son dynamics, but he could guess.

Alex was so focused on his thoughts, he ran right into Quinn, who had stopped in front of him. Quinn spun around and practically growled at him.

"This changes nothing! I am still going to bring you back to stand trial. Just because you have fae blood doesn't mean you are fae. You are still a grimy human, and you don't belong here. All this proves is that you are a danger to the safety and security of Osrealach." The venom in Quinn's voice punctuated each word as he glared at Alex.

Alex held up his hands and backed up a few steps in surprise. "I..."

Quinn spun back around and stalked away. "You better run back to Reyall and forget about all of this if you know what's good for you," he shot over his shoulder.

Alex shook his head and let him go without responding. Ronin caught up to him. "What was that all about?"

Alex shrugged. "I don't think he likes me, but what did I ever do to him? Besides not dying, that is."

Ronin chuckled, "He is probably a purist and sees you as a threat. He thinks fae and humans shouldn't mix, and half-breeds shouldn't be allowed in Osrealach at all."

"A few weeks ago, I didn't even know Osrealach existed, let alone being fae, having magic, and all the rest of this. How am I a threat?" Alex asked, bewildered.

Ronin shrugged. Alex was pretty sure Ronin knew more than he was saying.

Althenaea stopped outside the entrance into the mountain forge and waited for the rest of the group to catch up. Gremlore and Bailor chatted quietly as they arrived last. They nodded in agreement before Gremlore approached Alex and unslung the long pack he had been carrying. He carefully unwrapped each item and laid them out on a large, flat rock beside the entrance. Ronin whistled in admiration.

Gleaming silvery blue and white, five knives, a pair of battle axes, a sword, and a javelin lay before him. The amber light of the sunset made their blades appear to be on fire. Alex's breath caught as he admired the gifts. He looked from the weapons to Gremlore and back several times, trying to come up with something to say.

Gremlore chuckled. Bailor grinned broadly as Alex continued, struggling to find a response. Quinn looked just as stunned as Alex, while Althenaea looked like she had expected this. Mahkai practically sputtered as he stared at the artful masterpieces in the waning light.

Alex reached out and traced the intricate detail forged into the handle and blade of the nearest axe. As he touched the blade, a shock ran up his hand. He picked it up, testing its weight and balance in his hand, and swung it in a small arc to get a feel for it. It felt like it was made for him, like the knife earlier, an extension of his arm, moving with precision. He felt awed and unworthy to be holding, let alone gifted, such fine weapons.

Ronin stopped beside him. "May I?" he asked as he reached out to pick up one of the knives. Alex nodded. Ronin flipped it up with practiced ease, catching it mid-air with the blade pointing down his forearm. He grinned mischievously at Alex as he flipped it once more.

Alex snatched it out of the air and crouched low, ready and waiting to see what Ronin had in mind. Ronin's eyes glinted as he swung at Alex; his movements fluid, effortless. He wasted no energy as each attack flowed into the next.

Alex parried and ducked, trying to find an opening to attack. Their movements started slowly at first, but gained speed as each fought to gain an opening in the other's defense. It surprised Alex how well Ronin preemptively blocked his attacks; as if he knew what Alex was thinking and planning, but then he remembered Ronin had been there, as Bucephalus, for most of his training. Just as he was thinking about the move McCannon had used on him that he never learned how to counter, Ronin swept his legs out from underneath him.

Alex rolled to the side, narrowly avoiding Ronin's strike, but was off balance for his next pass. Ronin was able to get behind him. Alex felt his arm twisted behind his back before being flipped over his head, landing on the ground on his back. Ronin knelt on his chest with his knife to Alex's throat and pinned Alex's knife hand to the ground under his boot.

"You... that was you?" Alex wheezed. He stared up at Ronin, dazed, trying to catch his breath.

Ronin grinned as he stood up, offering a hand to help Alex up off the ground. He casually walked over to return the knife with the others. Alex dusted himself off as he watched Ronin, waiting for a response.

Ronin looked at Alex with a self-satisfied grin on his face. "I don't know what you could possibly be referring to," he said with feigned innocence.

Gremlore and Bailor chuckled at the exchange. Althenaea looked pleased. Quinn looked begrudgingly impressed. Mahkai watched with wide eyes.

Alex helped Gremlore place the weapons back in their respective sheaths but offered the last knife to Ronin. "I noticed you don't carry any weapons," Alex said by way of explanation.

Ronin reached to take it, but Quinn stepped between them. "He is an exile under trial for execution. He is not permitted weapons of any sort," Quinn said with a bit of an arrogant tone. "I would prefer you were not permitted to have them either, but since you are under the guidance of the Aqualite Master Althenaea, I will defer to her judgment," he said through gritted teeth.

Alex wanted to point out that Ronin was a weapon himself, but decided against it in the end. Quinn was already aggressive toward Ronin; he did not need to make it any worse. He turned and put the last knife in the top of his boot. He remembered, with a grimace, the times he wished he had thought to put one there sooner and was trying to decide where he wanted to keep the rest of them when he felt a hand on his shoulder.

Mahkai stood over him with an odd expression on his face. "Your sparring match was..." Mahkai trailed off as he removed his hand from Alex's shoulder. His face was only partially lit by the torches burning at the entrance. The others made their way through the doorway, and Mahkai turned to join them, but Alex stopped him.

"Mahkai," Alex paused, unsure how to say what he was thinking. "I want to apologize about earlier. I shouldn't have ignored you."

"Oh! I... appreciate that," Mahkai sounded surprised. "Apology accepted."

"I was so overwhelmed," Alex said haltingly. "Still am, if I'm completely honest. There were so many people around," he tried to explain. "I'm still processing everything, and I'm not sure what to think about all this.... but I'll try to tell you what I can," he offered.

"I had no idea. I am so sorry!" Mahkai said, mortified. "I was so focused on my notes and questions, it did not even occur to me that you might be overwhelmed or unable to answer."

Alex looked at his feet, feeling awkward and unsure of what to say next. "Shall we?" Mahkai gestured toward the door where the others had disappeared. Alex nodded and followed him inside.

CHAPTER 13

OVER the next few days, Alex spent every waking moment either training with Ronin and his new weapons or training with Gremlore and Althenaea, trying to learn to wield magic. Alex had fought with other knights before, but fighting with Ronin was a whole other level.

Ronin constantly changed up his fighting style, sometimes even mid-match, pushing Alex to adapt. Most of the time, he felt exhilarated to learn new skills and techniques. Today, though, he felt completely inadequate and out of step.

Quinn watched from across the room with his arms crossed, frowning. Alex wondered what was bothering him. He must have hesitated in his distraction, because he found himself, yet again, dumped in the dirt.

"You aren't paying attention," Ronin said, reaching his hand to help Alex up.

"I know, I'm sorry," Alex sighed.

"I take it your lessons with Althenaea and Gremlore aren't going as planned? Or is it something else?" Ronin asked pointedly.

"Abysmally," Alex quipped.

Ronin raised his eyebrows in surprise. "It can't be that bad, can it? What have you done so far?"

Alex shrugged and looked at the ground, pretending to inspect the toe of his boot, and muttered, "Nothing."

"Nothing… at all?" Ronin asked incredulously.

Alex didn't answer. He felt horrible about it. Here, he was supposed to not only be able to use all five types of magic, but he was supposed to be incredibly strong too. "Even the basics, like making water swirl or make a flame grow or shrink seem out of my reach," he said, sighing.

"The first time I met with Gremlore, he had this look of great expectation and excitement on his face. But time after time, I tried to do what he instructed but couldn't even do the simplest task he asked. Don't get me wrong, he is being incredibly patient with me, but I'm just so frustrated. I've tried everything he suggested. Nothing works." Alex's voice was barely above a whisper.

Ronin looked over at Quinn for a minute, thoughtfully. "You want to spar?" he called across the room. "No weapons," he added, holding up his empty hands.

Quinn scowled, then turned and stalked out.

"Now then, let's see where you are with your magic, since you are not in the right frame of mind to spar." Ronin beckoned Alex to follow him outside.

"Did you not hear a word I just said?" Alex asked in frustration.

Ronin did not respond and continued walking the way he was headed.

They emerged from a side tunnel into the clearing Alex had first met Saoirse and Quinn. Ronin slipped off his boots and sat down on the ground, crossed his legs, and placed his palms on the ground in front of him. Alex followed suit and did his best to mirror him.

"There are two parts to earth magic. There is the manipulation of what is already here, which is easier, and there is the creation of what is not, which is much more difficult and tricky." Ronin closed his eyes and took a few deep breaths. He was still for so long Alex was unsure if he was supposed to do something; so he just waited.

"Close your eyes and just listen. Listen to everything around you. Listen to the wind in the trees and grass. Listen to your slow, steady breathing. Listen to your heartbeat. Now listen deeper," Ronin said in a low, soothing voice.

Alex did as he was told. He sat and listened. He heard everything Ronin had said, but the last one made no sense to him. *Listen deeper? Listen to what?*

He sat so long, listening to everything and nothing; his legs fell asleep. He groaned internally. He was not going to enjoy trying to stand after this.

"Hey, no offense, but what am I supposed to be listening for? Ronin?" he asked. He peeked his eyes open.

"Hey!" He threw his boot at Ronin, who had dozed off. It hit him in the chest.

"What!?" Ronin said, sitting up straight.

"I thought you were supposed to be helping me," Alex accused.

Ronin looked at him sheepishly. "I was... until I wasn't." He grinned at Alex as he stretched his arms over his head.

"Well, you weren't. What was that supposed to accomplish, other than letting you take a nap?" Alex asked.

Ronin shrugged. "My instructor started my first lesson that way, so I figured it would work for you. Though, by the time he woke up, he was sleeping in a tree because I was so bored with not moving for so long, I figured it out on my own," he said mischievously.

Alex shook his head and picked a blade of grass and twirled it between his fingers.

"Well, what did you gain from this? Do you feel calmer, more centered, more yourself?"

"I guess." Alex half shrugged as he continued to stare at the blade of grass. "Everyone makes it look so... simple. I figured it would be like talking to dragons. That seemed natural enough."

Ronin looked at him sharply. "You failed to mention that earlier."

"To be fair, I almost died. If it hadn't been for the..." Alex stopped abruptly.

"The what?" Ronin narrowed his eyes. "What else are you withholding?"

Alex looked around to make sure no one was around before sliding his hand into his pocket and pulling out the "not rock." He held it out to Ronin. "This."

Ronin took it from Alex and turned it over in his hands, inspecting it from every side. When he reached the bottom side, he studied the inscription and almost dropped it in surprise. "Is this what I think it is? When did you get this? *Where* did you get this?" he asked incredulously.

"In the tunnels behind the waterfall. It's what I used to cut myself free," Alex answered.

"You... you..." Ronin sputtered as he stared at the rock in his hand.

"What?" Alex felt confused.

Ronin turned it over in his hand one last time before handing the "not rock" back to Alex. "Well, it depends on who you ask, but some say it is the first dragon's tear that lights the way of the lost. Others tell of a star that fell from the sky that gives wishes to 'the worthy.' Still, others say it was spewn out of the heart of a volcano and allows the holder to speak with distant lands. One says it was dug up from a deep mine and shows the beholder their soul. Another story says it was found in the center of a lightning strike on the beach and is just a pretty rock that people claim has magical properties... if you believe what the stories say.

"One legend says there were six powerful beings, gods to some in their own right. One of each earth, water, fire, wind, and two others... all not bound by the passing of time. They created the dragons and shaped the land and sea. They used to walk among the fae but, over time, withdrew as the fae seemed to need or want their presence less and less. They left behind a talisman called the guardian stone for the fae to contact them, but it was lost long ago. The guardian stone supposedly enhanced the magic of the one holding it, but only sometimes. Some think it is just a nice story. My favorite story says the three got into a fight, and one lost their nose." Ronin finished with a grin.

"That is a lot. How do you lose such an ancient and powerful talisman, if that is indeed what this is?" Alex asked.

Ronin shrugged. "Lots of things were lost or destroyed in the wars. I only know about it because my father was obsessed with finding it for a very long time," Ronin said, shaking his head. "Do me a favor? Don't let him know you have it… or anyone, for that matter."

Alex nodded and slipped it back into his pocket. "Okay, seriously though, am I broken? Why can't I seem to use magic?" Alex asked him candidly.

Ronin looked at Alex with the same look he had worn after the Revealing ceremony but was silent for a few moments before shaking his head. "I don't know," he said finally.

They sat in silence for a while. Alex got lost in his thoughts. He pondered over the sequence of events that had brought him here and the mysteries of his heritage, when his stomach rumbled loudly.

Ronin chuckled, breaking the silence. "I guess we should go in search of food, unless you have more magical food in your pockets again," he teased as he stood up.

Alex smiled and stood up, tentatively, testing to see if he had feeling back in his legs. Just then, a blast of air blew from the open tunnel door. Seconds later, Mahkai barreled out.

"Oh! There you are! Althenaea requests your presence," he said, before hurriedly returning the way he came. The clip-clop of his hooves quickly faded into the distance.

Alex moved to follow, but stopped when Ronin placed a hand on his forearm. "Don't worry about your magic. It will show in its own time."

"How do you know?" Alex asked.

"Call it a hunch."

"And how will I know if it does?"

"Oh, you'll know. Trust me, you will know." Ronin smiled mischievously.

CHAPTER 14

THEY followed Mahkai into an unfamiliar room. Not surprising, since the tunnels through these mountains were extensive. In the center of the room, a massive map spread out across a large octagonal table. There were little black stones scattered all over Reyall and the edges of Osrealach. Althenaea, Quinn, Gremlore, Bailor, and several other dwarves gathered around it with grim looks on their faces. Bailor placed another stone on the map as Alex looked it over. He noticed the newest addition was to Creedon. He looked up quizzically.

"What do these rocks mean?" Alex asked.

"These represent fae who have gone missing," Bailor said.

"Missing?" Ronin asked, looking over Alex's shoulder.

Bailor nodded solemnly. "This is getting out of hand. We need to do something - anything!" His normally quiet voice grew in volume and intensity as he spoke until he was almost shouting. He looked at Althenaea. "Why won't the council do something?" he demanded.

She sighed and shook her head. "The council does not see it as their responsibility to mount an investigation into the matters of humans and half-breeds. I have tried to change their minds, but they will not be swayed."

"There are so many! Who is missing in Creedon? And how have they gone missing?" Alex interrupted, still looking at the map.

Gremlore came up behind Alex and put his hand on his shoulder. "We just received word that Bronach has gone missing, lad," he said gently.

Alex spun around, searching Gremlore's face for evidence that this was some kind of joke. Finding none, he looked around the room. "How did he go missing? When? What can I do?"

"We do not know. We suspect it is the same group that abducted me when we first met," Althenaea said, referencing when Alex and Ronin had rescued her from the well.

"I have been wondering, what were you doing in Reyall when they captured you? How did they even capture you?" Alex asked.

Althenaea shook her head. "I was careless," she said.

Ronin looked like he wanted to tear something apart. Alex didn't know what he felt.

"I'm going. I don't need anyone's permission. And since I'm one of those 'undesirable half-breeds', the council won't object." Alex said, making up his mind. He knew he would be giving up his magic training and possibly would never be allowed in Osrealach again, but Bronach was the closest thing he had to a father. If he could possibly do something, he would try.

"I'm coming with you," Ronin said adamantly. Alex nodded at him gratefully.

"Good riddance," Quinn said from the corner, under his breath.

Althenaea nodded to Alex and Ronin. Relief flashed across her face. "You will go with them, Quinn."

He clenched and unclenched his jaw as he balled his fists at his sides, but bowed his head in acknowledgment.

"Mahkai, help them gather supplies for their journey. Any information you can give them would also be greatly appreciated," Althenaea said.

Mahkai perked up at this. "It would be my pleasure," he bowed before hurrying off down a tunnel.

Alex looked from Bailor to Althenaea. "Is this what you were referring to the first night we arrived?" he asked, putting a few pieces together. "What do you know that you aren't saying? What can you tell me to help me find these missing fae?" he asked, looking over the map again to see if he could discern any patterns.

Mahkai returned with two packs slung over his shoulder and a scroll tucked under his arm. He handed the packs to Ronin and the scroll to Alex. "I sketched this earlier for my own records, but it seems you need it more and I can make another."

Alex unrolled the scroll. It was a detailed replica of the map before him.

"You'll have to travel by foot. I cannot arrange transport without drawing unnecessary attention," Althenaea said.

Ronin nodded. "Do your sources have any leads as to when and where this group strikes? Patterns of whereabouts?"

Althenaea shook her head. "Nothing so far, but it is difficult. Every time our informants get close, they disappear as well. Maybe with your connections, you might get farther than we have."

Alex was distraught. He wanted to race home and start looking immediately. *How could this have happened? Does the king know about it? Surely I would have been informed if he did. Maybe that was what we were to discuss at the Summit I missed.* Guilt wrapped around his heart and squeezed. If he had been where he was supposed to, maybe Bronach wouldn't have been taken. None of this would have happened.

Ronin shook his head. "You can't blame yourself for all of this."

Alex looked up at him sharply. Sometimes he suspected Ronin could read his thoughts, but that was silly. Ronin was just good at reading people.

They discussed different strategies but ultimately advised they start in Creedon and go from there. After they finished their meeting, Gremlore asked Alex to meet him at his forge. Alex followed them out but overheard Althenaea. "Do not, under any circumstances, reveal the existence of Osrealach and the fae. You know what is at stake."

XXX

When Alex arrived, Bailor presented him with a tunic. Alex put it on and found hidden pockets and slits sewn into the tunic lining in various locations to conceal his knives.

He put a knife in the small of his back, one in his boot, one in the sheath made specifically for it on the leather strap that ran across his chest, holding the javelin on his back, one up his sleeve, and one next to the slots for hanging his axes from either hip.

He was debating where to put the last one when Ronin walked up. He discreetly slipped the last one to Ronin, careful not to let Quinn see. Bailor and Gremlore smiled knowingly.

"I'm sorry I was unable to train you in fire magic, lad," Gremlore said seriously to Alex. "When you come back, we'll have plenty of time to work on it, though."

"Bring our brother back," Bailor said to Alex and Ronin. "May your road be kind, and your arrows fly true. May the storm clouds part, and your skies be blue. May your waters be calm, and your troubles few. 'Til your journey's end, and your destiny finds you."

"How do you know that?" Alex asked in surprise.

"There are many versions I expect, but 'tis as old as my family remembers; as old as the dragons, perhaps," Bailor said.

XXX

"What does undesirable mean?" Alice asked, interrupting the story.

"It means unwanted or disliked, love," he replied, unbothered by the interruption. He took a shirt down from the drying line and handed it to her to fold and put in the laundry basket.

"Why don't people like Alex?" she asked.

"Because he isn't like them, and that scares them," he responded after a moment.

"Well, that's silly! I like him! He's my favorite. I want to be just like him when I grow up!" she declared, taking the shirt from him. She tossed the shirt into the basket without folding it. Instead, she picked up a stick and pretended to fend off an invisible attacker with it.

He chuckled, continuing to fold laundry while he watched her whirl around the yard. "Watch out for the sneak attack behind you," he said with a grin.

She spun around to press her advantage against the invisible foe. He picked up a stick of his own and held it at the ready. When she turned to face him, she narrowed her eyes as if sizing him up before charging at him.

"Aaaaaahhhhhh!" she yelled as she charged, driving him back.

He laughed as he let her push him further and further away from the laundry lines. Suddenly, he side-stepped and flipped her hair with the tip of his stick before dancing out of her reach.

"Hey! No fair, your arms are longer." She giggled as she chased him around the yard.

He let her catch him, and she pretended to run him through with her "sword". He fell to the ground dramatically, holding his wounded side. "Tell my daughter... I... love her," he said, pretending to gasp for breath before collapsing completely.

She laughed as she dropped her stick and dove on top of him. "I've got you now!" she exclaimed.

He caught her as she tackled him and wrapped her tightly in his arms. "Or maybe it is I who have you!" he said, laughing with her.

They sat on the ground breathing hard for a little while, trying to catch their breath from laughing so hard.

Alice looked up at him. "Where did Bronach go?"

"What, sweetheart?" he asked her as he tucked a stray lock of hair behind her ears.

"In the story, where did Bronach and the other fae go? You said they went missing," she said. "What are they going to do to find him? And why can't Alex use his magic?" she continued.

He kissed the top of her head. "Let's find out while we finish the laundry, shall we?"

CHAPTER 15

RONIN, Alex, and Quinn set out on foot after they finished gathering supplies.

"We could have at least waited until morning," Quinn grumbled.

"No." Alex would hear none of it.

"This is slow and ridiculous, not to mention a waste of time. The only reason we have to walk is because the useless human cannot fly or use magic," Quinn grumbled under his breath.

Ronin growled a warning. Quinn glared back at him and did not comment further. Instead, he shifted into a snow owl and flew high overhead until he was out of sight, leaving Ronin to carry his pack as well.

They walked in silence for the first few hours, each content with their own thoughts. The mountains and dense forest gave way to wide, open, rolling hills. Their path was lit well enough to see by the almost full moon.

"Hey Ronin," Alex started.

Ronin looked over at him thoughtfully. "Hmm?"

"Can you tell me more stories about the three beings?"

Ronin looked around. "I have an idea I want to test out," he said before shifting to his direwolf form.

"Alex?"

Alex heard Ronin say in his mind. He blinked in surprise. *"Wait, how does this work?"*

"This is how puka communicate. Since you said you could talk to the dragon, I wondered if you could also talk to us. I guess I was

right," Ronin said in a triumphant tone. *"You asked about the three guardians, any particular reason?"*

"I think Kynthelic, the sand golem I met in the tunnels, is one of the three guardians," Alex said.

"Oh…. that's interesting. Why do you think that?" Ronin commented after a long moment.

"I think I met three of them at my revealing ceremony. You know, when I touched the basin. I went… somewhere else," Alex said, not knowing what else to say.

"You WHAT?" Ronin yelled in Alex's mind.

Alex winced. Ronin looked back at him with something Alex guessed was as close to sheepish as a wolf could look.

"There was a water one and a lava one present, as well as Kynthelic. They all spoke to me, but it was in riddles. It didn't make a whole lot of sense." Alex picked up Ronin's bags and slung it over his shoulder with his own.

"Let's keep walking so Quinn doesn't yell at us for being too slow," Alex said aloud.

ⵝⵝⵝ

They walked all night and all day, not even stopping for meals until Alex needed to take a break. His feet were killing him, but his urgency pushed him to keep going. After he stumbled for the fourth time in an hour, Ronin suggested they take a break. Alex sat down in the long grass, took off his boots, and massaged his sore feet.

Ronin disappeared into the growing shadows, leaving Alex alone with his thoughts. He leaned against a lone boulder as he watched the sunset; his body too weary to do anything else. He thought about trying to start a fire but miserably remembered, he did not have his flint and steel. He wondered if his saddlebags were still under the tree on the edge of the forest, back in Reyall. Thus far, he had been unsuccessful in producing a flame with his supposed magic. He searched his pack but came up empty-handed.

He closed his eyes, trying to concentrate as Ronin had instructed. He listened to the wind in the grass and tried clearing his mind of everything else. Thoughts of Bronach kept rising to the surface, breaking his concentration, so he gave up. His mind drifted to when he was little...

He was hiding from the other children of the village. He knew they wouldn't think to look for him here, and even if they did, they wouldn't come in for fear of Bronach. They enjoyed tormenting someone or something. Usually, Alex was on the receiving end of their mischief. He'd lost count of how many times they had dumped him in the ocean or shoved his face in the mud or locked him in the smokehouse. He had gotten pretty good at climbing the tall trees rimming their village. They always found him and threw rocks until he came or fell down. It seemed they always knew where to find him until he had stumbled into Bronach's forge. If they knew he was here, they left him alone.

Bronach was tall and broad and didn't say much. He seemed a little gruff and frowned at the village kids if they came into his workshop. They told stories of how he had flames in his eyes, but no one believed them since they were known for telling tall tales. Peculiar things did seem to happen to the other children when they trespassed in the forge. A bird would poop on their head, or a goat would eat their favorite shirt.

Alex heard a sound and looked up. Bronach stood over him. Alex froze. Fear prickled his skin. He didn't know what to do. He was afraid Bronach would yell or throw him out, but he was more afraid of what the other kids had planned for him. He overheard them discussing the manure pile earlier.

Bronach frowned and studied Alex for a moment. His head snapped to the left as the other kids ran past the workshop, calling for Alex. Alex hugged his knees and tried making himself as small as possible, willing the ground itself to open and hide him so they wouldn't find him.

Bronach's face softened into a look of understanding and concern. He nodded once and walked back to his forge. Moments later, one of the braver children ran into the shop, looking for Alex. Bronach pulled a red-hot iron from the forge as he turned to look at the child. The boy skidded to a halt with a look of horror on his face and turned and ran away just as fast as he had arrived.

Alex stayed, watching Bronach work long after dark before going home, just to be sure they were not waiting outside for him. After that, any time the other village kids tried to come after him, he hid in Bronach's workshop.

The third time he visited the forge, and every time after, Bronach allowed him to hold the end of the rod, fetch things for him around the shop, or hold a particularly unruly horse for him to shoe. Even when Bronach had nothing for him to do, he still visited often.

Alex liked watching the flames flickering in the forge. They made him feel warm and safe, like Bronach's presence. Entranced, he liked to imagine he saw horses in the fire, dancing and prancing, rearing and kicking, and shaking their heads and snorting at one another.

"Alex! Wake up, Alex! ALEXANDER!" Ronin yelled distantly.

Alex's eyes snapped open. He had dozed off. Flames surrounded him, blazing high into the evening sky. Horses made of fire reared and pranced, exactly like he had just been dreaming about. All he could do was stare as they trotted and galloped around him.

A foal trotted up to him, pawed at the ground, and put its nose in his hand. His first instinct was to pull away. It was warm but did not burn him. After patting the foal for a moment, it ran back into the rest of the fire.

"How did you do that?" Ronin asked in shock.

"I don't know," Alex yelled over the wall of fire. "How do I put it out?"

"Your guess is as good as mine. What were you doing to start it?"

"I was dreaming about Bronach."

Suddenly, the wind kicked up, creating a cyclone around the fire circle and Alex. The horses disappeared as the flames climbed higher in the torrential wind.

"What are you doing?" Alex yelled, looking for the source of the wind.

Quinn appeared next to Ronin, his brow creased in concentration. "I have it contained. You put it out!" he yelled to Ronin.

Ronin complied. The grass parted and dirt sprayed up and folded over the base of the flames, smothering them instantly.

"You could have burned down the entire valley! What were you thinking?" Quinn snarled at Alex, then turned to Ronin. "And what were you doing leaving him unattended practicing magic?" he snapped.

Ronin opened his mouth, then shrugged. "I don't answer to you."

They surveyed the charred area around Alex. "You are lucky this is all the damage you did," Quinn seethed. "Didn't you learn anything?" Quinn continued to chastise Alex, but Ronin ignored him.

Ronin walked over to Alex in the center of the charred circle, took his boots off, and sat down. He looked up at Alex and patted the ground beside him. "Now is as good a time as any to see if you can tap into your earth magic too. Let's see if you can heal the damage."

Alex looked at Ronin, surprised.

Quinn sputtered incredulously, "No! Leave it alone. You have done enough."

Alex looked from Ronin to Quinn, uncertainly.

"Oh, shush, Quinn! What's the harm in it?" Ronin interrupted.

"C'mon, I can undo or counter anything you do," Ronin said gently to Alex.

Quinn growled back at Ronin but said nothing more.

Alex sighed and sat facing Ronin. He closed his eyes and pressed his hands into the dead grass between them. He did not know what he was trying to do, or what he was trying to feel for exactly. He let out another sigh. He couldn't concentrate with Quinn pacing back and forth. He thought he caught a glimpse of concern underneath Quinn's anger.

Alex surveyed the damage his fire had caused. Quinn was right; he had no control, and that made him dangerous. He was about to give up when he saw a little green shoot pushing its way up out of the black. He felt a hint of joy as he watched it grow before his eyes. What started as a tendril of green was rapidly growing into a young sapling in mere seconds. A bead of sweat rolled down Ronin's temple.

Ronin wiped his face with his sleeve, giving Alex a tired yet encouraging smile. Alex did not think he could manage a tree, but wondered if he could grow a single blade of grass. He closed his eyes and focused on the grass, willing a blade between his hands to grow like Ronin had done.

He felt nothing. He peeked open his eyes. Nothing had changed. His shoulders slumped. He drew his knees to his chest and rested his chin on them.

Ronin's face was unreadable. Alex thought about the feel of the soft grass under his feet outside his mother's cabin in Creedon. He loved to lie in the grass, staring at the clouds on a sunny afternoon after he finished his chores and listen to his mother work. It was one of the few fond memories he had with her, one of the few times she looked content, happy even. Most days, for as long as he could remember, she just looked tired and stressed.

He felt something tickle between his toes. He looked down, thinking Ronin was playing a joke on him. A solitary blade of grass, the glossy light green of early spring just after the last winter snow. He touched it gently, amazed and not quite believing he had actually grown something!

Ronin smiled and patted Alex on the shoulder as he stood up and put his boots back on. "I'll take it. It's a start, at least. Let's go, we have a long journey ahead of us," he said tiredly.

XXX

They walked until the sun had fully set behind the tree line, bathing everything in a blanket of gold and amber. Ronin led them to a clearing next to a stream with a well-used fire pit in the center. A torch of blue-green fire burned next to a stack of dry logs and sticks on the other side of the clearing. A dozen or more hammocks hung suspended between trees around the edge of the clearing. They were close enough to the fire to be warm but far enough away that stray sparks would not catch them on fire.

"What is this place?" Alex asked.

"It's left over from the war, an old sanctuary of sorts. Now, travelers use it as a resting place on their journey. There's residual dampening magic still lingering here, so anyone outside the ring of trees won't be able to listen in on conversations," Ronin replied.

"You can do that?" Alex asked, astonished.

Quinn knelt next to the fire pit and started building a campfire. Alex went to the stream to wash his arms and face and to refill his water flask. In the fading light, he gazed at his reflection. Black soot smudged his face. He scrubbed as best he could with the cold water running down his arms, but he could not get it all off. Eventually, he gave up when his face felt raw and his fingers were numb from the cold.

Back in their campsite, fire burned steadily in a ring of stones. Ronin cooked chunks of meat skewered on stakes suspended over the flames. Alex joined Ronin and Quinn around the campfire. They watched silently while the meat sizzled.

"Do you think it will take a long time for it to grow back?" Alex asked no one in particular.

"Longer than if it had never burned in the first place," Quinn snapped without looking up.

"Now listen!" Ronin lowered his voice to just above a growl. "I saw the fire. It hadn't burned anything until you interfered," he accused Quinn.

"Impossible!" Quinn argued back.

Ronin looked like he was about to fight Quinn, but Alex cut them both off. "Enough. What's done is done. I can't go back and undo it, so just drop it. Both of you. I'm sorry I brought it up," Alex said miserably.

They fell silent again. Alex watched the sparks rise and disappear into the starry night sky as Ronin poked a stick into the fire and stirred the coals.

After a few minutes, Quinn cleared his throat. "What is your plan for when we cross into the human realm?" Quinn asked. "You do have a plan, don't you?" he demanded.

Alex nodded. "We'll start in Creedon at Bronach's house and forge as well as ask around for information. We'll also need to find that tree where I left all our gear and my armor... if it's still there, that is."

"We will also need to acquire human clothes for Quinn. His guard uniform would draw too much attention," Ronin added. "And probably get a new saddle and bridle fitted."

Quinn looked down at his captain of the guard uniform. The yellow and orange trim standing out from the purple and fuchsia tunic and pants. "What is wrong with my uniform?" he demanded.

"Nothing... except it is a bit too, um, colorful for normal humans. People only wear bright colors at festivals, and usually only the acrobats and performers at that," Ronin replied.

Quinn's face turned red at the thought of being compared to the entertainment.

"Wait, Ronin, you said new tack? I can't ride you! Not now... now that I know you are not really a horse," Alex protested.

"I don't see why not," Ronin replied. "They'll be expecting you to have Bucephalus, or at least a horse in general. A real horse would just slow us down and cost too much." He continued, "Besides, I've had lots of practice, and we'll go a lot faster this way. I don't know about you, but Quinn and I have both been chafing at this slow pace."

Alex wanted to protest further, but Ronin would hear none of it. "It's decided," he said with finality.

Quinn rose from beside the fire and climbed into the nearest hammock. Ronin followed suit shortly after. He poked his head over the side. "We'll leave at first light. I suggest you get some rest. Don't worry about the meadow; it'll regrow in time." He added as an afterthought, "Oh, and congrats on finding your magic, by the way. Or, well, two of them at least."

"Thank you," Alex said quietly before selecting his own hammock. His thoughts raced, but his body was so tired it did not take long for him to drift off to sleep. His dreams were restless, but when he awoke the next morning, he could not remember them.

XXX

The sun had just peaked the horizon when Alex rolled out of his hammock. His foot caught the side, so instead of gracefully sliding out and landing on his feet, he landed on his face. He heard a snort to his right. Ronin was repacking his bag, trying to cover his grin. Alex untangled himself, stood up, dusted himself off, and shrugged. He could not help but grin and shake his head at his own clumsiness.

After a quick breakfast of cold bread and cheese, they left camp. Alex shouldered his pack and started down the path. Quinn and Ronin watched as Alex left camp.

"Shouldn't you be carrying my bag so I can fly?" Quinn called after Alex.

Alex looked back at them and Quinn's bags where it sat next to the cold firepit. "You can stick to the ground today. I'm sure you'll manage. Ronin, you too. I carried both of your packs yesterday, so you can figure out how to carry them yourself today," Alex said with authority that surprised even himself.

Ronin looked at Quinn, standing with his mouth agape, searching for a retort. "You heard the man, Quinn. We need to get creative if we want to keep moving. We could probably still wear them as our cat form. If you don't want to walk like a human, that is," he said thoughtfully.

Ronin walked to their packs, flipped them around, and adjusted the straps while Alex waited on the trail. Quinn shifted to his snow leopard form. Ronin considered the bag and then Quinn. He adjusted the straps a bit more before instructing him to lift his paw. Quinn acquiesced but made no attempt to conceal his displeasure as Ronin pulled the pack onto his back. Quinn raised his other front paw awkwardly and nearly stumbled as Ronin pulled the strap over and tightened it down onto Quinn's shoulders. Ronin inspected his handiwork before picking up his own bag and walking toward Alex.

"This seems doable, but I'll need an extra pair of hands, if you don't mind."

Alex grinned at Quinn. "Ronin, I never thought I would see a leopard wearing a pack," Alex said as he took Ronin's pack.

Ronin shifted to his panther form and lifted each paw, allowing Alex to adjust and tighten the straps down so it rested comfortably on his back.

"Everything seems fine," Ronin said in Alex's mind. *"This feels odd but manageable, I think. Shall we go?"* He shifted his weight back and forth. Quinn's growl sounded like a leopard's version of a grumble, but followed Ronin's lead.

They made better time that day since Alex wasn't weighed down by two extra packs, but by midday, the clouds that had gathered threatened to let loose. Alex looked up at the sky, then fished his cloak out of his pack. No sooner had he clasped it around his neck than the rain came in sheets. Quinn hunched his back and dropped his head, tail thrashing back and forth. Ronin didn't seem to mind the rain, or if he did, he didn't show it.

Thunder rumbled overhead. Alex marveled as the light streaked through the dark sky in a brilliant display. Lightning struck the ground on a hilltop off to their right in the distance.

"Do you think we should stop until it blows over?" Alex asked aloud.

"Nah, it won't stop for a while, and I don't want to lose time," Ronin said in his mind. *"We'll be fine,"* he added when Alex looked skeptical.

Alex glanced at Quinn, who looked miserable with the rain running off him in rivulets; his tail still thrashed, but he kept any complaints to himself. As they continued walking, he practiced talking with Ronin in his mind. He learned mind speech is heard by whom it is directed towards. Not like speaking out loud, so

Ronin could talk to Alex without Quinn or anyone else hearing them unless they use their actual voices.

CHAPTER 16

FOR the next two days, the trio walked steadily, not stopping to rest until it was almost too dark to see. Each night when they finally stopped, Quinn insisted on making the fire - not trusting Alex to do it. Ronin cooked, usually rabbit or other small game he caught throughout the day, and Alex practiced growing blades of grass.

They topped a hill just as the sun was setting. Alex was speechless and could only stare in awe. The sun sprayed its amber rays across the sea while it painted the clouds in pinks, purples, and fuchsia. Ronin shifted to his fae form and stood next to Alex, admiring the view as well. Even Quinn shifted to his fae form and stood with them for a moment. Alex admired Quinn's uniform, which seemed to reflect the scene before them.

"It is quite possibly the most magnificent view I've seen," Alex murmured.

Alex thought Quinn smiled in surprise, but it was gone so fast he doubted he'd seen it at all. A large waterfall spilled into a small cove down to his right. He knew where they were. He felt an odd sense of apprehension and homesickness, but refused to dwell on either of those feelings. Gripping the "not rock" in his pocket, he wondered if he could find the entrance to the tunnels again.

By the time they reached the cove, the sun had fully set. He could see well though, since the moon was almost full tonight. It cast its silvery hue to everything, giving off a magical and serene aura. Quinn and Ronin set up camp while Alex went to the water to wash.

His feet crunched quietly on the pebbly sand as he walked slowly around the cove. Near the waterfall, he slipped off his boots and waded into the water. He braced himself, expecting it to be icy cold, but was pleasantly surprised. The water was actually balmy and warm. He pulled his tunic over his head and tossed it next to his boots on the shore before diving underwater. The warm eddies in the current gently pulled and pushed him, tugging at him like it was coaxing or leading somewhere.

He resurfaced and swam slowly with long, sure strokes towards the waterfall. The mist beaded and ran down his face. He took a deep breath and dove under the water, pouring off the rocks from above, kicking his legs swiftly. This time, there were no tricks threatening to drown him. The thunder of the waterfall echoed around him as he pulled himself out of the water onto the path on the right side.

The tunnel was dark, with only the light of the moon to see by. Alex pulled out the "not rock" from his pocket, wondering if it would, again, light his way. It did not. He slipped the rock back into his pocket and felt along the tunnel wall as he walked. He thought he remembered where he first tumbled head over heels into the entrance, but after a few minutes of pacing back and forth, it simply wasn't there.

Alex pulled out the rock from his pocket. *Maybe I need to be holding it for the doorway to appear?* Still nothing. If he was being honest with himself, he was more than a little disappointed. He would have liked to talk to Kynthelic again. He needed answers to the plethora of questions buzzing around in his head.

He sighed deeply, then backtracked to the waterfall. He held out his hand and touched the flowing wall of water, letting the force of it sting his skin. *How did I get into the labyrinth before? Why not now?* He sat on the edge of the walkway and dangled his feet for a moment before replacing the rock in his pocket and sliding into the water.

Alex swam unhurriedly back to shore, but as he drew near, the eddies he felt earlier pulled more insistently further out to sea. The more he swam against it, the more the current pushed back. Something wrapped around his foot and dragged him down.

He managed to take a deep breath before being completely submerged. He struggled violently, but to no avail. *What is this?* There was nothing holding him captive, yet he was still being dragged further underwater. He was running out of air quickly, but the invisible assailant's grip had not lessened. So he stopped struggling and just let the water take him where it wanted, as if he were caught in a rip current.

Despite the water remaining moonlit, his ears popped from the increase in depth and pressure. *How is this possible? Was it this deep before?*

As suddenly as the force had appeared, it released him just as quickly, leaving him suspended in this watery void. His lungs burned, and he grew more and more desperate as he looked in every direction, but could not discern which way to swim. He wondered at it more than anything. *Should I be panicking?* Strangely enough, he was not. His lungs started convulsing, desperate for air. "*After all these last weeks, this is how it ends?*" he mused.

He should probably feel a little more distraught over his imminent drowning, but if he was being honest, he was tired. Tired of always having someone trying to kill him, tired of being an outcast, tired of not knowing the right thing to do or say. Most of all, he was tired of not feeling good enough for anyone, including himself.

"*Breathe, Little Defender.*" He heard in his mind as a shape formed before him.

Shocked, he let out the last of his air and accidentally breathed in water. He choked, gasping for air he knew his lungs would not find. "Help!" was all he could manage.

"*Breathe again,*" she said.

"*Breathe how?*" He demanded. Something was nagging at the back of his mind, but he was so focused on not dying, he ignored it.

A rush of cold water flowed around him, so cold it made him gasp another lungful of water. He realized he should have passed out by now. His lungs were full of water, and yet he had not drowned. He took another experimental breath of water and felt less lightheaded. He took a few more breaths and found it still uncomfortable, but he felt he could breathe in a way.

"*Now then, your journey does not end here, Little Defender. Your story has only just begun.*" The water golem from the Revealing ceremony floated before Alex.

Ronin had said the legends called them guardians. "*Are the legends true? Did you create everything?*" He pulled out the "not rock" and held it up to her. "*What is this?*" As he held it out, suddenly, the surrounding water emanated with bioluminescence.

"You may call it the guardian stone if you wish. 'Not rock' is also somewhat accurate, if you prefer," she said with a hint of humor.

The guardian stone glowed the same blue-green light. Alex looked at it with fascination for a moment before looking back at her. "I feel lost. The closer I get to home, the more lost I feel. I don't know who I am. I don't feel like I belong anywhere. I don't know what I want."

"Do you not?" she questioned simply.

He raised his eyebrows at her. "I don't understand."

"Do you not know what it is you want, young one?" she asked again. "When you know yourself and find what you seek, there your answers will be," she said gently.

"But what about Bronach and the other missing fae? Can you help me find them? Where should I look? What happened to them?"

"Listen to the sea. It will guide your way," she replied, slowly disappearing.

"No, wait!" he called to her, but she was gone. The bioluminescence faded, only it was not the lights fading... It was his vision. He was beginning to black out from exhaustion. His last thought was of Ronin, and how he would find Alex's boots on the beach and always wonder what happened to him.

✗✗✗

"No, Daddy! He can't die. He just can't!" Alice exclaimed, grasping his forearm with her little hands as he tucked her into bed.

"Why not, sweetheart?" he asked.

"Because he hasn't saved Bronach yet!" she declared. "He swims back to shore and sits next to his boots and tunic. Then leans back and stares thoughtfully at the starry sky as the cool night air dries his skin. After a while, the delicious scent of cooking meat makes his stomach grumble, so he picks up his boots and tunic and goes back to their campsite," she insisted. "That's what happens, Daddy. Say it. Say Alex is okay!"

He chuckled as he stroked her hair. "I can't say that. Sometimes things aren't always that simple, my love."

She huffed her displeasure.

"Do you want to stop for now and take a break?"

"What!?" she shrieked. "No, I have to know what happens. How can you expect me to concentrate on anything?"

He smiled and booped her nose, "If you are sure..."

"Very sure."

"Ok sweetheart, let's continue."

CHAPTER 17

ALEX dreamed he was falling. He dreamed he was home on his cot in the little shack on the edge of the tiny fishing village he grew up in. The waves lapped gently out his window. He threw off his covers, shoved his feet in his boots, and kissed his mother's cheek as he grabbed a couple of smoked fish wrapped in seagrass from the table and ran out the door.

How had he overslept? He had promised Fin to go exploring. He ran down the shore towards the woods, looking over his shoulder to make sure the other town kids weren't following him. When he turned back, he was at the little cove north of Creedon. How had he gotten here? He wondered. This wasn't where he was meeting Fin. He turned to run back towards town, but when he rounded the bend, he was back at the cove. Strange. Wasn't this the cove the sea monster Eirach had dropped him off in? Water dragon, not sea monster, he corrected himself.

He heard Fin's voice calling to him, "Alex. Aaaallleeeex!" Only it was not Fin's voice, it was someone else's. He thought he recognized the voice but could not place it. He closed his eyes. Suddenly, his head hurt and his entire body ached like he had swum to the reef and back in the midst of a storm. He groaned and tried to rub his temple, but his arms were too heavy to move.

He opened his eyes. Instead of the bright morning sun, the soft hues of dusk greeted him. His muscles screamed in protest as he tried to sit up. He lay there for a few minutes until a large dark silhouette with long hair, pointed ears, and bright eyes, reflecting the waning light, peered down at him.

He did not know how he got here. Just before, he was running along the beach to meet Fin. Why did his chest squeeze when he thought of her? They were friends. He blinked repeatedly. He must still be dreaming, for the large silhouette transformed into a human. Not a human exactly. Fae… right. Ronin.

Everything came rushing back to him. How he had saved the knights and gone to train as one. How Fin had married another in his absence, before Alex could tell her how he felt about her. How he had been tricked and captured by the fairies in the enchanted forest. The last thing he remembered, he was underwater talking with the water golem and then he blacked out.

He gasped a deep breath of air as he tried to roll over. The residual feeling of water in his lungs choking him made him cough, as if to dislodge anything still in his lungs.

"Easy, easy there. You're okay," Ronin soothed as he placed a hand on Alex's heaving shoulder. "Relax, you are okay."

Alex tried to speak, but could only cough at first. "Where am I? What happened?" he finally asked Ronin.

"I found you facedown on the beach, laying half out of the water, not breathing. I almost lost you there," Ronin said, concern written all over his face. "Where did you go? What happened out there?"

"I went to see if I could find Kynthelic in the tunnels, but the entrance wasn't there," Alex started as he found his voice.

Talking with his mind felt too taxing at the moment. He wondered briefly why, but was interrupted.

"What wasn't there?" Quinn asked suspiciously as he crouched down next to Alex. "The entrance to what, exactly?"

"Last time I went through the passage behind the waterfall, there was a maze of hidden tunnels I stumbled upon. But when I went back to find them again, they weren't there," Alex said.

Quinn frowned in thought.

"But what happened? You were lying *facedown* on the beach, *unconscious!*" Ronin insisted.

"I got pulled under. Last I remember is blacking out," Alex said. "How am I not..." He paused for a moment before continuing, "Dead?" he finished.

"If you had died..." Quinn began.

"I wouldn't finish that sentence if I were you," Ronin cut him off in a warning tone.

"... It would be much more convenient for me. Rather than going on this ridiculous quest to find a half-breed no one even cares about, I could be back home with my unit getting recognition due to me for having brought the notorious Ronin to justice," Quinn continued spitefully.

Ronin growled.

"You couldn't bring him in if your life depended on it!" Alex spat at Quinn with a venom that surprised even himself. "Ronin is twice the man you could ever hope to be; more skilled, more competent, a better leader, and more honorable. If you had half the honor you claim to, you would want to be here looking for all your missing people, not complaining about wanting to be back home in your cushy bed, surrounded by people who worship the air you breathe."

Quinn's nostrils flared as he clenched his jaw and fists, tension filling his frame. Next thing Alex knew, Quinn launched himself with a roar of fury. Alex met him head-on, letting out a deep guttural yell of his own. Quinn swung a fist at his jaw, but he deftly dodged the blow.

Ronin looked startled, frozen in place, gaping at his two traveling companions fighting. Alex ignored him, too angry and tired to think straight. All he saw was red. His body went into automatic defense.

He shifted his weight back, allowing Quinn to overextend himself. He deflected Quinn's arm out of the way, grabbing his wrist as his other hand grabbed the back of Quinn's head. Using his own body weight and Quinn's momentum, Alex twisted and dropped to a knee as he flipped Quinn over his shoulder, throwing him to the ground on his back. As he landed, Alex straddled Quinn's torso and pummeled his face as hard and fast as he could.

Quinn blocked with his forearms and lifted with his legs abruptly, knocking Alex forward and off to the side, rolling him over his shoulder. Alex tumbled forward, letting his momentum carry him to his feet, turning to face his opponent. He instinctively raised his fists, ready to go again. Simultaneously, Quinn rolled away from Alex. He crouched and started shifting into his snow leopard.

Ronin broke free of his daze as he recognized this brawl was about to become deadly. "That is ENOUGH!" Ronin boomed in his most commanding voice as he stepped between them.

Startled mid-shift, Quinn blinked at Ronin oddly, then shifted back. He still looked furious, but he no longer looked murderous.

Alex stalked towards Quinn, unwilling to yield and still blinded by his anger, but Ronin placed a hand on his chest. "No, not tonight. Go walk it off," Ronin said in a stern tone.

Alex resisted, attempting to push past Ronin, but he pushed back more firmly. "*Alex!*" Ronin said in his mind, finally breaking through to him. Alex took a deep breath and stopped resisting. The firelight flickered in Ronin's dark eyes as he gave him a pained look before stalking off into the surrounding forest.

XXX

Alex paced barefoot along the shore as he thought about what had transpired since he was last home. He picked up a handful of smooth pebbles and rolled them around in his palm as he walked. It seemed, not long ago, he had ridden out on Bucephalus on his way to the knight's summit, but also a lifetime ago, or another life altogether.

The warm evening breeze gently caressed his flushed skin as he turned to observe the moonlit horizon. He thought he knew who he was, and where he belonged in this world, so sure of himself. He didn't like the status quo, but at least he knew his place in it. Now he didn't even know himself. *So much has changed in so little time, and yet nothing has changed at all.* He sat on the sand, knees tucked to his chest. He clenched a handful of sand and let it fall slowly from his fist as he listened to the whisper of the waves gently lapping on the sand.

"Listen to the sea; it will guide your way," he shouted out loud in frustration. "What does that even mean?" he yelled into the surf. His feelings of homesickness and loneliness flooded the forefront of his mind and threatened to overwhelm him.

I don't know where I belong or who I am. What's the point of having magic, or whatever this is, if I don't know what to do with it? Or if it kills me first? Despair surged through him, making his chest feel tight.

"Defender sad?" Alex felt a gentle voice nose into his thoughts. *"Defender need family?"* the voice continued.

"Who are you? Why do you call me 'Defender'?" Alex asked back.

"Defender calls me Eirach. Guardians call you Defender. Fits." The silhouette of a colossal head and long, snake-like neck poked out of the water in the distance and advanced toward Alex. *"Defender come,"* Eirach requested. *"Defender meet family."*

Alex felt compelled to swim out to meet Eirach's ever-growing, dark form. It was better than brooding on the shore in self-pity while thinking in circles. Still, he hesitated, remembering his last water adventure. *What if it happened again? I can't control it. I don't understand it. This is crazy. I know the sea! I have spent my whole life in it. Why am I suddenly afraid of it now?*

Making up his mind, he waded out into the dark waters of the cove. As he reached the sea dragon, Eirach lit up with bioluminescence. "Oh!" escaped his mouth as he found himself, yet again, face to face with the sea dragon.

"Defender, quiet mind. Too loud. Too much," Eirach said in his mind.

"But..."

"Defender cannot meet family. Quiet mind. Eirach help."

Alex tried to clear his mind as best he could. He focused on the swells and his strokes treading water, and after a few minutes that felt like hours, he quieted his mind.

Eirach submerged and rose up under Alex until Alex was sitting on his back. *"Focus on family. Focus on feeling of family,"* Eirach said.

As Alex relaxed and tried to do what he said, he started hearing sounds all around him, voices and songs and music. Not around him exactly, but in his mind and from all different directions. Some were faint and quiet, others louder. Loudest of all was Eirach.

"There! Defender, meet family. Family, meet Defender," Eirach chirped a few notes as he finished speaking.

Alex heard other chirps join in. He felt minds and thoughts gliding along together, yet separate, some having other conversations as well as investigating this new one. He marveled at each having their own personality. Some felt young and bright and talkative, others felt more reserved, and everything in between. All simply accepting him. He thought he felt one ask about a school of fish, and another reply back. He was glad he was sitting, because he was suddenly overcome with emotions he didn't have a name for yet.

"Defender belongs here," Eirach said simply. And many voiced their agreement.

"How do I know which one of you is which? Do you have names?" Alex asked.

"Eirach only one with name. No need for names," Eirach said. "Defender feel all, everywhere."

"But how?" Alex asked

"Focus on all, yet each," Eirach instructed.

"How?" Alex asked again.

Eirach snorted a spray of mist into the air. "All yet each." He indicated the mist.

Alex thought he understood the concept, but still didn't know how he was supposed to do that. He tried anyway, trying to reach out with his mind to each voice. He gasped. They were everywhere! All over, even in places he didn't know existed.

Eirach nodded. "Hold family feeling, then use magic."

"Family feeling?" Alex asked.

"Strong feeling, strong magic," Eirach said as he touched the tip of his nose to Alex's chest. "Strong family."

Alex absentmindedly placed his hand on Eirach's nose, who shivered and half closed his eyes in pleasure. "I don't know what to do." He shrugged. "When I try using earth magic, I only manage a blade of grass. I accidentally used fire once and nearly caused a wildfire." He sighed, hanging his head in shame and defeat.

Eirach snorted, "Feelings fuel magic. Good feeling, good magic. Bad feeling, bad magic. Listen to self. Learn and understand feelings. Defender control feelings, feelings not control Defender."

Alex held out his hands and tried to focus on the new sensations he experienced with the water dragons. He couldn't think of anything to do but push the water in front of him. To his surprise, he saw it move. He tried it again and again until he felt comfortable with the exercise. Then he tried pulling until he felt comfortable with that as well. He put it together and pushed and pulled the water until he gathered it into a small ball between his hands.

Eirach nodded as he watched. "More."

Alex had an idea as the sphere of water hung before him. Instantaneously, the water reshaped itself into long, thin strands, weaving between his fingers.

"What is it?" Eirach asked.

"The children in my village call it a cat's cradle; only they usually do it with string. It's a game of sorts," he explained.

Eirach tilted his head back and forth as he watched. Alex let the water drop, finished.

"Dragonlings do more than this," Eirach teased gently.

"Okay," Alex let out a sigh, not sure what more to do. Althenaea had made doors and a boat out of water. Eirach bobbed his head encouragingly. Alex smiled as his idea took form in his mind. Out of the water rose a perfect replica of Eirach. It even mimicked his movements. He snorted in surprise and let out a series of chirps in pleasure.

Alex felt the strain on his body and felt himself losing focus with his mind the longer he tried to hold it. Eventually, he let it fall back to the sea and reclined in exhaustion on Eirach's warm scales.

After resting a while and listening to the rest of the sea dragons, he thanked them and withdrew his mind. Immediately, he felt strangely alone, so he reached out again. He was met with comfort, understanding, and encouragement. "We are still here, even when you cannot hear us," he heard several voices addressing what he hadn't asked.

He stood and rested his forehead on Eirach's nose, thanking him repeatedly. Eirach chirped his pleasure before slowly sinking into the water, leaving Alex to swim back to shore alone.

Climbing out of the water, Alex sat in the sand, looking out to sea. He wondered at what had been so near to him, yet so far away, all this time. The moonlight rippled across the surface of the water and the night breeze blew gently across his face. He sighed deeply, torn between going back to camp or staying here until sunrise. Making up his mind, he stood, letting the seawater from his clothes drip into the sand as he wrung out the worst of it. His damp shirt and pants clung to his skin as he trudged back to Ronin and Quinn.

Ronin looked up inquisitively at him from across the campfire as he arrived back at camp, but said nothing. Quinn glanced his way before pulling a blanket around himself and turned to face the other way.

CHAPTER 18

THE next morning, a chilly drizzle had settled in. Alex wrapped his cloak around himself tighter, grateful for the deep hood. He watched as Ronin kicked loose mud into the fire to douse the flames. Alex wondered why Ronin didn't just use magic to do it as opposed to getting his boots muddy, but he kept his question to himself. He must have let something slip in his thoughts, because Ronin glanced his way and shrugged. Quinn was in a brooding mood. He wanted to apologize for last night, but didn't know how to start, so he didn't.

"We should probably try to retrieve at least some of your gear, if it's still there, and see what is salvageable," Ronin said aloud to Alex. Alex nodded, and Quinn shrugged.

It meant delaying seeing his mom and the rest of Creedon for a day. He still hadn't figured out what to say to her, if anything at all. Should he act like nothing was different? Should he tell her everything? What did she know? How could she keep this from him his entire life? Where was his father? Who was his father? The questions swirled in his head with no answers.

They entered the enchanted forest, or Cinntire, as Mahkai had told Alex that night in his treehouse. The rain had slacked off to a light mist, so they were only occasionally dripped on as they walked.

Alex realized Quinn hadn't even so much as grumbled today. He glanced his way and was surprised to find Quinn staring at him. Nothing in Quinn's expression gave away what he was thinking. Ronin started humming a tune that Alex knew, so he joined in to distract him from his aching feet and ever-growing list of questions and things he didn't understand.

They reached the other side of the forest faster than Alex thought they would, but then again, he had never walked straight through it before. He also wondered if a bit of magic was involved.

They found the tree easily enough, maybe too easily, almost as if it wanted to be found. His armor was covered in pine sap and needles, as was to be expected when it sat unused under a pine tree for so long. His saddle was in better shape, but the same could not be said of his saddlebags and blankets. Mice had chewed them to pieces and taken up residence. His rations bag was almost indistinguishable because it had sweet grass growing out of it.

Ronin chuckled loudly, which startled birds and rabbits nearby. "I think the sweet oatcakes and grain sprouted."

"Aww too bad. I figured you were looking forward to a snack. They were your favorite." Alex grinned.

"Mmmm, stale grain, my favorite," Ronin said sarcastically and made a face.

Alex couldn't help himself. He reached down and grabbed a handful and shoved it beneath Ronin's nose. "Awe, c'mon, it's not that bad," Alex laughed. "You've eaten worse. Remember Ol' Eli?"

"Oof, don't remind me," Ronin shuddered.

Quinn hung back, not sure what to make of their teasing.

"Ol' Eli was known to never throw anything out. His stable hand was just as old as he, so their stalls hadn't been cleaned in probably 5 years. We and a couple of the other knights were invited."

"Mandated, more like," Alex retorted.

"Well, you could have said no, but you would have spent the next month cleaning all the weapons and gear with all the squires. I don't know, it might have been worth it," Ronin shot back.

"Speak for yourself. You wouldn't have had to do all the cleaning. You would have been pampered by the ladies while I had to do all the work," Alex responded, shaking his head, grinning. "You always did like attention," he teased.

Quinn chuckled. "Not much has changed then," he said under his breath.

Alex was stunned. He hadn't heard Quinn laugh before. He was starting to believe his face was perpetually stuck in a frown and was incapable of humor. "Has he always been like this?" he asked Quinn.

"Nearly," Quinn replied. "He always did have a knack for getting attention." He smiled slightly and shook his head. Then his face fell.

Ronin had a pained expression on his face. Alex looked between Ronin and Quinn. "What? I don't understand."

"Why?" Quinn's voice was strained as he looked at Ronin. "Why did you do it? Why didn't you wait?" he demanded.

"I..." Ronin sighed as he sank down to his knees. "I didn't know," he whispered. "It has tortured me these last 15 years. You think I haven't replayed that day over and over in my head? Wondering where I went wrong..." His voice was thick with emotion.

"You think I don't see their faces in my dreams at night or hear their voices in my head?" He looked up and Quinn. "If I could go back and change that day, don't you think I would? I would wait one more hour. I would ask more questions. I would send a runner to inquire if they were willing to have peace talks. I have thought about that day every day since, and all I have come up with is I didn't know and wasn't told... But that is no excuse." He sighed dejectedly.

"What do you mean you weren't told?" Quinn demanded. "They sent out messengers the day before, telling everyone to stand down. Everyone knew. Next thing we know, we hear you have not only gone against orders and engaged with them, but lost a whole unit under your command."

Ronin looked genuinely shocked. "The day before? The last runner I had seen was 3 days prior." Quinn frowned. Ronin's eyes glazed over, lost in thought.

Not wanting to intrude further into their conversation, Alex started to move his gear out of the forest and into the meadow. This was going to take a while to clean anyway. He sat and unwrapped his leather cleaning supplies, which had thankfully remained intact in his absence.

After an hour, Alex heard footsteps behind him. Ronin crouched down beside him and looked at the progress he had made.

"Think it will still fit?" Alex asked, indicating the saddle.

"Well, let's find out, shall we?" he said with a mock flourish before shifting into Bucephalus. He snorted and pawed at the ground before kicking up his heels and tearing around the meadow, then dropped down to roll. *"I always did love a good roll in the grass,"* he said in Alex's mind as he stood up and shook the grass, clinging to his glossy black coat.

Alex chuckled as he threw the saddle up on Bucephalus's high back. To his surprise, it fit beautifully. He attached his armor to the saddle and stared at him for a long moment.

"Well, what are you waiting for?" Ronin urged.

"This feels weird," Alex said back. Bucephalus snorted, rolled his eyes, and pawed at the ground. "Okay, okay, I'm going, I'm going," he said as he climbed into the saddle, just like he had a million times before. It felt the same, yet he knew everything was different.

A grey, almost white, stallion emerged from the forest as they swung around and started towards Creedon. *"Home,"* Alex thought. He nodded to Quinn, admiring him appreciatively before Bucephalus took off in an easy canter.

XXX

The rest of the day passed quickly. When they arrived in Creedon, the sun had just set, and the light was slowly fading. The calm waters reflected the brilliant colors still lingering from the sunset. Alex could hear many voices singing and talking loudly from the main hall and guessed quite a group gathered in it. A few individuals sat by small fires near their boats, mending nets or lines. They looked up inquisitively as they rode in. Alex didn't stop, but rode straight to Bronach's blacksmith shop. He would talk to them later.

He dismounted and removed his gear from Bucephalus and started grooming him out of years of habit. His hand stopped mid-stroke and Bucephalus looked back at him indignantly.

"*Don't stop now. This is the best!*" Ronin said to him and nudged Alex's hand with his nose.

"But it's... weird," Alex said haltingly.

"*Just think of it like you are scratching my back,*" Ronin responded simply.

Alex resumed brushing, happy for the delay in seeing his mother and giving his hands something to do. Without thinking, he brushed Quinn as well, moving his soft brushes in long, sure strokes down his side.

Quinn flinched away. "*What do you think you are doing? No.*"

Alex stopped and backed away.

"*You should try it. You might actually like it,*" Ronin chimed in.

"*Absolutely not,*" Quinn was adamant.

Alex shrugged and put away his brushes.

"*Do you want us to go with you?*" Ronin asked.

Alex sighed. "No, I think this is something I have to do myself. Thank you though. Do you want me to bring you anything to eat?" Alex asked aloud.

"*It's okay. We'll just raid Bronach's stash of goods. Unless she makes gravy,*" Ronin added. "*We'll look around here and see if we can find anything that would give us a lead on who took Bronach, or where they might have gone.*"

Quinn eyed the sweet grain in the bucket hanging in his stall with disdain and suspicion.

"Bucephalus, I mean, Ronin always likes it; you might give it a try. I used to add some to my porridge in the mornings," Alex said with a shrug. He smirked, patted Quinn on the shoulder, knowing it might annoy him, and left.

The short walk to his house ended too quickly, as Alex found himself standing at the door he knew so well. He could hear his mother humming inside. She sounded content. He cringed with guilt, knowing he was about to shatter that. He took a deep breath and lightly knocked as he opened the door.

"Hi Mama, I'm back," he said as he poked his head in the door.

"Alex! Welcome home, love. If I'd known you were coming, I would have made something special for you." She stood up from her chair, set down the shirt she was mending, and wrapped her arms around him, squeezing tightly before letting go.

"It's okay, Mama," Alex said as he hugged her thin frame back. The top of her head only came to his shoulder.

She stepped back and looked him up and down. "Have you been eating enough?" She put water in a kettle to boil. "Tea?"

Alex smiled affectionately. "Yes, and yes."

He took off his boots and set them by the door before sitting in the only other chair in their small house. He looked fondly at their meager living, the only home he had ever known. Two wooden plates and two cups rested on a simple table near an old stove. The lofted bunk bed he slept in when he was in town was made neatly, like he had just made it that morning.

Two tattered and worn leather chairs sat near a clean but well-used fireplace. Its chimney rose to jut at an angle out the roof. The floor and walls were bare, but tidy. Light sun-bleached wood reflected the firelight, making flickering shadows dance across the room like fireflies at dusk. Alex took a deep breath. It smelled of salt and sea, smoke and pine, fresh baked bread and tea. It smelled of home.

After she finished making tea and handed him a mug, she sat facing him in her chair with her legs tucked under her and sipped on her tea.

"You wanna talk about it?" she asked simply.

She always did have a knack for knowing something was on his mind. She didn't press him, she just asked and gave him space to talk or not.

Alex sighed before pulling his ring out from under the collar of his shirt. He heard his mother take in a sharp breath before slowly letting it out. He couldn't bring himself to look her in the face, so he studied the familiar ring like it might spill its secrets. "Tell me about my father."

CHAPTER 19

THE next morning, as he exited his house, he saw several of the village children peeking around the corner of a nearby building. He smiled at them and crouched down, opening his arms. Two little boys and a girl came dashing towards him, giggling.

"Uncle Alex! Uncle Alex!" they cried as they tackled him to the ground. "You've been gone forever! Did you slay any more dragons?" they said over each other.

"Lydia, Tom, Garrett," He laughed, "I missed you too!"

"Where did you go this time?" Tom asked.

"Can we see Bucephalus?" Lydia asked.

"Why, of course, you can," Alex said to Lydia. "Let's go see him, and I'll tell you all about my adventures," he said to Tom.

"Okay!" They dashed toward the blacksmith shop.

"Hey Ronin, Quinn, you are about to have visitors," he said to them in his mind. *"Be nice,"* he said as an afterthought.

He stopped and picked up a few tools where they had been left out and brought them into the shop to put away. Bronach must have left in a hurry or didn't leave of his own volition. He would never have left his tools lying around.

When he walked into the stable part of the shop, he saw Tom sitting on Bucephalus's back calling down to Garrett who was swinging a wooden sword around in front of them, like he was fighting a great beast, and Lydia braiding ribbons into his tail. Alex grinned and chuckled as he sat down on a stool.

Quinn watched warily with his head hanging over the door of the stall next to Ronin. His ears swiveled, questioning Alex.

"Be careful of this one. He's mean and bites," Alex said to the children. Quinn snorted, making Alex smirk. "That reminds me, do you know where Bronach is?" Alex asked Lydia.

"The scary men came and took him," she replied.

"What scary men? What did they look like? Which way did they go? Have you seen them before?" Alex asked rapid-fire.

"One had a scar down the side of his head, like he got into a fight with a shark or something!" Tom gestured from the top of his head to his jaw.

"Did you see that one of them was missing an ear?" Garrett asked Tom.

"Oh, yea!" Tom exclaimed. "They all carried weapons, like swords and stuff, but they were all rusty and not at all nice like yours are."

Alex crouched down near Garrett. "Do you know why they took Bronach?"

Lydia chimed in, "They were trying to pick a fight with everyone. I don't think they cared who. First, they were kicking stuff and being disrespectful."

"Yea! And then when Papa tried telling them to stop and stood up to them, they knocked him out cold flat on his back," Garrett said emphatically.

"Then Bronach came stomping over. His papa is big, but nobody is as big as Bronach. I've never seen him so angry. He fought all of them at once!" Tom chimed in.

Garrett interrupted. "Bronach would have won too. He had them all on the run, but one of them whispered something to Bronach, and he just stopped. Like when Mamma dumps cold water on Reggie when he's going to go do something stupid."

"Then they put those prisoner cuffs on him, and he just went with them," Lydia finished.

Alex paced, every once in a while stopping to just look at Ronin. "Do you know which way they went?"

The children shook their heads. Tom slid down from Ronin's back and dangled from his mane as Ronin lowered his head and placed the boy gently on the ground. "Are you going after them?" Tom asked.

"Yes, as soon as I refill my supplies," Alex said decisively. Dread trickled down his back like a cold bead of sweat. He knew this day might come. His past mistake had finally come back to haunt him. "Can you run and get me some bread, cheese, and dried fish, and fill up this bag with as much sweet grains and oatcakes as you can?" He asked all three of them as he picked up some spare saddlebags. They nodded. He handed one to each of them and they took off in different directions.

"*Well, that's interesting,*" Ronin mused in Alex's head.

"*What is?*" Quinn demanded as he looked back and forth from Alex to Ronin.

"*We've had a run-in with those two particular thugs before. They were part of a band that used to ambush merchant wagons on their way between cities. They became a big enough nuisance that a knight was sent to deal with them,*" Ronin said.

Alex blew out a breath in frustration and rubbed his face with his hands. "We captured most of the gang, but those two got away. I was so focused on taking back the ones I had already apprehended. I wanted the accolades for my accomplishments, for once. I was afraid the other knights sent to help me transport them would take credit. No one besides McCannon believed I could, and he was gone." Alex looked at Ronin. "You wanted to go after them. I should have listened to you."

Quinn said impatiently, "*Regret won't change the past. Hurry up. Let's go already.*" He walked out to stand in the yard by the shop. He pawed at the ground and thrashed his tail.

Soon after, Garrett and Tom came running back and handed Alex the full saddlebags. "Mamma added some dried fruit and nuts in there too," Tom said proudly. "She said if you were going after the bad men, it was the least she could do."

Alex had just finished tacking up Bucephalus. He tied the bags across the back of the saddle. Bucephalus snuffled Garrett's pockets until he pulled out an extra oatcake and fed it to him. Bucephalus rubbed his forehead on the boy's chest in thanks. Alex smiled at their antics as he finished tying on his javelin, a pike, and two spears he had gotten from Bronach's storeroom.

"I have half a mind to make you carry gear too. Come here." He motioned to Quinn as he picked up a soft harness off a hook on the wall.

The saddle blanket connected to a chest plate and girth to keep it in place. It was specially equipped with strings and metal loops meant for attaching things.

Quinn snorted indignantly and turned his hindquarters towards Alex.

"I'm not asking," Alex said firmly as he walked toward Quinn.

Quinn attempted to kick and bite Alex, but he stepped out of the way and flicked him on the soft part of his mouth.

Quinn snorted in surprise and pinned his ears. Alex took that moment to attach a rope halter to him.

"C'mon, it's your turn to carry things," he said aloud as he attached the harness.

"*I'm regretting letting you talk me into this,*" Quinn complained. "*Why did I have to be the one sent on this mission? I couldn't have been tasked with other things... No, I had to be stuck babysitting...*" He continued grumbling as Alex finished balancing the packs on his harness.

Ronin had wandered out into the yard. "*Hey guys? You might want to come out here.*"

Alex led Quinn out to join Ronin and saw most of the town had gathered. He made a show of tying the lead rope to his saddle for the sake of all the eyes watching him. He nodded to them as he finished making sure everything was secure.

Garrett's father limped towards him, his arm in a sling. Old bruises marred the side of his face and neck.

"My boy says you are going after the..." He glanced toward the children. "...men who did this and took our people," he finished.

Alex nodded solemnly. "Who else did they take?"

His stomach tightened. Sadness and outrage churned in his chest. He didn't realize how attached to this town, his home, he had become. He'd always felt like an outsider, but now that someone had invaded, he felt like they had stolen something from him personally.

As Garrett's dad listed off four others besides Bronach, Alex felt his throat tighten and his fists clench. This was his fault. He would make it right.

Ronin snorted and bumped his arm. *"Hey, hey, easy. We'll find them,"* Alex heard in his mind.

Alex rested his hand on Ronin's glossy black neck. "I vow to bring all our people back and make those cowards pay for their crimes," Alex said gruffly, his voice husky with emotion.

"We know you will, son. We believe in you. You have become a fine man that will make us proud." Alex's mother, Rose, placed a hand on his shoulder.

She directed her attention to Quinn and Ronin, who were observing everything attentively. "You keep him safe, both of you. Don't let him get into anything over his head," she whispered, standing close but not quite touching them. She gave Alex a quick hug and handed him a small bundle. "Open it later."

"Thank you, Mother." Alex tucked it into one of his bags, then mounted up. The rest of the townspeople gathered and raised a hand as he passed them. He nodded to each of them in turn.

"They care for you in their own way, Alex," Ronin said simply. Alex couldn't respond, still overcome with conflicting emotions.

Lastly, they passed Fin, standing by the road by herself, very pregnant with her first child. Her husband was one of those taken with Bronach.

"I'll bring him back, Fin!" he declared with more strength than he felt. Her red puffy eyes gave away the fact that she had been crying. He wanted to go to her and comfort her, but knew she wouldn't want attention drawn to her. He wasn't ready to move on yet, but Ronin had already started moving away.

"Old lover?" Quinn asked.

"Missed opportunity. I chose a different path." Alex sighed.

✗✗✗

Alex spent the rest of the day in his head, alone with his thoughts. He was grateful Ronin and Quinn seemed to understand his need for silence. That evening, when they stopped for the night, Alex relieved them of their burdens.

Quinn shifted into his fae form and groaned as he stretched. Alex raised an eyebrow at him. *Dramatic much?*

"Why don't you carry all the packs tomorrow and play the role of the dumb beast and see how you feel," Quinn snapped.

Alex realized he had spoken out loud, but struggled to bury his feelings of irritation. "Why did you even come?"

"I was given a direct order. I don't know about you, but I am not in the habit of defying my superiors," Quinn quipped back.

"You can just hang out in the forest for a while or pretend like you lost us," Alex said sarcastically.

Althenaea hadn't given either of them a choice, nor had she shared her reasoning. A great number of things frustrated Alex; he didn't know where to direct his attention first. Without another word, Quinn shifted into an owl and took off into the night.

Ronin lit a small campfire and hung a hammock between two trees.

"Care to share?" he asked after he finished and sat down by the fire.

"Not really." Alex still didn't feel like he had anything sorted out enough to share.

"I know he was being dramatic, but after what you said the other night, you could be a little more gentle with him. He drives me crazy too, but this isn't easy for him either," Ronin said.

"That's rather diplomatic of you," Alex retorted.

"We are looking for trouble in unfamiliar territory for him. If we continue to fight amongst ourselves, we will never find Bronach or the others," Ronin continued.

Alex looked at him for a moment. He wondered when Ronin had become the peacekeeper of their group. "Alright. For Bronach," Alex conceded.

Ronin nodded. "We headed to Arageyll?" he asked.

"Might as well. It's as good a place to start as any. They had to stop somewhere. Maybe someone saw them," Alex suggested.

Ronin shrugged. Alex hung his own hammock and crawled in. He mulled over things as he closed his eyes, but he was asleep within minutes.

His lungs burned as he ran. He didn't know why he was running, only that he couldn't stop. His legs were sore and tired, but desperation drove him to keep up his speed. Running down a dark, stone corridor, he could hear running water off to his right, but he couldn't slow down to look. He spotted a light up ahead and felt relief. He was almost there. He was going to make it! He pushed his tired body faster. As he rounded a corner, he saw the entryway, but as he drew closer, he sensed something was wrong. The gate was still closed!

He didn't know why he thought it should be open, but he was certain it was supposed to be. He felt deep and utter despair as he slowed to a stop. He tried the lock, but it was still securely fastened. He looked around for a key or anything to pry it open with. At any moment, they would discover him missing. He had to hurry!

He heard a shout, back the way he had come. He had been found! Throwing caution to the wind, he yanked on the iron bars. They didn't budge. He threw himself at it and slammed his shoulder into it as the sound of footsteps and voices grew louder. Again and again, he threw himself at the bars, hoping and praying to both Nocturne and Fiera to save him. To let him go free.

He felt hands roughly grab him and wrestle him to the ground. The shock of cold from the stone floor lanced through him. He fought back and yelled, but his body would not cooperate. They were too strong and easily overpowered him. These demons who held him captive. Why would the gods create such beings? They bound his hands and feet behind his back and dragged him back down the corridor. All his will to fight… gone, replaced with overwhelming dread. He would never see Fin again. Why was he thinking about Fin?

Once they finally dropped him next to the other prisoners and their footsteps retreated, he turned over to face them. What!

Alex jerked awake. He was in his hammock. His clothes were drenched and clung to his skin uncomfortably. His heart pounded and his body ached.

The fire was burning low, so he got up and added a couple more dead branches to it. He sat as close as he dared next to the fire. He couldn't get that last image out of his head. Why was he dreaming about being captured by minotaur? Why was he thinking about Fin? It didn't feel like a normal dream. It was like he was watching it happen through someone else's eyes.

That person didn't know what minotaur were and saw them as demons. They prayed to both Nocturne and Fiera and thought about Fin. How was he dreaming about Fin's husband? He wrestled with it more while he stared into the fire until he nodded off. Then he crawled back in his hammock and slept dreamlessly for the rest of the night.

XXX

The next morning, Alex awoke with a start. Ronin was gone, and Quinn was crouched next to the cold remnant of the campfire. Alex still felt irritated at Quinn, but he also felt ashamed of his own behavior. Of how he had lost control of his temper and lashed out. Everything he disliked about the other knights, he had resorted to himself. His face burned as he thought about it.

"Uhh look..." Alex began, unsure of what to say exactly. He rubbed the back of his neck as he struggled to find the right words. "I'm... sorry," he finally said.

Quinn inhaled sharply, but Alex cut him off before he could respond, "Wait, let me finish, then you can say whatever you want and I'll listen... Please?" Quinn looked at him suspiciously.

"I don't know who I am, where I'm actually from, what all this is, why me, or why the world is suddenly different from what I thought it to be," he began. "I didn't ask for this, and I don't feel like I have done anything to deserve any of it."

"I envy you. I woke up one morning and found everything I knew flipped on its head. Like waking up from a dream, and I have this feeling that this is only the start. You have known about magic your whole life. I know I can't ask you to see it from my perspective, because to you, this is all normal, like breathing. I envy that."

"I envy your ability to have confidence in knowing the world you live in and where you belong in it. I envy your life, in that you were fortunate to grow up in a world full of magic and wonder. A world of infinite and unimaginable possibilities," Alex spoke quickly, not caring that he was rambling.

Quinn stood up and faced him, but Alex kept going. "I am sorry you got dragged into this. I'm sorry you have to be here at all. I know Bronach means nothing to you. I know you don't want to be here. I know you hate me, what I am, what I represent, and that I'm nothing to you either," he trailed off.

"If you want to leave, I won't stop you. If you want to take me back to the council to stand trial for whatever grievances you feel I have committed, fine. I'll go with you... But please, just let me find Bronach," Alex ended quietly with a tone of desperation.

He held his breath and twisted the hem of his tunic between his fingers, afraid to look Quinn in the face. He didn't know why he felt nervous. After a moment, he let out his breath and looked up. Quinn stared back at him, his face unreadable.

"You..." Quinn never got to finish his comment. He was interrupted by a loud snapping of branches behind him. He whirled to face it, his hands shifting into claws. Alex drew two of his knives as he naturally stepped up next to Quinn to cover his side; a move drilled into him from his knight's training.

The underbrush rustled violently in front of them as they silently stalked forward in unison. Quinn thrust out a hand and sent a whirlwind into the trees toward the sound. Alex heard a dull crash of something large being sent flying and then, "Oh! Oh my, oh dear!"

They raced towards the voice, both poised to attack, but stopped short. Quinn let out a frustrated growl and relaxed his posture, letting his claws return to hands.

Alex almost laughed at the sight before him. Hanging upside down, helplessly tangled in vines and branches, was Mahkai. Books and papers were scattered haphazardly around in the branches and on the ground beneath him. His little owl peaked out of the top flap of an olive-green knapsack, hanging from a branch nearby.

"Great! This is just what we need!" Quinn threw up his hands before stalking away.

"Mahkai, what are you doing here?" Alex asked, turning from watching Quinn walk away. He wanted to know what Quinn had been about to say.

"Ah, um, I… I have come to offer my assistance in your quest," Mahkai stammered as he tried to disentangle himself to no avail.

"No offense, but you are not exactly inconspicuous here… among humans," Alex said as he tried to help. He cut through a few of the vines until Mahkai could wriggle himself out.

Mahkai landed on his side with a thud as he dropped to the ground. Twigs and leaves poked out of his clothes at odd angles as he did his best to straighten his vest. Alex helped him gather his books and papers strewn about and handed him his little spectacles as well.

"I know, but, you see, my cousin, erm well… a few of them actually… they seem to have, well…"

"Mahkai…" Alex prompted, trying to be patient with him, but he was tired. The emotions of this day and last while were wearing on him. He also felt the loss of the conversation left unfinished with Quinn. He didn't know when or if he would get Quinn to talk straight to him again.

"Right, right. Sorry. A group of rogue minotaur, mostly youths mind you, left Osrealach for Reyall and seem to have vanished. They made quite a fuss before leaving, so I followed them out of, well, honestly curiosity, but also out of concern for my cousins. I lost their trail not long ago, and that is when I found you. Or well, you found me, I suppose. It was quite the fortuitous coincidence that I ran into you."

"Why would minotaur be in Reyall? If they are here, where could they be? Minotaur would be seen as monsters and hunted on sight, if people even knew they–you–exist outside of old lore and myths."

"I do not know. They were unhappy with the way things have been since the peace treaty, but aren't we all? I never imagined they would leave. Oh my, do you think they could be connected to all the missing people?" Mahkai chewed on his bottom lip.

"Mahkai, I don't think…" Alex started.

"Oh dear, I must tell the clan leaders and the council, or at least Amsah and Althenaea, at once. I apologize Alex. I must leave you, even though I have just arrived. If you need anything, send word. I shall endeavor to assist you from afar. Strength and wisdom, my friend," Mahkai said as he stuffed the last of his papers in his bag and slung it over his shoulder. He hurried away, crashing through the underbrush deep into the forest.

Alex shook his head as he watched the minotaur depart, then returned to their campsite.

CHAPTER 20

THEY were coming up on the crossroads headed toward Arageyll, when Alex saw other riders approaching. As they drew closer, he recognized the four knights. He groaned under his breath.

"Well, well, well! If it isn't Sir Can't-be-bothered-to-show-up," Fintan said to the knight on his left. The knight snickered.

"Fintan," Alex kept his tone neutral. "George, Robert, John." He greeted each of them, barely inclining his head.

"Cole wanted to send search parties out after you when you didn't show up to Summit. We told him it would be a waste of time, that you were probably in some ale house or locked up for impersonating nobility," Fintan said haughtily. "Looks like we were right. He had nothing to worry about." The other knights chuckled.

"Seems to me like you prefer horse thieving, because as Nocturne is my witness, there is no way you could afford either of these two fine animals," Robert said as he rode a circle around them, scrutinizing Quinn with obvious jealousy. "Tell you what. We'll take that grey off your hands for you in exchange for pretending like we never saw you," he offered, pointing to Quinn.

"*Over my dead body!*" Alex heard Quinn say in his mind.

"*Tell him he doesn't want him, he has a bad attitude, and he bites,*" Ronin said to Alex. Quinn pinned his ears at Ronin. Alex smirked at their antics.

"*He couldn't handle Quinn. His riding instructor isn't here to tell him which end is which,*" Ronin continued the commentary. Quinn shook his head, and Alex had to cough to cover his laugh.

Robert reached out to take Quinn's lead rope attached to Alex's saddle. Ronin and Quinn danced out of his reach. Fintan moved his horse forward to block them from moving further while Robert reached again.

"If you touch that rope, we will have a fight on our hands," Alex said in a serious warning tone.

"What are you going to do?" Fintan asked. "There are four of us. We can do what we want. No one will believe you anyway." Fintan gestured to John and George; they moved forward to surround Alex.

"*Alright, how do you want to do this?*" Alex asked Quinn and Ronin.

"*Tell them they need to roll for initiative first,*" Ronin joked, referencing a popular game Alex had learned while traveling with McCannon during his knight's training. Alex grinned.

"What's so funny?" Fintan asked suspiciously.

Alex shook his head. "Nothing."

Fintan moved to Ronin's head and seemed to notice the absence of a bridle for the first time. Ronin pinned his ears, then lunged toward Fintan's horse. The horse stumbled out of the way, barely managing to avoid Ronin's teeth. Quinn kicked out at the two knights behind him. Robert jumped from his horse at Alex and managed to snag Quinn's lead rope, but the halter slipped off his head. Robert scowled as he dodged out of the way of Ronin's hooves and pulled out his sword.

Alex pulled out one of his spears and began using both ends to drive the other knights away from him and Ronin. Quinn was separated from them and seemed to be hindered by the packs tied on him.

"C'mon. What do you need with two horses anyway? All you do is sit around taking credit for things you didn't do while the rest of us do all the hard work. Give up already," Fintan taunted as he tried to maneuver Alex toward the other knights.

Run! Alex yelled to Quinn in his mind. *Make for the trees and shift when you are out of sight of anyone. Don't kill them.* He added for good measure.

Quinn didn't argue, he just took off at a flat-out gallop. Alex resisted the urge to watch him leave, but kept his attention focused on Fintan and Robert.

"John, George, after it!" Robert called angrily.

Alex saw Robert's horse run off without him just before Fintan tried ramming Ronin with his horse straight on, but he wheeled just in time to only be grazed. Alex alternated between stabbing at Robert on the ground off to his right and parrying blows from Fintan on his left.

"You are thinking too much!" Ronin scolded Alex through their mind link.

"What do you mean?! I'm trying to keep us from getting killed!" Alex said exasperatedly.

"Just like McCannon always said, 'Let your body feel the rhythm of the fight. Let it flow and breathe through you. Like a dance, a very lethal dance,'" Ronin instructed with wry humor.

"This is not exactly the best time to make jokes," Alex pointed out as he parried and jabbed. *"They fight well together,"* he added with a hint of admiration.

"We used to fight better until you stopped trusting me!" It was Ronin's turn to sound exasperated. *"We took down a land*

dragon for crying out loud. And a big one at that! These two sorry excuses for fighters aren't nearly as skilled as that was."

Alex hesitated. *"That was a dragon, like Saoirse?"*

"No! But can we talk about this later? We are kind of in the middle of something here. My point is, we worked together perfectly in sync because you trusted me. Trust me now!" Ronin yelled.

Alex's ears were ringing even though it was all in his head. *"Okay... What do you want me to do?"* Alex took a deep breath.

Ronin was right, and he knew it. Alex consciously relaxed a little as Ronin started pointing out weaknesses in the other knights' fighting style or guard. Parry here, redirect there, stab, slash, wheel, charge, back, charge again... Alex's strikes and blocks became stronger as he felt Ronin shift his weight and momentum at the perfect time to aid him.

None of his energy or power was wasted as Ronin used every movement to flow into their next one. It did feel very much like a dance. Alex found himself grinning as they drove Fintan and Robert further and further back, creating more space and not giving them any room to strike back.

Fintan backed off and watched Alex and Ronin for a few seconds before he put his weapons away. Alex could have sworn a flash of something resembling surprise and begrudging respect flashed across his features briefly and was gone. They were in a standoff.

"Let's go, Robert," Fintan said, finally.

"What? You can't be serious!" Robert argued, out of breath, but Fintan cut him off.

"No, we are going. C'mon, we need to find your horse anyway." Fintan turned to go.

Alex and Ronin watched them leave. Both of them were breathing hard, but Alex couldn't keep himself from smiling. *"That was amazing!"*

"Yea! See what I mean?" Alex felt Ronin tremble beneath him.

"Hey, you okay?" Alex asked.

"Yes, fine, let's go find Quinn." Ronin broke into a lope towards the forest.

As they loped, Alex replayed the feeling of power and balance he'd had felt when he and Ronin moved as one. It was intoxicating. He wanted more.

"Is it always like that?" He broke their silence.

Ronin didn't answer. Alex felt him sway beneath him and immediately knew something was wrong. Ronin slowed to a stumbling walk.

"Quinn!" Alex called in his mind, hoping he wasn't too far away. He dismounted and found a gash running from Ronin's shoulder to his flank. He tried to remember when that could have happened, but it was all a blur.

Alex took off the saddle as fast as his shaking hands would allow. The adrenaline, still in his system from the fight, made doing anything that required fine movements difficult at best. When he finally slid the saddle and blanket off and set it on the ground, he inspected the wound. It wasn't too deep. "Hey, are you still with me?"

Ronin hung his head and swayed, eyes dull and listless. Alex didn't know what to do. He was powerless to stop him if Ronin fell while in his horse form.

"QUINN!" This time Alex yelled in his mind.

"What!" Quinn finally responded tersely. Alex could feel his annoyance.

"Ronin is wounded and not responding."

"Describe it to me."

"It's like all his fire has gone out. He's just standing here swaying."

"Inspect the wound closely! Is there anything in it? Any shards or bits left behind?"

Alex pushed on the skin around the gash as he moved toward Ronin's shoulder. It wasn't bleeding a lot, but was quite swollen. "I'm sorry for this," he said as he pushed on a spot with the worst of it. Ronin didn't even react.

"I don't see anything, but it's really swollen already. I've never seen anything like this so quickly after an injury."

"Iron. If he was cut with something iron, especially if there is still a piece in there. It would cause this."

"Without digging around in there, I can't tell. There is nothing on the surface that I can see. This might need an actual healer."

"Keep going to the town you were headed towards. I will catch up!" Quinn said in a tone Alex hadn't heard from him before. He couldn't quite place what it was.

"Okay." Alex didn't know what else to do. He was hoping a healer would know what to do, but Ronin wasn't really a horse. Carrying his packs and weapons slung over his shoulder, he led Ronin on foot. He would yet again have to leave his saddle and armor behind and hope it wouldn't be another month or more before he could come back for it.

Alex urged Ronin to walk as fast as he could get him to move. The closest healer was in Aberdeen. They were still half a day's ride, and he doubted they would make it before nightfall at this pace.

Alex refused to stop as long as Ronin kept putting one hoof in front of the other. He offered him water or grain several times, but it was as if his body were just going through the motions, and his mind wasn't there at all. Alex was frustrated at his lack of skills. He didn't want to just start blindly cutting into him. He was sure that would only harm him more.

It was well past midnight when he finally crested the hill before the granite city of Aberdeen. He hadn't heard from Quinn all day, no matter how many times he had reached out. They made their way to the gate, and the guards called for them to halt.

"State your business," one guard commanded gruffly as several guards with torches approached.

"My name is Sir Alexander, and I'm here to see a healer," he responded absently as his eyes adjusted to the light. His mind was full of worry for Ronin.

"I don't know of a 'Sir Alexander.' Sorry, lad, you'll have to wait 'til morning," the guard said dismissively.

"No, you don't understand. My horse is injured and can't wait 'til then." His voice grew desperate.

One of the guards whistled appreciatively. "That is a very fine horse, sergeant." He looked at Alex intensely. "Tell me, was he injured before or after you stole him from the knight you are trying to impersonate?"

"Wha…" A sharp blow to the back of his head cut off his question. Everything went black.

CHAPTER 21

PAIN lanced through Alex's head. His body ached all over, as if he had slept on rocks all night. When he opened his eyes and managed to get them to focus, he saw that he had, in fact, slept on rocks all night. A stone floor in the guard prison, to be precise. He groaned as he sat up. He heard footsteps coming towards him, but when he turned his head to look, his vision swam, and he felt a stabbing pain in the back of his head.

"Ah, good. You are awake. I have questions for you," a voice said.

When Alex's vision finally cleared, he saw the sergeant from the night before standing over him, holding his sword.

"How does one such as yourself come across such a fine horse and blades whose craftsmanship equal none as I've ever seen?" he asked Alex. He was a broad, stocky man with grizzled features and a pockmarked face. He looked like he had seen his fair share of combat.

"They are mine. I didn't steal them, if that is what you are thinking," Alex commented. His voice sounded hollow and far away to his own ears.

"Yeah, likely story, lad," he said, as he continued to admire Alex's sword.

"Really, you have to believe me!" Alex tried to argue. "Where is Sir Cole? He knows me. He can clear this up."

"*Captain* Cole is busy with the tournament and doesn't have time to be bothered with the likes of you," the sergeant said as he turned to leave. "It's a pity about the horse. I'd imagine he was magnificent in his health," he added, before closing the door behind him with a thud.

Alex suddenly felt very cold as if ice water had been poured down his back. "What do you mean?" he called after the guard. "Hey! Speak with Captain Cole! Or any of the other knights…" He trailed off. He felt helpless. *Part of my reasoning to become a knight was so I wouldn't feel helpless anymore,* he thought angrily.

"*Ronin!*" he called with his mind. Ronin couldn't be dead. He just couldn't! "*Ronin! RONIN!*" he yelled with all his might. No response. "*Quinn?*"

"*What? Alex, I don't have time for this. I'm busy.*"

"*Where are you? Is it true? Is Ronin dead? Where were you last night?*" Alex channeled all his fear, anxiety, and grief at Quinn. He knew it was unfair of him, but he didn't care. Despair and grief threatened to overwhelm and choke him. He let his head fall and buried his face in his hands.

"*Not yet, he's not,*" came Quinn's reply a few minutes later.

Alex's head shot up. "*How do you know? The guard said…*"

"*Guard? Where are you? And no, he's not dead. At least not yet anyway.*"

"*I'm stuck in the guard prison,*" Alex said.

"*What are you doing there? I need another pair of hands. Get here as soon as you can. We are in the stable,*" Quinn said with finality.

"*But…*" Alex started. He was on his own. His head was pounding, and his balance was still off, but he managed to stand after a few tries. He breathed heavily as the floor tilted at odd angles, so he leaned against the wall for support. He closed his eyes as he checked himself for his weapons or anything he could use to get out of his cell. They had taken everything, even his hidden blade, and the "not rock." He deeply felt at a loss over that and took a moment to understand the depth of his feeling but didn't have time to process it beyond that. He needed to get to Ronin.

He looked around his cell, only now fully taking in his surroundings. He was in a small stone cell, roughly the breadth of his arms wide and twice again as deep from front to back. There was a small, dirty-looking straw pallet on the floor against the back wall. Just above Alex's head, a small rectangular window was cut into the rock at ground level. Alex could see it was still early morning, as the sun had barely risen. He was glad it wasn't raining, because it looked like the ground outside around the window sloped toward it and would effectively channel any run-off into the cell.

Think, Alex, think. But found nothing useful to use. He grasped the iron bars of his cell and tried to lift it off its hinges, but it was too heavy. He felt his pockets again and pulled out one of the fruit gems that had been deep in the bottom of his pocket. That wouldn't help unless the guards came back and he could bribe them to let him out.

Alex felt along the wall, testing every block to see if he could pry it free with his fingers, but none of them budged. He felt along the floor on his hands and knees, but they were also solid. Feeling defeated, he closed his eyes and buried his aching head in his hands.

He sat there for a while until he felt the sun on his back through the small window. He was running out of time, and Ronin was dying.

"*What is taking you so long?*" Quinn clipped his words impatiently, startling Alex, and interrupting his wallowing.

"*I can't get out,*" Alex said dejectedly. "*I don't understand why they won't believe I am who I say I am.*"

Alex heard Quinn sigh. "*What kind of lock is it? Describe it to me.*"

He got up and looked at it and described what he could see.

"*Use your magic to move the tumblers or break the lock.*"

"*How? I can't control my fire magic, and you have seen my abysmally lackluster ability with earth, and there is no water nearby that I can see. Also, it's made of iron.*"

"*That shouldn't matter. Use air magic.*"

"*I don't know how.*"

"*I can't believe I'm doing this. Don't make me regret this!*" Quinn said forcefully. "*Roll up your sleeves or take off your shirt.*"

"*What? Why?*"

"*So you can feel the air around you,*" Quinn said as if it were obvious. "*Now feel with your skin and your mind. Take several deep breaths and feel the air as you breathe.*"

Alex took off his tunic and tied it around his waist. He shivered in the cool, damp air of the cell and moved to stand in the little sunlight coming through the window. He closed his eyes and focused on his breathing, trying to feel the air around him. The longer he concentrated, the more he thought he could feel the slight eddies and currents in the air, like ocean currents.

"*Good, now command it to go where you want it. Be firm and specific,*" Quinn continued after a moment.

Alex attempted to move it like he had the water. At first, nothing happened, so he stretched out his arms from his sides and imagined that the air was water flowing in the lock and turning the tumblers. He heard a creak as he felt the air around him moving. Releasing the air, he opened his eyes and tried the bars. Still locked. Frustrated, he reached out again, and rather than be gentle, he thought to wrench the lock with the air. He poured the force of all his hurt, frustration, and worry into channeling the air and directed it at the lock.

Suddenly, he was thrown back against the cell wall and heard a terrible wrenching sound. When he opened his eyes, he saw a twisted mass of iron bars where the wall had been before. The feeling of wrongness alarmed him, and the sheer power of it terrified him. Someone would have heard that.

He staggered as waves of exhaustion hit him. Not waiting for them to come to investigate, he stepped around the mass and found where the guards had stashed his stuff. His sword was missing, as was his "not rock." He would need to track them down, but later, after he had helped Ronin.

"How did it go? Did it work?" Quinn asked.

"It worked! I'm on my way," he answered back as he put his tunic back on and slung his weapons and bags across his shoulders. As he left the guard prison, he looked around cautiously. No one was around or paying attention. He rushed towards the stable, trying not to run. Running would draw unwanted attention. Minutes later, his heart pounded in his chest as he slipped into the stable unseen.

He found Quinn and Ronin in the back stall. Ronin was lying flat on the ground, still in his horse form. Quinn was kneeling over him with a pair of pliers in one hand and his claws on the other. He looked up at Alex. "I have found most of the iron fragment flakes, but I need your help for the last one," he said, in all seriousness.

"What do you need me to do?" Alex asked as he set down his gear in the corner of the stall.

"Take the pliers and hold this side open while I open it up a little more," Quinn said, indicating an especially nasty section on Ronin's shoulder.

Grey tendrils spider-webbed out from the wound, looking like roots of a tree spiraling and spreading outward. Alex did as he was instructed while Quinn used one of his claws to cut the wound open a little more. Alex could see the tip of the iron down in the wound and reached to grasp it with the pliers. After the second try, he finally got it and slowly drew it out. Ronin's whole body shuttered in response, and the grey tendrils faded.

Quinn let out a sigh of relief. "I think we got it all. Go look in the tack room for a needle and thread. I want to sew this up as best I can."

Alex wiped his hands in the straw and went to look for the tack room. He found it easily and had no problem locating several needles and some thread. He found the groom's stash of alcohol and brought that too. He thoroughly doused the thread and needles with the alcohol before handing the bottle to Quinn. Quinn looked at him with an odd expression.

"What is this for?" he asked.

"Pour a little on the wound. It will help keep him from getting infected," Alex answered.

Quinn sniffed it and made a face. "What is this?" he demanded. "It smells terrible."

"Some people drink it." Alex shrugged.

Quinn grumbled something about stupid humans and drinking rotting dead things, but poured a little on Ronin's wounds anyway. Together, Alex and Quinn sewed it up as best they could. They had just washed their hands and Alex was thanking Quinn when a shout rang from outside the stable.

"I wonder what that is all about?" Quinn said.

Alex sighed and rubbed the back of his neck. "They probably just found what remains of the cell I was in."

"What do you mean? What did you do?" Quinn demanded.

"I... might have completely destroyed the bars in my attempt to turn the lock." Alex still felt dazed and exhausted, but now he was starting to feel the shame he had felt after burning the meadow. Quinn looked a little impressed, surprised, and concerned.

"I don't think..." Quinn was interrupted.

"I'll check in here. He couldn't have gotten far." Footsteps jogged toward the stable.

Quinn shifted to his owl form and flew up into the rafters as two soldiers charged in. "We found him!" One cried as they rushed towards him.

Missing his sword, Alex pulled out his axe and a dagger. "Listen, there has been a misunderstanding. I am Sir Alexander. I'm a knight in the Knight's Order. I don't want to hurt you." He stepped further away from Ronin's stall.

"*I'll watch over him,*" Quinn said. "*I'd highly recommend not using magic to fight them though.*" He added from his perch.

Alex nodded as he continued to advance. He couldn't run. He couldn't kill them, so he had to try to reason with them. The soldiers drew their swords and came at him.

They weren't very skilled, and in two strokes, Alex had disarmed one of them and had them backing out of the stable. Out of the corner of his eye, he saw Quinn hop to a rafter that gave him a better view of the entrance and outside the stable. He glanced behind the two soldiers as he drove them back, blocking whatever blows came his way.

They stepped out into the late morning sun. Four more soldiers and two guardsmen headed his way. They had drawn their swords as they quickly approached and fanned out in a semicircle around him. They were well-trained as a unit, but their individual footwork was sloppy and sluggish. Alex disarmed a couple of them and sent one sword flying.

A large guard, who towered over him, slashed down with an especially powerful swing. Alex blocked it easily enough, but felt the impact down his arm. The guard was very straightforward with his attacks as he slashed again and again at Alex. Rather than take all of that force, Alex opted to dodge when he could. The disarmed soldiers retrieved their weapons or acquired new ones and rejoined the fray. Alex parried and dodged, rolled and lunged; his feet seeming to move of their own accord. He silently thanked Ronin for training with him the last few weeks. These soldiers weren't difficult to fight, and one on one, they wouldn't have stood a chance, but the sheer number of them began taxing Alex's already exhausted body. His head throbbed, and he fought to stay focused.

Then the sergeant arrived. The guardsmen suddenly grinned sinisterly at Alex as they made room for the sergeant to join their ranks. A ring of soldiers with shields fell in behind them. Alex stepped back to catch his breath as he surveyed the new challenge.

"I really don't want to hurt any of you!" Alex begged them to listen. "I am Sir Alexander of Creedon. Knight in the king's employ. Why won't you listen to me?" he practically pleaded, panting hard.

The sergeant stepped forward, brandishing Alex's sword. "Careful Sarg, he might have more explosives." Another guardsman eyed him warily. The sergeant nodded without taking his eyes off Alex.

"It seems I underestimated you before, but you are outnumbered, lad. Why don't you put down your weapons and come quietly? I'd rather limit the bloodshed today," he said.

Alex understood his logic. "I'd rather there be no bloodshed as well, but the facts still remain. I am who I say I am, and you have my sword. So hand it over and leave me to my business, and I'll pretend like none of this ever happened," he spoke with confidence he didn't feel. If he were being honest, all he really felt like was a hot bath, a hot meal, and to sleep for a week, but the likelihood of that happening was dwindling by the minute.

The sergeant scoffed, "Have it your way then." He stepped back in line and they advanced toward Alex together.

Alex rolled his shoulders and crouched, looking for weaknesses in their line. As a unit, they moved together seamlessly. He took a deep breath, cleared his mind, and let his body "dance" as Ronin called it. He attacked them first, not waiting for them to reach the stable. Trying not to hurt his opponent when they were trying to kill him was more exhausting than just outright fighting, he decided.

He never stopped moving, attacking their flanks to keep them from completely surrounding him. He disarmed four of them and caught one sword broadside, shattering the blade. He was astonished he was doing so well. Maybe "well" was a bit of an overstatement, because he was steadily losing ground to keep from feeling the bite of their blades.

They drove him into the entrance of the stable. He couldn't spare a glance to see if Quinn was still in the rafters. *"Are you still here? What are you going to do if they actually try to kill me?"* Alex thought to Quinn.

"I'll step in, of course, but that would effectively end your quest for your friend, as I would need to take you immediately back to the council to stand trial for your crimes," Quinn answered matter-of-factly.

Alex dodged a sword and parried another. *"What were those again?"* he asked as he kicked an overzealous soldier in the chest and sent him sprawling. Another soldier over-extended his swing, so Alex used the hilt of his axe to knock the sword out of their hand. He kicked it, sending it flying backward behind him.

Just then, Alex heard a clattering of hooves on the cobblestones of the yard. He glanced up. The sergeant and the largest soldier took advantage of his momentary distraction to step in his guard. The sergeant knocked Alex's weapons from his grasp. The large soldier dropped his own weapons and tackled Alex to the ground.

In the blink of an eye, Alex was on his chest with his face pressed into the sawdust floor and his arms twisted behind his back. He was hauled to his feet. He tried to struggle, but the soldier gripped him tightly. "Bring him," the sergeant said, turning crisply on his heels and marching out of the stable.

Alex blinked in the bright sunlight as he stumbled to keep his footing while being roughly pushed from behind. Cole dismounted and handed his reins to his squire, then turned to address a silver-haired man dismounting next to him.

"Cole!" Alex yelled. Cole's head snapped toward him.

"Quiet!" the sergeant punched him in the stomach. "And that's Captain Cole to you, you disrespectful snipe."

Alex doubled over in pain as his breath whooshed out and tears streaked the corners of his eyes. He coughed and yelled again, his voice hoarse, "Cole!" He squeezed his eyes closed and braced for another beating.

"Who is the senior officer?" Cole's voice drew closer. Alex met his eyes. "Alex?" Cole asked incredulously. "Alex! It is you!" he exclaimed, putting a hand on Alex's shoulder when he reached him. "Release him, soldier," he commanded.

"Sir!" the soldier holding Alex's arms abruptly let go.

Alex swayed. The edges of his vision turned black. Cole caught him before he completely collapsed and slung Alex's arm over his shoulders and around his neck. He half carried him towards the nearest building.

"But sir, he's dangerous." The sergeant challenged Cole.

Cole stopped and turned slightly. "I should hope so," he said before continuing on.

Alex felt consciousness slipping from him.

"He should be locked up. He was caught impersonating a knight and was in possession of stolen weapons and a horse. He even destroyed his holding cell," the sergeant continued less confidently.

"Bring me the weapons, the horse, and anything else found on his person," Cole commanded without stopping.

Cole said in a low voice that only Alex could hear. "I'm glad you're alive."

Then Alex completely blacked out.

CHAPTER 22

"Daddy?" Alice said.

"Yes, my dear?" he replied.

"They aren't going to die," she said with certainty.

He laughed. "Now how do you know that?" he asked, feigning surprise.

She giggled and skipped down the path without answering. He shook his head and smiled at her antics. He took one of the water skins out of his pack and drank deeply before replacing it. The mid-afternoon sun streamed through the trees, giving everything a golden glow. They were taking a hike as was their annual tradition.

As he emerged from the lush green forest into a small meadow, he breathed in deeply the scent of wildflowers. Alice ran back to him with a large bouquet of fresh flowers and offered them to him. He grinned.

"For me?" he asked with exaggerated surprise and gratitude.

"No, silly. Can you make a crown for me?" she asked sweetly, looking up at him expectantly.

"Oh, silly me, my mistake," he said, taking the flowers from her. He quickly braided the flowers together with practiced ease. When he had finished, he dropped to one knee and presented the crown to her.

"Does this please my lady?" he asked, his eyes twinkling with affection. He let her look at it a moment before placing it on her head, securing it with a few hairpins he produced from his pocket.

"Thank you, Daddy!" she exclaimed as she twirled around. "It's beautiful!"

"Anything for my princess," he said with a flourish and a deep bow.

"Dance with me?" she asked as she twirled around. He twirled around, holding his arms out from his sides. "Not like that." She laughed as she caught his hand and halted his spin.

He faked dizziness and staggered a step. "Oh, thank you. You saved me. I thought I might twirl forever, caught in a mischievous spell of a fairy circle"

She giggled as she took his other hand and placed her feet on top of his. He hummed as they danced, and in a moment of crescendo in the song, he picked her up and twirled her around above his head before dipping her.

They danced a few more songs until they breathlessly collapsed to the ground in the sweet-smelling flowers and soft clover, laughing until their sides hurt.

Finally, when they had both recovered, he began unpacking food and water out of his pack for a picnic. He spread out bowls of dried and fresh fruits, nuts, boiled eggs, a loaf of bread, and a wedge of cheese.

"Can we stay here tonight, Daddy?" she asked thoughtfully between bites.

"I don't see why not. I brought a hammock for that very possibility," he said with a knowing smile.

After dinner, they made a small fire and crawled into their hammock. He pointed out the stars and constellations and told her the stories behind each one.

"Okay, I'm ready for the next part of the story. Tell me what happens next." Alice snuggled closer to him with her head on his chest.

Their hammock swayed in the warm evening breeze as he continued his tale.

✗✗✗

Footsteps approaching alerted Alex he was regaining consciousness. A heartbeat later, he thought he heard the faint whoosh of wings fade away. The door opened and the footsteps stopped next to him.

He opened his eyes and immediately shut them again. His head felt like someone had cracked his skull. He groaned internally, but he must have made a sound, because he heard a sigh, then liquid pouring. Hands pulled him up to sit, then pressed a cup into his hands and lifted it toward his lips.

He swayed, but the mystery hands braced him firmly. He drank deeply, not even tasting whatever was in the cup. When he emptied it, the mystery assistant refilled it again. This time, he drank a little more slowly and wished he hadn't. It tasted bitter, but he felt a little better, enough to open his eyes again.

He blinked to focus his eyes and turned to look at the person attached to the mystery hands. He saw a lanky lad, almost gangly and with large hands, watching him with wide eyes. The lad ducked his head and flinched as if waiting to be punished.

"I..." Alex cleared his throat. His voice sounded raspy. "What is your name, lad?" he asked, unsure what to say or ask first.

"Page Justin Avery the 3rd of Salar, sir," he answered.

"Where am I, and how long have I been here?" Alex asked.

"Sir, you are in Captain Cole's guest suite, sir, and a day and a half, sir," Justin answered.

"A day and a half!" Alex repeated with alarm and sat up straighter. His body ached all over, like the time he'd been bucked off and dragged. He unsuccessfully tried to stifle a groan as his body objected to his movements. He took a deep breath.

The page watched him openly now. "I've never seen anyone take a beating with so many injuries as you did and still live." He cringed and shut his mouth, pressing his lips together. He aimed to run, but Alex stopped him.

"I'm not going to punish you for talking to me," he said quietly. Alex had heard that some of the other knights liked to punish the pages and squires for simply being there.

Justin paused his retreat. "You're different from most the other knights."

Alex smiled to himself. If he only knew… "I'll take that as a compliment."

"Oh, yes, sir!" the youth said emphatically. "I saw you fight," he said reverently. "Where did you learn to fight like that?" he asked after a pause.

"From…" Alex paused. What was Ronin to him? Friend, ally, acquaintance, comrade? "… My brother," he answered finally. "*Ronin!*" he thought with a start. "Do you know how my horse is? He's big and black and was injured when I arrived."

"The magnificent destrier is yours?" Justin looked at him with open wonder. "Captain Cole had the healers look at him, just after you collapsed and they brought you here. I can go check on him if you want or have one of the younger pages do it. If you still need me here, that is," he said eagerly.

Alex smiled at him. "He is magnificent. He's saved my life more times than I can count. If I can give you one piece of advice?" he asked.

"Yes sir." Justin nodded emphatically.

"Treat your animals well, all animals for that matter. You never know, they may one day save your life because you were kind," he said, with a bittersweet thought. He was grateful Bronach had taught him that lesson. Bronach knew.

"Aye, sir, I will, sir," he said, bowing deeply.

"No, no, there is no reason for all of that. I appreciate your respect, but there is no reason to bow and call me sir all the time. Alex is fine. Unless we are around the other knights. I don't want to give them a reason to punish you," he said thoughtfully.

"Oh! Begging your pardon, sir. I mean Alex, sir. Captain Cole said I was to report to him as soon as you were awake." he practically scampered out the door.

Alex shook his head and smiled. He stretched a little and felt his joints pop throughout his body. His muscles were very sore, but he decided to try to stand anyway. Movement would help him heal faster, or so he told himself. At the same time, he tentatively reached out with his mind to Quinn.

"Quinn, How is Ronin?" Alex asked.

"Ask him yourself," Quinn responded.

"Thank you!" he responded. *"Ronin?"* he asked hesitantly.

"Alex! You're alive!" Ronin practically yelled in his head.

"I'm alive? You're alive! I thought I was going to lose you there for a minute," Alex replied, laughing with relief.

"Same here. Quinn told me what you did and even went to see your cell door," Ronin said.

Alex could almost hear the unspoken questions, and it made him ashamed and a little afraid. *"I don't know what happened, but I must have done something wrong. It didn't do what I asked it to,"* Alex said.

"What do you mean?" Ronin asked gently.

"I only meant to unlock the door, not destroy it, but I was afraid I was losing you, and I didn't know what else to do. I was so frustrated. They didn't believe I was a knight. They thought I had stolen you." Alex felt the familiar tension rising in him, but pushed it from his mind.

He saw his "not rock" sitting with his weapons on a table next to the bed. More than a little relieved, he picked it up.

"Powerful emotions create powerful magic, Little defender." A gravely voice rumbled in his mind. *"You choose to harness negative emotions: anger, fear, frustration, loneliness... or positive ones: community, security, loyalty, contentment... but the negative ones do far more damage and are less controlled and unpredictable. Use wisdom and caution when choosing what to harness your magic with. You may find yourself with unintended consequences,"* Vesuviius advised. *"Not that those emotions are bad in and of themselves, but acted upon, they can be quite dangerous,"* he finished.

Alex felt the "not rock" warm in his hands and looked down at it. It looked like it was made of molten metal. The warmth spread up his arms and throughout his chest. He felt many of his aches lessen and even saw some of his bruises fade in the space of seconds. *"Thank you,"* he said, as it faded to a slate-grey pyramid once again.

"*That was amazing!*" Ronin exclaimed. "*Do they always talk to you?*"

"*What was that? Who was that?*" Quinn interjected to both of them.

Startled, Alex nearly dropped the "not rock." "*You both heard that?*" Alex asked.

"*Yes, now explain,*" Quinn demanded.

"*You don't have to tell him anything,*" Ronin cut in before Alex could respond.

"*He might as well know,*" Alex said as he slipped the stone into his tunic pocket, hanging on the back of the chair.

"*Know what?*" Quinn demanded.

"*You know the legends about the Guardians?*" Ronin inquired.

"*Yes. Everyone does. What about them?*" Quinn clipped his words impatiently.

"*They aren't just legends,*" Alex interjected quietly.

"*What? Are you sure? How do you know?*" Quinn's voice cracked. He cleared his voice and continued, "*What did they say?*"

"*Which time?*" Alex asked, then began to fill him in on some of the interactions, leaving out anything to do with the guardian stone. "*This time it was Vesuviius, and you heard what he said,*" Alex finished.

Quinn was quiet for a long time while it sank in. "*Why you? What is so special about you that they would talk to you and only you?*" he asked angrily.

Alex had just finished getting dressed and strapping on his different weapons. He picked up his sword and inspected it thoroughly, wiping off any fingerprints he found until the blade's natural sheen practically glowed. Just then, Cole strode through the door.

"*I don't know,*" he answered Quinn quickly.

"*What? That's it?*" Quinn demanded.

"*I gotta go.*"

"*We're not done talking about this. Alex?*"

"Alex!" Cole greeted him and placed a hand on his shoulder. "You look... well... for having spent the last day and a half unconscious on Nocturne's door." Cole shook his head in surprise as he surveyed Alex up and down.

Justin openly gawked right behind him. Thanks to Vesuviius, Alex felt significantly better. He must have looked it too, based on the page's reaction.

"Cole!" Alex responded with apprehension. He slid his sword into its sheath and strapped it on his back. "Thank you for making them return my belongings, by the way," he said sincerely.

Cole waved his hand. "It was nothing. Things have a tendency to go missing with this bunch." Alex raised his eyebrows in surprise. "But never mind that! You are alive! I thought you had been killed or kidnapped, but we never received a ransom note, so I knew it couldn't be that. Where have you been? You missed the Summit! Where is your armor? What happened to Bucephalus? Did your blacksmith make these for you?" Cole said, gesturing to Alex's new weapons.

Alex nodded, not sure which to answer first. "I've been following up on missing persons reports. It seems like all across Reyall, people are going missing, including my blacksmith and others from my village. But the trail has run cold, though," he said with a sigh.

"The healer said you sewed Bucephalus up really well for how nasty those wounds looked. How did that happen? I don't think I've seen him lame for even a day. It's a shame. I was going to invite you to compete in the tournament coming up," Cole said.

Alex shrugged. "Some thugs we tangled with got lucky."

It was Cole's turn to raise an eyebrow. "You took down a large dragon single-handedly, but some thugs got the better of you? Alex, you seriously think I would believe that?" he asked incredulously.

Behind him, Justin's eyes grew wide, and his mouth hung open as he stared in open wonder.

Alex fidgeted and looked away, unable to meet Cole's gaze. "It wasn't that big." Having stood next to Saoirse, he knew the little land dragons they had here were tiny by comparison.

"Was it Fintan again?" Cole asked quietly.

Alex shot him a look.

"What? You think I don't know there is bad blood between you? Everyone knows he hates you, and if I remember correctly, he threatened you after the last incident in Arageyll."

Silence stretched between them until Alex sighed and shrugged. "Fintan, Robert, and their two lackeys." Alex's stomach chose that moment to growl loudly.

Cole nodded. "What do you say we eat while you fill me in on what you have to go on for the missing people? That is a serious issue. I will see if I have any contacts for you. Avery, get my request letters from my personal quarters and have food brought to the officer's mess. Ink and paper as well."

Justin took off immediately. When the slap of his footfalls had faded, Cole stepped a little closer to Alex and dropped his voice. "Where were you really? Knights came in from all over Reyall and even Keirwyn, and none of them had seen you." His eyes searched Alex's face.

Alex rubbed the back of his neck with one hand and reached into his pocket to touch the "not rock" with his other. It still felt warm. He mulled over what to say, but couldn't come up with anything that didn't sound remotely crazy. He didn't like the idea of lying to Cole. "I'm not sure you would believe me if I told you," he said finally.

"You aren't going to tell me you got kidnapped by fairies, held against your will, and somehow escaped by sheer luck and cunning, are you?" Cole said jokingly with a grin. Alex gave him a sharp look and narrowed his eyes. "Alex?" Cole looked stunned.

"I'm not ready to talk about it yet," Alex said, feeling very uncomfortable. He was still struggling to believe it, and he had seen and felt it for himself, so he had no idea how he would make rational sense to anyone else.

Cole studied him for a few moments. "You are different somehow. I can't quite put my finger on what it is, but you have definitely changed. Not in a bad way, just different." He stared at Alex a little longer, then seemed to understand he wouldn't get any answers right now.

"When you are ready, you know you can always talk to me," he said finally. "Come, let's go eat and talk about the tournament and this quest of yours," he said, gesturing toward the door.

CHAPTER 23

THE next couple of weeks passed rather quickly. They moved Ronin to a large paddock where he continued to get stronger while his wounds healed. Alex spent most of his time either training near Ronin or working with Cole for leads about missing people.

At one point, he noticed Justin watching his training sessions, so he motioned for him to pick up a sword and spar with him. For all his lanky limbs, Justin wasn't that bad. Alex patiently helped him fix his stance or grip and ran him through the same drills Ronin had put him through. He wondered to Ronin if he was this bad when he started out.

Ronin was conspicuously quiet, but Alex saw the humorous glint in his eyes as he watched them spar. He occasionally offered Alex advice on how to adjust Justin's technique. Quinn was nowhere to be found, but Ronin didn't seem worried, so Alex tried not to think about it too much. During the evenings, Alex spent his time in the stable with Ronin, practicing his magic.

When he was almost fully healed, they began discussing where they would travel next. Cole's runners had, one by one, returned to report more missing people but no solid leads. The circumstances behind each of the missing reports differed. Alex tried to keep his spirits up and distract himself, but his feelings of unease grew by the day.

One afternoon, Alex was sparring with Justin when Quinn flew overhead and landed in the trees nearby. Taking advantage of Alex's distraction, Justin neatly disarmed him and held him at sword point. Alex grinned proudly and congratulated him. He was about to suggest they go get something to eat when he saw Quinn striding toward them.

Justin saw Quinn as well and looked at Alex questioningly.

"What are you doing? Where have you been?" Alex asked Quinn in his mind. Ronin trotted over to them.

Quinn looked at Ronin, then Alex. "We need to go. Now!" he said with a tone of urgency.

"What? Why? What's going on? Where have you been?" Alex asked.

"Is your friend still here, the captain?"

"Cole? No, he left yesterday. Why?"

"Did you leave anything in your room?"

"No, it's all here or in the stable."

Quinn swore. "We don't have much time. The two that jumped us outside the city arrived and have been stirring up the other knights and soldiers against you. So unless you want more bloodshed, which is fine by me, but I know how you feel about that, I suggest we leave immediately."

Quinn noticed Justin standing there and let out another curse. "Are you going to be a burden to bring along, young one?" he asked as he grabbed him by his tunic collar. "Or should I put you out of your miserable short existence here and now?" Quinn held a wicked-looking dagger in his other hand and raised it.

Before Alex could intervene, Ronin stepped in and head-butted Quinn on the shoulder. Ronin's eyes blazed. He pinned his ears and bared his teeth at Quinn before nudging Justin with his shoulder. Justin only sputtered, his eyes wide.

"That won't be necessary. He'll come with us. If he stays, they'll probably kill him out of spite anyway," Alex said quickly. "Ronin, take Justin to the river, and we'll meet you there. Quinn and I will go get the rest of our supplies."

Ronin snorted and nodded. Justin only protested a little as Quinn reached over and tossed him up on Ronin's back as if he weighed nothing, and Ronin was a small pony and not an eighteen hands tall war horse. Justin grabbed a handful of Ronin's mane to keep from falling off as they thundered toward the treeline.

Alex and Quinn sprinted toward the stable. They could see a few soldiers patrolling like normal, and several more lounging outside the barracks. Alex's pulse pounded in his ears as they snuck quietly into the stable. They quickly gathered the rest of their supplies and belongings. Every sound made Alex flinch and seemed like it would alert the soldiers to their presence. He had his hand on the door latch when it swung open of its own accord. The Sergeant, Sir Robert, and a couple of soldiers were standing just outside the doorway.

"Well, well, well, what do we have here? Someone trying to make a run for it now that your precious captain isn't here to protect you, I see?" Robert sneered. The sergeant and soldiers laughed.

Alex knew he couldn't fight them without drawing others, but they were standing between him and the way out. He heard an angry whinny and the thud of hoofbeats behind him. He barely registered a white blur before it slammed into the soldiers. Using their momentary surprise, Alex grabbed onto

Quinn's withers and slung himself onto his back as Quinn kicked out at another soldier. As soon as he was on, Quinn bolted toward the forest, easily clearing fences and other obstacles along the way.

The wind stung Alex's eyes, making them water, but soon the sounds of pursuit faded away until all he could hear was the wind whistling in his ears as they ran. He bent low over Quinn's neck and tried to stay as still as possible. Quinn slowed his pace only by a fraction when he reached the trees. Alex marveled at how much smaller Quinn was than Ronin. He had a similar feel of power and grace as they dodged trees and roots. When they finally reached the river, Quinn slowed only when they had crossed to the other side.

Alex slid down to the ground. His legs ached and felt a little wobbly, but held him. Quinn shifted to his fae form and began moving piles of leaves with his air magic until it covered their tracks. They heard a gasp and whirled toward the sound in unison. Alex reflexively drew his knife and unclipped his axe. Quinn's hands shifted into claws. Justin stood next to Ronin, who was still in horse form.

"How did... What... Who are you?" Justin finally managed to ask.

Quinn ignored him as he uncovered the roots of a few large trees and gestured to Ronin. Ronin shifted and stepped towards the trees. Justin gasped and his feet slid out from underneath him as he tried to backpedal away from them. "Demons! Nocturne, save me. I've been abducted by demons."

"No, not demons, Puka. But I can see how you would think that, given the bedtime stories you were probably raised with," Ronin responded with a smirk.

"You... you... you're a... this whole time?" Justin sputtered again.

Ronin winked. "Your secrets are safe with me, kid."

Justin stared open-mouthed, unmoving.

"You are taking it better than I did." Alex placed a hand on his shoulder.

"We don't have time for this!" Quinn urged, motioning to Ronin. Ronin knelt next to the tree and placed a hand on the gnarled, twisting roots. They began to move, reshaping themselves into an opening just wide enough for a person to squeeze through. Through the opening, Alex saw the beginnings of stairs and a tunnel.

"How long has this been here? Are there other such tunnels?" Alex asked.

Ronin's head snapped up. "We don't have much time. They are entering the forest." He motioned for Alex and Justin to follow as he slipped into the hole.

Alex crouched as he entered the opening and half-crawled down the tunnel a little way. It expanded enough for him to stand upright, shoulder-to-shoulder with Ronin. Ronin brushed past Alex and Justin and closed up the opening as Quinn finished covering their tracks. It was almost pitch black in the tunnel, with the only light coming from cracks around the roots of the tree woven across the tunnel opening. Hoofbeats thundered above them moments later. Alex held his breath until the sound faded into the distance.

Ronin's hand rested on his shoulder. "Any chance you can light our way? Quinn and I can see in the dark, but you and Justin will be blind."

"Is that... safe? You know how last time went..." Alex trailed off as shame, tinged with a hint of fear, rose in his chest.

Quinn started to say something, but Ronin silenced him with a look. Ronin turned Alex to look him directly in the eye. Mere inches from his face, Alex could see his silver eyes reflecting the light from the opening. He looked calm and confident. "I trust you," he said, barely above a whisper.

With those three words, Alex felt a surge of warmth and confidence run through him. His fear and shame drained away as he thought back over what Vesuviius had said. It must have shown on his face. Sensing a change in his demeanor, Ronin took Alex's left hand and held it palm up then stepped back.

Alex took a deep breath and thought back to all the times he felt safe and secure. He thought of quiet nights by the fire with his mother, of working with Bronach in the forge, and of early mornings out on the water while the rest of the world still slept. He felt his hand tingle, and his body relaxed with warmth. When he opened his eyes, hovering just above his palm, he saw a small flame-colored foal dancing and prancing in place. It shook its head, rearing and pawing the air.

Justin inhaled sharply and stared at the foal in Alex's hand. He rubbed his eyes in disbelief before letting out a low whistle. "I'd have never believed it if I hadn't seen it for myself. I'm dreaming. I'm dreaming... I must be. I'm going to wake up on my pallet, and this is all going to be a crazy dream. Whatever I ate last night must have been bad. That's the only explanation." He shook his head and leaned against the tunnel wall.

"We need to get going," Quinn grumbled and made shooing motions to Justin.

Ronin nodded then took the lead with Alex following right behind him, firelight flickering along the tunnel walls.

ХХХ

Alex didn't know how much time had passed while they were down in the tunnels. It felt like forever. They walked until they needed to rest and ate as they walked. The flickering light from his little fire foal was strangely comforting his nervousness from being unaccustomed to spending so much time underground. It didn't take nearly as much energy as he thought it might. Though when they stopped for a break, he released it and instantly felt somewhat drained. Accessing his magic became easier each time he mentally reached for it until he barely had to consciously think about it.

Every once in a while, they came across other tunnels branching off the one they followed. Ronin pressed a hand to the wall and closed his eyes then chose a tunnel. Occasionally, they encountered a blocked or caved-in tunnel, but Ronin made short work of clearing it out.

They stopped for a rest by another tunnel entrance. Alex heard running water as he followed Ronin out into the evening dusk. They had just finished the last of their supply, so this came as a relief. They found a small stream nearby, cutting through rocky terrain. After filling up, Alex took off his tunic and gear and splashed the frigid water on his face and arms.

"Where are we going?" Justin asked Ronin as he sat on a boulder with his legs dangling.

"We are following some leads on missing people," Ronin said cryptically.

Justin looked thoughtful, if a bit puzzled. Quinn shrugged noncommittally. Alex had to give the lad credit. Not once had he complained or grumbled or even so much as sighed in malcontent.

Alex took in their surroundings in the dimming light as he redressed and checked his weapons. They had emerged from a small cave entrance, hidden in an outcropping of rocks. Even from here, he wouldn't have known it was there if they hadn't walked out of it.

"There's only a little further left of the tunnels before the mountains. We'll need to find something warm for Justin to wear, or he'll freeze," Ronin said aloud.

"We could spread out and look for game. That will replenish our food as well," Quinn suggested.

"That's not a bad plan," Ronin mused. "Food will be harder to come by in the mountains."

Quinn shifted to his owl form and took off into the night sky.

"I'll never get used to that," Justin said in wonder.

"Mmm... I know what you mean," Alex agreed with him. "Do you want us to set up camp for the night?" he asked Ronin.

"Pardon me, sir. Not to contradict you, sir, but aren't we going to go hunting?" Justin asked Alex nervously.

Alex laughed, "You don't have to call me sir, and they don't need our help hunting."

Ronin grinned with a feral glint in his eyes before shifting to his dire wolf form. Justin let out a string of oaths in surprise. Alex laughed so hard tears gathered in the corners of his eyes. Ronin bared his teeth in a wolfish grin as he silently melded into the shadows and disappeared.

CHAPTER 24

ALEX and Justin gathered firewood and set up camp under the natural, curved overhang of a rock face. Justin stacked the branches near the ring of rocks Alex had set up and sat back on his heels as he stared intently at Alex. Tension and curiosity emanated from the young page.

"Yes?" Alex asked without looking away from his pile of shavings he was creating.

"Are you… Can you…" Justin stammered. He cleared his throat, then continued, "Can you teach me?"

Alex looked up at him thoughtfully. "I don't know how I can do it and am just learning myself, unfortunately."

"I… oh. I understand," Justin sounded a little disappointed. Alex went back to cutting kindling for the fire.

"But I can teach you other things, if you are willing. What do you want to do with your life? Why do you want to be a knight?" Alex asked quietly as he lit the fire with his flint and steel, out of habit.

Justin looked at him with a hopeful expression. "To make my family proud. To bring dignity and honor to my family name. When I was younger, right after I was brought to Aberdeen for training, a dragon killed and chased off all of our farmers and took up residence in the forest on part of our land."

"It killed our livestock without discretion, almost as if it thought we were keeping them for it. Every time people tried to work the fields near the forest, the dragon would attack them. My father tried to gather some men to chase it off or kill it, but they were unsuccessful, and he was gravely wounded. He offered increasing sums for anyone to remove it, but the way he describes it, the monster was massive and vicious." Justin stared into the fire as he spoke.

"My family's livelihood was ruined, and some of the other noble houses started spreading rumors that it was a sign we had fallen out of grace with the gods. Just before the knight's summit, I received a letter from home saying someone had slain the dragon, and my family could finally start rebuilding." He looked up at Alex. "That was you and Buchephalus... I mean Ronin. You saved my family from further disgrace and gave them the chance to start over. For that, I owe you my gratitude and my service..." he said as he moved to kneel in front of Alex and bowed his head. "If you'll have me..."

Alex was stunned. "I... I think you have the wrong guy. I didn't slay the dragon out of a sense of duty or trying to save your family or anything honorable really..." He paused and sighed deeply, "If I'm being completely honest, I was only trying to get the other knights to finally respect me, to prove myself out from under McCannon's shadow and protection. I'm not the man you think I am." He continued, "And now we've kidnapped you and endangered your life in more ways than you even know. I don't think you'll be taken seriously or allowed to become a full knight squired to me."

"But..." Justin looked up at him with a pained look on his face.

"What about Cole?" Alex continued. "He would be a much better knight to oversee your training."

"He already has two squires and..."

"You don't want to tie your life to mine," Alex said.

"It's too late for that, Alex," Ronin said quietly as he approached the fire. He had a deer slung around his shoulders and held a brace of rabbits in his left hand. "I..." he paused. "I'll think on it." He looked away, then back at Justin to judge his response.

Justin gave Alex a look, then got up quickly and started helping Ronin clean the animals. Alex watched them working together seamlessly, as if they had known each other for years, not weeks. Justin seemed to know intuitively what Ronin needed before he asked. He marveled at how quickly Justin had gotten over his fear and wariness of Ronin.

"Why can't you take Justin as a squire?" Ronin asked gently.

Alex did not answer. He was still figuring that out for himself.

Quinn returned a while later with a fox and a coyote. He laid them in front of Justin, glanced in Alex's direction and frowned, and walked away without a word. Alex called to him in his mind, but Quinn acted like he didn't hear him. Alex felt confused and a little irritated. He thought Quinn had been warming up to him, but now they seemed right back where they started.

XXX

The next morning when Alex awoke, Quinn was gone. Again. Alex rubbed his eyes and trudged over to the stream to wash his face. The icy water felt invigorating. He had missed running water.

While he was grateful they had gotten away from Aberdeen, he dreaded going back into the tunnels. It had forced him to use his fire magic, but he hated not being able to see the sky. He had started feeling like the walls were closing in around him.

"Is Quinn out scouting or hunting again?" Alex asked Ronin.

"He muttered something about being called back on a special assignment," Justin piped in. "Back where?"

"Best if you didn't know," Ronin cut in, giving Alex a look. "You cannot give information you don't have if you are captured and interrogated."

"Don't get me wrong, it will be nice not having his brooding presence around with his ever-present threat to kill me hanging in the air, but why now? What is more important than finding the missing people and figuring out what is happening to them?" Alex asked grumpily. "Is that why he seemed so... preoccupied and distant last night?"

"I'm sure my father has his reasons, even if he doesn't care to share them," Ronin replied.

"Your father?" Justin asked curiously.

"Ronin's father is on The Council," Alex replied.

"Is that like The Convocation?" Justin asked.

"I don't know what that is," Ronin said.

"It's a group of the eldest, most powerful families of nobles in Reyall. They like to pretend they have power, but mostly they just throw fancy parties and gossip," Alex replied to Ronin.

"No, it's more like if the king, earl, duchess, knight commander, and the lord marshall were all equals in power and made decisions jointly. Or they're supposed to, but in my experience, they do what they want, usually in spite of or in secret from one another."

"Oh, wow... okay, that sounds complicated," Justin said. "Until recently, I've never known any different. How is a monarchy better though, giving one person the power to determine the fate of an entire kingdom?" Ronin asked.

"I don't know. Like you, I've never known it could be different," Justin replied. Ronin "hmmmed" thoughtfully.

All three were quiet. Lost in their own thoughts as they finished their tasks. Alex distributed the meat strips they had cooked and dried overnight. Ronin brought the pelts over to Justin and helped him wrap leather cords around them to keep them secure as he walked.

They broke camp and covered their tracks before heading into the rocky hills at the base of the mountains. By midday, Alex's legs were aching from the constant uphill climb. Before the last month or so, he would have considered himself fairly fit. Justin, to his credit, didn't complain.

Alex looked at the peaks looming in front of them. He had seen them from Aberdeen, but their sheer size was overwhelming. As they walked, it grew colder. Alex rubbed his hands together to keep them warm. Ronin noticed and gave him a funny look.

"What?"

"Why are you cold when you can warm yourself?"

"Wait, really?"

Ronin chuckled and shook his head. "Sometimes you surprise me."

"Hey... why do I feel like that's not a compliment?"

"Magic is about imagination and creativity, just as much as it is power and concentration. I've seen lesser fae do way more than even the masters because of their creativity. A gentle nudge of a butterfly can sometimes be more effective than a tidal wave."

Justin watched them with open curiosity as Alex focused on thinking warm thoughts. "Can everyone do magic where you are from?"

"To some degree, yes," Ronin said.

"Oh, that must be nice. I bet it's an amazing place to live... no conflict and everyone works together as equals," he trailed off.

Ronin laughed bitterly and shook his head. "I don't think it's like that anywhere. There is still a hierarchy of people who believe they are better than everyone else. The 'haves' and 'have nots,' if you will, but it's more determined by the strength of magic than just what family you were born into." Alex gave him a disgruntled look. "I'm not saying I agree with it, just that is the way it has been for a long time," he continued.

Ronin held up a hand to silence them. He shifted to his falcon form and took off into the sky. Justin gave Alex a questioning look. Alex shrugged and watched Ronin until he disappeared from view. He didn't hear or see anything, and Ronin hadn't given an explanation.

He unclipped an axe from his belt to be prepared, just in case they were ambushed. Something made a noise up ahead but, as he listened closer, he relaxed. It was only melting ice falling from the rocks. He kept his axe in hand but motioned for Justin to follow him as they continued up the narrow trail.

They followed the trail through several switchbacks. The ground on both sides of the trail rose steadily into jagged, rocky walls and the snow deepened underfoot. Alex clenched his left hand, trying to concentrate on his surroundings as well as keep himself warm. The wind, like an icy breath, blew directly into his face, making it hard to see. He shut his eyes against it as he felt Justin grab hold of his pack. He felt his way along the walls to guide his steps up the path. They turned a corner, and suddenly, the wind died down, and he blinked at his surroundings.

They stood in the mouth of an ice cave. Grateful for the shelter, Alex re-clipped his axe to his belt and searched for something to build a fire with. "We'll wait for Ronin here. No sense getting lost out there in the snow."

Justin looked relieved as he walked further into the cave and sat down. "That snow came out of nowhere. I thought my nose would freeze off." He breathed into his cupped hands to warm them.

"The mountains are dangerous in and of themselves. The weather is just as inclined to kill you as the animals. McCannon didn't like the cold, so he never brought me up here." Alex shrugged.

"I heard some of the knights boasting about their bravery for spending a night in the mountains. They liked to tell stories, to scare us pages and squires, about the labyrinth of trails and monstrous beasts that would devour the unwary traveler." Justin shivered as he rubbed his hands together and stuck them back under his furs.

Not finding any branches or kindling, Alex followed the cave tunnel further. He didn't get far, though. The cave ended a hundred yards in. Water trickled somewhere in the walls, but he didn't see a way through the wall of ice and stone. He wondered briefly if he could warm the ice enough to melt it to see if there were more tunnels beyond, but he was already tired from the climb and keeping himself from the verge of frostbite.

"I'm not seeing anything to burn," he called to Justin as he turned to head back to the entrance. No response. "Justin?" He walked faster. Alex rounded the bend in the tunnel and saw Justin standing, staring out of the cave. Justin didn't say a word as he slowly raised a hand to point to the clearing. Alex didn't see anything but ice and snow at first glance. Then it moved.

Alex froze as fear sliced through him colder than the icy gale blowing across the cave mouth. Before them crouched a mound of jagged ice and rock with two large intelligent eyes staring back at them. It unwrapped a tail covered in long spikes of ice as it rose to its feet. It looked like a horned lizard Alex had seen near the southern desert, except those lizards were cute and brown and fit in the palm of his hand. This was like that, but the size of a cottage and made of ice and stone.

Alex's heart pounded as it just looked at them. He saw Justin slowly reaching for his weapon. "No, wait!" He reached out to stop Justin, but he was too slow. Justin pulled his sword and charged the ice lizard, chopping at its eyes. At the last moment, the lizard swiped a massive clawed foot and batted him to the side like a fly. It continued to watch Alex as Justin stumbled to his feet and came at it again. He staggered. His blade glanced off the end of an icy horn.

The beast roared and flung Justin aside with its tail. Its mouth displayed terrifyingly jagged, pearlescent teeth, glittering in the afternoon sun. Justin hit the side of a rocky outcropping and slumped to the ground, unmoving. Alex ran and slid to a stop on his knees next to him. Justin was unconscious and had a gash above his eye. It was bleeding profusely, but he was still breathing. Alex faced the ice lizard, protectively putting his body between it and Justin. He didn't think it would do much good, seeing as it could easily swat him out of the way if it wanted.

The wind picked up again. Alex needed to get Justin back into the cave and keep him warm while he stopped the bleeding. He eyed the lizard, but when it made no move against him, he picked Justin up by his shoulders and dragged him back into the cave. He braced for an attack, but it only seemed inclined to watch him with its dark, glittering eyes.

Alex took out some bandages from his pack and pressed them against the wound. He wrapped the rest of it around Justin's head and tied off the ends. It wasn't pretty, but it would do for now. The lizard watched his every move, but remained where it was. Confident it was not going to strike, Alex pulled out some jerky and his canteen, but it was frozen solid. He sighed and held it between his hands trying to melt it. He flinched as he saw movement out of the corner of his eye. The lizard tilted its head to the side like a curious dog, unsure of what he was doing.

Shivers wracked his body as the icy wind howled through the cave. Alex was torn. He needed to keep Justin and himself from freezing, but also protect from the lizard if it chose to attack. So far, it had only defended itself and not attacked, but they were cut off from any possible escape. Not that he would get far, dragging Justin's unconscious body.

He held out his left hand and reached down deep for his fire magic. At first, nothing happened. His emotions were all over the place. He closed his eyes and concentrated. His little fire foal flickered to life and pranced in his hand. He focused on making him bigger, hoping he could warm Justin as well as himself.

Alex kept his eyes on the lizard but resumed his attempt at using his fire magic. "Where is Ronin?" he wondered aloud to himself. "How will Ronin find us?"

His fire foal blazed larger until it was the size of a real foal. It pranced in the snow, leaving little melted hoof prints. It danced out of the cave, over near the lizard of its own accord, stretched its little neck up, and sniffed it. The ice monster remained motionless, ever watchful, and let out another breath of steam. Alex's foal sneezed and shook its head, then trotted over to stand near Justin.

Alex watched tensely, with wide eyes, unsure what to do. The snow melted around the foal as it lay down. Justin moaned, but did not wake. Alex settled down next to Justin to share body heat. His eyelids felt heavy. He fought to stay awake and watchful, but he was so tired. He'd only rest his eyes for a moment.

The crunching of snow and ice awoke him. Instantly, he jumped to his feet, ready to fight. He hesitated. The ice monster had moved to fill the entrance to the cave. They were trapped. Fear spiked in his chest again. His fire foal must have gone out when he fell asleep. That made sense since it took concentration to keep his magic active. He reached for his weapons. The lizard's onyx eyes narrowed. Steam escaped its nostrils, but it made no movement toward him.

Sweat trickled down his temple. The air no longer hurt to breathe. With the mouth of the cave shielded against the biting wind, the warmth from his fire magic lingered. "Thank you," he croaked, finally finding his voice. "May I know your name?" he asked hesitantly.

It blinked at him. The cave rumbled from an earthquake. Something shattered further in the cave, followed by a scraping noise. A gentle breeze caressed his face, down his arms, torso, and legs as if searching for something, then left. It smelled of damp earth, minerals, and metal. He pulled his sword from his back and turned to face this new potential threat. But nothing came. His heart thundered in his ears. Slowly, he followed the tunnel to the back where the wall of ice had been earlier. Chunks of ice lay scattered throughout the tunnel, but no assailants jumped out at him.

The icy floor gave way to damp stone that edged a small pool of water. Steam rose lazily off the water's surface. Confident no one was going to attack him, he sheathed his sword and eyed his new icy companion as he trudged back to Justin. "Did you know there is a hot spring back there all along?" Alex asked no one in particular.

It didn't respond. He knelt down and checked on Justin's wound. It had stopped bleeding and he was warm but not feverish. Alex was a little concerned he hadn't woken up on his own yet and wondered if he should try to wake him. Exhaustion pulled at him again. Maybe he could just rest for a little while and wake him after.

He sat down next to Justin against the cold stone wall and draped his cloak over them both, too tired to even try using his magic. He gazed at the ice lizard still watching him. *"You're on guard duty,"* he thought more to himself than to it. As he closed his eyes and drifted off, he dreamed it replied, *"What do you think I've been doing?"*

XXX

Alex felt a hand on his shoulder, shaking him awake. "Sir Alex, wake up," Justin whispered. "We have been trapped by the beast."

Alex rubbed his hands across his face as he sat up. "What?" He felt lightheaded and groggy, and his mouth was dry. The lingering feeling of his dreams faded. He felt like they were important and was frustrated that he couldn't remember them. His canteen had thawed, so he gulped half of it without stopping for a breath.

"It sleeps, but we must find a way out of here before it awakens," Justin whispered insistently. He crouched in front of Alex, worry etched on his fine features.

"If it was going to kill us, it would have done so by now," Alex said in full voice, waving a hand in the air. "Besides, we aren't trapped; it saved us from freezing by using its body to cover the opening." He stretched his cramped legs and climbed to his feet. "Here, look what is in the back of the cavern."

Alex beckoned Justin to follow him to the back of the cave and showed him the hot spring. Justin knelt and felt the water with his hand and proceeded to strip. Alex followed suit and slowly lowered himself into the steaming water. The pool was large enough around for three people, but only waist deep. He knelt and submerged himself until it covered his shoulders. Justin let out a sigh.

"How's your head?" Alex gestured to Justin's wound.

"It aches a bit, but not too bad. What happened?"

"You collided with some rocks," he said simply.

"So why hasn't it killed us yet?" Justin asked after a few moments of contemplation.

"Your guess is as good as mine, honestly," he shrugged. "It seems intelligent, though."

Something was nagging at him. He had this feeling he was missing something vital.

"What is it?" Justin asked.

"Hmm?" he asked as he moved his arms around in the water.

"You have a pensive look on your face. What are you thinking?"

"Just that I feel like I'm missing something," he said as he used a touch of his water magic to make a tiny sea dragon poke its head out of the water and swim around.

"What is that?" Justin asked, amazed.

"It's my friend, only a much smaller version." He smiled as he thought of the sea dragons with fondness. "He wouldn't fit in here." He laughed as he gestured to the little pool. "They are sea dragons. If you ever visit my home with me, I'll introduce you."

"Dragons!?" Justin asked in a voice laced with fear and disgust. "Your friend?"

"No, no. Not like you are thinking. There are several types of dragons: fire dragons, sea dragons, the land dragons you know about already..." he trailed off.

"Is that what you think this one is?" he asked as he gestured back up the tunnel.

Something clicked in Alex's mind. "That's exactly right. I can't believe I didn't see it before." He stood up and started climbing out of the pool.

"Where are you going?" Justin asked as he followed Alex out of the pool and started putting on his clothes.

"To talk to it, of course."

"Talk to it? They can talk?" Justin sputtered.

"Well some can when they want to, but only with whom they want." Alex shrugged. "Ronin acts like it's a big deal, but they all seem inclined to talk to me, at least a little. Some can be very… cryptic though."

"Incredible!"

They finished getting dressed. Alex rubbed the inside of his hood on his hair to dry it. It had gotten long, longer than he'd let it grow in years. His dark curls hung in his eyes, now extra curly from the water.

"Couldn't you just tell the water to not stick to you?" Justin asked curiously as he struggled with his sleeves sticking to his damp skin.

"I don't know… I suppose I could. I hadn't thought about it," Alex mused. He ran his hands through his damp hair. "I don't mind, honestly. I grew up in a little fishing village at the edge of the Cobalt Sea, so I'm used to it. The water beading on my skin, the feel of water dripping out of my hair, the droplets sparkling in the sunlight… It reminds me of home." He lifted a few drops of water into the air and let them swirl around him. Homesickness welled up in him, followed by faces of his town that were counting on him to find their family members. He straightened and released the water as he turned back toward the entrance.

Justin watched and followed him without a word. The ice dragon was still there, eyes half closed. The light coming through the translucent, icy walls was dimming. With the sun going down, Alex expected it must be even colder out there than before. But inside, the cave was warm enough that Justin didn't need to wear his furs.

"Uh... hi!" Alex said uncertainly to the ice dragon. He couldn't be sure, but he was pretty sure it blinked at him, but it didn't move or respond.

"Alex, tell her to let me in. I'll be right there," Ronin said.

"Where have you been? Oh, we found a hot pool! She who? How did you find us?" Alex asked.

"That's awesome! She, the dragon that is blocking the cave entrance... who else do you think I mean? Let me in; It's cold out here."

"I knew it. I knew it was a dragon!"

Alex looked up at the dragon. "Would you mind letting my friend in?"

It flared its nostrils but didn't budge. *"Excuse me."* He tried again with his mind this time. *"My companion is out there, would you please let him in?"*

"You look like you are having a staring contest with it," Justin commented.

"Oh, sorry, I'm asking her to let Ronin in."

"He's here? How do you know? Her? How do you know it's a 'her'?"

Alex just shrugged and looked back at the ice dragon. She still acted like she didn't hear him. Alex wondered if he was doing this right. Could she even hear him? He remembered when he met Saoirse and talked to her, he had been holding the "not rock."

He slid his hand into his pocket and held it loosely. Its warm shape, familiar and comforting in his hand, sent a tingle up his arm. He felt his shoulders relax as some of the weight he had been carrying seemed to lift.

He cleared his throat and squared his shoulders, *"Hello, lady dragon of the ice. My name is Alexander, and if you would be so kind as to allow my companion to enter, I would be most appreciative."* His words were more formal than he intended, but he bowed slightly anyway.

The dragon raised her head, then inclined it towards him. *"Well now, that is better."*

Alex inwardly cringed. Her voice in his head reminded him of the noble ladies at court. They acted like they were better than everyone else, and it was a privilege to be graced with their presence. Alex took a deep breath and braced himself. He had never been very good at court nuances, but neither could the ladies at court kill him with a backhanded slap.

"Now that you have properly addressed me, I believe an expression of gratitude is also in order for keeping you from freezing to death," she continued.

Alex sighed. *"Many thanks, lady dragon. You are most kind,"* he said smoothly, trying to hide the irritation from his voice.

"What is taking so long?" Ronin chimed in.

"You sure you don't want to stay out there? You remember Daphne?" Alex asked him.

"You mean that wretched wench of a noble who insisted that she be allowed to ride a warhorse, and it was below her station for anything less? I hated her. Why do you ask?"

"This dragon reminds me of her."

"Oh."

"Very well," the dragon conceded, unaware of the conversation Alex and Ronin were having. She moved just enough for Ronin to slip in.

The air from outside rushed in, instantly freezing everything. It hurt. It hurt to breathe. It stung his eyes, and his body shook violently from the cold. He called his fire magic to warm them and wondered if he could make a shield of some kind with it. Immediately, the wind stopped and the cold abated.

"Thank you," Ronin said to no one in particular. He shook the snow off himself and pulled his hood back. "We've a meeting with King Yukiharu in the morning. She'll continue to guard and escort us 'til then," he said, tilting his head in her direction. "What happened to you?" he asked Justin.

"As long as she doesn't try to kill me again," Justin grumbled heatedly.

Ronin looked stonily in her direction. "Is that so…"

The dragon snorted, steam hissing out of her nose.

"Who is King Yukiharu?" Alex asked, bewildered. The only king he knew was the king of Reyall and lived in Ocelum. This didn't look like Ocelum in the slightest.

"The king of the ice dragons. They call themselves the Okami," Ronin explained.

Alex followed him to the back of the cave where he crouched to touch the water. Ronin glanced up at him as he removed his boots to dangle his feet in the water. He closed his eyes, leaned back on his hands, and let out a sigh.

Alex sat down, facing him with his back against the cave wall and a knee tucked up to his chest. A thousand questions ran through his mind, and he was trying to decide what to ask when

Ronin broke into his thoughts. "You are thinking so loud I can almost hear it. Spill."

"How have they been here for so long without anyone knowing they exist? For that matter, all of the fae? What are you expecting to happen tomorrow? Will they help us? What will they want in return? We can't fight them. She almost killed Justin with a light swat. Why do all the other dragons let the land dragons run unchecked? Is this King Yukiharu who you believed wanted to meet me? Why? What does he want with me? Why bring me here? Do they have any leads about the missing people? How could they? Where did you go all day? You just left without a word. What other kinds of dragons are there? Do all ice dragons act like her?" Alex's words came tumbling out in a rush.

Ronin held up his hands in mock surrender. "Okay, okay, I asked for that," he chuckled.

"Well..." Alex prompted.

"First off, they, like the rest of the fae, keep their existence a secret to protect themselves, but more so to protect the humans. Can you imagine what chaos would ensue if humans knew of the existence of magic?" Ronin shook his head. "It wouldn't be good. It is fairly easy to stay out of most humans' attention as they see what they want to see. If they see something they don't think is rational, they rationalize it away as a trick of the light or a dream or the wild imaginations of children."

That made sense to Alex. Their legends had to come from somewhere, even if they were entirely inaccurate.

"As for tomorrow, I don't know what to expect or what they want. Dragons keep their own council and operate in an entirely foreign logic to me, so we'll just have to see. Land dragons are a difficult topic. They are very much like wolves or bears, in that they operate on animalistic instincts, but they have a right to live and exist the same as everything else, I suppose."

"What other dragons are out there?" Alex asked.

Ronin shrugged. "I don't know. The Ardra might have known at one time, but other than you, they are gone. I know of sea dragons, fire dragons like Saoirse, land dragons, and the Okami, or ice dragons. My dad told stories about ancient dragons. He said a long time ago, there were lightning dragons, moon dragons, and night dragons, and even a sun dragon with scales that shone like liquid light."

"What does that look like?" Alex asked.

"I don't know." Ronin chuckled. "Father said the histories don't go back that far, so they are probably just myths."

"I think I'd like to meet more dragons," Alex said after a minute. The idea of more of these creatures simultaneously terrified and excited him.

"Such an Ardra thing to say," Ronin teased.

They sat in companionable silence, each lost in their own thoughts, until Alex heard Justin's shuffling footsteps approaching. The cave was almost completely dark, lit only by the pale moonlight coming through the walls. Justin handed him his cloak and bag, then unrolled his bedroll next to him. Alex murmured his thanks before following suit. He never heard Ronin move, but a few moments after he closed his eyes, he felt Ronin's back against his. He fell asleep to memories of the times he had done that with Bucephalus.

CHAPTER 25

BITTER cold air bit Alex's face as he trudged behind Ronin's giant direwolf form. He was tempted to press himself into Ronin's warm furry side for warmth, but stopped himself. Ronin was a person, not his pet.

They approached a jagged mountain, looming taller than the rest around it. Ice and rock spires jutted out all around them, like a frozen branchless forest reaching for the sky. He had to remember to pay attention as he walked. More than once, he had almost impaled himself on spikes angled across the path by letting his mind wander.

Justin looked in wonder around them as he walked. "Diamonds would be put to shame and look dull compared to this." He gestured to the nearest spike. It caught the light and painted everything around it with sparkling rainbows.

Alex nodded in agreement, not trusting his voice. If he spoke, he was afraid he would say how he really felt, and he didn't want to offend their guide. As pretty as it was, if Alex were being honest with himself, he was tired of the glare of ice, the blinding, endless snow, and the cold.

He missed the sea; the way the colors of the water shifted and changed with the light. He missed the trees, and their comforting greens and reds and golds. He didn't know why anyone would choose to live here. He was being irritable. The ice didn't respond to him like the water and fire and even air did. He didn't like it. It didn't make sense to him. Could he even use ice magic or was it only dragons? Was there such a thing as ice magic? What were they called? What about the other types of dragons he hadn't met, was their magic so wholly different from his, or was it the same, and he just needed to learn to use it like everything else... if they still existed or even existed in the first place.

If they did, what were they like? Were they all this cryptic? No, the sea dragons he met weren't cryptic at all. With a pang, he thought of them and wondered if they could hear him from so far away. He hoped so. He craved their presence. Was that normal?

Opening his mind, he thought of them. Remembering how he had touched the mountain and the "not rock" and called to all the dragons accidentally. He thought he could hear something, but it sounded garbled, like trying to listen to someone underwater. Could he do it again? Only this time, focus only on the sea dragons? He wanted to try.

He stepped over to the ice spire before him on the side of their path and released the fire magic he was using to keep warm. He shuddered. He would have to be quick or risk freezing to death. Grasping the "not rock" in his pocket, he tentatively touched the ice while thinking of the sea dragons.

Suddenly, the world tilted and shifted. Colorful fish swam around him throughout a coral reef and seagrass waved in the undersea current. Many other sea dragons, much larger than Eirach, glided regally through the cerulean water.

It was disorienting. *This is new.*

"Hello," he called out with his mind.

They greeted him with feelings. They felt different, like he was feeling them through someone else. Stronger somehow. It felt like he'd been wrapped in a tight embrace.

He was moving now, swimming. He sensed not only the temperature and current, but also the pulsing of tiny heartbeats around him. A single strong beat echoed through the water as though all around him. There it was again. He counted out the seconds; it beat in time with his own, though much slower than he was used to. It thrummed again.

He was acutely aware of where all the other sea dragons were; they glowed and shimmered as they swam. Do all the sea dragons' hearts beat together? Why did he feel different this time? How could he see them? He felt Eirach's laughter as if it were his own. Was he seeing through Eirach's eyes? How?

They snatched up a fish and swallowed it. He tasted it on his tongue. He knew, without knowing how, these were Eirach's favorite.

He sensed a different electrical pulse through the water. Suddenly, the dragons were on alert. They directed each other through images of coves and rocks and underwater locations.

Three tiny slivers appeared on the surface far above him. He felt a surge through the ocean as the water became dark. There were boats headed across the sea toward Osrealach.

"The storms will stop them."

Storms? Alex wondered as he saw storm clouds appear out of nowhere.

Lightning streaked across the sky, and the ocean began to churn. *"Are you doing this?"* Alex asked in fascination. Eirach poked his head above the surface and surveyed the three ships. ballista bolts shot past him, just missing him. The ships were shooting at Eirach. Alex felt a nudge in his mind. *"Defender, go."* Eirach was kicking him out.

"No, I want to stay! Will you be okay?" He felt reassurances from the sea dragon and a stronger nudge, then an outright shove.

Suddenly, he was blinking at the bright sunlight sparkling off the ice, blinding him. He felt stiff and out of sorts from the abrupt disconnection. Something was wrong. He couldn't move. He called his fire magic to warm him, but it didn't feel very warm. Panicking, he focused on strengthening it.

"Alex, Stop!" Ronin cried right in his ear.

Alex tried to turn his head but was unable. "Ronin, I can't move. My fire magic isn't working."

"It is working fine! Too well, actually. Release it," Ronin sounded upset and something else he couldn't place.

Alex released his fire, and something shadowed his vision. Ronin's face came into view. He was clearly concerned and… was that fear? His face looked odd though, like looking through glass. Alex tried to raise his hand, but remained restrained. "Ronin, why can't I move?"

"You trailed behind, and when I realized, I came back for you. You had one of the Okami by the horn and weren't responding. She carried you here and said you were with the Umi. You were dangerously cold, and your heart was beating really slow. Then as if your body knew it, you flared with heat and started to melt her. The other Okami wanted to kill you, but she wouldn't let them. She didn't know what it would do to the Umi you were connected to."

"What? Connected to? Could she see what I saw?"

"Hello, Little Defender, yes, I was there with you as well. Eirach, as you call him, is delightful. Thank you for the honor of that adventure, though I'd appreciate it if you would ask first next time. And maybe have more control over your fire, though your companion tells us you are still a young pup yet."

"Why can't I move?"

"You can." She made a sound Alex felt was meant to be a chuckle. "Release the guardian stone. I asked them to prevent you from harming me or my kin."

He did, and suddenly he was freed. The hand he had been clutching the "not rock" with burned, and his other hand tingled painfully. The glass between him and Ronin vanished, and Ronin caught him before he collapsed to the ground. "You did? How did you do that?"

"You were connected to it and me, so when I sensed you didn't know what you were doing, I asked it for help so it encased you and insulated you so neither of us would die."

"Who are the Umi?" Alex asked.

"The sea dragons as you call them."

"Wait, how were we connected?"

"You used me to call them, so, naturally, I was connected as well. That was fun! After the other Ardra disappeared, I never thought I would get to experience the sea. Zora never does anything so amazing. Can we fly next?"

"Kaida! You will do no such thing. Release the human."

Alex felt someone else talking to her as if in his head as well, then instantly cut off. His hand tingled less but felt oddly colder than the rest of him. They were in an elaborate cavern made entirely out of ice. The ice spire before him moved suddenly, though not before he noticed a handprint melted into it. An Okami stood before him, surveying him with eyes full of wonder and mischief. For some reason, she reminded him of the little girl from Arageyll.

A giant ice dragon stepped into view and glared at him with disdain. Kaida stepped back and lowered her head, in deference to the large one.

"I am Yukiharu, King of the Okami. You have not only invaded my kingdom without permission, but have accosted my daughter and corrupted her. You are a danger to my people, and I have passed judgment on you. You will be imprisoned in ice to live out your short days in a cave of our choosing."

"He has the guardian stone, Papa."

The king closed his eyes and let out a huff of steam. He did not respond for long enough that Alex wondered if he was going to at all.

"That is interesting. Does the Council of Fae know you have it? No, they would not let you keep it if they did." King Yukiharu mused aloud to himself. "Very well, you may live, but leave my kingdom. Your presence here with it will draw attention we have been working so hard to avoid."

"Before today, I didn't even know you existed. I apologize for my actions that have possibly damaged you. I didn't know what I was doing, or that it was you. I thought you were just some ice. My deepest apologies for intruding on your kingdom." He attempted to bow, but staggered.

Ronin gripped him tighter. He watched the exchange warily. Alex knew Ronin wouldn't have let them encase him in ice for the rest of his life, but at what cost? A thought occurred to him. "So, when we were walking here through all those ice spires, those were all dragons?" Kaida grinned toothily and nodded. Alex felt himself go cold again. They had passed thousands of ice spires, and he had seen many thousands more all the way to the horizon.

"I accept your apology. I will require something of you, Ardra, keeper of the guardian stone, friend of the Umi," Yukiharu's voice rumbled through the cavern.

Alex swallowed and took a deep breath.

"This will be interesting," Ronin said in his head.

XXX

A few hours later, they trudged through the snow again. Kaida led them through the snowy landscape, toward a hidden pass in the mountains. They claimed even humans did not know of its existence.

Walls of ice rose on either side of them. Alex was grateful it kept the wind from tearing right through them. Justin shivered and stuck close to Ronin, back in his direwolf form.

Alex's mind reeled from what the Okami king had asked of him. It seemed impossible. Essentially, the king said they had reached maximum population density and had nowhere else to go. They couldn't leave the mountains for fear of the humans finding out about them, but also because they simply wouldn't survive in a warmer climate.

He had also said they can change their surroundings somewhat to accommodate their needs, but it might kill anything not suited to the cold and ice. He wanted Alex to convince the humans to move further south or find somewhere else for them to go, and a way for them to get there.

"Ronin, I just don't know what to do."

"I don't like that he asked that of you. It is not only unfair but also almost impossible. Why did you agree to it again?" Ronin's growl echoed throughout the ice canyon.

Justin whipped his head back and forth, looking for an unseen enemy.

"What is it? Where? What's out there, Ronin?" Justin asked. He gripped the hilt of his dagger.

"Nothing, Justin. Ronin and I were just conversing. Sorry to alarm you." Alex laid a hand on his shoulder.

Justin relaxed slightly. "Did you have a chance to think over what we talked about? I'd still really like to be your squire."

Alex sucked in a breath quickly. He had been so caught up in everything that had happened recently that it had slipped his mind.

"Alex, say yes. Take him on as your squire. I like him. He is sharp and a quick learner. And, in spite of everything we have put him through in the last few days, he is still here," Ronin's thoughts echoed in Alex's mind.

Alex let out his breath. "Alright. If you are sure about this."

"Yes. Thank you, sir." Justin knelt in the snow before Alex. He bowed his head and placed his fist over his heart. "I, Justin Avery the third, page of Aberdeen, do pledge myself to thee, Sir Alexander of Creedon. I swear to follow you wherever your journey takes you. To uphold your honor and the honor of this rank you have so graciously bestowed upon me, with my words and my actions so that my conduct will ever reflect well on you, M'lord." Justin gushed.

Alex blushed and coughed awkwardly. He had no idea what to do or say.

"Ronin, a little help?"

"Didn't you learn anything? How do you not know this? Tell him to rise and call him Squire Justin." Ronin made a sound like a chuckle. *"Then say something magnanimous like a king would say."*

"Right. Magnanimous? I grew up in a fishing village. I don't know any flowery, fancy words."

"Just say something."

"Rise, Squire Justin," Alex said seriously. "I vow to train you to the best of my abilities, so that you may be prepared to not only pass the Knight's Trials, but in whatever else you choose to pursue."

Justin looked up at Alex with hope and pride in his eyes as he rose. They grasped forearms. Ronin nudged Justin in the back and gave him a wolfish grin.

"First thing."

"Yes M'lord?" Justin responded.

"Stop with the 'M'lord' business. I'm not a lord and have no land or holdings."

"Oh, yessir!"

"Justin."

"Yes, Sir?"

"Just call me Alex, please?"

Justin looked perplexed for a moment, then nodded.

"Great. Now that that is handled, let's get out of this cold." Ronin nudged them after Kaida, who was waiting a ways away, watching them.

"The first of many supplicants for your new kingdom has pledged themselves to you? Well done," Kaida's approval drifted into his mind.

"Supplicant? New Kingdom? What are you talking about? I just agreed to train him," Alex asked, bewildered.

She remained silent.

Justin asked Alex questions over the next few hours until night had fallen. They stopped at a dead end.

"I thought there was supposed to be a way out of here," Justin commented, shivering shamelessly. He pressed into Ronin's side for warmth.

"We will stop here for the next few hours until the moon is beyond the mountains. Then I will lower the pass for you to exit."

Alex relayed what she said to the others. Ronin chuffed, then laid down in the snow. Justin burrowed against him and tucked his face into his fur.

"Hey Ronin. You've been really quiet. Everything okay?"

"Yea, everything is fine. I'm just cold and looking forward to getting out of the ice and snow for a while. I need to shift into something else soon."

"Is there something wrong? Can I do anything?"

"It's a puka thing. No, but thank you," Ronin replied lethargically. *"Here, might as well make a puppy pile so we can all keep warm."*

"Was that wolf humor?"

Ronin chuckled. Alex wondered if his fire magic would continue to keep him warm if he slept. He was still contemplating that as his heavy eyelids drifted shut of their own accord.

A few hours later, they awoke to the sound of shifting ice. Alex rose and brushed off the snow that had accumulated while they slept. Justin groaned and slowly stood and stretched. His teeth chattered as he stamped his feet.

Ronin whimpered in pain, then growled.

"Ronin, are you alright?" Alex asked, concern lacing through him.

Ronin's eyes looked wild, like a real wolf's eyes, for a moment. He blinked a few times and shook his head, then slowly started shifting. Alex's worry grew. Ronin had never taken so long to shift before. Had he gotten injured? Was there iron around here somewhere?

After Ronin had finally shifted back to his fae form, he stayed on his hands and knees in the snow, head hanging, breathing hard. Alex crouched next to him and placed a hand on his shoulder, willing his warmth into him. Ronin's breathing calmed, and he finally looked up at Alex. His eyes seemed troubled. He smiled tiredly and allowed Alex to help him stand, then took his pack from Alex and slung it over his shoulders.

"Let's do this." He strode toward the ice dragon, who stood next to a small hole in the ice wall.

"This will take you back to the human realm. It was interesting to meet you, Ardra. I look forward to our next meeting," Kaida said to him as he left.

"And you as well, Princess Kaida," Alex responded.

The ice tunnel led them out into a scraggly stand of trees. The air was significantly warmer here, and Alex released the strand of fire magic he had been holding onto. Relief and tiredness flooded him on the heels of a feeling of loss.

A large wall of smooth stone rose high into the sky before them. "Did we really travel all the way to Ocelum? That is the only other northern walled city, so it has to be." Justin looked astonished.

"There's no guard on that wall. Why?" Ronin asked.

"Because nothing lives in the frozen north, and nothing can get through all that ice, so why bother. As far as they know, there is no reason to guard this side of the city," Justin responded.

"Let's get some rest, then enter the city in the morning," Alex said through a yawn. He felt like he had been walking for weeks, not days.

Ronin and Justin agreed. They picked a tree to sleep under for the rest of the night. Alex hesitated for a moment before laying with his back against Ronin's like they had in the ice cave.

CHAPTER 26

ALEX, Ronin, and Justin approached the gates to Ocelum. Brightly colored banners flapped in the breeze along the high, marbled white and black walls. They joined a steady stream of carts, wagons, and people both mounted and on foot, approaching the gate. As they drew nearer, the throng of people slowed to nearly a standstill.

"Is there an event or celebration that we are unaware of?" Justin asked his two companions.

Ronin shrugged. Alex couldn't think of anything. The summer solstice was still weeks away.

"You must be new to the city?" a brightly colored trader nodded to them.

"Why yes, how did you know?" Alex responded in surprise.

The short, round man smiled pityingly. "Best find a place to hide those pretty weapons of yours before you enter the city, or better yet, leave them with one of your companions out here." He gestured to Alex's sword sticking up over his shoulder and his two axes hanging off his belt. "I'm no swordsmith, but I can recognize fine workmanship when I see it. You'll not be getting those back if you check them with the city guard."

"What do you mean, check them with the guard?" Ronin asked suspiciously.

"Oh, didn't you know? There are no weapons allowed inside the city unless you are either city or royal guard," he responded.

"Why?" Alex asked in surprise.

"How did you know we weren't?" Ronin asked.

The man chuckled. "They have their own entrance and passes. They don't deign to stand in line with us common folk either." He pretended to put on airs and look down his nose at them.

"Oh," Ronin grunted.

"I heard from the knights that they were strict, but nothing about no weapons," Justin commented thoughtfully.

"Aye, they have been getting more stringent as of late. Makes doing business difficult. If it weren't that they pay top dollar for my wares, I'd go south. By Fiera, I'd even brave the roving marauders, battle lines, and crossing the river to trade with those southern barbarians..." he trailed off and wiped his brow. The morning sun beat down on them.

Alex and Ronin traded glances. Justin looked worried.

He frowned and dropped his voice to barely above a whisper as a shadow crossed his face, "If you want my advice, whatever business you have in the capitol, you best conclude as quickly as possible. Or better yet, forgo it altogether if you can. Scuttlebutt is that the king's gone mad."

Ronin quirked an eyebrow, but kept his thoughts to himself.

"Well, thank you for the information." Alex unstrapped his sword and both his axes and handed them to Ronin. *"Maybe hide these under a tree and fly in ahead of us?"* Alex said in his mind.

Ronin nodded and took Justin's weapons as well. He disappeared into the forest. They followed the crowd slowly snaking toward the entrance. As they drew near, the noise of merchants, craftsmen, and traders with their animals and wares rose until it was almost deafening. The crowd pressed uncomfortably around them, with people impatient to enter the capitol.

The sea of people parted respectfully around the white and black robes of Fiera and Nocturne's Priests and acolytes as they threaded their way through the throng. Two acolytes dressed in black passed closely by Alex, one nearly brushing his arm. She stumbled. Without thinking, Alex put his arm out to steady her. She looked up at him, her eyebrows raised in surprise. Her hand on his forearm radiated heat like standing too close to the fire. It was his turn to look at her in surprise.

She jerked her hand away and quickly followed the other acolyte. The crowd closed behind her quickly, cutting off Alex's view.

"What was that?" Justin practically yelled in his ear to be heard over the din.

Alex gave him a perplexed look and shrugged. He had no idea. He was still mulling over it when they reached the gate.

Each person before them in line read a scroll resting on a small raised stand and marked it before being allowed to enter. The guards took any weapons and gave them a small piece of leather and attached a matching one to the relieved weapon.

When it finally came to Alex's turn, he stepped up to the scroll. In bold, heavy lettering, he read:

Hello and welcome!

This is a safe space. We want everyone here to feel comfortable, safe, and happy. To assist us with our endeavor, please leave all weapons, sharp objects, opinions, humor, personality, sarcasm, and -by the Twins- sass at the door. Non-

compliance will not be tolerated. Please see a guard to assist you with your weapons.

Thank you, and have a happy day!"

Below another larger scroll had been attached:

"Supplemental Laws & Schedules:

No frowning, no expressing negative emotions of any kind, no disagreements, no arguing, no yelling, no crying, no sharp objects, no weapons, no stealing, no harming yourself or others, no laughing too loudly, no expressing your opinions (so as to not offend anyone), no getting offended, no boiling water (you could burn yourself or others), no spitting, no uncovered sneezing, no uncovered coughing, no smiling with your teeth, no wearing a hood or disguise, no public intoxication (best not get intoxicated at all), no eavesdropping, no lying down in the street, no using vulgar or profane language, no rebelling, no gathering of five or more unless attending an authorized event, no dancing, no impersonating another person, no lying, no fighting, no throwing things, no singing loudly. All meals must be eaten on the schedule posted below, all citizens are to be at their place of residence by sundown, no exceptions, somber colors are forbidden, religious robes are to be worn exclusively on holy days unless you are a member of the religious orders."

"Is this a joke?" he asked the nearest guard. The smiling guard shook his head. His smile looked more like a grimace, permanently affixed to his face. He appraised Alex.

"Please remove yourself from the line and attend to your garments before attempting to re-enter the capitol." He pointed to the last line on the scroll. "No somber colors. Are you a member of Nocturne's religious order?" he asked.

"No," Alex looked down at his mostly black and grey attire.

"Then amend your garment color choices before you will be permitted on the premises. No exceptions."

"But this is all I have at the moment."

"Not my problem. Step away, please. NEXT!" The guard gestured for the next person to step forward.

The openness that had been on the trader's face was gone; a fake smile plastered in its place. "Happy day to you," he said through tight lips as he signed the scroll and led his horse and cart through the gate.

Justin moved to step out of line with Alex, but Alex shook his head. "You go on. I'll wait out here for you."

Justin signed his name and let the guards pat him down, throwing an apologetic look over his shoulder at Alex as he stepped through the gate.

Alex wandered away from the line and the gate and settled down in the shade with his back to a tree. While he waited, several figures left the line with various weapons and gear and emerged from the treeline empty-handed. He wondered how many people forgot which tree or bush they hid them under and made a mental note to ask Ronin later. He almost reached out to him several times over the next few hours, but stopped short each time. If Ronin was busy, he didn't want to bother him.

The sun was setting by the time Ronin emerged from the treeline with their weapons. "How'd it go? Did you see Justin? I wonder who he talked to that could be taking this long?"

Ronin shook his head. "I didn't see him, but I also had a hard time getting in anywhere. They have the entire city on lockdown. The only open window I found was in the highest tower." He pointed to a tall, skinny tower rising above the rest.

"What is in there? Did you see the king?"

"I saw him, I think. He talked to me, even."

"Really? What did he say? Will he send help?"

Ronin gave him a pained look. "I don't think he is in his right mind. And definitely not able to send help, let alone run the city and kingdom. I never shifted. He talked to me as my falcon. He paced around his room ranting and pulling out his hair. He looked awful."

"That's odd. What was he ranting about?"

"He just kept repeating 'They are coming. Ash and dust. We are all going to burn.'" Ronin shrugged.

"What does that mean?"

"Your guess is as good as mine."

The trader from earlier exited the city just then. He paused when he saw them and shook his head. "Your companion won't be joining you. The young lad was taken by a group of knights, spouting something about fulfilling his oath. They left out the other gate hours ago." He massaged his face.

"Knights? Which knights?"

"The main one had a half sun. You know, like it was rising or setting."

"Fintan. Do you know where they were taking him?"

The trader lifted a shoulder in a half-shrug. "Best guess is Aberdeen or Drevantor"

"We have to go after him." Alex started toward the trees, but Ronin stopped him with a hand on his shoulder.

"That is back the way we came. We can't. We need to finish this and hope he is okay until then. Bronach and the others might not have that much time." He sighed. "I'm sorry, Alex."

Alex felt torn, but he knew Ronin was right. They had to keep going. With his throat tight and shoulders slumped, he said nothing.

"Which way you headed? I'm headed south to Salar. I wouldn't be upset to have some able-bodied individuals who know their way around a blade, such as yourselves, accompany me. Never can be too careful with the increased reports of bands of rogues in the area. I'll make it worth your while."

"If you wouldn't mind the company, we'd be happy for the transport." Ronin looked relieved at the possibility of riding in a cart rather than having to walk.

"It's settled then." He gestured for Alex and Ronin to climb onto his cart.

CHAPTER 27

THE trio arrived in Salar two days later. Their journey with the trader, Jeb Trimbalson, as he introduced himself, was rather uneventful. He'd inquired into what they were doing and they'd told him about the missing people. He didn't have any leads, but promised to keep an eye out and ask around.

Alex was polite but didn't feel like chatting much, so he'd kept to himself. Leaving Justin behind weighed heavily on his mind. He wondered, not for the first time, if they had made the right choice.

Ronin shot him several inquiring looks throughout their journey, but left him alone to his thoughts. As they made their way into the sprawling city, Jeb offered to have his partner make them a home-cooked meal before they went on their way. They agreed.

Jeb's house, attached to the Wayward Barque Tavern, resided at the top of a hill overlooking the harbor and the bay. Warm lights spilled out of the open door and windows of the cozy grey stone and roughhewn wooden building.

While Jeb unhitched the cart and tended to his horse, Alex admired the view of the city spread out below them. The salty sea breeze caressed Alex's face, causing his chest to tighten. He'd missed the sea. Ronin stood silently behind him as he stared longingly at the horizon. The sun dipped out of view, painting everything in soft amber and rose gold.

"I'd offer to let you stay with us, but we only have one room, and the kitchen is a bit cramped." Jeb shouldered a small pack as he emerged from the stable. "After dinner, I'll take you to the Bonny Caravel, the best Inn on this side of Salar. The owner is a bit, um… eccentric." He leaned in and whispered, "They say she's from Keirwyn, the southern kingdom, and she practices their…" he paused for a moment, as if looking for the right word. "Religion."

"Well, I don't honestly care who she prays to, as long as it's halfway clean and comfortable." Ronin shrugged.

"That it is." Jeb nodded.

They followed him into the tavern and sat on tall stools at the bar. A golden-haired man grinned and waved at them. He hugged Jeb and greeted him warmly before introducing himself as Lionel, Jeb's partner.

While they introduced themselves, Jeb told their travel story. Lionel placed three mugs of a steaming, dark liquid before them. "Here, try this and tell me what you think. I've been trying to perfect it and think I've almost got it."

It smelled unlike anything Alex had ever tried before. Earthy and nutty with smoky undertones. "What is it?" he asked as he tasted it. It was delicious, sweeter than he might have thought from the aroma. He found himself drinking the entire cup and asking for a second.

Lionel chuckled and brought Alex another one. "It's called coffee. In my travels, before I started the Wayward Barque, I came across a little shop called 'Legends & Lattes' that sells this drink made from roasted beans. I've been trying to recreate it ever since. I'm so glad you like it." He beamed.

After dinner, Alex slipped out while Ronin and Lionel chatted. Jeb had been called away by business associates, promising he would show them to the Bonny Caravel when he returned.

The sea was calling Alex, drawing him to it. As he neared the water, he pulled off his boots and tunic, dropping them on the pebbly beach. There were a few others by the shore enjoying the view. A stooped, older gentleman strolling along the beach nodded to him as he passed.

Alex waded out waist deep, then casually swam until he could no longer touch the bottom. The water was so frigid it made him gasp and shiver, but he didn't care. He finally let himself relax, immersed in the dark, gentle waves. The quiet surf centered him, bringing him a small measure of peace. Closing his eyes, he submerged completely and was reminded of his encounter with Chantara. Had he really breathed underwater? Could he do it again? He tried to remember how it felt, but it went completely against his natural instincts. The thought of breathing in water made him panic, so he gave up and resurfaced.

After a short while treading water, the cold seeped into his muscles. He shivered as he slogged toward shore. The night air felt warmer than the water he had just swam in. He considered using his magic to warm and dry himself, but decided against it. In the end, he opted to sit on the shore as the night air drifted around him. His head felt clearer, as it always did after a swim, and his thoughts drifted like the wind. Where to look for Bronach. Was Justin alright? What was all that about in Ocelum? Was the king really insane?

He took a deep breath and turned to make his way towards the door of the tavern when something caught his eye down the shore. A pair of shadows moved alongside one of the small boats tied at the small dock. Fishermen work all hours of the day and night, so he wasn't surprised to see people around at this hour, but it struck him as odd because they had no torch or lantern. Like they intentionally didn't want to draw attention. He took a step in their direction, to investigate when the older gentleman who had nodded to him earlier suddenly tripped and fell. Alex rushed to his side. "Are you alright, sir?" He knelt down to help him to his feet.

"I'm quite alright, young man. My pride is more bruised than my side I'm afraid, but thank you."

"Can I help you on your way, sir?"

"No, no. I think I'll sit here and enjoy the evening air for a few more minutes before I go my way."

"Alright. Good evening, sir."

"Good evening, young man."

"*Hey, have you finished swimming with the fish yet?*" Ronin teased gently. "*Jeb is back.*"

"*Yes, I thought I saw…*" He glanced at the tavern before turning back to the boats, but the figures were gone. "*Never mind. I'll be right there.*"

He shouldered his pack and walked up the hill to meet Jeb and Ronin.

They walked on cobblestone streets through the edge of Salar as most of the town slumbered, with only the occasional pair strolling by. They nodded to or greeted Jeb warmly. Everyone seemed to know him. He explained that most of the people on this side of town were somewhat regulars at the Wayward Barque. They followed a path out to the point of the bay where a two-story building nestled up against the cliff-side, attached to a lighthouse towering above it.

The warm glow from the lanterns and light spilling out of the windows, beckoned them in with promises of comfort. As

Alex approached the stairs leading up to the front porch and wide double doors, he felt a familiar curious breeze swirl around him then disappear.

Upon entering, he immediately forgot about the odd breeze. The room was lined with shelves and shelves of strange items, random odds and ends, knickknacks, books, scrolls, and the occasional weapon. He was so enthralled that he ran into Ronin, where he had stopped next to Jeb.

"Jeb, you old rascal, what are you doing here?" A middle-aged woman with a flour-covered apron called to him from behind a high counter. She wiped her hands on a cloth and embraced him warmly.

"Good to see you too, Sereia. Lionel needs more pastries, and my escorts need a place to stay for the night, so I thought I'd come pay you a visit." He grinned warmly at her as he held up a small sack. "I brought you some of his latest to try."

"I have a batch that just came out of the oven, if you care to wait while they cool." She took the sack and disappeared through a door. Alex assumed it was the kitchen, based on the delicious aromas that wafted out when she opened the split doors. She came back carrying a large tray of steaming mounds of golden flaky pastry in the shape of crescent moons.

Alex's mouth watered as he noticed the wall behind the counter covered in skeleton keys hanging on tiny hooks. There were approximately two score keys on the wall. Large, small, brass, silver, ornate, simple, decorative, and plain; no two keys were alike.

"Pick one," Sereia directed, as if she were used to this reaction.

Alex felt her watching him as he contemplated. Ronin took out a pouch that jingled, but she held up her hand.

"We don't take coin here." Alex's face must have reflected Ronin's confusion because she continued, "Stories, items, errands, tasks, information... that sort of thing. Only gems and gold if they have a story to them, but..." She trailed off and seemed to be lost in thought for a moment before she refocused on Alex and Ronin.

"You look like you have quite the story, if you'll tell it." She scrutinized them with sharp eyes that seemed to miss nothing. She took in Alex's exotic weapons, attire, and even his posture, then she held his gaze with an intensity that made him feel exposed and completely naked.

He tried to keep eye contact and not shift nervously. When she finally slid her attention to Ronin, Alex slumped into the nearest chair. He felt he had just passed some unspoken test. Jeb watched in silence, with twinkling eyes, from where he sat on a barstool at the counter.

"What are you in town for?" Sereia inquired as she poured four glasses full of bright green liquid and handed one to each of them.

Ronin sniffed the liquid, then tasted it. *"This is really good!"* he told Alex.

"We are looking for missing people from my village, as well as reports of missing people from all over the kingdom," Alex replied to Sereia.

"Is it that widespread?" Jeb asked in surprise.

Alex nodded as he tasted his own green drink. "I have a feeling it is not just happening in Reyall."

Jeb rubbed the back of his neck. "So, you think it is an organized group?"

"It has to be, doesn't it? And they seem to be taking advantage of the lack of unity and communication between towns and cities," Alex said, taking a long swallow. It tasted of exotic fruit with a hint of a nutty aftertaste.

"What is this? It is delicious. I've never had anything like it," Alex asked Sereia, holding up his mostly empty glass.

She smiled, "Something from home. I'm glad you like it." She refilled his glass and then her own.

"What is your plan, then? Lionel and I can ask around here for any word on missing people, if you like. Lots of people come through our tavern. We'll have to be subtle about it though, don't want to raise unnecessary alarm and frighten people. That would cause more harm than good, and you will be hard-pressed to sort through what is real, and what is just the overactive imaginations stirred up by fear." Jeb said, sipping his own drink.

Alex nodded in agreement. "Thank you. Any help is much appreciated."

Ronin drained the last of his glass as he studied the wall of keys. "That one," he said, pointing to a simple bronze key.

She unhooked it from the wall and handed it to him. "And what about you?" She turned to Alex. "Do you prefer to share a room with your comrade, or would you like to choose your own room?"

Alex debated for a moment. "I'm perfectly fine in his room, but thank you." A bed sounded nice, but he had gotten so used to falling asleep near Ronin it wasn't a tough choice. He was used to sleeping on the ground, so the floor would be fine.

Also, he wasn't sure he wanted to tell his story to "pay" for the room, but he wasn't sure what else he had to offer her.

She dipped her head and busied herself, putting things away and straightening up.

They finished their drinks, said goodnight to Jeb, and followed Sereia upstairs to their room. Ronin unlocked the door and strode in without ceremony. He seemed to be in a mood. Alex hesitated in the hall. Maybe he should ask for his own room to give Ronin some space. Did Ronin want his own room? Why was he overthinking this?

Sereia's voice broke into his internal debate. "When you get to Moradon, speak to Foxglove and Nightshade. If something is happening, especially in their territory, they would know about it."

"Are those their real names?"

Sereia lifted a shoulder in a half-shrug and smiled.

"How do I find them?" he wondered as he committed their names to memory.

"I suspect you can just ask around and they'll find you."

"Do you think they are behind it?"

"Oh, no. They don't trade in people, just difficult to obtain supplies or items, and information. If you know what I mean. If you need help, send word and I'll do what I can from here. Unfortunately, this place is not like my last..." she said cryptically as she laid a hand on the doorframe and sighed deeply. A look of deep affection etched her face. She winked at Alex before she turned to go downstairs.

XXX

THE next morning, Alex came down to breakfast and returned their key. A little boy perched on a stool next to the counter, covered in flour.

"My rolls don't ever come out like yours," he said to Sereia as he rolled out the dough.

"That's because you have to talk to it."

"I do."

"Then you must speak to it how it wants to be spoken to."

"But how do I know how it wants to be spoken to?"

"You know."

"But I don't know."

"Then you don't."

He sighed dramatically but started asking the dough how it wanted to be talked to, shooting them a daring look to say something.

Alex smiled and said nothing as he sat down on a stool near the other end of the bar near the door.

"She reminds me of Saoirse," he said to Ronin with his mind.

"Who is Saoirse?"

"The fire dragon with the twins…"

"Oh, yes. How so?"

"She's cryptic and says one thing, yet means another."

"It is not nice to talk about someone in front of them like they are not in the room, Little Defender," another voice chimed in.

Ronin paled and choked on his drink.

Alex looked at her sharply in surprise. Laughter echoed from far away.

"I told you he would figure it out," a second voice joined in.

Sereia smiled mischievously. *"Yes, yes, you did. I like him."*

"I thought you might."

Ronin whispered, "What is going on?"

"The dragons are talking, sssshhhhh," Alex whispered back in alarm. Ronin gave him a wary look and darted his gaze to Sereia. Horror and outright fear shadowed his face as what Alex said sank in.

"Right, you…" she pointed to Alex, "have somewhere to be. And you…," she pointed to Ronin, "have someone to meet."

"But…"

"I said what I said. Now go. Here, take this with you." She handed each of them a small package before making shooing motions out the door.

Ronin practically stumbled out the door. Alex thanked her and turned to follow, but was stopped by her hand on his arm. She stepped closer, cradled his chin in her hand like his mother did when she wanted him to hear what she was saying, and looked him in the eye with her intense gaze. He saw amber flames blazing in her eyes and wondered how he'd missed that particular detail before.

"It's not your fault. You made the right choice," she said quietly.

Alex's brow furrowed in confusion. "What choice?"

"You couldn't have changed what happened. You made the right choice. Remember that." Sadness shadowed her features for a moment.

"Okay…?" Alex didn't know what she was talking about, but accepted it. She released his chin and patted him on the shoulder.

"Oh, and when you are ready to learn how it works, come find me."

"How what works?" Alex was tired of the cryptic messages of dragons and guardians.

"You'll know," she said, the mischievous glint returning to her eyes. She turned back to the little boy and helped him place the pieces of dough onto a tray.

Why can't they just speak plainly? He wondered as the door swung closed behind him.

"Now where's the fun in that?" Sereia and Saoirse chuckled in his mind.

He shook his head. "Dragons..." He muttered under his breath as he approached Ronin, waiting for him a few steps away from the porch.

They stopped by the Wayward Barque on their way out of town to say farewell to Jeb and Lionel and to have one last mug of coffee. Lionel also gave them a small package with an assortment of cheeses in it with a small note on how to eat, cook, and prepare each one.

They parted ways a little before midday and continued on foot until the sun began to set, then made camp. They didn't talk much, each lost in their own thoughts. Before they turned in for the night, Ronin offered to spar with him. "It'll take the edge off."

"I think I'll pass. I'm exhausted, but thanks."

Ronin studied him, then shrugged and walked away into the treeline. "I'll take first watch tonight."

Alex didn't argue and was asleep within seconds after he lay down.

He awoke with a blade to his throat. "Best ye don't move or ye'll be breathing out o' new hole," a gruff voice said in his ear. Alex gagged at the stench of breath from his would-be assailant but held still. He slowly rotated his left hand under the blanket until he could grasp the hilt of his dagger in the small of his back.

"Good one!" chuckled another voice off to his right. Alex could hear him rustling around, looking for something. "Who doesn't carry valuables with them? They've nothing worth taking. Let's go. Don't want to draw the attention of the 'Phantom.' He'll eat a man whole, leaving only his socks."

"What are ye on about? Ye know that's just a made-up fairy tale meant to scare children not to stay out past dark. There's no Phantom."

"I'm tellin' ye, there is. They say he prowls the forest as a great cat, its coat as dark as midnight. The only thing ye see is the glint of its eyes before he strikes. They say he is Nocturne, death incarnate. Other stories say he's a great wolf the size of a house and can devour a whole village."

"That's nonsense. Maybe they be carryin' their valu'bles on 'em!" Alex felt more pressure on his throat as a hand started patting him down. They snagged the chain around his neck. "Well, well, what do we 'ave 'ere? Not a bust after all. Looks fancy. I think I might just relieve ye of this. Seein' as ye've been so accommodatin'."

Alex made his move. He slapped away the knife at his neck as he snatched his ring from their hand and knocked the rogue to the ground with one swift motion. He pressed his foot to their neck and pinned their knife hand with his other foot. In the pale moonlight, he could just make out the figure, half hunched over Justin's pack. He slipped the chain back over his head and drew another knife.

"I think you'll be leaving here empty-handed tonight, though I'm of a mind to relieve you of a hand as well," Ronin's voice growled from the dark. The man beneath Alex froze.

"I... I know that voice..." The other figure stood bolt upright. His voice raising an octave, "The last time I 'eard that voice, the 'phantom' got my crew. Never saw any of 'em again." He dropped whatever was in his hands and scrambled toward the road.

As the footsteps faded into the night, Ronin silently stalked toward them. He stopped short of stepping into the moonlight filtering through the trees. In a flash, he shifted to his panther form and pounced on the man, knocking Alex to the side.

Ronin snarled and snapped at the man, now lying pinned under his great paws. The man whimpered as Ronin dug his claws into the man's arm and ran a claw down the man's cheek, drawing blood. Then he leaped off the man and stalked back to the shadows. As soon as he was free, the rogue scrambled to his feet and sprinted away.

"The Phantom? Why is this the first I'm hearing about this?" Alex demanded.

Ronin gave a half-shrug and prowled away. *"Had to pass the time somehow. This was at least entertaining. Go back to sleep. I'll finish the watch for tonight."*

"What were you doing before... not keeping watch clearly." Alex bit out at him.

When Alex didn't get an answer, he shook his head and sheathed his knives. He spread out his disturbed bedroll and climbed back in and went back to sleep. His dreams were filled with panthers stalking in the dark just on the edge of his vision. The next morning, he awoke tired and sore with Sereia's words echoing in his mind.

CHAPTER 28

ALICE sat cross-legged before him as he plaited her hair back out of her face.

"Ronin is the Phantom? What kind of things did he do? I bet he caught and punished all the bad men. Did he make people angry?"

He smiled. "I think he made a lot of people angry, but a lot of other people happy."

"I like Sereia. She seems fun. Do you think if I talked to our food as we made it, it would turn out better?"

He laughed deeply. "I don't know, but why don't we find out tonight." He finished her braid and tied the end with a teal ribbon. "You can take the lead, and I'll assist so you know I didn't interfere. There. All finished."

She hopped up and gave him a peck on the cheek. "Thank you, daddy," she said as she raced to the kitchen.

He followed her and rolled up his sleeves.

She was pulling out ingredients and placing them on the table. "I know just what I want to make, too. And you can keep telling the story while we cook."

CHAPTER 29

ALEX and Ronin stood in the receiving room of the palace, feeling dirty and out of place, despite the fact that Alex was wearing his best tunic and only pair of clean pants. He fidgeted with his hem as they waited.

The polished marble floors gleamed in the early morning sunlight. Everything was either carved marble or encrusted with gemstones and gilded accents. Tall, ornate pillars stretching from the floor to the lofted ceiling lined the outer portion of the room. Despite the obvious display of wealth, the room had a light and airy feel. It reminded him of his visit to Fiera's temple at Drevantor. The throne sat empty on a small raised dais at the end of the room.

Alex quietly blew out a breath of frustration and shifted from one foot to the other impatiently.

"Like I was saying, the Duchess is very busy and isn't receiving anyone today. You understand. Please come back next month on the appointed receiving day and she will hear your request." Viktor, Duchess Korynna's assistant, told a pair of merchants in front of them.

When they approached his small desk, he didn't even look up. He repeated the same line he had given the merchants before them.

Alex introduced himself as Sir Alexander of the Knights Order here to request an audience with the Duchess. Viktor looked at them skeptically over the rim of ostentatious spectacles perched on the bridge of his nose.

"You don't look like a knight. Might I remind you that impersonating one of the king's knights is treason and punishable by imprisonment and even death."

"I thought you might not believe me." He pulled his ring from under his tunic and showed the assistant. He had used it as his heraldry. Now he wondered at the wisdom of using a symbol he didn't know the history of... now that he knows it belongs to the fae. "Also, you can send a letter of inquiry to the retired Commander McCannon. I believe he makes his residence here in Moradon. He will vouch for my credibility."

"Very well..." His smile didn't reach his eyes as he narrowed his gaze. "I will inquire as you say. Come back five days hence. I should have an answer for you then."

They were clearly dismissed.

"Does the 'Phantom' have any contacts here while we wait to see the Duchess?"

"Hmmm," Ronin said thoughtfully. "He might, actually. We might as well look for Foxglove and Nightshade too while we're at it, and I could use some food. I know of a place down by the docks. Maybe you can talk to some of the workers there. You know, fish to fish." He winked at Alex and nudged his shoulder teasingly.

Alex grinned. "You're just jealous."

"Mmhmm sure, sure. I don't have saltwater in my veins like you do." He grinned back.

A bit later, Alex and Ronin strode down a smaller street off the main thoroughfare. They didn't know where to begin to look for this Foxglove character.

As they passed a rough-looking tavern, someone hurled through the only window out on the street. Another figure followed the first, bellowing curses and brandishing a broken chair. The worn sign hanging above the door read "Harpy's Hollar." He was so absorbed in watching the fight, he didn't notice the three figures standing before them until he heard Ronin say, "Watch where you are going."

"Pardon?" a distinctly feminine voice answered him.

"Don't be rude, Ronin," he said to his companion. "I... Oh!" Before him stood Duchess Korynna dressed in common clothes flanked by a pair of guards, also in common clothes. He blinked in surprise. *What is she doing here?*

"Not a word. Follow me," she commanded and spun on her heel to walk down the street, not watching to see if they followed.

Ronin protested, but Alex shook his head and followed her. *"That's the Duchess."*

"Wait, what? Really? What is she doing here? Why are we following her?"

"That's what I was wondering. We wanted an audience, well, here's our chance."

She led them through a maze of narrow streets to a small staircase in a back alley. It led to a small, clean, but sparsely furnished apartment with bunks and hammocks lining the walls of the common room, and a small stove against the wall in the corner to the right. It reminded Alex of one of the safe-houses McCannon had used occasionally.

She gestured for them to sit down and took a position standing by the only window. Her guards stood on either side of the doorway, ever vigilant.

"What do you want? Why are you here? How did you find me? Did my brother send you? Does Viktor know where I am?" She glared down at them, though her small stature made her only a little taller than Ronin sitting down.

"No, Viktor told us you were busy and to come back in five days to meet with you."

"My Lady, if he knew where you were, he wouldn't have sent... them," one of the guards interjected.

"True," she mused. She looked at them with cold, calculating eyes. "Well...?"

"We just came from Ocelum, by way of Salar, M'lady. We are looking into reports of missing people. We hoped you might have resources we could utilize in our quest," Alex tried to sound as much like McCannon as he could summon, remembering the way McCannon slowed his speech and added emphasis on certain words to give them more weight.

"You sound like him." She glanced at one of her guards, then back to Alex. The guard nodded as if to affirm her unspoken question.

"Sound like who? If you don't mind my asking." He reminded himself that he was talking to the sister of the king. "Your Grace." She could greatly assist them in their search, but if stories were to be believed, she was inclined to have them thrown in the dungeon, for interrupting her or some supposed insult.

"McCannon." A small smile played at the corners of her mouth, and her eyes seemed to soften for a moment. "Does he know you are here?"

"Not yet. We've only just arrived and came to see you first."

"What were you doing on the west side, then?" Her eyes became hard and calculating again.

"We were given a couple of names for potential contacts who might have information to help with our search. Apparently, if something passes through here, they would know about it. Do you perhaps know where we might find one, Foxglove or Nightshade?" Alex asked.

One of the guards coughed.

"They are a myth. A bedtime story told to children to keep them from sneaking out at night." Korynna dismissed a little too quickly.

"You mean like dragons and the 'Phantom'? I can assure you, M'lady, they are very real," Ronin countered. "Makes me wonder what other bedtime stories are real too; they have to come from somewhere, I suppose."

"*She's hiding something,*" Ronin accused. Alex had come to the same conclusion. "*Does she know who this Foxglove is... Where to find them? Why would she hide that? Maybe it's someone close to her.*"

"*There's got to be a way to get her to talk,*" Alex mused to Ronin.

"Yes," as if she had made up her mind. "I will give you resources to help you find these missing people, but first I need you to run an errand for me," Korynna said after a pause.

"What?" Ronin exclaimed. "Don't you have servants for that?"

"What do you need us to do, M'lady?" Alex said at the same time. Ronin shot him a disgusted look.

"I do," she said, frowning at Ronin. "How else do you prove you are worthy of my help?" she said loftily.

Ronin glared at her then Alex. "*We don't need her help. I'll not be ordered around by some entitled royal.*"

"We can use this as an opportunity to look for Foxglove."

The look on Ronin's face said he relented, but wasn't happy about it.

"We'll be happy to help, Your Grace," Alex said to Korynna.

A sly smile flashed across her face for an instant. "Go to the Salty Rose and ask for Alyse. Tell her I sent you."

"Yes M'lady." Alex stood and bowed deeply.

Korynna nodded to her guards who opened the door and held it open for her. When Alex made to follow, the remaining guard stopped him.

"Wait, how will we contact you when we are finished?"

She continued down the stairs as if she hadn't heard him, raised her hood, then stepped into the street at the end of the alleyway, disappearing from view.

"You don't." The large man ushered Alex back into the room and shut the door. "One of her people will find you. She will send someone to fetch the item from you. Do not, under any circumstances, go searching for her in the palace. Do not speak to Viktor or any other knights, nobles, or royals about your meeting with her or the existence of this room. If you do, she will deny any knowledge of your existence, and it will result in the termination of her assistance and your life as you know it." He reached into his pocket and held out a small key.

"You are permitted to use this for your residence while you are under the employ and protection of Her Highness the Duchess. Leave it as you found it. Don't bring anyone else here."

"So she'll help us then?" Alex asked. Uncertainty laced his words.

"What does she want from us in return? It can't be as simple as running an errand," Ronin broke his silence, his voice heavy with suspicion and distrust.

The guard grunted and set a small coin pouch on the table by the door. "For any expenses you may have. Scuttlebutt's Folly makes a decent meal." With that, he looked them both over once more, then exited, leaving them in stunned silence.

Ronin prowled over to the window and surveyed the street below, a pensive look on his face. He chewed the inside of his lip.

"Well, do you want to get food first then go to the Salty Rose or go straight there?" Alex slipped the key on the chain around his neck, next to his ring, then tucked it beneath his tunic once more. He opened the coin pouch and whistled. Ronin peered over his shoulder and made a "hmph" noise.

"I'm going to try some of my old contacts and see what I can dig up while you do *her* bidding," Ronin said.

"Oh, I thought…" Alex trailed off. "Alright. Meet back at Scuttlebutt's Folly this evening for dinner then?"

Ronin nodded. He stowed his pack in the corner, far under one of the cots then reached for Alex's packs. He paused, staring at Justin's bag in his hands, then met Alex's eyes. "He's a good kid. Smart, resourceful… He'll be okay," he said as if he could feel the weight of Alex's guilt following him around like his own personal cloud.

Alex took a deep breath and let it out slowly. He didn't want to talk about it. He knew he probably should. If anyone would understand, it would be Ronin, but he held back. Ronin finished stowing their packs, and Alex hid both of his axes under the mattress, but kept his sword and knives. Alex locked the door after they left, and they went their separate ways.

XXX

It took him a while to find the Salty Rose. He got turned around several times and had to ask for directions repeatedly. Finally, he arrived at a row of large houseboats-turned-storefronts and shops attached to each other, gently bobbing attached to the dock.

The Salty Rose turned out to be a tailor shop situated between the Soren & Son's Cobbler and Hattie's Haberdashery. A little bell jingled, announcing his arrival as he opened the door and stepped inside.

A small, stooped lady with salt and pepper hair and a round face looked up from a table covered in strips of material. She bobbed a curtsey. "I'll be with you in a moment," she said around the pins she had pinched between her lips. She finished pinning the piece she was working on and removed the other pins from her lips before making her way over to him.

"Are you Alyse?" he asked.

"Turn please." She held up her finger in the air and drew a circle.

"I... oh, um, what?" He stumbled over his words, completely caught off guard. "I'm not..."

"Tut tut, you don't have to tell me." She wrote something on a scrap of paper produced from her pocket. "The craftsmanship on your garments is excellent, but needs mending. I don't have anything in your size for formal attire if you'll be needing something for this evening, but I could have them done by week's end, if that's agreeable. Possibly by the morrow, but that will cost extra; you imagine." She held his arms out from his sides and wrote more notes, circling him. "Mmhmm! If you step into the back..."

"Pardon me, ma'am. I believe you have mistaken me for someone else."

"Oh?" she gave him a stony, appraising look.

"I was sent here by Duchess Korynna to find Alyse. She didn't say what I needed to retrieve for her actually..." his cheeks burned with embarrassment. He felt a little foolish, but by the whole interaction and for forgetting to get more details about what he needed to do. He had been so caught up in meeting Korynna so suddenly that it had completely slipped his mind.

"Ahhh, that explains it," she said with a small smile. "I haven't quite finished it yet as my shipment has been delayed. Please fetch it for me, and I'll mend your tunic while I wait?" it was phrased as a question but she made it sound like he didn't have a choice in the matter. "You'll find a simple tunic and pants behind that curtain to change into. They should fit."

"But..." he started to protest.

"I really must insist. It's the least I could do." She turned him and gently pushed him toward a dark green curtain in the corner.

He quickly changed into a pair of dark brown pants, a cream-colored shirt, and a medium brown jacket. The jacket was large enough that it hid two of his knives in their sheaths, but not the rest. He stepped out from behind the curtain and handed her his clothes, still holding on to his sword.

She tsked, "They'll do for now I guess. Anything you would like me to alter while I mend?"

"No, but thank you. I'll be back soon," he said.

"Your belongings will be safe with me, I assure you." She nodded toward his sword.

He stared at it in his hands, debating for a moment before placing it on top of the pile of clothes in her arms, then exited without another word.

Go to the Harbor Master's post. Go down to the end here and over a few rows. It will be the big one on the end. You can't miss it. Tell them Alyse sent you.

Her directions were precise, and he arrived a short time later. He presented himself to the elderly gentleman sitting behind the desk and stated his purpose for being there.

"Ah yes, Alyse's normal shipment was delayed, but I believe..." He looked at Alex over the rim of his tiny spectacles then back down to a pile of papers strewn across the desk. He picked up several and rifled through them before squinting at one in particular. "Ah yes, here we are. Her parcel is being unloaded currently. You may wait here or on the dock outside until it is ready for you, if you'd like."

Alex thanked the man and stood in the corner, out of the way of the people coming in behind him.

He tried not to listen in on the conversations, but in such a tiny room, it was impossible. "Ah, Mr. Lars, good morning to you. What a pleasant surprise!"

"Good morning."

"Where is young Xander today? Gave him the day off? He didn't take ill, did he? I heard a nasty cough is going around."

"No, no, none of that. I don't know where he's gone. He disappeared without a word."

"That's not like him at all. I always thought him the responsible sort. I hope nothing bad happened to him."

"And I as well. Now I have to train a replacement."

They continued to chat about the weather and their aching joints and the upcoming social events, but Alex tuned them out as he thought more about the missing boy. Could it be a coincidence? People went missing all the time, but he had a strong hunch that they were all connected.

He was about to approach the man about it when another man burst into the little room holding his arm. He had a nasty-looking gash on his arm that was trailing blood.

"Will! What happened? Are you alright? You look like you need a healer! Mr. Lars, would you mind sending for the healer?"

"Straight away!" Mr. Lars pulled out a cloth and handed it to Will, then left quickly.

"Oh, it's naught but a scratch. A crate had a stray nail that caught me. I'll be right as rain. Not to worry. Though Kieran will be stuck unloading the rest on his own, I expect."

Alex stepped toward Will. "I'm not a healer, but I know my way around cuts and the like. I can take a look at it for you, 'til the actual healer arrives."

Will nodded. "That'd be fine." He held out his arm to Alex and removed the cloth.

"Here." Herman offered him an empty bucket and a jug of water and moved his chair over for Will to sit in.

Alex washed the gash, and after making sure there weren't any splinters in it, he placed a new cloth that Herman handed him over it and instructed Will to keep pressure on it until the healer arrived.

"Thanks," Will said.

"Alex," he finished for him.

"I'd offer to shake your hand, but..." he trailed off then chuckled.

"Sorry I can't do more, but without a needle and thread and proper bandages, I'm afraid that's all I can do."

"You've done more than most, and I'm grateful," Will said, nodding.

"I can help unload some of the crates, if that would be alright?" Alex offered. "I'm waiting for a package off the..." He looked at Herman.

"*Morning Delight*," Herman offered.

Will nodded again. "That's the one we were working on when this happened." He looked down at his arm.

Alex looked to Herman. "It's alright by me. She's the third one on the left. You'll see Keiran unloading. If you don't see him, he's probably fallen asleep somewhere." Herman looked at Alex in surprise and looked at him more closely for a moment then turned back to the papers on his desk.

Alex found the *Morning Delight*, but the dock and deck were empty, as Herman suspected. He climbed onto the ship and went below deck in search of Keiran for instructions. The hold was half-filled with crates of all sizes and shapes. Some marked with what he guessed to be names, and others with contents. He didn't find Keiran, so he grabbed the nearest stack of crates and carried them up the ramp in the meantime.

He was mostly done unloading crates and had to pause to catch his breath and wipe sweat from his eyes. He'd removed his jacket and rolled up his sleeves at some point, but he was still overheated from the exertion. A hand thrust a canteen of water into his face. Will had a freshly bandaged arm and an odd look on his face.

"Where's Keiran?"

"You are the first person I've seen." Alex shrugged.

"You did all this yourself?" He gave Alex an appreciative glance before surveying the crates. Alex had organized them by name and contents where he could.

"Hey, Will! What happened to your arm? Been drinking on the job again?" Two men approached them from down the dock. From their clothing, Alex guessed they were sailors.

"You know, it was the craziest thing, a crate just jumped out of nowhere and bit me," Will shot back with a grin.

"You know he don't touch the stuff," the other man said to the first. They nodded to Alex. "Where's Kieran? Who's the new guy?"

Will shrugged. "Haven't seen him since this happened, and this is Alex. He's just helping out today. There were some shady lowlifes hanging around the docks this morning. Anything missing?"

"Won't know 'til I check the manifest again, but don't seem to be." He looked over the scattered piles of cargo.

Will looked at Alex. "This is Rod and Reg, Captain and first mate of the *Morning Delight*."

Alex nodded to them.

"You do good work. If you find yourself with an overabundance of time and under-abundance of coin, you are welcome here anytime, Alex." Rod held out his hand. "We'll finish from here,"

"Much appreciated," Alex clasped forearms with Rod. "This evening we're gathering at the Scuttlebutt's Folly for drinks and food. You'd be welcome at our table," Reg said.

"I don't know where that is, but sure. You are the second person to mention it today," Alex said.

"You're not from here. Everyone knows where the Folly is." Reg laughed. "Where are you from? What are you in town for, if you don't mind me asking?"

"I'm originally from Creedon, and I'm looking for a Foxglove. Supposedly, they have info I need."

The three exchanged glances. Alex opened his mouth to ask, but Will interrupted. "Let me find the crate for Alyse for you, and you can be on your way. I'm sure she's expecting you."

Reg headed to the office, and Rod started to follow, but paused. "We'll see you at the Folly tonight then?" he asked Alex.

Alex nodded, and Rod turned back to follow Reg into the office. Alex followed Will down into the hold of the ship. Will produced a tiny box from within a larger crate and handed it to Alex. "I appreciate your help today, both the work and my arm. Like Rod said, you are welcome here any time as well. Tell Alyse I said hello," Will said.

With the tiny box tucked under his arm and jacket slung over his shoulder, he rolled his shoulders to loosen the tension in them as he walked back to the tailor shop. When he entered, she was exactly where she'd been earlier, complete with pins in her mouth. Only this time, she was holding emerald green and turquoise fabric as opposed to the black and red from earlier. On a stand-off to her left, an ornate black and red gown now hung on display. The stand directly behind that one caught his eye: a black, long-sleeved tunic with ornate gold embroidered cuffs and collar, with a matching black cloak draped over it. He'd seen nobles at various events wear outfits such as this, but never up close. The workmanship was exquisite. Usually for him, clothes were just clothes. Too many people cared more about what they wore than the plight of the people they were responsible for.

"Will says to say hello," he said as he set down the little box next to her. She smiled warmly around the pins in her mouth, the corners of her eyes crinkling. He stepped closer to the tunic and cloak and reached out to touch it, but pulled back when he saw the state of his hands.

He looked up to find her watching him, the little box open in her hands. It was full of golden buttons. "Do you like it?"

Alex gaped at her. "It's magnificent! All your work is amazing!" he said with a sweep of his arms to include the whole shop.

"Those are for a special client and they are almost finished," she said, rising with the box and approaching the black cape. She took two buttons and quickly sewed them on and attached a small golden chain. She set down the box and walked to a stool in the corner and picked up a pile of folded black fabric and his sword. "I was able to mend yours and had some extra fabric, so I imitated the design as best I could and made you a second one," she said, handing the bundle to him. "I'm not finished with Her Highness's order yet, so you'll have to come back tomorrow I'm afraid."

"What do I owe you for these?" he asked.

"Oh, nothing, my dear. It looks like you've worked hard enough to more than pay for it. I hope Reg and Rod didn't give you too hard a time." Alex's surprise must have shown on his face because she laughed. "I've known those two since they were small boys, same for Will. Any work you did for them is payment enough for me." Alex protested, but she just laughed and waved her hand. "I'll hear no argument."

Not wanting to soil his newly mended clothes, he buckled his sword across his back and carried the bundle in his arms. As he reached the door, he turned back to see her still watching him. She waved then turned back to her work. He started to say something then thought better of it and turned back to the door.

"Ask your question, Alex of Creedon," she said gently.

He took a deep breath. "Do you know anything about missing people? Or how to find a person that goes by Foxglove?" he asked.

She shook her head. "No, but much can be gleaned from being in the right place at the right time… or, I suspect, the wrong place at the wrong time, to be more accurate."

He sighed and opened the door. "Tomorrow, then."

"Perhaps revisiting places when those who wish to remain unseen are more likely to go about their business," her voice called after him.

Alex felt tired and dirty when he arrived back at the room. He contemplated going for a swim, but his growling stomach reminded him he hadn't eaten in a while. He stripped his dirty clothes he'd gotten from Alyse and used a sponge and water basin to clean up as best as possible before putting on the new tunic she'd made. It fit perfectly and was surprisingly soft and comfortable. It even had identical slits and pockets for his knives. He had just finished redressing when he heard footsteps on the stair outside, followed by the scrape of metal in the lock.

He drew a knife and stood behind where the door swung open, and just before he lunged, the figure turned to close the door. "Oh!" the girl cried, dropping her large wicker basket. She stepped back, wide-eyed, and held up her hands. "I didn't know anyone would be here. My sincerest apologies." She ducked her head and shoulders like she was trying to make herself smaller and less threatening. Alex thought it seemed slightly forced, but let it go. He sheathed his knife and closed the door.

"I apologize for scaring you. Can I help you?"

"Oh, I'm just coming to tidy up and take any washing. Do you need anything washed?"

Alex was stunned that the duchess would send someone for that. "Um, yes actually, thank you."

She held out her basket for him, and he placed his sweaty clothes from earlier in it.

"It'll be back by morning, sir." she curtsied, then picked up her basket and hastily walked to the door. Alex opened it for her and closed it behind her when she left. He had just stepped away from the door when it opened again. Before he had time to react, he saw Ronin's dark hair peek in.

"Ah, you are here. How was being an errand boy to the duchess?"

"Surprisingly eventful." He filled Ronin in on his afternoon. "What about you? Did your contacts have anything useful?"

Ronin looked worried and started pacing. "No, nothing. I couldn't find any of them. They were all gone. Which is strange. A few of them I understand, but all of them? Something's really wrong to have chased them all off."

He told Ronin about the two missing people from this afternoon and finished with what Alyse had said.

"Well, it sounds like we'll be dining with your new friends at the Folly tonight and then have some night stalking to do." Ronin said with a feral look of glee.

CHAPTER 30

VOICES and laughter spilled out into the road from the open door of the Scuttlebutt's Folly. Will, Rod, Reg, and the Duchess's guard sat at a table, having a lively discussion when they walked up. The guard nodded to them over his mostly empty mug.

Will rose and grasped Alex's forearm with his. "Hey! You made it. Wow, you clean up well. You look…" he trailed off, appraising them. "Who's your friend?"

Ronin studied each of them, his gaze lingering on the guard as if he wasn't sure what to make of him.

"This is Ronin." Alex introduced, unsure what else to say. He couldn't say where he was from, that he was his former steed, or the Phantom.

"I'm Will. This is Rod, Reg, and Colin. Delilah, Colin's wife, runs the kitchen. If you need anything, just ask her." He pointed toward the counter where a broad-shouldered lady hoisted a keg over her shoulder and placed it in an open space on the wall lined with various other kegs.

Rod pulled a couple more chairs over to their table and held up two fingers over his head. A girl across the room nodded, then turned to fill two tankards before bringing them over and placing them on the table. Alex tried to offer her several coins, but she looked at Colin then refused them.

Colin smiled affectionately at her. "Thank you, Darling."

"You're welcome, Papa," she smiled back at him. "Mama says the pies should be ready soon if you want to come pick which one you want. Do your friends want anything to eat, too?"

He looked at Ronin and Alex before he said, "Yeah, whatever your mother has fresh."

"Okay, Papa. Oh, can I go to the market with Lily and Grace tomorrow?" she said, twisting her apron between her hands nervously.

"What did your mother say?"

"She said to ask you."

He chuckled. "I don't see why not, as long as you take Devin with you, and you are back before dinner."

"Devin? But why? He hates the market and always hurries us along and ruins the mood." She pouted and folded her arms across her chest.

"You know why. Either you take Devin with you, or you don't go at all."

She sighed dramatically. "Fine, but I'm not waking him up. If he's not awake by the time we leave, then it's his own fault and he'll have to catch up."

"I'll make sure he's up."

"Thank you, Papa," she said over her shoulder as she threaded her way between tables back to the bar.

A small boy shuffled over, balancing a tray full of plates of food larger than he was. Panting, he set the teetering tray on the table between Alex and Ronin. Clearly related to Colin, Alex guessed this was his son or nephew. The boy carefully transferred the plates to the table one by one. Alex returned his attention to Rod, who was telling them about his last trip to Salar. He felt a tug at his pocket.

Ronin's arm snaked out, catching the boy by his scruff. His chair scraped the floor noisily as he lifted him into the air. It tipped over, hitting the floor with a thud. The room went completely still.

Holding the "not rock" in his hands, the boy looked at Ronin in sheer terror as his legs dangled in the air. Ronin's eyes had turned a dark, greyish silver, and reminded Alex of his wolf form.

"Colin Samuel Cavanagh Jr., what is the meaning of this?" Colin bellowed in the silence. He rose to look the boy in the face. "What did I tell you about stealing?" He demanded.

The boy flinched but didn't take his eyes off Ronin. He dropped the "not rock." Ronin snatched it out of the air almost too fast to see and handed it to Alex without looking.

"Thieves lose a hand when they are caught taking what isn't theirs," Ronin threatened in a low voice. "Where I'm from, they say the Phantom will steal you away and feed you to the fairies," Ronin whispered something in the boy's ear before setting him down.

Colin Jr. trembled violently; his eyes wide with fear.

"Go help your mother with the dishes and any other chores she asks. If I hear you complained, even once, there will be severe consequences." Before Colin even finished, the boy tore off, disappearing through the door to the back.

Ronin picked up his chair and sat down. Colin grunted and sat as well. After a moment, the rest of the room went back to their own conversations and food.

Colin sighed heavily. "I apologize for my son. I don't know what has gotten into him lately."

"No harm done," Alex said, digging into his food.

Reg looked at Ronin. "The 'Phantom', huh?"

Ronin shrugged. "Seemed like the right thing to say. It's interesting how everyone has their own unique lore. What are the tales and legends you have around here? What about Nightshade and Foxglove?"

Their laughter gave way to seriousness. Reg leaned in. "Best be careful where you use those names." He said in a hushed tone. "Word is you don't find Nightshade. They find you and you don't want them to find you, if you catch my meaning."

Colin considered them a moment before he rose, saying something about pie. He returned shortly with a steaming fruit pie, sliced and ready to be eaten.

They swapped various tales and legends over pie and drinks long into the evening. At some point, Ronin slipped out, muttering about needing to retire for the evening.

"Let me know if you need me," Alex said to him in his mind.

"I will." Ronin rested his hand on Alex's shoulder, then he left.

A little while later, the group dispersed their separate ways. Rod and Reg carried Will between them, more than a little tipsy. He slurred a version of the bard's last tune as they trudged down the street.

"Care for some company?" Colin followed Alex out of the main door of the tavern.

"If you'd like." Alex could feel his efforts of the day taking their toll on him. He was tired.

They walked in silence for a few streets. "I appreciate your compatriot's mercy with my son tonight," Colin started. Alex only nodded, not sure what else to say.

Colin continued, "You did good today. I trust Will with my life, so if he trusts you, then it's good enough for me." Alex blinked at him in surprise.

"She won't tell you this, but some of our people have been going missing, as well as quite a few from all over the city. Whoever is taking them is good. Really good. In and out without notice or even so much as a footprint." He rubbed the back of his neck. "We actually thought it might be the Phantom, but reports placed him outside of Salar two days ago at the same time as people went missing here."

"How many?" Alex asked quietly.

"By our count, just under ninety," his voice was strained.

"That many?" Alex gasped. "That's a lot more than a few scattered missing people. Wherever they are keeping them has to be near Moradon."

"You may be right... hmmm." He stroked his bearded chin as he seemed to contemplate that thought.

They arrived at the alley below the apartment a few moments later. Alex hesitated at the base of the stairs and turned to face Colin. "We'll find our people." Emotions made his voice thick and husky.

Colin nodded. "I'd say 'be safe', but safety is an illusion wielded by the powerful to control the masses." He turned and walked to the end of the alley, disappearing around the corner.

Alex took out his key and unlocked the door. The hairs on his arms prickled just before he pushed the door open and stepped in, shutting it quickly behind him. He leaned against the door and shook his head.

Thoughts and concerns about the day's events crowded his mind. Each one vying for priority over the others. His body and his mind were exhausted. He was very much looking forward to sleep. He locked the door behind him, then trudged to sit on the edge of the bed.

"I locked the door. Are you coming back tonight?" He hoped Ronin could hear him, but after a few moments of silence, he decided to try again with the "not rock." He pulled it out of his bag from under the bed and cupped it in both hands. The white tendrils weaving through the glossy obsidian glowed silver in the moonlight streaming through the window.

He concentrated on Ronin. *"Hey, are you okay? Are you coming back tonight?"*

"Leave the window open."

Ronin seemed distant and focused on something, so Alex left him alone to whatever he was doing. Crossing the room, he unlatched the small window and opened it a fraction. He slipped off his boots and curled up on the bed in the corner with his back to the window, not bothering with the blanket.

He traced the silvery white veins along the "not rock" surface with his fingers. His mind still raced, but within moments, sleep pulled him under. His last thought was of Quinn as he wondered where he was and if he was alright.

✘✘✘

He crouched next to the fireplace, stirring a pot of delicious-smelling stew. A man with dark, curly hair approached him. "They'll be bringing the next batch in later. Where do you want to put them?"

"With the rest of them. We'll sort them tomorrow."

"What about the broken ones?"

"Burn them."

"But…"

"Did I stutter? I don't remember giving you permission to ask questions." Venom laced his words, meant to intimidate, but pained him to say. He wondered what was coming over him, but pushed it aside. He had a job to do.

"No, sir. It will be done, sir."

The man left. He watched the fire flicker for a while, then dropped a few flowers into the stew and stirred it. "Food's ready," he called to a strangely dressed guard. The guard nodded and called down the hallway for others before entering the room and serving himself a bowl.

He didn't wait for the others; he needed to go now. The strangest feeling came over him and suddenly, his vision changed. His body felt different, lighter, his vision clearer. He could see through the night like it was day, and the details from far away came into focus. With a mighty leap into the air, he was weightless; the wind pressed against him. It was breathtaking, exhilarating, yet familiar - like it was a part of him. He reveled in it.

He surveyed the area, noting everything as it should be. He circled the buildings higher and higher, making sure his presence wasn't missed, then took off toward the distant horizon, holding onto those feelings. Calling the wind to him, it propelled him along at impossible speeds.

XXX

Alex woke with a start and sat up abruptly. His eyes were crusty and his face felt stiff, but he couldn't shake the memory of soaring high in the sky with the wind flowing over and around him.

Ronin leaped to his feet instantly with the knife Alex had given him in hand. When he saw there was no immediate danger, he laid down again, grumbling under his breath.

Alex still held the "not rock" It had left an impression. He must have been gripping it tightly all night. Unable to fall back asleep, he lay staring at the ceiling, thinking about his dream. A soft knock rattled the door. Ronin rolled over and grumbled, pulling the blanket up over his head.

Alex slipped on his boots and opened the door. Colin stood there looking annoyingly fresh and awake. Without a word, Alex stepped to the side to let him in. "I can't stay but a minute, but I thought you might like to know four of the night dock-workers disappeared last night. The Duchess has multiple units of guards looking into it for the moment." He nodded in Ronin's direction. "Did your friend happen to come across anything last night while he was prowling?"

"I don't know. We haven't had a chance to debrief yet."

Colin nodded. "If you do find anything, my daughter will be at the market. Give her a message, and she'll make sure I get it. Or you can always stop by the Folly. My wife is usually around." He collected his spear leaning against the wall outside, and left.

Alex closed the door with a soft click. He hadn't heard him move, but Ronin stood by the window, silently watching the street below.

"Why do you trust them so easily?" Ronin's words were bitter, icy, and clipped.

"Where did that come from?" He asked, confused by the venom in Ronin's voice.

"Why do you trust them?" he repeated, ignoring Alex's question.

"Why don't you? They want the same thing we do."

"Do they?" He turned from the window and stalked toward Alex. "How much do you really know about your precious duchess?" Ronin growled.

"Ronin, what are you talking about? Where is this coming from?" Alex fought to keep his tone even. "She's the king's sister. Colin is her guard. They are trying to find the missing people… same as we are."

"Are they? Korynna is the one behind the missing people, Alex. She also has a whole smuggling operation going on. You were right that she was protecting Foxglove, because she *is* Foxglove."

"What! You're mistaken."

"Am I? I followed her last night, down to the docks." He paced the room angrily. "She met with several shady individuals. They opened hidden compartments in the ships full of crates, boxes, and even a few people. PEOPLE, Alex! Like they were goods to be traded." He faced Alex, outrage written all over his features. "Why else do you think she was wearing commoner clothes when we met her, and she hauled us here when you recognized her?"

Alex shook his head. A dull ache was building at his temples and forehead. "There's got to be another explanation." He needed there to be.

"Why? You don't want to believe that your leaders would never do something so corrupt?" Ronin sneered. "You want to hold on to your innocent belief that they would never use their position of power for personal gain? Grow up, Alex. It might work that way in your little village, but this is the real world. Humans and Fae alike are greedy and power-hungry." He seethed and stalked across the room again.

"Just because you wish it differently doesn't make it so. Your dreams are just that. It is time you accept that this is the way things are, whether you like it or not." He raked his hands through his long hair. "She is using you. To what end, I haven't figured out yet, but I don't wish to stay long enough to find out." Ronin knelt and pulled out his bag from under the bed and set Alex's bag against the wall.

Alex couldn't breathe. He refused to believe Duchess Korynna would do any of that. Sure, some of the knights were corrupt, and the nobility seemed to look the other way if they weren't complicit, but they would never... Would they? And kidnapping people? No. He shook his head and met Ronin's glare with his own. "No, she wouldn't; you are mistaken. I'm staying. She promised to help find Bronach and the others. I believe her."

"Alex, that's what she wants you to believe," Ronin pleaded. His eyes implored Alex to listen to him.

"You're wrong, Ronin," Alex's voice was hard as he held his ground. Ronin had to be mistaken. He had to be. Alex didn't want to believe that the king's own sister was involved in slave trade. He didn't want to face that possibility.

Ronin frowned, shouldered his pack, and stalked to the door. "I won't stay here any longer. Stay if you like. You know how to get a hold of me if you change your mind."

"Ronin, don't be like that. Ronin!" Alex followed him to the top of the stairs and watched his companion stalk around the corner.

He sighed and leaned his forehead against the door frame, rubbing his temples. That was not how he'd imagined this morning to start. He hadn't even told Ronin about his too-real dream. Footsteps trod up the stairs. He looked up, hopeful Ronin had come to his senses and come back to talk through it. He couldn't help but let his shoulders slump in disappointment.

The laundry maid with her basket he'd met last night. "I know I'm not the most attractive person, but I don't usually get that reaction. Sometimes I'm met with loathing and curses, but disappointment? That's a new one."

He cringed. "I'm sorry, it's not you. I just thought…"

"That your friend had come back to work out whatever you were fighting about?" She finished for him.

He looked up sharply. "How did you know that?"

"I pay attention, and it's hard to miss two angry men in a lover's quarrel."

"We're not lovers."

She raised an eyebrow, then dipped her head. "As you say. Your clothes are done. Shall I lay them out for you?" She moved to enter the room.

"No, it's okay. I can dress myself."

"It's no trouble."

"Tell me, you know Duchess Korynna better than I? Do you think she is capable of nefarious deeds?" he said as he moved to let her through the doorway.

"I think our duchess is capable of a great many things. It's her station to make decisions that seem less than favorable to us common people but have far-reaching consequences."

"But what about kidnapping and…"

"She's not behind the missing people, if that's what you are asking," she said quietly. After a pause, she said, "She instructed me to escort you to her, whenever you are ready."

"But I don't have her items from Alyse yet. I'm supposed to pick them up from her this morning."

"We can stop by there on the way, if that is acceptable to you. Though we don't want to keep her waiting."

Alex nodded then gestured for her to exit. "If you don't mind, I'll change into these before we go."

She looked at his attire. "You don't look like a local or a knight." Alex gave her a strange look.

"Is she in the habit of inviting locals and knights to stay in her secret apartments? I'm Alex, by the way."

She tilted her head to the side then stepped out the door. "Change quickly, Alex By-the-way. Such an odd title that..." she trailed off with a smirk as she closed the door.

Alex changed quickly and stowed his extra clothing and weapons under the mattress again. He hesitated to leave the "not rock" here again. He walked to the door then, at the last minute, retrieved it out of his pack and slid it into his pocket before stepping back over to the door.

She appraised him before turning to walk down the steps without a word. Hurriedly, he locked the door and ran down the steps, taking them two at a time. Something had been nagging at the back of his mind since yesterday. She didn't act like a servant. Who was she?

As he followed behind her, he noted her confident, fluid stride. They turned a corner onto a familiar street. They were nearing Artisan Row, as he'd been informed it was called last night.

He stayed a step behind her, pretending to take in his surroundings as he watched her. She moved with an intentionality that reminded him of Ronin. He stopped abruptly as an icy chill trickled down his back. The way she moved reminded him of Ronin.

A warrior. A predator.

His mind replayed their conversation about Nightshade at the Folly last night. "You don't find her, she finds you," they had said. Suddenly, he wasn't so sure she was taking him to see Korynna.

"Hey Ronin."

"Are you ready to admit you are wrong?"

"No. Are you?"

"No."

"But…"

"I don't think we have anything to talk about."

"Fine."

"Fine!"

Alex let out a frustrated breath. He was on his own. *Well, she found me;* he thought as he resumed walking. This was what he wanted, right? He would prove Korynna's innocence to Ronin.

XXX

CHAPTER 31

WHEN they arrived at the Salty Rose, Alex quickly ducked inside. He took a deep breath and let it out slowly to steady his nerves and racing heart. Alyse watched him curiously from her workstation.

"You... are early," she commented. "I'm not quite finished yet, but if you would be a dear and deliver a letter for me, I should have enough time to finish."

"I... um," Alex hesitated.

Alyse smiled knowingly. "You can use the back. I'll distract Talia for a while."

"Talia?"

She chuckled. "The young lady with the basket outside. The one you are currently hiding from..." she trailed off. Her eyes danced with humor.

"Thank you!" Alex breathed out a deep sigh.

She handed him a small scroll tied with a red velvet ribbon and sealed with the same rose insignia from the sign out front. "Take this to Maywind at the Clever Potter in the market. She'll give you something to bring back for me."

He tucked it into the inside pocket of his jacket and headed for the back. Just then, the front door opened and the little bell chimed. "Ah, hello my dear, Grace!" She greeted the young girl warmly with a hug and handed her a small package.

"Good morning, Alyse. Mama and Papa send their thanks and regards." Grace smiled shyly.

"Grace, this is Alex. Alex, Grace. He's new in town and still getting his bearings. Would you mind so much taking him by the market to Maywind's shop?"

Grace bobbed a little curtsy and blushed as she noticed Alex for the first time. She gaped at him until Alyse cleared her throat. "Oh, um, yes. I am to meet Lily and Rachel at the market anyway." Her blush deepened.

Alex looked away, uncomfortable with the doe-eyed way she gazed at him. Alyse gave Grace a firm nudge toward the door. "Send Talia in, would you? Please?"

Alex followed Grace out the front door and stepped aside as Talia stalked past him. She refused to meet his eyes, annoyance palpably radiating from her. He wondered if she'd heard their conversation from out here.

Grace strolled in nervous silence as she led them to the market. She fiddled with the edge of her package and occasionally opened her mouth to speak, blushed, then closed it again. Alex didn't know how to handle the awkward situation, so he remained silent and hoped it would ease or be over soon.

Throngs of people joined them on their trek to the market. As they drew near, delicious aromas teased him, making his mouth water. The smell of freshly baked bread, hay, animals, fish, spices, and flowers wafted around him, mixing with the salty sea air.

Brightly colored banners and streamers waved and snapped in the breeze. Minstrels playing instruments while shop owners called out their wares. Children chased each other, winding through legs and under carts and around stalls, tables, and blankets ladened with everything imaginable. If something could be traded, he surmised he would find it here.

He saw a familiar figure, Colin's daughter, Rachel, standing with another girl about her age, and a slightly older boy. He looked half asleep and bored. She caught sight of them a moment later and waved to Grace before saying something to the girl next to her. She must be Lily. They hurried over to Alex and Grace.

"Who's your new boyfriend?" Lily asked Grace.

Grace's face turned a bright shade of red as she stammered, "He's not my boyfriend. Alyse asked me to show him the market."

"Oh, well, if you don't have dibs, do you mind if I claim him?" Lily grabbed Alex's arm and looped it through hers possessively.

Alex cleared his voice as he gently tried to free his arm. "Excuse me, M'lady, I really must complete my task and be on my way back."

"But you just got here." Lily pouted and held his arm with a surprisingly strong vise grip. "I bet you've never been to a market like this one. I can show you all the best parts."

"You are correct in that I have never seen, much less been to, a market such as this."

"Well, it's settled then. You are coming with us."

"Really, I can't…"

"Lily, that's one of my papa's friends. I don't think your father would be pleased," Rachel commented.

"Are you betrothed or have a special someone?" Lily looked up at Alex through her dark lashes.

"No, but I…"

"See, no harm done," she interrupted, dragging him further into the market.

"Devin, say something!" Rachel demanded.

"Does this mean I can go back to bed?" he asked hopefully.

"Devin, you're no help. And no. Papa would be angry if he found out you left us."

Whatever Devin responded, Alex missed because Lily pulled into a tightly packed shop.

"Here, taste this. It is so good!" Lily said sensually, as she stuffed something sticky and sweet in his mouth.

It was good; a buttery, flaky roll dripping with honey. He felt trapped and helpless. He could wrench himself free of her but risked hurting her or drawing unwanted attention; which he would rather not do if at all possible, so he went along with it. He'd been in much more uncomfortable situations before. He could handle this.

He wondered where Ronin was. As Bucephalus, he'd always seemed at ease in these types of situations and enjoyed the attention.

Alex spent the rest of the morning being dragged from stall to stall, tasting various foods and beverages, and looking at the various trinkets and wares. The three girls went into every shop and stall, Lily never letting go of his arm or hand. Devin trailed behind them in resigned silence, uninterested in anything the market had to offer.

"Which stall do your parents run?" Alex asked Devin.

He glared at Alex in surprise. "Not my parents. My aunt and uncle, and that one." He pointed to a large booth, overflowing with a rainbow of colorful bolts of cloth. "How did you know?" He narrowed his gaze warily, truly taking in Alex for the first time. His eyes stayed on the hilt of Alex's sword sticking up over his shoulder..

"It was a guess. Only someone who grew up coming here regularly could be disinterested in all the wonders this place offers."

Devin nodded, not taking his eyes off Alex's sword. "Lily, I think it is time to let him go on his way." Devin's voice took on an icy tone. "You've had your fun."

"But Deviiiinnn," Lily whined.

"Now Lily, or we are going home." Something in his tone must have gotten through to her and told her he was serious because she let out a huff and reluctantly let go of Alex's arm.

Lily, Grace, and Rachel watched Devin and Alex, concern etched on their features.

"It has been my pleasure to explore the market with you ladies, but I really must complete my task and return to Alyse." Alex dipped his head and met each of their eyes.

Grace blushed again when his eyes met hers, then turned away. Rachel raised an eyebrow but said nothing. Lily was still pouting like she had just lost her favorite toy. "I hope to see you around again." Devin herded them away toward his aunt and uncle's stall.

Alex sighed and shook his head after they left and looked around to get his bearings. He finally spied a sign that said "Clever Potter." The cool, earthy smell of clay greeted him as he entered. A tall, slender man wearing a colorful apron stood behind a wooden table, wrapping a large bowl in an old sackcloth. He secured it with twine, gave it to the waiting couple, and bid them farewell. They nodded to Alex on their way out.

"Can I help you find something specific?" The shopkeeper asked in a heavily accented voice.

"I'm here to see Maywind," Alex replied, pulling out the scroll and holding it up. "Alyse sent me to deliver this to her."

"Oh, she is just in the back throwing more bowls. I will fetch her for you." He disappeared behind a tan curtain and reappeared a moment later. "She said to send you on back. Please, do be careful not to break anything," he said as he held the curtain back for Alex to step through.

Alex walked down a narrow hallway lined with pottery in various stages of completion, careful not to bump into anything. The hallway opened into a small, fenced yard with a large kiln in the center. A lanky woman sat at a potter's wheel off to the side. She tilted her head and sized him up as he walked towards her; her hands never stopped moving and shaping the clay.

"Can you read?" she asked in a reedy voice.

"Pardon?"

"Yes or no? But given your response, I'd assume yes," she said as she dipped a hand in a muddy water bucket next to her and continued to mold and shape the mound of clay on her wheel.

"Um... yes?"

"Did you already read it?" she asked, her voice accusatory.

"No, of course not!"

She chuckled. "No, I don't suppose you did or I suspect you wouldn't be here. Read it to me."

Suddenly, he was grateful his mother had insisted he learn and made him read every night before bed. He cleared his throat, broke the seal, and read out loud:

Greetings Maywind,

I hope this finds you well. Your last shipment was exquisite. Please accept the bearer of this letter as my thanks and payment.

~ Alyse

Alex coughed and read it twice more in his head. What did she mean? He looked up at Maywind in confusion. Her eyes sparkled as she grinned at him.

"Have you had a midday meal?"

"Pardon?" Alex gaped back and forth from her to the page. He was the bearer of the letter. She couldn't possibly mean... Could she?

"Have you eaten, yes or no?" she said impatiently. "Gerald, would you please set another place setting? We have a guest," she called out.

"She didn't... but I... I don't understand."

"It's alright dear, Alyse has offered your assistance to me. Not to worry, we'll eat first." She waved him over to a low table, surrounded by cushions and set with mugs and plates and bowls filled with fruit, green leaves, and fish.

"I'll be finished shortly, and Gerald will just close up the front then will join us. Please have a seat."

He did as he was told. He marveled as she turned a mound of soggy, grey clay into a small bowl with a wavy rim. She removed it from the wheel with a small wire, then set it aside, next to other similar bowls on a stone tray. She opened the large kiln door and carefully slid the tray inside.

Gerald emerged from the back of the shop, bearing another bowl and plate filled with fruit and fish, and set them down in front of Alex. "I'm Gerald, as you may have heard. Welcome to our table." He sat across from Alex, folding his long legs and crossing them under the table. He offered Alex a jug of fruit juice after pouring some into the third cup, presumably for Maywind.

Maywind washed her hands then picked up her bowl of fish. Alex watched quizzically as she took several pieces and placed them in a small dish on a raised pedestal. She repeated the process with her bowl of fruit.

"She is making an offering to Zamin, one of our gods, for protection and prosperity as we do every meal," he said by way of explanation.

Maywind sat and nodded. Gerald began to eat and gestured to Alex to do the same. The fish was delicious. It was smoky and sweet and had a hint of tartness. He was about to ask how they prepared it when a shadow passed over them. A large, familiar black falcon landed on the pedestal and snapped up pieces of the offering.

"*Ronin? What are you doing?*"

Maywind and Gerald gasped.

"*Oh, hey, Alex, what does it look like I'm doing? I'm eating,*" he said as he snatched another piece of fish from the dish. "*This is really good! Have you tried this yet?*"

"*You can't eat that! It's their offering to their god.*"

Ronin shrugged a very unbird-like shrug. "*Oh, are you going to eat that? Thanks.*" Ronin flew over to perch on Alex's arm and ate the fish from his bowl as well.

"*Hey, that's mine. What are you even doing here?*"

"I could ask you the same thing."

"I'm running an errand for Alyse and now I'm eating lunch before I help these two."

Ronin made a sound like a bird's version of a chuckle. He bobbed his head to Alex's two companions, then took off into the sky. *"Talk later, gotta fly."*

"Ronin? Ronin!" He sighed at his mostly empty bowl.

"The gods have found favor with you!" Gerald gasped in awe.

"Zamin has blessed us!" Maywind looked pleased.

Alex finished what was left of his food. Gerald cleared away the dishes while Maywind led Alex aside and handed him a small, painted clay figurine of a rearing horse. "I need this delivered to Calamine at the royal livery, if you would be so kind?"

"I..."

"Thank you for joining us for lunch." She sat at her wheel again and prepared to make more pottery. He was clearly dismissed.

Alex found the royal livery, The Golden Shoe, easily enough. It was hard to miss the giant golden horseshoe hanging on the corner just off the main square. The market was still bustling with people, so the sudden quiet of the stable was a welcome relief.

He wasn't used to so many people in one place. Several times he had almost dropped the figurine when he had been jostled roughly in the crowd.

"Can I help you?" a delicate female voice called out from the stall to his left.

"Hi, Maywind sent me to deliver this." He held up the figurine as he stepped to the open stall doorway.

"Put it over there on the shelf above the bridle hooks," she said without looking up from the horse's leg she was wrapping a bandage around.

He did as he was told and walked to the door to leave when her voice stopped him. "Where do you think you are going? I need you to fetch some bits from Embers."

"Where is Embers?" He attempted to keep the frustration out of his voice. He felt like he'd been sent on a wild goose chase instead of what should have been a simple errand for the duchess. Why did these people presume he was there to run their errands, too? He would never hear the end of it from Ronin.

"Embers isn't a where, they are a who. Don't they teach you anything? Honestly, I can't do everything myself. I won't." She sighed.

"I'm not…" he started.

"The Iron Crucible. Now, stop wasting my time. Go and hurry back," she interrupted with a clipped tone.

Alex sighed and trudged out the door. He had no idea where to even begin looking for this Iron Crucible. Back out on the street, he looked for signs or markers for the Iron Crucible.

He ran into Colin making rounds. "Hey, Alex, what has you over here?"

"I'm looking for the Iron Crucible. I'm supposed to ask someone named Embers for bits to take back to the Golden Shoe, so I can go back to the Salty Rose to pick up something for Her Highness, the Duchess." He sighed and shook his head.

Colin chuckled. "Ah! Oh, I heard you escorted my daughter and friends to the market earlier this morning. Thank you for that. I apologize for Devin. He can be a bit overprotective sometimes."

"It was not a problem. I enjoyed getting a look around the market."

Colin's name was called from down the street. "Well, I need to go. Keep going down this road 'til you see the Rusty Rooster Inn, then take a left and follow that lane to the end. You'll smell and hear it long before you see it. Can't miss it."

"Thank you!"

Alex followed his directions, and a few hours later, he finally found it. It was a large, open-sided building with a billowing forge in the center. Weapons, shields, and various pieces of metal were strewn about in piles, on racks, tables, and workbenches in all stages of completion. Several silver pieces, delicate and decorative, as well as larger pieces, lay on a different workstation.

A sandy-haired youth ran back and forth from the bellows to the fire and back again. He was struggling to keep the fire hot enough while he tried to work the metal.

"Here, let me help," Alex offered to take over the bellows for the lad.

"Oh, T'anks very much. I was having a bit of a go wif it." He pulled a chunk of metal out of the fire and beat it wildly with a hammer.

Alex watched as the lad warped and bent the piece of metal haphazardly. Clearly, this lad was an apprentice, and a new one at that. Alex cringed as the tongs slipped from the boy's hands, dropping the red-hot piece of metal on a small pile of straw. It instantly caught on fire.

Alex released the bellows and grabbed a nearby bucket of dirt to throw on the fire before it spread further. He stamped out the remaining embers.

"M' names Grogan."

"Alex." He nodded to him while he made sure the fire was completely out.

"Pleasure! You seem to know your way around a forge."

"Yeah, I grew up around one. I always liked the peace and the methodical routine of it."

"Mmm yeah, I know what you mean. Like you know what is expected, and you just do it. Once you get the hang of it, that is..." Grogan blushed with embarrassment and dug his toe into the dirt floor.

"We've been getting a lot more orders since the master blacksmith went missing. He always wins the Artisan's Festival competition, but this year he didn't show. Nobody seems to know what happened to him. He just vanished. Like a lot of other people seem to lately. Nessa said people are disappearing left and right and the guard don't even know who dun it."

"Who's Nessa?"

"Oh, she's the kitchen girl who lives next door to me. She's nice. She brings me the burned or singed bread they normally throw out. I don't mind singed bread. Everything tastes burnt to me after a full day here, anyway."

"Here, do it this way." Alex changed Grogan's grip on the tongs.

"Oh, that's much better. T'anks! Saul says I need to pay attention better when he is instructing me, but he always chooses to tell me the important bits when Cam is doing the interesting things with silver. It's so captivating. I can't help it. Saul wants me to choose him and do blacksmith work, but Cam's work is always so pretty. I don't want to make horseshoes all my life, ya know what I mean? Don't get me wrong, it's good, honest work... Or so my papa says. He says it'll keep me out of trouble. I can't help but wish I could be more than just a farrier, day in and day out. That's where Saul is now. He went to the livery to deliver some bits and shoe one of the warhorses."

"The livery? As in the Golden Shoe?" Alex asked, irritated.

"Yeah, why?"

"Never mind. So you are not Embers?"

Grogan laughed. "Not exactly. But I'm training to be. Saul and Cam won't be back 'til tomorrow, so whatever you need from them will have to wait."

"So what is Embers, anyway?"

"Oh, I thought you knew," he laughed and genuinely seemed happy to have something he could teach someone else. "Embers is a code name for us in a network of contacts. We help make sure the right things or information get to the right person."

Alex tried not to look too interested in case the lad clammed up. But Grogan seemed happy to have someone to listen to him. "So if I wanted to send a message to the Clever Potter for instance, who would I address it to?"

"Shards, of course. If you needed to send a message to Nails, that's Kit at the Golden Shoe. She can get a message to anyone."

"Kit doesn't seem to like me."

"What makes you say that?"

"She didn't even look at me."

"Oh no, she's just like that. It's nothing personal. I think she is aiming for a promotion."

"What about Nightshade and Foxglove?"

"No one wants to send a message to Nightshade. It's better for you if they don't know you exist. And no one sends a message to Foxglove. Very few people have even seen them and know who they are." His voice took on a tone of awe and reverence.

"Foxglove started this whole thing. It's rumored that they take in all the strays or relocate them if they want to." He dropped his voice to barely audible. "I've even heard they recruit shabbies from prisons and save some meant for execution. Word is, if you are in line for hanging or execution, get a message to Foxglove's network, our network. And someone will come to review your plight, and maybe they'll spring you." He puffed up his chest proudly.

"I heard Foxglove has a ghost ship that feeds on the souls of the dead, and if you catch a glimpse of it, your soul is forfeit. It sails on the mists and clouds at night." He straightened and looked at the setting sun. "Oh, I must close up here and be off before the sun sets! Nice to meet you, Alex. See you around."

"I need to be going too. Nice to meet you as well, Grogan."

"Oh, hey wait. What did you need with Saul and Cam anyway?"

"Oh, nothing. Thanks." Alex walked quickly back the way he came, needing to get back to the Salty Rose before nightfall. He didn't bother going back to the Golden Shoe or the Clever Potter. He was starting to wonder if he had been set up to meet people in this network. Clever.

Alex arrived at her shop as the sun was sinking low in the sky. Alyse was just finishing wrapping something when the little bell on the door announced his arrival. He had a burning question to ask Alyse.

"Ah, here you are. Perfect timing. Thank you so much. I expect your efforts were fruitful?" She handed him several packages and held open a large brown sack for him to carry them in.

"You could say that." He blew out a breath of frustration.

Her eyes sparkled. "Good. I believe Duchess Korynna will be most pleased." She nodded to him and turned to put away bolts of fabric.

He noticed the red and black formal attire was no longer on the racks they had been on earlier and found he was a little disappointed. Not that he could afford it or had anything to wear it to. He looked at her, weighing if he should ask his question.

"I can't read your mind, you know, Alex of Creedon. Speak your mind."

"Are you Foxglove?"

"Oh, dear me, heavens no!" she chuckled after a moment of surprise. "I can see why you would think that though. No, I'm Needles." Her smile grew into a grin. "I believe many of your questions will be answered soon. It was nice to meet you Alex. If you need anything tailored or mended, I do hope you'll come to me first. It was a delight working with you." She ushered him to the door and closed and locked it behind him.

"Finally!" Talia materialized in front of him. "Let's go!"

He flinched in surprise. Hesitantly, he followed her to a storage warehouse meant for keeping shipments before they are loaded onto the boats.

She unlatched the door and slid it open, stepping aside for him to enter. He paused a few steps through the doorway to let his eyes adjust. The interior was much darker than outside, even in the dimming light. Her basket rammed into his back, sending him tumbling in the darkness. Disoriented, he rolled over on his side and began to stand when he felt the prick of cold metal against his neck.

"I'd stay still if I were you. I would hate to mar that pretty face of yours." Talia's voice had lost its soft, lilting accent and took on a hard, commanding edge. He held perfectly still.

"*Uh… Hey Ronin!*" His voice sounded strained even in his own mind. "*I could use some backup, please.*"

"*Where are you?*" Ronin's voice sounded tense. Something in Alex's voice must have told him something was wrong because he didn't demand Alex admit he was right.

"*Down in the last warehouse, on the left of the main harbor.*"

"*I'll be right there, I'm not far.*"

"*Oh, and Ronin, I think I found Nightshade.*" Ronin let out a string of sounds, and what Alex could only guess were curse words and expletives. He kicked himself for not listening to his instincts. *Why did I follow her here?*

"Talia? What's going on?" He could make out her silhouette from the dimming light coming through the large door. The setting sun blinded him to everything else through the open doorway.

"If you so much as breathe the wrong way, I will slit your throat," she said in a low voice. "Tie him up," she said slightly louder.

Hands roughly pulled his arms behind his back. The blade was removed from his neck. Their mistake. He kicked his legs out and sent himself crashing into the person behind him, then rolled over them, pulling his dagger free from its place on his calf in the process.

He reached for his sword on his back, but it was missing. The figure on the floor before him grunted, then rose quickly, pulling out their own blades.

They wove in and out of piles of crates and burlap sacks as they fought until something slammed into his chest, knocking him to the ground and driving the air from his lungs. He heard four snicks and found his arms and legs pinned to the ground.

His chest heaved as he tried to catch his breath. Where she had come from? One minute she was standing by the door watching, the next she'd stepped out of the shadows. She stood over him and made a show of testing his sword's balance. She picked up his daggers and looked at them appreciatively before they disappeared into folds in her clothes.

Three figures joined her and his opponent. The four of them hoisted him from the ground and tied his arms behind him and his ankles together. She stepped forward and relieved him of his other two daggers and emptied his pockets. When she pulled out the "not rock," it flashed in the light from the still-open door reflecting off it. She stared at it, unmoving for a long time.

"Nightshade, what are your orders?" one of his assailants asked.

She blinked and looked up with a dazed look on her face, then dropped the "not rock." It clattered on the floor. She turned on her heel and walked to the door. She glanced over her shoulder, then nodded once. They pulled a hood over his head and something sharp pricked his neck. Everything went dark.

CHAPTER 32

RONIN reveled in the wind as it buffeted him and sent him soaring high above the city. Alex drove him crazy like no one else. For all his 150 years, what was it about this human that affected him so? How could Alex be so blind and trusting? Always willing to see the best in everyone. Ronin hated to admit it, even to himself, but it was also what made Alex so endearing. Had he ever been that unjaded and innocent? He shook his head. No. His father had seen to that. Everything came at a price. No one was as they seemed. Everyone wanted something from you. Smiles, gifts, and pretty words hid deceit and selfish ambition.

He hated it.

He hated politics, always had. His father had wanted him to join the court, to be someone powerful's personal assistant. Something or the other that would let his father spy on his opponents. When it was his turn in rotation to learn military tactics, he had been thrilled when it came naturally. Just like his magic. He could see strategies and maneuvers clearly like he never had with political endeavors.

The thought of being limited to small house magic or minor architecture made his blood boil. He smirked. He remembered the look on his instructor's face when he had grown a full tree, rather than the delicate weaving he'd been instructed. He loved that tree; loved the feel of the dirt and rocks as they slid along his magic; loved the thrill of growing complex and sprawling tree systems. It sang to him, called to him.

He missed Osrealach and its wild, lush beauty. He missed the clean air, practically humming with magic, with life. Reyall was nothing like that, and it tormented him for these last twenty years. Ten years left in his exile, or there were until he had followed Alex and the two fairy children through the waterfall. Now, he suspected he could never go back. And for what? Whom.

For Alex. And given the choice, he'd do it all over again.

Ronin's sharp falcon eyes caught the glint of fish scales just below the surface of the water. He wheeled and dove for it before he realized what he'd done. He banked steeply and rose aloft once more.

Focus. If he wasn't careful, the natural instincts of his falcon form would creep up on him and make shifting to anything else really difficult and eventually impossible. He couldn't stay in this form too long. This one was especially challenging for him because he didn't have the earth and trees to ground him, reminding him of who he was.

Every Puka family had stories of family members who stayed in one of their forms too long, either intentionally or unintentionally, and never shifted back, eventually losing all sentience.

There had been a time that he had tried, even welcomed that fate, but he couldn't settle on which one to be, so he had switched back and forth for a time until he met Bronach. He owed everything to Bronach. He had helped him start to heal. He had given him purpose, something to focus on, and this person he now called a friend. This infuriating, reckless, ridiculous, stubborn, headstrong man that he'd been traveling with these last 5 years. This strong, gentle, warm, kind, compassionate, funny... he needed to focus. Right. Focus. He forced all thoughts of Alex out of his mind and made himself focus.

Ah, there they were. A group of dancers and musicians came to town, which was not really odd, but something seemed off about them and it was bothering him. He landed on the edge of a building and watched as three men unloaded a barrel off their wagon and carried it into a squat, stubby building, not much more than a shack squished between two larger buildings. *What are they doing? What is in that building?*

A youthful voice called out in fear. What *were* they doing? The voice cut off with a dull thump. Moments later, the three men rolled the same barrel back out onto the street and loaded it into their wagon. A moment after they disappeared back into the building, he swore he heard more thuds coming from the barrel. If it weren't for the iron bands around it, he would have just asked it to open. *Curse these humans and their iron on everything!* He needed to get a closer look.

"*Uh... Hey, Ronin!*" Alex. He sounded strained and... was that fear? "*I could use some backup, please.*"

Icy dread slithered down his spine. "*Where are you?*"

"*Down in the last warehouse, on the left of the main harbor.*"

What was he doing there? "*I'll be right there. I'm not far.*" He wasn't really all that close, on the other side of the city, to be precise. What could he have possibly gotten himself into now?

"*Oh, and Ronin, I think I found Nightshade.*"

Ronin swore with every word and phrase he knew and even made up a few. She was not someone Alex could beat in a fair fight, or even an unfair one. The way shadows seemed to envelop her as she moved. Even Ronin hadn't mastered her level of silence and stealth. Guardians! Why couldn't he have convinced Alex to walk away from Korynna and this whole mess?

Everything blurred as he flew faster than he'd ever flown before. He didn't believe in gods or deities, but he found himself praying to anything that might listen he'd get there in time. If anything happened to Alex, he didn't know what he'd do.

He swooped into the warehouse from an open hatch in the ceiling and shifted to his panther form just before he landed soundlessly in the rafters.

"*Alex!*" he called in his mind. "*I'm here, Alex. Where are you?*"

He scented the air; his heightened senses of his panther form told him the only beating heart in this warehouse was his. Silently, he dropped to the floor and prowled around overturned crates, boxes, a shredded net, and splinters of something. Alex had been here recently, but he wasn't here now. Based on the scents all over the room, Alex had put up quite a fight and hadn't gone quietly, Ronin was sure of it.

He found Alex's favorite little blade he normally kept hidden in the small of his back, buried to the hilt in a crate. Ronin shifted so he could pry the blade out and slipped it into his pocket. He stalked the warehouse again, making sure he didn't miss anything. He growled in frustration. Anguish threatened to overwhelm him. Alex was his friend, his brother, and he'd not been here to protect him again.

A shard of stone glinted on the floor. Ronin picked it up. He knew this stone; he'd held it once before. The guardian stone. Mixed feelings swirled in him as he knelt to pick up four more pieces. Alex would never give this up willingly.

How did it break? What had happened? Where was he now? Helplessness, fear, old pain, and deep anguish coursed through him–feelings he had been stuffing down and rigorously holding in check were no longer held in check.

His vision blurred as a memory overwhelmed his senses.

Ronin munched on sweet grass by the river as Alex and McCannon practiced on the ridge above. He snorted at a blade of grass tickling his nose as he contemplated going hunting while they practiced. Suddenly, the edge of the ridge gave way in an avalanche of dirt and rock. Alex yelled as he plunged into the river below.

Ronin watched for Alex to resurface. Something was wrong. He should have resurfaced by now. He must have hit his head or gotten caught on something. Ronin looked to McCannon to intervene, but McCannon raced away from the edge to the trail leading down to the water. He would never make it in time. The trail to the river was steep with several switchbacks that required caution to traverse.

Ronin glanced around once more, then dove into the water, shifting as he went. The icy water bit his skin as he searched the murky river for Alex. There. Alex's armor was caught on a submerged tree limb. Ronin launched himself forward and yanked Alex free. His lungs ached for air as he kicked to the surface, dragging Alex with him. He pulled him out of the water and checked to make sure he was breathing, then shifted back into Bucephalus.

Alex sat up, coughing the last of the water from his lungs. His eyes landed on Ronin. Ronin froze. Had Alex seen him shift?

Ronin took a deep breath. Unsettled, he felt like he'd been back there, as if it had happened all over again. His vision blurred again as he felt himself pulled into another memory.

Ronin paced next to the campfire, attempting and failing to not worry about Alex. He had never seen Alex react like that before. His fight with Quinn earlier that night had surprised him.

Quinn hadn't said another word and gone directly to bed, but Ronin could see Alex's words had hit their mark. He had refused to look Ronin in the eye, so he let Quinn work it out on his own. Quinn looked conflicted. What was it about Alex that made people question everything? Ronin had watched Quinn grow and train with singular focus Quinn's entire life and had even trained the younger puka himself. Never once had he seen even a hint of anything other than sheer determination and grit.

He paced all night, playing the conversation and the events leading up to this fight over and over in his mind. Quinn woke unconcerned Alex had not come back yet and left to hunt for breakfast.

Ronin sighed. Alex should have been back by now. He decided to go look for him, his worries getting the better of him. He worried more fairies had captured him, or he'd fallen into an old trap forgotten and left from a time long past, or some other terrible fate. Alex loved the water, he would have gone to the sea. As he jogged lightly to the beach, he tried and failed to convince himself Alex had just fallen asleep watching the stars.

His steps faltered. A dark figure lay half out of the water, unmoving. His heart pounded in his ears as he sprinted down the shore, contemplating shifting to a faster form. He kicked himself for not coming sooner. How could he be so stupid? He would never forgive himself if he was too late. As Ronin drew closer, he knew for certain the prone form on the beach was Alex.

He slid to his knees in the sand and turned Alex on his side. He was breathing, barely, but it was there. What had happened? He hoisted Alex onto his shoulders and carried him back to camp, hating the *helpless feeling surging through him. Not Alex. He couldn't bear to lose him too.*

Ronin felt the memory fade, but the emotions remained. He was just getting to his feet when another, much older memory forced him to his knees.

He stood on the crest of the hill with his back to camp, his camp, his unit. Men and women who looked to him to make the right decisions and make sure they came home after all this. He had studied human warfare and their bloody wars and excessive need for death and bloodshed. The Fae had long since found other ways to fight their wars without anyone dying.

Any day now, messengers should arrive announcing the completion of the peace negotiations. His orders were to hold this ridge until told otherwise. He spied movement in the trees down below. The minotaur would be crazy to attack. He looked again, and there they were. Brightly visible and scaling the base of the ridge with torches in each of their hands. He bristled. They brought fire with them? He recognized one, a renowned Ardere with powerful fire magic. They meant to burn the whole forest down around them?

Over my dead body! But the peace talks? Had they failed? He signaled for his unit to ready themselves to fight. Their questions flooded his mind, but he shut them out. They would defend this ridge and its forest as they had been ordered.

Flash forward…

Ronin knelt in the grass with the bodies of his unit strewn around him interspersed between the bodies of the opposing minotaur. Their faces twisted in charred anguish. The histories would say this was a victory but with too high a cost. All for what? Tears for his slain comrades and friends streaked down his face as his shoulders shook in silent sobs.

He dried his face and quieted his breathing when he heard muffled footsteps approaching. The council guard picked their way around the bodies and still smoldering trees and charred boulders. His father was with them, surveying everything with a grim look. His unreadable gaze met Ronin's.

Ronin's pain and grief only deepened when his father pointed to him and said, "Restrain the Bacia."

Death bringer.

Ronin shuddered and gripped the pieces of the guardian stone as the second memory faded. He braced himself for more, but none came. Breathing deeply to calm his emotions, he fiddled with the pieces until he could make out the inscription.

"What you wish will be reflected.
What you are will be revealed.
The pure of heart hold the key
To that which has been sealed."

Odd riddle. His father never told him there was an inscription on it. Did he even know? Bitterness and resentment rose to the surface of his raw emotions. His father had pinned all the deaths on him. He'd made it seem like Ronin had instigated the battle. His own father! For what? A seat on the council? He hated this stupid rock. It reminded him of his father's obsession and lack of presence in Ronin's childhood.

Bitterly, Ronin thought about throwing the pieces into the ocean where his father could never find them. He didn't see why everyone made such a big deal over it? It was just a rock. Even so, Alex was fond of it. He had even clutched it in his sleep last night.

Instead, Ronin calmed his mind and reached for the quiet place where his magic resided. He looked closely at the stone in his hands like he did anything he wanted to mend. He expected to see the minerals of what it was made of, intent on coaxing them to link back together, but that wasn't what he found. It pulsed and flowed and shifted, not wholly there. It moved like water or molten rock, yet felt solid in his hands. He blinked and shook his head.

"Is this what you truly wish?"

A strange yet familiar voice filled his head and resonated through him. *"What?"*

"This path you would choose. Is this what you want?"

"I don't know this path from another."

"That is true. I will show you."

Colors, sounds, and smells whirled around him, sweeping him up, suspended and weightless. Scene after scene, picture after picture, and place after place washed over him. He tried to make sense of it, but was overwhelmed.

"You have seen but a fraction of what could be. Will you still choose it?"

"I don't understand what I saw, but this is not for me. It's...his," he felt the truth of his words resonate through him, freeing something in him he didn't realize had been there at all.

"You would choose this path for him, then?"

"I would never. He should be free to choose for himself."

"Wise words, Wandering One. You will find what you are searching for."

In a flash, everything faded. The surrounding stillness seemed to seep into his very soul and ease his raw emotions and something deeper.

He looked at the pieces in his hands once more. The edges glowed as they knit back together. Its black, glassy surface seemed to disappear. Tiny pinpricks of light, like starlight, sparkled up at him like the night sky. He blinked, and it looked like an ordinary rock again.

CHAPTER 33

RONIN prowled through the darkness, his panther feet silent on the boards of the dock. He had followed Alex's scent to this dock yesterday, but had lost it to the wind. He spent the better part of the day watching the comings and goings of this particular dock and now tracked the low hum of voices moving steadily toward the end of the pier.

Why this dock, though? From what he could see, there was nothing special about the small merchant vessel anchored further out. A steady stream of boats ferried boxes and crates of trade goods back and forth, but there was nothing special about those either. He would know. He had inspected every inch of that ship. But something about this dock and these people had him convinced they were connected to Alex's abduction.

A dark figure carrying a lantern strode past him, completely unaware of how close they had come to him. He smiled wickedly, more a baring of teeth than a smile. His smile faded as he caught sight of their face and arm in a sling. It was one of the men from the tavern.

What had he said his name was? Will. He continued to watch as Will stopped beside a small rowboat and conversed with a hooded figure standing in the boat. They exchanged something. Ronin caught the glint of a dagger on the hooded figure's hip. He would recognize that hilt anywhere. He had stared at its twin for countless hours since Alex had given it to him.

This dagger had been forged by dragon's breath in the ancient halls. The twins were masters in their own right, and their skill was far above that of anyone else. The forge in the mountains of Thoria was ancient, a legend that predated anything even the master of histories could access. Only the dragons were old enough to remember who had carved those halls.

And now she had it.

Ronin watched from the shadows as Will strode back down the dock. The hooded figure cast off from the pier and rowed toward the merchant ship, but instead of stopping, they continued on further. Ronin lost sight of them as they rounded the end of the ship. He shifted to his falcon and launched into the air to follow.

He caught sight of them again, rowing steadily out to the edge of the harbor. He glided silently on the night breeze, careful not to cross in front of the moon and give himself away to his prey; he was aware that if someone looked up, they might note the oddity of a falcon hunting at night. Humans wouldn't think anything of it, but they weren't the ones he was concerned about.

As they rounded the rocks at the far edge of the harbor, Ronin noticed a large ship tucked into a small alcove. It was hard to make out exact details in the moonlight, but as he flew closer, he read its name, the *Oleander*.

He chanced landing on the mast as he watched the activity on the deck. A handful of sailors moved about the deck with ease and skill, but they made very little noise. He heard the barest murmur of voices in quiet exchange as the hooded figure climbed up the side of the ship. He tracked their movements to a door, presumably to the captain's quarters if this ship was like others. They disappeared inside.

He needed to find a way down there without drawing attention to himself. He could always shift to his otter form. It wasn't large or dangerous, and he generally got himself in more trouble than not with that one, but it seemed like the best choice. He shivered once, then concentrated.

It took him longer to shift for this one because admittedly, he practiced shifting to this one the least. Finally, after what felt like minutes, he scampered along the rigging and down to the deck. He hadn't figured out how to open the door yet, but he would improvise.

As luck would have it, a burly sailor with thickly corded muscles exited as he reached the door. He slipped through the open door before it slammed shut behind him. The corridor was dimly lit, but bright light shone from under the door at the end. He could hear voices as he peeked under the door.

"Send Rai and Diego on the next run. They did well on their last assignment, and I think they are ready. They could also use some time off ship, but as usual, have them followed."

"For their safety or ours?"

"Both."

"The other news I have…"

"Yes." There was a long pause. "Talia, what is it?"

"One of our raids was interrupted a couple of nights ago. I think it was the Phantom."

"That's not good. Are you sure?"

"No, but we never can be. They don't leave a calling card, but it fits their usual methods," Talia recited.

"I want you to go ahead with this next one, but set it up so if the Phantom does show, we'll be ready."

"It will be done."

Muffled footsteps shuffled toward the door. Ronin looked for somewhere to hide, but there wasn't anywhere. He opted to shift to himself and pulled his knife as he pressed himself against the wall. If he timed it right, he would catch them off guard just as they opened the door.

"Oh, Kor, the new one is awake."

"Okay, thank you. I'll handle him."

"Be careful with that one."

"Aren't I always?" Kor laughed.

"I'm serious. He didn't fight like a knight... just be careful, okay?"

"T., you worry too much, but thank you."

The door opened, and Ronin made his move. He darted in and held his blade to the hooded figure's throat as he wrapped his arm around her, but she ducked around his blade. She somersaulted across the floor and crouched, holding Alex's knife in one hand and a curved, wicked-looking dagger in the other. Out of the corner of his eye, he saw Korynna rise from a desk, cutlass outstretched. He contemplated using magic, but there were no plants or seeds, no living things he could manipulate. There were metals and stones, of course, but manipulating them took more concentration than he had to give at the moment.

He needed to incapacitate at least one of them in these close quarters. He could take two at once but not quietly, and he didn't need the entire ship coming to investigate. There was always retreat, but that wouldn't get him any answers and might hurt Alex since Korynna knew they were together.

They looked at him expectantly, waiting for his next move, he realized. He wanted to free Alex, but he also needed to stop their entire operation. He could straight up demand they release Alex. And then what? No. He needed to get them to reveal their hand.

"I won't let you get away with this." He cringed. It hadn't come out the way it sounded in his head.

"And what exactly am I supposed to be getting away with?" Korynna eyed him like she would a troublesome colt.

"You know what you are doing," he said stubbornly. What was he saying? This wasn't going at all like he wanted it to.

Korynna smirked and turned back toward her desk. She laid down her sword on the desk next to her in easy reach should she need it, but the message was clear. She didn't see him as a threat to her. That annoyed him more than he wanted to admit. He wasn't used to being dismissed by humans. Stuck up royals with an over-inflated sense of importance.

The need to prove to her he was a threat surprised him. *Get it together Ronin, you aren't a young initiate anymore. She is baiting you.* He forced himself to relax a bit and grinned what Alex called his predator grin. He lowered his hand holding his knife and relaxed his fighting stance a little.

Talia didn't move. She watched him like he was a viper, ready to strike at any moment. Smart. Ronin returned his attention back to Korynna. "Release Alex and all the rest of the people you have taken captive."

Her hands stilled and her shoulders stiffened, but she didn't turn towards him. "I can't do that," she said in a low voice.

"What has Alex done to you? You are the sister to your king, and he is a knight of your kingdom. Why would you do this?"

Slowly, she turned to face him and studied him with sharp eyes. "It's not what he has done, it is what he will do for me." She paused and tilted her head slightly, as if contemplating a puzzle. Finally, she said, "Where is your kingdom then, I wonder?"

Ronin froze and swore in his head. How could he be so careless? He had just single-handedly told her he wasn't from Reyall. Rookie move.

Korynna continued. "You're not from Keirwyn. Your bone structure and coloring are all wrong. And you have the wrong accent." She gestured to him. "So then where?" Her eyes widened then narrowed. "My brother was right. There is something else out there. Somewhere."

Talia cursed out loud.

"Where is it? How do you get there?" Korynna demanded.

Ronin's options just narrowed to two. Run and try to find Alex without getting caught, before they drag the information out of him, and hope they never found Osrealach. Or stay and fight and ensure these two can't tell anyone else. He thought of all the bodies lying around him on the battlefield, of children playing innocently, of the peace they had finally achieved after so long. He couldn't risk it. He refused to be the reason more people died. Another war started. Because there was no way humans invading Osrealach wouldn't start another war. They had to die. Now.

Something on his leg burned. He pulled the guardian stone from his pocket. It was glowing. It burned his hand, so he dropped it. Talia flinched. Flinched! Korynna watched with surprise. When it hit the floor, it didn't bounce or break; it turned into a pile of sand. Startled, he took a step back. All three stared at each other and the shrinking pile on the floor. Well, that was interesting.

"What is that?" Korynna breathed when it was apparent it wasn't an immediate threat.

"I don't... It's just..." *the hell?* Words seemed to be failing him today and now was no different.

"You?" Talia's question caught him off guard.

"What?" Ronin was confused.

"Talia, what is it?" Korynna's voice was softer with concern.

"That rock, it..." Talia seemed just as lost for words as Ronin was.

"*Ronin?*" Alex called in his mind.

"*Alex? Where are you? I'm coming to get you out! I'll get everyone out. I just need to kill Korynna and Talia first.*"

"*Ronin, you can't. Don't. Please, I'll explain. Just don't kill them.*"

"*I can't let them keep doing what they are doing.*"

"*Ronin, listen to me.*"

"*There is more. They figured out I'm not from here. I can't expose Osrealach to humans. I won't. They can't live.*"

"*Ronin, where are you? I'm coming to you. Don't do anything until I get there.*"

"*Captain's quarters. You better hurry. And Alex...*"

"*Yes?*"

"*I'm glad you're okay.*"

"*Me too.*"

The pile of sand had completely disappeared. Korynna was looking back and forth from Talia to Ronin. "Talia, explain. What was that?" She demanded.

"The knight had that rock on him when we acquired him, but when I took it, it showed me things. Places. Events I don't think have happened yet. It's hard to describe what I saw. It was in my head. It knew things. It took over all my senses, like... like I was there, but I wasn't. I thought I was going crazy." She spoke barely above a whisper.

Ronin felt uneasy. What was that rock? What had he done by fixing it? Did it just break again? Where did it go? What game was this? Was it really connected to the guardians? What did they want?

Ronin heard footsteps approaching the door to his back. *"Ronin, I'm coming in, don't stab me, please."* He chuckled.

Talia tensed and raised her daggers again, seeming to remember he was there. The door swung open and Alex peeked his head into the room.

"How did you get out? Who let you out?" Talia demanded.

CHAPTER 34

ALICE awoke with a start. His head pounded like he had been thrown into a stone wall. He groaned when he opened his eyes. The bit of light that filtered through struck his eyes; lancing pain added to the throbbing ache. He tried to move, but didn't get very far. He heard the chink of metal and felt heavy cuffs on his wrists and ankles. Where was he? How did he get here? Why was he chained up? Why was the world tilting at odd angles? He must be dizzy. No, the rocking was too rhythmic. He listened closer and heard the gentle lap of waves nearby. He was on a ship.

He groaned again. He remembered his fight with Ronin. Running errands for Korynna and everyone else, it seemed. Alyse and her package. Talia! The warehouse! Oh, he remembered now.

"Ronin? Can you hear me?"

Nothing. The iron in the manacles must be blocking his ability to talk to Ronin, or Ronin was also captured. He didn't like that thought.

He must have drifted back to sleep because he awoke with a start when someone started banging on metal. The clang reverberated through his head. His headache was somewhat lessened, though. When he opened his eyes this time, it was mostly dark except for a small lantern hanging just outside his cell. The light didn't hurt his eyes anymore either, thankfully.

"Hey, you awake?" A gruff voice off to his left asked.

Alex grunted, not trusting his voice to speak. His throat felt dry and scratchy. A small cup and pitcher of water sat next to his head. He sat up slowly, wary of his dizziness, willing it to go away. He poured himself a cup, downed it, and poured another. He ended up drinking the whole pitcher before he finally started to feel better. What had they knocked him out with?

"Hey, you over there. New guy, you awake?"

"Are you talking to me?" Alex mumbled.

"Yeah, the rest of us have been here a few days. So, therefore, you are the new guy."

"He's not very bright. Where'd they pick him up, I wonder?" another, slightly higher voice joined the first. He sounded younger or smaller.

The first voice chuckled a deep baritone laugh. "It might be the stuff they knock us out with too. I'm not one to judge. I'm here just the same as everyone else, so he must have done something wrong… or right, depending… You know."

Alex didn't really understand. "What do you mean?"

"Didn't they tell you anything?" the second voice sounded incredulous. "Foxglove makes deals with us, and we agree to her and Nightshade's 'methods.' It seems to be effective, so whatever works, I guess."

"They feed us good. I'm out of the elements and I even have a blanket. So I'm not complaining. Better than I can say for my last place."

Alex was appalled. "What do you mean your last place?"

He heard a sigh and shuffling of feet. "Prison work camp, lad."

"Oh." Alex tried to figure out what to say, but everything he came up with sounded either accusatory or disingenuous.

"Go ahead, ask. Everyone wants to know, but there is no easy way to ask. I understand. What did I do to be sent to work camp prison? Is that what you want to know?" The deep voice rumbled.

"Yes? No. I mean…" Alex trailed off. He was curious, but he was more curious about why they were here, and what Foxglove and Nightshade wanted from him.

"I killed someone. Plain and simple," he said matter-of-factly.

Alex breathed in sharply. "Why?"

"Just someone who wouldn't take no for an answer."

"I don't… understand." He said haltingly.

"One of the king's knights was harassing my neighbor's daughter every time he was nearby. He wouldn't leave her alone, so when I heard her screams coming from the alley, I intervened with a permanent solution, if you know what I mean. He had it coming, if you ask me. I was just the one to be Fiera's justice this time."

The penalty for murder was imprisonment and even possibly execution. The work camps were only a delay of execution, really. They were not known for taking care of even basic needs. Most prisoners who were sent to work camps didn't make it more than four seasons. If the poor food and lack of shelter didn't kill you, the other prisoners were just as likely to take whatever you had. Alex shuddered.

"How did you end up here?"

"Why, Foxglove, of course. Same as everyone else."

"I still don't understand."

"You mean to tell me that you didn't ask to be here?" the voice hummed in contemplation.

"I don't even know where *here* is."

Another chuckle. They stopped when footsteps shuffled toward them. Alex backed away from the cell bars as best he could. A figure stepped into the small pool of light. A woman dressed in a loose maroon shirt tucked into dark pants with tall chestnut-colored boots to her knees held a tray with several bowls on it in one hand. She took out a ring of iron keys and stepped to the cell next to Alex's. "Here you go. Bread?" she said in a gentle, lilting voice.

"Can I trade it for a kiss?" the higher voice crooned.

She rolled her eyes. A smile played at the corner of her mouth. "Ever the charmer. Eat your supper."

The other voice chuckled at the mock disappointed sounds of the younger voice. "Thank you, miss."

She nodded her head. She moved to the cell on the other side of Alex's and unlocked that door, and set down a bowl and chunk of bread on the floor before closing and locking it back. Finally, she unlocked Alex's door, slipping the keys back into her pocket. She stepped in a few paces and held out the last bowl and chunk of bread to him.

He eyed her warily. "C'mon. I don't have all day. I have other tasks to do, you know," she insisted impatiently. "Do you want to eat or not?"

He stepped closer and reached to take the bowl, but his hands stopped just short. He was chained to the back wall. His chains clinked as the cuffs bit into his wrists. It struck him, he hadn't heard chains clink from everyone else. Either they were really good at muffling the sounds, or they weren't wearing any.

She stepped a little closer so he could reach the bowl. Her eyes widened when the lantern light illuminated his face. She made a little sound and hurriedly backed out of the cell, locking the door behind her, and rushed away.

Alex was confused. *What was that all about? Do I have something on my face?* He was starving and the wooden bowl in his hands was warm. The smell made his stomach grumble. The best he could tell in the dim light was it was a thick stew. The bread was a little stale, but in the absence of a spoon or utensil, it worked well to dip and scoop with.

After he finished licking out his bowl, he slid it as close to the cell door as he could. He glanced up. A shadowy figure stood at the bars, watching him. He hadn't even heard them approach. He must have made a startled sound because the two voices he had heard earlier started swearing.

"Sweet Fiera, it's a demon come to claim my soul." "Nocturne, save me. How did it even get here? Is this ship haunted?"

Alex knew that silhouette. Talia. Nightshade. Growling, he lunged for the cell bars. Anger driving sense out of him. He hit the end of his chains with a yelp and crashed to the floor. She dropped her hood and smirked at him. Assessing him with a shrewd gaze that gave away nothing. After a moment, she turned on her heel and glided away, making no sound at her retreat.

"Who was that?" the baritone voice asked after a moment of silence that seemed to stretch on for longer.

"Nightshade," Alex said in a low voice as he surveyed the cuffs and chains. He winced at the raw skin he felt on his wrists where the cuffs had dug into him.

"What did she want with you? Were those chains I heard? Why are you chained up?"

"I don't know."

"My name is Griffin Torson. My friends call me Griff."

"Alex."

"Just Alex?"

"Just Alex."

He hummed, but let it drop.

"I'm Kenzo," the second voice introduced themself.

"Kenzo and Griff, so what are we here for?" Alex asked them.

"I think we'll find out soon enough."

Someone blew out the lantern. Alex laid down on the little pallet, grateful for a wool blanket. He let his mind wander as he laid staring into the dark. How had he gotten himself into this situation? Korynna. That's how. Where was Ronin? Was he even worried, or was he grateful to have gotten rid of Alex as a burden? Alex admonished himself as soon as he thought it. Plenty of times Ronin could have left and not come back, but he didn't.

XXX

The next morning, Alex awoke to another pitcher of water, a wedge of cheese, and a chunk of what might have been jerky in a past life. The bowl from last night was gone. They weren't rocking as much as they had been yesterday. Gulls in the distance. The hatch to the deck was open, and sunlight streamed through the opening. Alex inhaled deeply the salty air. It made his blood surge and joy bubbled up in his chest. Something about the ocean called to him. It settled his restlessness and gave him a spike of energy, simultaneously.

He took this opportunity to look around at his cell. There wasn't much. A small bucket sat in the corner opposite his pallet and blanket. Iron bars separated him from the rest of the ship.

A pair of bare feet stepped into view from the stairs leading up to the deck. A girl, no more than thirteen, dressed in a dark crimson skirt over dark leggings with a cream-colored blouse, stepped completely into view. A scarf tied back her unruly black curls that threatened to spill over the top. She hummed as she skipped to Kenzo and Griff's cell.

"Captain says you are free to roam. Just stay on the ship. Cook will send someone for you in a bit when they need your help." She unlocked their door and turned to leave again.

Alex watched as a large balding man in torn pants cut off at the knee emerged into view and followed her to the stairs. He was bare-chested, which showed off various healing bruises and old scars. A smaller man with long, tangled brown hair and hawkish features followed him. His tunic looked better for wear than Griff's, but he had definitely seen better days as well.

"What about me?" Alex asked hopefully.

All three turned to look at him, pity on their faces as they surveyed his chains. "Sorry, Captain only said these two." Kenzo and Griff followed her up the stairs without another word.

A short time later, two burly men stomped down the stairs carrying a figure with long black hair between them. Alex's breath caught. For a moment, he thought it was Ronin, but as they drew closer, he saw it wasn't him. This person was thin, almost gaunt, with a sickly pallor to their skin. Their clothes, not much more than rags, hung off them.

"Thank you." a frail feminine voice whispered as the two men exited the adjacent cell.

One of them turned back with a gentle look of concern. "Of course," he said before closing the door without locking it.

Quiet sobs broke the otherwise silence of the hold.

Alex stretched and flexed to exercise his sore, cramped muscles unaccustomed to disuse. He contemplated escape, but then what? He was on a ship, who knows how far from shore. His thoughts drifted to Eirach. He wondered if the sea dragons were out here too.

XXX

"Why are we packing again?" Alice asked as she sat on the floor with her clothes and pack strewn around her.

"I told you, we are going on an adventure. A trip to a very special place. It should be very exciting." He handed her a hair comb to put in her pack.

"No, Daddy, it's not. Trips are boring. Your feet get tired, and you walk forever, and dirt gets everywhere." She complained dramatically, waving her comb around. "Do we have to go?" She dropped it on her growing pile of things.

"But you'll see some of your friends when we get there. You can swim in the lake. Think of all the yummy food you'll get to eat… And I'll tell you more of your favorite stories on the way. The time will pass by so fast; we'll be there before you know it."

"Yay! Alright, I guess it won't be so bad," Alice relented.

He knelt next to her and took some of her clothes to fold. "Here, let me help. I'll fold. You put them in your pack. And I'll continue our story where we left off."

"Okay, Daddy." She picked up her bag and held it open for him.

CHAPTER 35

ALEX lay on the floor, staring at the ceiling, when something landed on his face. He brushed it off. It felt gritty, like sand. What were they doing up there? More sand trickled onto his face, so he rolled over out of the stream of it. It pooled on the floor strangely, with an iridescent shimmer. Odd. *What is this?* He picked up a pinch of it and rolled it between his fingers, trying to place where he'd seen this before. He scooped up more of it.

"What are you?" he wondered out loud. "Certainly not normal sand. Can you, by any chance, fetch a key for me?" What was he saying? He didn't even know why he said it. He did need a key, but to ask this mysterious sand for one? He really was losing it.

He chuckled to himself. *It is just sand, Alex.* He told himself as he let go of his handful. Something thunked on the floor in front of him. Sand definitely did *not* thunk. He opened his eyes and blinked at the shimmering key laying in an ever-growing pile of iridescent sand. *What the…?*

Gently, he picked it up and held it in the light to inspect it, uncertain of what just happened. *C'mon, Alex, this is by far not the strangest thing you have seen.* He shrugged and tried the key in the locks of his manacles. They sprang open and clattered to the floor. Elated and confused, he unlocked the cuffs around his ankles next. He needed to tell Ronin where he was.

"Ronin?" he called as soon as he wasn't touching iron anymore.

"Alex? Where are you? I'm coming to get you out! I'll get everyone out. I just need to kill Korynna and Talia first."

"Ronin, you can't. Don't. Please, I'll explain. Just don't kill them." Alex begged. This was not good. Not at all.

"I can't let them keep doing what they are doing."

"Ronin, Listen to me." He begged. He had to get to Ronin before he did anything rash.

"There is more. They figured out I'm not from here. I can't expose Osrealach to humans. I won't. They can't live."

"Ronin, where are you? I'm coming to you. Don't do anything until I get there."

"Captain's quarters. You better hurry. And Alex..."

"Yes?"

"I'm glad you're okay."

"Me too."

Alex turned back to the pile of sand to scoop up and take with him, but it was gone as if it had never been there. Very odd. He didn't have time to deliberate, though. He needed to get to Ronin.

Miraculously, his new key worked on his cell door as well. He shoved it in his pocket as he took the stairs two at a time up to the deck and raced to the captain's quarters. He passed Griff on the way.

"Hey, they let you out! About time! Congrats! We should celebrate... Alex? Where are you going in such a rush?"

Wordlessly, Alex sprinted to the door and wrenched it open. Griff followed with heavy steps. He'd deal with that later. Alex's legs complained at the sudden use after days of inactivity. Still, he relished the feeling of excitement and danger racing through his body. There was something wrong with him, he decided.

He skidded on the newly clean and still-damp floor as he fought to keep his balance in his mad dash down the short hall. *"Ronin, I'm coming in. Don't stab me, please."* He twisted the handle and poked his head in.

"How did you get out? Who let you out?" Talia demanded. She sounded pissed. Not good, but she wasn't the one he was worried about right now.

"Hey, Ro." Alex winced. *Ro? Where did that come from?* Ronin's eyebrow quirked up, but he didn't seem to hate it. Alex's chest heaved as he tried to catch his breath. Korynna gave him a suspicious look, but seemed more intrigued than anything else. "It's not what you think. She isn't behind the kidnappings. Well, not the ones you are thinking of anyway." He said to Ronin.

"Are we really having this conversation again, Alex? Here? Now? I know what I saw," Ronin said aloud.

"Where have you been? Are you okay? Is that blood? What did they do to you? I will end them!" Ronin said in Alex's mind. Ronin snarled at Korynna and Talia after seeing the dried blood.

"It's fine. I wasn't being smart with the manacles. I'm okay, Ronin," he said aloud, more for Talia and Korynna's benefit than anything.

"Manacles? Alex..."

"Do you mind if we sit?" he said, gesturing to the chairs.

Several sets of footsteps stomped down the hall toward the door. Griff and who knows who else. Ronin tensed next to him.

"Fine, have it your way," Ronin seethed. "This was exactly what I was trying to avoid. Having to fight the whole damn ship." He glared at Alex.

"Trust me. Please," Alex begged.

He couldn't interpret the look Ronin gave him just as Griff and a couple of other crewmen burst through the door, weapons drawn. Korynna glared at everyone in the room, seeming to grow and expand to much larger than her small frame would suggest.

"Everyone out. Now!" she commanded menacingly.

Talia snapped to attention and immediately moved toward the door, past Ronin and Alex. She eyed them warily before slipping out the door. Griff flinched away from Talia as she swept by. The rest of the crew moved to let her pass with almost reverence, then scurried after her.

"That means you too," Korynna addressed Alex and Ronin as she pointed to the open door. Alex ducked his head and turned to leave. Ronin grasped his forearm, stopping him.

"We aren't going anywhere until we have answers," Ronin ground out.

"And you will have them. Now, if you'll excuse me." She turned back toward her desk and rifled through some papers.

Alex gestured to the door with his head. Ronin glared at Korynna, but followed Alex into the hallway. When they stepped out onto the deck, they found it a flurry of activity. The crew rushed around, preparing the ship to set sail. A team of four turned a large spindle, raising the heavy chain attached to the anchor.

Ronin leaned against the wall near the door with his arms folded across his chest, watching everything and nothing with feigned disinterest.

"Ronin…"

"Alex, I don't know whether to punch you or hug you right now. I'm of the mind to do both. I thought I'd lost you.

Again. For good this time." Several emotions warred on Ronin's face, then slipped behind his mask of nonchalance.

He really had been worried for Alex. "Ro, I..."

Alex was cut off as Ronin crossed the short distance between them and wrapped him in a tight embrace. His whole body stiffened, then slowly relaxed into the hug. He had been expecting to be punched, if he were being honest. Slowly, he wrapped his arms around Ronin and hugged back. He wasn't used to physical affection. With anyone else, it might have been awkward, but this felt right.

"Don't do that to me again. Please. I can't lose you too," Ronin whispered after a long pause, then released him.

"Lose me too? What do you mean?" Alex searched Ronin's face for a hint.

Ronin sighed and rubbed the back of his neck. "Ask me later when we can have some privacy and aren't surrounded by murderous pirates who may try to kill us."

Alex nodded and surveyed the ship's main deck, now that he wasn't in a mad dash to get somewhere.

It was old and weather-worn. It had definitely seen better days and more than its fair share of storms and battles, but it was well cared for. The dark mahogany rails gleamed as if freshly polished. The decks were clean and well organized. This ship had been quite beautiful when it was newly built. He looked closer at the hand-carved details of swirls and swells of waves, clouds, birds, and fish on every surface. Who had this ship belonged to previously?

Korynna stepped out of the door. Immediately someone called, "Captain on deck!" The entire ship froze, waiting and watching to see what she would say or do.

"As you were. Once we are out on the open sea, pull up a barrel. It seems we are in need of a family meeting," Korynna's voice carried across the ship. The crew sprang into action. Everyone seemed to know their task and moved to complete it with purpose.

"Someone, go tell Cook. He'll want to know," she added as she spied Alex and Ronin on the side. Tendrils of her flaming auburn hair blew away from her face in the gentle breeze as she strode toward them with the confidence of being in command and perhaps a little swagger.

"Family meeting?" Alex asked.

"Despite what you seem to think of me, of us," she swept her arm to include the surrounding crew, "We are not behind the disappearances. Like I told you a week ago, some of my people are missing too, and I'd like to deal with those responsible as much as you do."

"And what is your explanation for kidnapping Alex, Silver Tongued Mistress?" Ronin growled, narrowing his eyes. Korynna glared back.

Alex stepped between them. "What matters is we are here now. We need each other. Let's put our differences aside for now. Then you can go back to being at each other's throats."

"What happened to you these last few days?" Ronin appraised Alex, looking for anything to gain insight.

"Some of the crew shared their stories with me. Everyone here was in a prison camp or in line for execution or some other horrible fate. Korynna and the rest of the *Oleander* crew saved them and gave them a home, a family, a purpose."

"And that is? From what I've seen, you are just a bunch of pillaging pirates, skimming off the top of shipments or outright commandeering them. I'm all for stealing from the rich and all that, but what about all the people I've seen locked up in your cargo holds? Explain that too while you're at it, Fox," Ronin spat.

"I don't have to explain myself to you, Rogue," Korynna countered.

"You do if you want our help."

"I don't want your help, nor do I need it. Get off my ship, Phantom," Korynna spat back.

The crew listening in to their argument seemed startled. The ship was sailing further and further from shore. Only the strongest swimmers might make it back unaided, but even then, the dark water would be treacherous.

"Okay then, Alex, let's go." Ronin seemed unfazed. He stalked toward the rail. A slim lad coiling a length of rope stood between Ronin and the rail; he darted out of the way, looking uncertainly between his captain and Ronin.

Alex watched him go, unmoving. Ronin turned, a questioning look on his face. *"Ronin, I'm staying, and I need you."* he said in his mind quietly, silently pleading with him to stay. He hated that they had fought. He hated the haunted, tortured look on Ronin's face when he saw Alex. He knew Ronin's past haunted him, but a possible future without Bronach haunted *him*. A future where he had to face his village, knowing he hadn't done everything in his power to help get his people back.

"I don't trust them, Alex."

"Then trust me."

Ronin searched his face a heartbeat before relenting. *"Fine."* He sighed and stalked back to stand next to Alex.

Korynna looked between Alex and Ronin with interest, like they were a puzzle she couldn't quite figure out.

A few minutes later, Korynna called for them to drop anchor. The crew assembled and sat or leaned against barrels and railing, giving Korynna their rapt attention.

She called out station rotations and introduced Griff and Kenzo as the new crew members. Alex could feel the curious stares from the other crew members at the lack of their introduction as crew. If they weren't crew, who were they, and why were they here? Why was Alex charging across the deck before?

Korynna gestured to them. "This is Sir Alexander of the Knight's Order. He's on special assignment to lend aid to our search for our missing crew and people in our city. As you know, there have been reports of missing people all over the city, but it has reached across all of Reyall. He's here to investigate. We plan to put an end to it."

"Aye, but why is he here on our ship?" a voice called out.

Korynna nodded. "I vetted him through our normal channels." A murmur went up through the ship. "And the other one?" another voice called.

"He's with me." Alex stepped forward. "I vouch for him on my honor and with my very life." Ronin furrowed his brow in surprise.

"There you have it. Anyone have an issue with this?" she challenged. She was met with silence. "Talia will pair you up for shore leave and mess duty. Under no circumstances is anyone to go anywhere alone. Is that understood?"

The crew assented with a chorus of aye's and yes's.

"Welcome aboard the *Oleander*." She turned and strode away.

Alex followed her to the stern. She gazed out over the water with a faraway look in her eyes. He stood next to her and silently marveled at the stars reflecting on the water.

"I'm not the monster you think I am." she murmured.

Alex wanted to tell her he knew, but let her continue uninterrupted.

"I became Foxglove to protect my people from the real monsters. From the time I was little, expectations were placed on me as a princess. I was the youngest, so everyone knew I would never rule, but I was still expected to play the part. The pretty, silent girl who was seen but not heard, quiet and demure and did as I was told. I'll admit, I was spoiled a bit too. I learned who to ask to get my way, to get an extra treat, more riding time, or whatever.

At first, I rebelled. I'll be the first to admit I was unruly, defiant, and prone to moods. So much so, my father called in the only person he knew could handle me. McCannon. He taught me to use my silence, to weaponize it; to listen to what was said, but also for what wasn't. I learned how to blend in so people forgot I was there, let their guard down, and spilled their secrets.

When I was frustrated with useless dance lessons, he taught me how to fight and use the footwork I learned to help me wield weapons. When I was bored from too many speeches or parties, he instructed me to read people and learn their weaknesses and desires to use like weapons.

After my father died, and my brother took the throne, McCannon was sent off to do whatever whims my brother had. I felt stifled again, so I would go down to the docks to watch people and practice my skills. One of the old deckhands saw me watching them day after day and offered to teach me to sail. After that, I was inseparable from the sea. Until someone recognized me and reported me to my brother.

He threatened to lock me up, but I told him I'd run away and he'd never see me again if he did. Alric, my other brother, recommended I be given a role in running the kingdom, so Reggy said if I liked the sea so much that I would be given responsibility for everything sea-related. Sea trade and the new navy to combat the growing threat of pirates harassing our merchants. He thought I would refuse, or that it would keep me busy enough to keep me out of trouble.

It did for a little while, but then I saw how the people weren't actually being taken care of with this new navy. They only cared about the possible conflict with the south and protecting shipments to the capital. I tried telling my brothers, but they were always too busy. The system was failing our people. My people. If a princess couldn't make the changes needed, then maybe a monster could."

She turned to look at him, a mischievous smile on her lips. "We start and feed most of the rumors going around. And those we like that we didn't come up with, we expand on. In their downtime, the crew like to come up with 'ghost stories' to spread when they go into town."

Alex laughed and shook his head, content to listen.

"As Foxglove, I am free of all the politics and social constraints. I am free to do as I see fit, to do what is best for my people. As the sister to the king, I am expected to be just a pretty face and to host balls and parties. As Foxglove, I am feared, yes, but also adored."

She turned to face the rest of the ship and leaned against the rail. "You might notice I give my crew the freedom to challenge me... most of the time, anyway. It keeps them honest, and they respect me for it. I don't have to worry about dissent in the ranks. They outright tell me when they don't agree. All of them came here from hopeless situations where they had lost any choice or control over their lives. Some never had it to begin with. So where I can, I let them decide what they are a part of and what they aren't. They know I'm ruthless with my enemies but fiercely loyal to my crew and people." Korynna watched her crew with fierce pride shining in her eyes.

Ronin walked over to them and leaned against the rail on Alex's other side. Korynna feigned indifference but tracked his every movement until he was out of her direct line of sight. Ronin watched her with narrowed eyes. Alex found it rather interesting and slightly amusing that her indifference seemed to get Ronin so riled up.

"You saw a problem with the way things were and did what you had to in order to make the change you wanted. I respect and admire that." Alex turned his attention back to their conversation. "There are so many things I want to change. I dream of a place where everyone is equal and valued, regardless of their birth. I hate that you have to be of noble birth to become a knight." He clenched his fist at his sides in frustration. "Why? Who decided that only nobles have the skills to be a knight? Or what if a noble wanted to be a baker or a musician instead?"

"Are you not common born and yet, here you stand, a knight of the order?" Korynna challenged him.

Alex looked at Ronin briefly before addressing her. "Except I'm not. My mother is Rose Callaway, the sole heir to

Lord Callaway. I was raised in a tiny fishing village on the edge of the kingdom with no knowledge of this until recently. So it turns out that even I am no exception to the rule." He paused in contemplation. "I wonder now if McCannon knew that when he offered to train me. I've never met my grandfather, have you? Do I look like him?"

Korynna studied him for a while before answering. "I'd never have picked up on it if you hadn't told me, but yes, you do a little, in your eyes and mouth. Do you favor your father in looks, then?"

Alex shrugged. "I've never met him either. He left before I was born."

Korynna nodded as if that explained everything. "I remember hearing whispers, nothing more than rumors and idle conjecture, as to what happened to Rose Callaway. This dream world of yours," Korynna changed the topic. "What would it look like? If not by birth, then how?"

"I'm still working that out." Alex blew out a breath. "I don't know how to fix it yet, but I want to figure it out."

"Change takes time," Ronin interjected quietly. "And a strong will to wrest power from those who wield it for their own gain. They do not give it up lightly, not without a mighty driving force behind the change. And they will do *anything* to keep it." He had a haunted look on his face again.

Alex nodded and breathed deeply as he gazed at the night sky. Voices of singing and laughing crew carried across the deck. Griff clomped toward them, carrying four large mugs. Wordlessly, he handed one to each of them. He bowed slightly to Korynna and nodded to Alex before clomping back the way he came.

"I look forward to the future where your dream becomes reality." She raised her mug in a toast. "To the world in our dreams."

Alex raised his mug. "And the one that made us."

Ronin raised his mug as well. "And this one here and now."

They drank in silence for a few minutes. Alex was lost in his thoughts of Mahkai and how he also desired to change the status quo. Was there a way to change both their kingdoms? How? What would it look like? Until a question that had been burning in Alex's mind for a while finally drowned out all the others. He blurted out, "What do you think they are doing with all the people they kidnap?"

"Labor of some sort would be my guess. Given the number of people taken," Ronin responded.

Korynna hmmm'd her agreement. "That was my working theory as well. Mines maybe? It would be easier to conceal a large number of people underground, and an easy place to dispose of bodies after their usefulness has run its course."

Ronin leaned around Alex and gave her an appraising look.

"What?" she asked, raising an eyebrow at him. "It's what I would do."

"I don't know whether to be appalled or impressed," Ronin sounded amused.

Korynna shrugged with feigned indifference. "I don't care much either way."

Ronin scowled and turned away.

"You still haven't told me where you are from, Ronin. Or should I call you the Phantom?" she said.

Ronin grunted and walked away. Korynna looked expectantly to Alex for answers. He sighed and shook his head. "It isn't an easy topic to discuss for him, and it's not my story to tell."

"You are close." It wasn't a question.

Alex's smile was strained. "We are something. Most days I don't know what."

"How did you meet?"

"Bronach, my father figure growing up. He introduced us. Said we'd be good for each other," Alex chuckled. "We were at odds right from the start, but I think that is just how Ronin is with everyone," he trailed off. "Bronach was one of the ones taken from my village."

"I'm sorry," she breathed.

He felt the familiar pain of helplessness wash over him and suddenly desired to look into the soothing flames of his fire magic. He pushed away from the rail and started toward the stairs to the deck below. "Give him time. I think he'll come around," he said over his shoulder. "Good night, Foxglove."

"Goodnight, Alex."

CHAPTER 36

"SAILS! Ship ahoy!" The cry came from the crow's nest. "Picaroons inbound. Looks to be headed across."

Alex, Kenzo, and Talia were standing on deck discussing weather patterns and navigation. "What do they want? Do you think they will just pass by? Where are they headed out here so far, I wonder?" Kenzo commented.

"Let me have a look." Talia reached for the spyglass in Alex's hand. She stared at the smudge on the horizon for a moment. "That's the *Gull's Envy*. They have skilled archers and ballistas. They beat us to our last haul. Better watch out for them." She looked again. "But if they want a fight, we'll give it to them. Battle ready!" she commanded.

Crewmen darted across the ship and retrieved various weapons from hidden compartments, and took up strategic positions. Kenzo and Griff slid wooden panels into slots to form a wall, or sterncastle, for added protection from arrows from behind. Some of the crew uncovered ballistas, oversized crossbows mounted to heavy wheels, and rolled them into position, securing them in place.

He was riveted. Fascinated. He'd seen them used in mock battles when the soldiers demonstrated war games, but this was very different. As the *Gull* sailed closer, they raised a flag with three dots inside a circle on a white background, the flag of peace. They weren't aiming for conflict.

Alex watched as the crew disassembled and stowed the ballistas and weapons. By the time the *Gull* was within visual range, they looked like nothing more than a merchant vessel. "Why not show them you can protect yourselves rather than hide it? Doesn't that encourage them to attack if you look defenseless?"

Talia smirked. "You would think that, but oftentimes it is easier to let them in close and take them by surprise. Less chance of them running away with their contribution to our cargo. That, or cut and run ourselves if we are outmatched."

"Are you often outmatched?"

"Only with the navy vessels and the *Bellum*."

"What is the *Bellum*?"

"The *Para Bellum* is a ship crewed by cutthroat savages who are without honor or code of conduct. They are as inclined to steal from their own as from anyone else. Pray to Chantara, or whoever your gods are, that we don't encounter them."

Alex gave her a sharp look, and she quirked her head at him. "Chantara?"

"You know, the ancient goddess of the sea? I thought you lived in a fishing village. Do they not teach you about her on the edge of the world?"

Alex smirked and rolled his eyes. "Yes, I know Chantara. I'm just surprised to hear you reference her."

"I know most people of Reyall worship the twins, Fiera and Nocturne, but my... the people that raised me had a little shrine to her down by the sea that I liked to visit when I was little," Talia continued. "We should be arriving at Isla del Sol before nightfall." She left like that was the obvious end to their conversation.

Alex shrugged. *"How are you doing up there?"* Alex checked in with Ronin.

"Much better. Great idea. I wish I'd thought of this sooner."

Ronin was currently perched on the lip of the crow's nest, having spent the better part of the day battling seasickness. Alex had the idea for him to shift and fly to get rid of it. He flew for a bit and went fishing.

"Tell them to sail faster. You are too slow."

"That's not how it works, Ronin. They can't just conjure wind in the right direction, or the water to propel them faster whenever they want. They are reliant on what happens naturally from the weather."

Ronin harrumphed impatiently. Alex busied himself, watching every aspect of sailing the ship the crew would allow. The biggest boats he'd been on were fishing boats. Everything about the *Oleander* fascinated him. Korynna said she would teach him more maneuvering tricks and tactics when she returned from her trip.

She was headed to Salar, then on to Ocelum for "some family thing" for a few days. Korynna was sailing with her navy ships. Understandably, she couldn't very well show up to the capital city on her stolen ship with her crew of stolen criminals. While she was gone, the *Oleander* and crew were going to be selling or distributing their stolen goods to the various islands in the Divina Iles. As first mate, Talia was now in charge.

✕✕✕

They had spent the day loading and unloading cargo off the ship, hopping from island to island. Alex didn't even know there were this many islands, and there were people living on most, if not all, of them. Some of them he met were born and raised on their island and planned to never leave. They weren't interested in the "mainland," as they called it. They were happy and content to stay in their little community and their tiny huts made of driftwood and seagrass.

"But what about storms?" he asked one lady who was busy fixing her roof that had collapsed. "Don't you tire of having to rebuild after every storm? Don't you wonder what else is out there? Don't you want to see more, explore more?"

She smiled pityingly at him. She pitied him! "You have been bitten by the wanderlust fish. I can see it in your eyes, though not as much as your friends and the lady captain. Some of the children wander out too far into the shoals and across the sandbars when they have been told they shouldn't. They are usually bitten too."

"Bitten?"

"Bitten, stung… I'm not quite sure because, as you can see, I've not been. So I don't know, and those who have don't remember. You see, it can sometimes take time before the venom really sinks in. For some, it's days. For others, it may be seasons or even cycles of seasons. The venom spreads through their entire body, under their skin, and throughout their lifeblood. It calls to them and whispers in their ear. It gives them dreams and notions of adventure and excitement. I've seen even the strongest succumb to its call. They always leave and never return. The mainland doesn't give; it only takes."

"But if it only takes, then what about us? We are here and providing you with supplies you need." Alex replied, shocked.

"Yes, dear, but then you will leave again and may come back for a time, but eventually, you won't. The lady captain has been coming the longest, but one day, even she will cease to come again."

Alex was about to respond when he caught sight of a wooden structure sticking out of the sand between huts. "What is that?"

"Oh, that is the temple of Chantara. It is where she dwells."

"Really? May I see it?"

"She keeps it locked, but all may pray by her hut and be heard. Come," she set down her armful of woven seagrass and led him toward the structure.

He reveled in the feel of the warm sand under his bare feet. After the first island, he had removed his boots and left them in the chest by his hammock. She led him to what looked to be the bow of a ship sticking straight up out of the sand. Around it, woven baskets of seagrass and little bundles of grass decorated with pieces of shell and bones were scattered and piled in the sand. As they drew closer, he saw they were little figures made to look like people or animals. One bowl made from a shell larger than his palm caught his eye. Instead of braided grasses, it held pieces of colored stones, sea glass, and various shapes and sizes of pearls.

"Ah, that is the dark one's offering. She brings a piece each time she visits. Beautiful for one so dark."

"The dark one? Is she another goddess?"

She chuckled, "No, but some would think she is the daughter of a god or goddess with the way she shifts and melds with the shadows and night."

That sounded familiar. "Talia?"

"Do they not also call her Nightshade?"

She had a point. He nodded to her silently, taking in the way the pieces were resting in their shell, intentional, like Talia had placed them in a precise way. It was beautiful how it caught the light and sprayed its surroundings with flecks of colored lights, like it was highlighting the surrounding offerings.

She led him to the far side, where a small canopy of woven branches and grasses had been erected before a single door in the old wood structure. Several islanders knelt in the sand or on woven mats under the canopy with their heads bowed. Now he understood what she meant by locked.

"You may approach, but don't disturb the others. I trust you to be reverent and respectful, even though you do not follow the way of the sea," she said, halting just under the canopy.

He was tempted to correct her, but thought better of it. Better for her to think him an ignorant mainlander. He would be leaving soon enough, anyway. He was really curious about the door. When she said it was locked, he'd immediately thought of the key in his pocket. He approached, careful not to bump or kick sand at the kneeling islanders. He placed his hand flat against the door and felt it push back a little as a deep thrumming filled his entire body.

He snatched his hand away and looked over his shoulder to see if she was still watching. Her head was bowed in prayer. He placed his hand on the door, and the thrumming resumed. It made his body tingle, and he shivered even though it was blazing hot midafternoon.

With his other hand, he turned the doorknob, curious to see if it would open. It didn't. Keeping his hand flat against the door, he reached into his pocket. As soon as he touched the key, the door became liquid, not unlike Althenaea's door. He tumbled through it, sprawling and sliding on the sand within.

He got up and brushed the sand off. Dim light filtered through the cracks in the boards. It seemed bigger inside than it appeared on the outside. The ground sloped down before him. He was torn between going back and continuing on. Would they notice he was gone? Did they see where he went? Would they be concerned?

Ronin had to see this! He was on a neighboring island helping give out supplies so he could easily fly here and back before he was missed.

"Hey, Ronin, I found this structure in the middle of the island. The islanders worship at it and believe it is Chantara's shrine. I… may have touched the wall and fallen through… A lot like behind the waterfall." He was met with silence. *"Ronin?"* Maybe whatever kept people out also kept him from talking with Ronin.

He decided that if Ronin were here instead, he would definitely continue exploring. So could he. He would for them both and tell Ronin about it when he got out. Maybe they could come back and explore more together.

He started making his way down the slope. The deep sand sucked at his feet, making it difficult to stay upright. After a few minutes of fighting the sand, he sat down and tried to scoot or slide his way down. Once he got going, he slid faster and faster toward the far wall. Just before he reached it, the sand banked right and dipped out of view.

Suddenly, he was free-falling, and the light faded into inky blackness. Then he felt nothing. He couldn't tell if he was still falling; the air around him stilled. He reached out, but felt nothing. It was eerie and lonely, if he was being honest. The silence yawned before and around him. He called his fire magic to him, but nothing happened. He called his water magic, still nothing. He tried each of his magics and even wondered how he would call on his magic of histories, but still nothing. Panic surged as despair and hopelessness took root in his chest.

There was no beginning, no end, no forward, and no back. There was nothing but him. He had no way to measure the passage of time.

His mind wandered. They called him Little Defender, but what was he supposed to defend? And how was he to defend it from here? *Is this all there is? Is there a way out?* "What do you want from me?" he demanded in the silence of the void. "Why am I here? Why me?" He cried out until his throat was raw, but was only met with more silence. His mind continued to wander, leaping from thought to thought until finally, there was nothing. All his rage and fear spent, he sat in the stillness for the first time and accepted it.

He closed his eyes and sighed. When he reopened them, something glimmered beside him in the darkness. A light radiated from something near him, on him. Reaching into his pocket, he pulled out the key. It glowed brilliantly. Holding it in the flat of his palm, he watched as it grew and changed shape, turning into a pool of bright, golden liquid in his hand. It looked like it burned from within with a kaleidoscope of colors. He felt joy and hope surge within him, then snuffed out all at once, like the wind blowing out a flame.

Alex blinked in the sudden darkness after the brilliant light. He felt its loss deeply like he'd felt nothing else. Sorrow surged through him, and tears ran down his face. He didn't understand why he felt so strongly. Except... for the moments while the light had burned, he had no longer felt alone. Tears landed on his palm and rippled in the puddle in his hands.

Tiny pinpricks of light shone from the pool beneath the ripples. He watched in amazement as stars winked into view. Soon, all the dark spaces within the pool had been replaced by light until he held a pool of pure, liquid starlight.

Emotions flooded through him so fast he couldn't process them until all he could do was laugh with delight. He laughed, because he was afraid if he didn't laugh, he would cry and be consumed by sadness he didn't understand.

He gazed affectionately at his little pool of starlight, cherishing it and holding it like a lifeline. He didn't want to be left alone in the darkness again. He then wondered at the space around him. Could he light up more of it? He dipped his fingers into the pool and flicked them like flicking water from his fingertips or a painter might flick paint.

The droplets sprayed from his fingertips and danced around him. He flicked some more, and they, too, joined the swirl around him. He continued dipping and flicking his fingers until the surrounding space glowed with soft light. His little pool was quickly diminishing, but he didn't care. This was worth it. He wondered if this was what the artists and painters felt when they created their art.

He marveled at how the droplets sparked like diamonds in their shared light. They were connected, each glowing of its own accord, but lending its light to all the rest. He stopped when he had only a coin size pool left in his palm. He wanted to keep it for himself, but felt he should still do something special with it.

He let his mind wander, trying to decide what to do with it. He thought of Ronin and wished he could see this, wished he were here. His mind shifted to the memory of their magic lesson outside the mountain forge. He thought of Ronin's story about growing a tree.

A tree. He would make a tree. He dipped his fingers into the starlight and painted in the air before him. In his mind, he imagined a large tree, broad and tall. Broad enough to give shade and shelter, tall and stately so it would be seen and known and found.

As he painted the tree, adding branches and leaves, he thought about his conversation with Korynna and Ronin. What did he want the world to look like? He knew he wanted everyone to be valued for their actions and choices and things they could control, rather than things out of their control like birth family and magical ability, gender, race, etc. He knew he wanted people to be free to explore, create, learn, and grow. An idea formed in his mind, and he began to shape the space around him.

Sometime later–he couldn't be sure how much later–he sat in the shade under his tree and surveyed his surroundings. He felt tired, but more focused and sure of himself than he'd ever felt before. He had been sharing his thoughts and feelings out loud to the tree as if it understood him until he had nothing left to say.

He still had yet to figure out how to get back to the *Oleander* and her crew, though. While here in this place of his own creation, he knew no hunger or thirst. He wondered at the passage of time, but it didn't feel important. Though something in the back of his mind was starting to nudge him that he had stayed here too long. He began to feel an urgency to return to his world, but he felt sad at the thought of leaving this one.

He stood and placed a hand on the tree, and sighed. "Well, my friend, I have some things left unfinished. I hope to return. Would you know how to leave, perchance?"

The next thing he knew, he lay in the dark on his side on warm sand. He felt a sharp pain in his side as someone tripped over him. A voice grunted in surprise. They rolled to a crouch, dagger extended toward him. His gaze followed the length of the dagger to the face of its wielder. "Talia! It's me, Alex. Don't stab me!" he hastily crab-walked backward out of her reach.

"Alex. Where have you been? Where is everyone?" she asked, rising from her crouch.

"I was about to ask you the same thing. I was in the shrine and…" he trailed off, not ready to talk about it. It felt like a dream now, but a part of him knew it wasn't, just like he knew the guardians were real and not a dream. As he stood and brushed himself off, something caught his attention out of the corner of his eye. He looked down at his hands and noted the creases of his fingers glimmered with an iridescent sheen of starlight. He smiled and traced the lines on his palm. Definitely not a dream.

"In the shrine?" Talia looked at him sharply. "What is in there?"

"Nothing. Sand." He shrugged. That was true. When he had entered, there had been sand and nothing. A lot of nothing, in fact.

They traversed the rest of the island, but only found abandoned campfires and huts with things scattered around, as if interrupted. Talia spotted footprints in the sand leading to the water, but no boats were in sight. "Where did they go and why? What would cause everyone to leave so abruptly? Did you hear anything while you were in there?"

Alex shook his head. "Maybe they were called to another island. Ronin and some of the others were over at Isla Cielo. Maybe they know more."

Talia nodded. "My boat is on the north side. You row, I'll navigate." She didn't sound like it was open for negotiation.

As he rowed in the dark water, he surveyed the starlit sky. His chest tightened a little. For a moment, he paused rowing and cupped his hand in the water, staring at the reflection of the stars and moon in his palm. He let the water trickle through his fingers, then resumed rowing. Talia watched him silently from her seat at the tiller, her gaze inquisitive.

A short while later, they neared the shore of Isla Cielo. "Odd." She inclined her head and peered into the darkness. "Stop rowing, don't make a sound," she whispered.

He twisted to look over his shoulder. Very few torches and campfires dotted the shore. No movement or sounds reached them beyond the sound of the surf.

"Ronin, where are you? Something weird is going on. All the islanders and crew abandoned Isla Cielo. Are they there with you?" He was met with silence. Now he was worried.

They drifted closer; the waves pushed them toward the shore. As they ran aground, they leapt from the boat, dragged it up on the beach so it wouldn't drift away, and went in search of their missing crew.

The village was destroyed. Broken boards and pottery shards lay strewn about. What they had taken for campfires were the smoldering remains of burned huts and trees.

Unmoving forms lay scattered across the sand. Talia made a strangled sound when she rolled one of them over. Griff's eyes stared back at them, unfocused.

One by one, they identified five more crew members and eight islanders, all dead. Alex felt a little part of him relax slightly. Since they had found the first body, cold dread had been building, waiting for the next one to be Ronin's face staring back at him. Something told him he would feel Ronin's death. He would know somehow. Just like right now, he knew none of them were Ronin. He felt guilty for being relieved.

As they explored the rest of the island, it painted a grim picture. The island had been ambushed. It was hard to tell how many exactly, but numerous footprints had churned the sand between the village and the shore. There were some drag marks as well, as if someone or something were dragged to waiting boats.

Alex continued calling out to Ronin in his mind, but was met with silence each time. As he investigated one of the unburned huts, a sound startled him. He whirled around, expecting the worst. When he looked closer and held a torch in the dark corner, he saw a small figure huddled behind some crates.

"Hey, I'm not here to hurt you," Alex said in a gentle voice as he crouched down to make himself less imposing.

A young boy crawled out and shook before him. "You don't sound like 'em. Or look like 'em neither. Are you going to take me away, too?"

"Sound like who?" Alex asked.

"The pirates who came and took everyone away and burned down my village and hurt people. There was so much screamin' and yellin', and I didn't know what to do, so I hid. Auntie always said I was the best hider, so that's what I did."

"Did you hear them mention what ship they belonged to? Any names?"

"I don't remember. I was too scared." He trembled harder.

Alex found a blanket and wrapped it around the boy's slim shoulders. "It is okay. I'm here with a friend. Can you be brave for me and come with me?"

The boy nodded and followed him out of the hut. Talia met them in the center of the village. When he saw her, he ran to her and wrapped his arms around her waist, and pressed his face into her side. Alex couldn't make out what they said. Then it occurred to him they were speaking a language he'd never heard before.

Talia swore a string of colorful language. "He says he thinks one of the villagers was a relative or informant of someone on the *Para Bellum,* and they tipped them off somehow that we were here. It was the *Bellum's* crew that raided. He said he heard them laughing and congratulating themselves that they had drugged an entire island and took no losses. That someone paid them and pointed them in the right direction."

The boy said something else to her animatedly, waving his arms around. "He says the one they called the 'Phantom' fought like a beast of the night, unlike anyone he'd ever seen. Says his eyes glowed and looked like one of the great cats in his books from the mainland. Says he took down several of them before they overwhelmed him and finally subdued him." She looked at Alex sharply. "That doesn't sound like any of my crew," she said pointedly.

Alex let out a groan. "Did he say where they planned on taking them?" Ronin had a habit of coming to his aid. Well, now it was his turn to rescue Ronin.

Talia shook her head. "When Foxglove gets back tomorrow, she can make some official inquiries. I'll do what I can through my contacts. We need to get back to Moradon."

"Wait, tomorrow? I thought she wasn't due back for a few days."

Talia had started walking, but stopped and turned slowly to inspect him. "Where have you really been? Were you passed out drunk? It has been almost a whole week since she left."

Alex staggered and sank to the sand. He felt like he'd been kicked in the chest. Days! He'd been in there for days. Talia strode toward him. In the firelight, he could see her face was a calm mask, but from the set of her shoulders and her clenched fists, he wondered if she was actually seething underneath. She crouched in front of him; her face inches from his. He could see the barely contained fury raging in her eyes. She thought he'd done this.

His eyes widened, and he opened his mouth to say something, anything, but what could he say? "I didn't have anything to do with this, if that's what you think."

"Then explain yourself," she demanded in a low voice. He never saw her draw her dagger, but felt the tip of it prick the skin on his neck.

"You wouldn't believe me if I told you."

"Try me," she said, her voice barely audible.

"I was in Chantara's shrine, like I said, but it's…" he trailed off. He couldn't finish the sentence. *"Help me,"* he called in his mind to anyone listening.

"What would you have me do, Little Defender?" Chantara's voice soothed in his mind.

"I don't know why I feel this way, but I can't betray what is in there, the new little world. I feel this world was not meant to know about that one. It would taint it, maybe? I don't feel like my life is a worthy enough reason to trade for it."

"You would be its guardian then?"

"I don't know what that means or entails, but yes, I would if it meant keeping it safe from this one."

"Very well."

"What did you say?" Talia abruptly pulled away from him; wonder and fear etched her face.

Alex didn't understand until he realized she wasn't staring at him, but over his shoulder. He spun sharply. Chantara rose from the water in all her bioluminescent glory.

"He was with me, Daughter," Chantara's voice carried to them on the wind. She stepped onto the beach and glided toward them.

Alex relaxed a little. Talia remained rigid, deathly still, as if frozen to the spot. The boy watched silently, eyes wide and mouth open. Chantara approached the boy, placed a hand on his slim shoulder, and smiled at him. He blinked a few times, then smiled back at her with a boyish grin. His face flushed, and then he nodded. Alex assumed they were speaking mind to mind.

Chantara nodded once, then turned to Talia and Alex. She reached her hands out to both of them. Alex took her hand without hesitation. She helped him stand. A tendril of water slid up and wrapped around his forearm for a moment and squeezed before gliding back down to pool in his palm. The iridescence on his palm glowed faintly through the water.

"It will be with you even when you are apart," she said gently.

Alex nodded, unable to speak. Talia still knelt on the ground, looking up at Chantara's outstretched hand with awe and fear. She hung her head and stared at the ground. Chantara released Alex's hand and reached down to cup Talia's chin, tilting it to look up at her.

"Look at me, Daughter."

"Why do you call me that?" Talia's voice was bitter.

"Because you asked it of me all those years ago. Do you not remember?"

"Yes, but that was then, before... I'm not the same as I was." Talia's face reflected grief and agony. She tried to turn away, but Chantara held her from moving.

"You are still my daughter, no matter what life has thrown at you," she said gently, but firmly.

A tear rolled down Talia's face as Chantara knelt in the sand before her. She placed a hand on either side of her face and looked deeply into her eyes. Talia shuddered, and more tears streamed down her cheeks.

Alex felt like he was intruding on a private moment, but Chantara stopped him. "Little Defender, stay. You are not intruding."

She stood and helped Talia to her feet as well. "You will need this, I believe." She gestured in a sweeping motion to the sea. He saw bioluminescent waves propelling a dark shape in the water. With a flourish of her hand, the glowing, blue-green light spread across the silhouette, revealing the *Oleander*, now glowing from the rigging, mast, and hull.

"Thank you," Talia breathed and embraced Chantara.

"Though you choose to use the darkness, do not forget your light," Chantara said to Talia. She turned to Alex. "A fitting way to use the guardian stone. We have not been surprised in a very long time. Well done, and thank you." She glided back to the water, the waves greeting her like a lover, caressing her.

"But how will we sail? There are only three of us," Talia called.

"It is enough," Chantara said without turning. She lifted a hand over her shoulder in farewell and sank into the waves. The glow of the waters and on the ship faded moments later.

Talia let out a deep breath in a whoosh and stared out at the *Oleander* for a long time without moving. "Well, shall we?" she turned to him at last.

"Are we not going to talk about what just happened?" Alex asked.

She shrugged. "I don't see why. She told me to trust you. So I will."

"Just like that?"

"Just like that. Listen, I don't know about you, but when the goddess deigns to step out of the sea to grace me with her presence and gives me an order, I don't question it. There are a great number of things I question, but not her."

Alex couldn't argue with her, so he shrugged and started wading toward the *Oleander*. Talia and the boy followed. By the time they climbed onto the ship, Alex was tired and hungry. He slumped to the deck. His body felt like he hadn't eaten or slept for several days.

Talia strode away on light feet. Despite being soaking wet, she made no sound. Ever the confident bearing of a person comfortable in their own skin, and an authority figure used to being followed, even though there was no one here to command. He closed his eyes and leaned his head back against the railing.

Not long after, he felt the boy curl up next to him, still damp and shivering. Without thinking, he called his water magic and drew the extra water from his and the boy's clothes out and over the side, giving it back to the ocean. He thought of the sun's warmth on the leaves of his tree and willed his fire magic to warm them both. The boy tucked himself in closer to Alex, and Alex rested his arm around the boy's bare shoulders, now warm and dry.

Alex didn't know how long they rested, but a while later, he felt a hand on his shoulder. He blinked his eyes at Talia in the dim, pre-dawn light. She held out a small object to him wrapped in dried seagrass. He took it, not sure what to do with it.

She watched him and chuckled, then bit into hers. She showed him the inside. It contained cooked grain, and what looked to be fish or meat. He took a bite and savored the simple yet delicious food.

"Thank you! What is this?"

"It is called onigiri. My island used to make it."

"Your island? You are from the islands?"

She nodded with a far-off look in her eyes.

"Chantara said three of us are enough to sail back to Moradon. I'm not sure how since it takes seven at minimum usually, but who am I to question? I'll take the helm if you'll join me." She nodded to Alex. "Let's haul up the anchor first. Do you want to fly with the crows?" she asked the boy.

He nodded and scampered eagerly over to the rigging to begin his climb, but paused. "But how will we sail with no one to man the sail and rigging?"

"Chantara will provide," Alex said. He knew what she meant, but he wasn't willing to show them his magic. It was easier for them to think Chantara would be the one propelling the ship. And she might very well. Alex wouldn't stop her if she wanted to, but he felt she meant him.

They took up their position and waited. Alex instinctively called his water magic to him, but paused while he worked out exactly what he wanted. At first, nothing happened. He felt the water moving, but it wasn't moving the ship. They were drifting freely, but not in the right direction. He tried a few different things until he felt the ship finally move forward. Talia navigated, and he helped her steer since turning the wheel took two people without the aid of sails to maneuver.

At one point, he was so far lost in his thoughts and concentrating on keeping them moving, he didn't realize he had stopped responding until Talia waved a hand in front of his face. "Sorry, What?"

"Where did you go?"

"I was just thinking over what Chantara said," he said tiredly.

"I can keep us steady if you need to go take a break," she offered. "The current in this part of the water is usually strong and flows in the general direction we want to go, anyway. It shouldn't need much correction." He was tired, but he didn't think he could keep up the magic while sleeping.

"I'm alright. I might just sit for a while and rest my legs, though." He must have dozed off, because the sun was past its zenith when he opened his eyes next. They had slowed a little, but Talia had been right; the natural current was carrying them without any direction from him. He noted Talia curled up under her cloak an arm's length away from him.

It struck him how young she looked when she slept. He wondered at how they had gone from her trying to kill him, to being comfortable sleeping in each other's presence in the span of a little over a week. He looked down at his hand and traced the lines in his palm thoughtfully. A lot had happened in a week. He glanced up to find Talia silently watching him.

"The rock I had in my pocket when you 'acquired' me… what happened to it?" He had a strong suspicion, but he wanted to test his theory.

"Ronin had it last in Korynna's cabin. Then he dropped it. It was the weirdest thing; it turned to sand and poured through the cracks in the floorboards."

"Ah." He was right. The magic sand was his "not rock." He stroked the lines on his palm absentmindedly. "It is a key and not a key," he chuckled under his breath. "Yeah, no kidding."

"What?" Talia asked.

"Just something someone said to me when they gave it to me."

"It seemed important to you. I'm sorry you lost it," she said, genuinely apologizing.

He shrugged. "It… is alright, but thank you. I suspect it served its purpose."

She watched him, a look crossed her face too fast for him to read. She rose to her feet and stretched. "We should be close to the cove soon. This ought to be interesting to navigate."

"What do you mean?" he asked curiously.

"Well, to get in or out of the cove, we need to pivot the ship and cut speed at just the right time. Almost impossible to do without a crew."

"If we try and fail?"

"We either overshoot it and have to go around and try again, or we slam into the cliffs on either side and get wedged in. Or, we don't risk it and drop anchor outside of it and swim to shore to collect more crew to assist us."

Alex rose to his feet and saluted. "I am at your command, Captain. Tell me what you need me to do."

"Hold on to something and be ready to drop the anchor on my mark. Let's hope the current is kind."

If he hadn't known it was there, he would have never seen it. It looked like they were sailing straight toward a sheer cliff face. Talia expertly maneuvered the ship into the opening and turned the *Oleander* into the first switchback. He heard her hiss just before they bumped into one of the cliff faces and sent the stern swinging back the wrong way.

Alex concentrated on getting the water to slow the ship's movements and put them back on track. He felt a bead of sweat trickling down his temple from the effort. They bumped into the cliff face on the other side, but barely, and Talia got them pointing in the right direction. They had lost all their speed, so Alex nudged them forward just a little.

They came to the second switchback. Talia counted and braced her feet, wrenching the wheel. This time, they glided through with no issue. They picked up speed. Talia's knuckles were white from gripping the wheel and her face set with a look of grim determination.

"What is it?" he called to her.

"We are going too fast. We won't make the turn without scraping or crashing into the cliffs."

"What can I do?" he asked as he was already asking the water to push back against the ship to slow its speed.

"Grab an oar and try to push us away from the side if we get too close," she said, pointing to a couple of oars lashed to the side of the railing. "As soon as we clear the turn, I'll give you the signal to drop anchor, so be ready."

Alex's palms were sweaty from exertion, so he wiped them on his pants. He grabbed one of the oars and resumed his position. Looking up, he saw the boy had an oar in the crow's nest, and was ready as well. Their speed slowed. He hoped it would be enough.

"Here we go!" Talia said as she wrenched the wheel one last time.

The jagged rock face loomed closer and closer as the *Oleander* sliced through the water, pivoting faster than Alex thought a ship this size could. He held his oar ready, imagining a wall of water between them and the sharp rocks that would surely tear them to pieces. He imagined the water cradling the ship, gently guiding it through the narrow opening. His body was tiring quickly from the lack of sleep and food.

They were still going too fast, so he pushed harder. All at once, a wall of water rose all around them, shielding them from the cliffs. They slid into the cove and stopped gently next to the dock. Alex released his hold on his magic, grateful for the oar he held propping him up. The water crashed as it fell and receded. Talia studied him intently. His vision swam. He staggered, then slumped to the floor.

"What was that?" Talia's voice sounded like it was coming from a distance away. He felt his face smacked repeatedly. "Your eyes glowed, and you spoke in the language of the gods. Did you do that? Was it Chantara?" She sounded concerned. "You don't look so good."

"Admittedly, I don't feel so good," he mumbled as darkness crept into his vision.

"Oh no you don't. Stay with me." Talia smacked his face a couple more times. "Boy, go get some water."

Alex felt the slap of bare feet reverberate away from them as waves of fatigue rolled over him. He was so tired. He would rest his eyes, just for a little while. The familiar lap of waves against the shore soothed him. His body slowly relaxed as he let the black claim him.

Alex drifted on the dark ocean tides in his mind for an eternity. He felt calm and at peace. It was wonderful. He wrapped it around himself like a warm cloak and let himself drift. The darkness called to him. Beckoning him to give in to it. Whispering promises of safety with its sweet caress of silence.

Yes. He would like that. He was tired. Tired of running and fighting. Tired of not being enough. Here, he felt there were no expectations he could fail. No one he could disappoint.

"What do you want?" a voice whispered softly in the silence.

That voice. It sounded familiar. Those words. He had heard them before.

What did he want?

"Alex."

He heard his name whispered.

"Please. I can't lose you too," a voice from a memory.

"Alex. Alex... ALEX!" His name echoed louder and louder around him.

"Ronin?" Alex called out.

He couldn't stay here. He had to find Ronin. The darkness wrapped around him and constricted. He felt he was being smothered, whereas moments ago, it had felt comforting. No. He had to find Ronin. He fought the darkness, rejecting it. He tried to tear free of it. "I don't want this!" he yelled into the darkness.

"So, this is your choice then?" a voice whispered back.

"Yes. This is what I want," his voice hoarse and rough.

"So be it."

He felt the darkness recede like the water before a typhoon. Fatigue and pain racked his body. His muscles spasmed and cramped painfully. His skin felt like it was on fire.

Cool water touched his lips and ran down his chin and neck. A hand held the back of his neck, supporting him, encouraging him to drink.

"Stay with me, Alex. There you go," Talia's voice murmured in his ear.

The tang of salty sea air blew in his face. He swallowed, letting the water cool his parched throat. He blinked his eyes as they slowly adjusted and brought Talia's worried face into focus.

Her breath whooshed out. "For a moment there, I thought we'd lost you."

"How long was I out?"

She frowned and searched his face. "Only a moment or two... Why?"

"Oh... It felt... longer," He said quietly.

A lot longer.

CHAPTER 37

KORYNNA paced the length of her room furiously. Talia slouched calmly at the window, looking out at the night. Alex had just caught Korynna up on the basics of what happened. Though he and Talia thought it best to leave out the part about Chantara.

She wanted answers they didn't have. They didn't know who had tipped off the *Bellum*, where they had taken everyone, and why they didn't just kill them all. They also didn't know where the *Bellum's* crew docked, but it didn't matter anyway. The *Oleander* was out of commission getting repaired, and Korynna couldn't simply requisition a navy vessel without giving away her network and operation.

Korynna stopped pacing when they heard a knock at the door. She had dismissed her servants for the night, so she went to answer it herself. Alex glanced at the window, but Talia had already disappeared into the night. Just before Korynna reached the door, it flew open, and Viktor sauntered in.

"Korynna, there you are! I've been looking everywhere for you. You missed dinner. The emissary and the ambassador were here." His words sounded cheerful, but his tone was condescending and reproachful, as if admonishing a child, not addressing the king's sister.

Alex grit his teeth and looked anywhere but at Viktor. He noticed a figure standing in the doorway, a look of uncertainty on her face. Her sapphire eyes met Alex's, and a look of surprise flashed across her face before disappearing behind a calm mask of indifference. He took in her unusual attire. She wore mostly shades of tan, brown, and cream; except for a bright blue sash that matched her eyes, wrapped around her waist and tied at her hip. She wore lightweight, loose pants tucked into boots just below her knees, and a similar long-sleeved shirt with dark leather bracers.

His first thought was the bracers could hold hidden blades. He unconsciously moved to place himself between her and Korynna. His second thought was she didn't look like she was just an emissary. He couldn't explain why, and it bothered him. Viktor seemed to notice his presence for the first time.

"What are *you* doing here? This is highly improper. I must ask you to leave immediately." His voice grated on Alex's ears.

Alex bristled at "improper." He really didn't like that word.

Viktor rambled on. "You see, the Duchess is a betrothed woman now, and it is improper and invites assumptions of scandal…"

There was that word again. Wait, Korynna was betrothed? He looked to her for direction. He didn't know what to do. She stood rooted to the spot, staring at the wall to the right of the door. She blinked once, and he watched as the Korynna he knew disappeared behind a mask. Her eyes dulled, and her chin lifted haughtily. She looked down her nose at everyone with slight disdain.

"There will be no such thing. Everyone knows I wouldn't sully myself with the likes of a knight," she huffed, her voice dripped with entitlement and boredom. "I tire of your presence. Leave." She flicked her hand in dismissal without even looking at him. "But don't wander too far. I might need an escort or amusement."

Viktor looked pleased and a little smug. Alex resisted rolling his eyes as he left. He hated court politics and all the games they played. Colin was standing guard a few paces away from her door. He rolled his eyes at Alex, and Alex tried not to smirk and settled for shaking his head instead.

Alex stood guard until Viktor and the emissary left. He was hungry and had also missed dinner, so he went in search of the kitchen. The kitchen staff greeted him formally. They were polite but distant. They offered to pack a meal for him to take with him. He was pretty sure they were trying to get him to leave as soon as possible. As he was about to go, he overheard one of the cooks address a girl by Nessa.

He turned to face her. "Are you Nessa?"

She curtsied stiffly, leaving flour handprints on her dark brown skirt. "yes'sir."

"Are Grogan's Nessa? He speaks highly of you." Alex smiled gently, hoping they might let him stay to eat since he had nowhere else to go.

"He's a good mate, Grogan. I guess you're alright then." She grinned back at him.

Like magic, the entire room seemed to let out a collective breath and relax. Everyone went back to their respective duties and left him alone. Some of them stared with open curiosity, while others tried to hide their sidelong glances.

Several offered him bits of food to taste and asked for his opinion. One of the cooks gave him a bowl of stew she was working on. Another set out a tray piled high with sweet and savory rolls that looked a little misshapen. "Can't serve these to the royals and their guests," the cook said with a kind smile. He placed the "perfect" ones on a silver platter to the side.

Alex sat down on a barrel in a corner out of the way to enjoy the ever-increasing pile snacks beside him. A boy dressed in the house staff uniform wove his way to him and silently handed him a letter. It bore Korynna's seal and was addressed to him; he broke the seal and read its contents. She invited him to a Masquerade Ball in celebration of her engagement three days from now.

He read the contents again to see if he was missing something. They needed to find Ronin and the rest of the *Oleander* crew, not throw a party. He rubbed his temples with his fingers and saw the boy expectantly standing before him. "Is there more?"

"Yes, sir. Follow me, sir."

"Are you hungry?"

"Sir?"

"Have you eaten? Because I haven't, and I would like to eat what these lovely people have prepared for me." He gestured to the various plates of food on the barrel next to him. "And I don't think I can eat it all by myself. I would hate for it to go to waste, wouldn't you?"

The boy gaped up at him. "We aren't supposed to, sir." He hesitated.

Alex winked and held up a finger to his lips. "I won't tell if you don't." Alex saw the barely hidden smiles of the staff, pretending not to notice and watching out of the corner of their eyes.

The boy grinned and helped himself to a meat pie. After they finished every last crumb, the boy, Alastair, led him to a hallway of identical doors. Korynna's guest wing, he was informed when he inquired.

Alastair approached the third door on the right and produced a key. He handed it to Alex and bowed. Just before he ran off, he raised a finger to his lips and grinned.

Alex unlocked the door and stepped inside. The room was lavish and extensive, elegant and almost opulent, with arched doorways and pillars making up the far wall that led to a large balcony overlooking Moradon and the bay. Through another set of arches and pillars draped in dark, shimmery fabric was a bath, if you could call it that. It had a waterfall cascading into the grand oval pool.

Adjacent to the bathing chamber, another room was lined with empty bookshelves and comfortably arranged seating with cushions and blankets. He stepped onto the balcony and rested his palms on the wide marble rail. Off to the side in the corner, a hammock hung under a potted tree with broad leaves— to provide shade during the hottest part of the day, he assumed. He returned inside to continue exploring.

The bed was a massive affair. He guessed he could lie sideways and never reach the sides. Did one need a bed this large? There was a note on the bed next to a black silk half mask with matching silk ribbon to secure it. The note was blank except for the symbol of the Salty Rose and an oleander flower. He wondered what this meant. Was it code?

In the massive, ornate wardrobe, he found the tunic he had admired from the Salty Rose. He smiled as he stroked the fabric appreciatively. Alyse, that sly fox. He laughed under his breath and shook his head. Had Korynna been planning this from the start, or did she have other plans and adapted them for this? Or had Alyse seen him gazing at it in her shop and recommended it when Korynna sent for something for him? Alex moved on to the other articles hanging in the wardrobe. There were two more black tunics like the one she had made him, a dark brown and lighter brown tunic, and, surprisingly, a white one. He wondered at an occasion to wear white. He was more accustomed to blending in with the background and being overlooked. White would call attention to him. Only priests and priestesses of Fiera, royalty, or the Knight Commander wore white. Alex always thought it impractical, as it would get dirty immediately. Though Quinn seemed to wear it without issue.

His thoughts slid to Quinn, and, not for the first time, he found himself wondering where he was and what he was up to. Was he alright? He chastised himself almost immediately for that thought. Of course he was. He was Quinn, captain of the guard of the Council of Fae. He was lethal even without his shapeshifting and air magic. Still, he couldn't help wondering.

Maybe he should tell him Ronin had been captured. No, he rejected that thought. He was sure Quinn would want to know, but he was hesitant to involve him until Korynna had a chance to locate the missing crew.

Alex hated all this sitting on his hands and waiting. He wanted to be doing something. A shadow appeared in his window and realized he had been pacing. He stilled and waited, hoping it was Ronin or Talia. Hope and fear lanced through him. What if it wasn't Ronin *or* Talia? Anyone else who would climb through his window couldn't have good intentions. He palmed the hilt of his dagger, ready for the worst-case scenario.

He didn't have long to wait as the shadow materialized into Talia as she stepped from the window fully into his room. He breathed a sigh of relief. She cast an appreciative eye around his suite before throwing herself onto one of his chairs by the fire, draping her legs over the arms. A smile quirked his lips, but he suppressed it. Here was one of the most deadly people he'd ever met sprawled across one of his chairs like she had not a care in the world. Yet he knew, in the blink of an eye, she could move across the room and either disappear into the night or address any threat with lethal precision.

She still intimidated him, but since the islands, they had an easiness and awareness between them that surprised him. He found himself wanting to share his secrets with her, confident she would accept them, if not understand to some degree. But something held him back, and he didn't know why.

He thought about the people who had suddenly entered his life lately. How he couldn't think of going back to the way things were without them, even Quinn, he realized. He missed the brooding silence and blatant, gruff honesty. He never had to wonder where he stood with Quinn.

"Any luck tracking down where they are holding them?" Alex asked.

Talia blew out a breath. "Yeah, I found them."

"You did? Where? Let's go get them!" Alex headed for the door, checking his weapons.

"Hold up. It's not that easy. There is a timing to this."

"Does Korynna know?" He looked back at Talia, who hadn't moved and was still slung across the chair, staring at the mural painted on the vaulted ceiling.

She nodded. "I just came from her room." She wrinkled her nose.

"What?"

"It's nothing."

Alex walked toward her and dropped into the chair opposite her, content to wait her out. He propped his elbow on his thigh and leaned his chin on his fist.

Emotions crossed her face in rapid fire. "It's just that for as long as I've known her, Korynna has been a fighter and a planner. Always two steps ahead of everyone, even me. Why didn't she see this coming? Where is her blind spot?"

He said nothing as he let her work it out. It took everything in him to keep still and in the chair. He wanted to demand she tell him where Ronin was being held and storm his way in to release him. He wondered how Ronin wasn't out yet. Maybe he was and was looking for him.

A darker thought occurred to him, but he rejected it. No, Ronin wouldn't leave without him, and he definitely wasn't involved in the abductions. He couldn't be. The thought haunted him. How well did he really know Ronin? He shook his head. Where were these thoughts coming from?

"They are in the dungeon." She held up a hand before Alex could interrupt. "Korynna is going to use the ball as a distraction to get them out."

"Why? We should go now! Why wait? What if they are injured? What if they are executed before we can get to them? What if…"

"Alexander! You are not helping. Korynna has a plan. We have to follow it."

"Why? We shouldn't even need to talk about this. We should be on our way down there!" He was yelling, but he didn't care. He was tired of being told what to do. Tired of his life and those of the people he cared about being in someone else's hands. In danger.

"Don't you think I don't feel the same? That she does as well? Our people were taken too, if you remember. Our crew, my family!" Talia hissed. "Do you think I like the idea of waiting to free them, knowing that they could die in the meantime? My hands are tied. We need to wait for the right time. Kor has a plan, and we need to trust her." She sat up and glared at him.

He could see the fear and anguish clearly in her eyes. She cared deeply about the crew of the *Oleander*. He nodded his assent.

"For now, we wait. We prepare, and we wait." Her eyes glittered with lethal intent. "And then we make them pay," she snarled quietly.

CHAPTER 38

THE ball was to be a grand, lavish affair. Peering out of his mask at the guests entering, Alex saw they had spared no expense on their wardrobes. The cost of one of these gowns alone could feed his entire village for a month. He grit his teeth. He hated social functions. McCannon had always said you get used to them, eventually. Still, there were far too many people in a small space for Alex to be comfortable.

He fidgeted with his outfit for the thousandth time since he'd put it on. It was amazing. He looked great, and it was the most comfortable formal outfit he'd ever worn, but that wasn't saying much. He thought formal attire was too constricting, and, quite frankly, fashion was a bit ridiculous. But Alyse was a master at her craft and even sewed a couple of hidden pockets for two of his knives. He reminded himself to thank her when he saw her next.

He waited outside the door to the main entrance of the ball, waiting for Korynna to arrive. She had been held up by some of her advisers and sent word that she would meet him here. He went over the plan in his mind again to keep it straight. They were to make a grand entrance and dance a little. Then she would make her rounds with her subjects as he faded into the background. She would toast and announce her engagement, and that would be his signal to leave. He would have two hours to meet with the guards and crew she had assigned on prison guard duty for tonight and help them escape to the waiting boats to take them to the cove.

He fidgeted again. He'd never been particularly good at standing guard, either. He sighed, hearing McCannon's voice in his head telling him to focus and discipline himself. He couldn't help it. The only time he truly felt still and at peace was in the water. He knew the look in Korynna's eyes when she felt her ship and the sea calling her. He felt it.

He sighed again.

"You must be waiting on a woman with as much sighing as you are doing."

Alex startled at the voice next to him. Viktor looked just like he had on Alex's first day in Moradon, except dressed a bit more lavishly, if that was even possible. His orange half-mask sparkled as he moved. It clashed with the bright yellows and oranges of his robes, making him look like a cross between a tropical bird and a candle. Alex coughed to cover his snicker.

"Why yes, I do believe I am. She should be here any minute, though." He hoped Viktor took the hint and kept walking. If not, he needed to think of a way to get rid of this man as soon as possible. There was no way he would suffer his condescending tone for very long without getting violent.

Ronin was rubbing off on him. Right, Ronin. That was why they were here. To create a distraction while the crew of the *Oleander* infiltrated the prison below and sprung Ronin and their other crew members.

Viktor frowned. "And who might that be, if you don't mind my asking? I know every name on the guest list." He pulled out a list from the folds of his oversized robes.

Of course he did, Alex groaned inwardly.

"Me." Korynna's voice echoed down the long hallway. She wore *the* red and black dress and looked every bit the regal duchess, sister to the king, as she glided down the hall effortlessly. The soft swish of her dress was the only sound she made as she approached.

Viktor's fake smile turned into a scowl. Alex made a point to ignore the looks Viktor gave him. Alex bowed deeply to Korynna. He stepped toward her and offered her his arm like he'd seen some other men do for the ladies at court. She placed her hand on his forearm and dipped her head in the slightest of nods to Viktor before facing the main doors.

"Shall we?" she said softly.

Alex nodded, and the guards opened the large, gilded marble doors, announcing their arrival. He led her into the room as everyone bowed or curtsied to them, to her. Alex couldn't shake the feeling of foreboding crawling down his spine as the doors closed behind them.

XXX

Alex sprinted down the steps of the palace and out into the street. His heartbeat pounded in his ears, drowning out the sound of his leather boots slapping on the cobblestones. He had to get away. All else was driven from his mind except escape. He couldn't breathe. He stopped as he reached the part of town where the cobblestone streets turned to hard-packed dirt.

They had been set up. Somehow, someone had been tipped off. Alex knew something was wrong when Colin approached Korynna and whispered in her ear before her speech. To her credit, she had only blinked then flicked her eyes to Alex and said something back.

Alastair found Alex not long after, made some excuse as to needing his presence, and then filled him in on what Colin had just informed Korynna. They had attempted to break Ronin and the crew out of the prison, but when they got there, the prison cells were completely empty. Not a single soul.

Alex had remained hidden in an alcove, trying to master his frustration, when he overheard Viktor bragging about how he had captured the crew of the infamous *Oleander* and their captain, none other than the Phantom, also known as Foxglove. And then dispatched them to the ends of the kingdom. The courtiers had congratulated him on his cleverness and begged to know where he'd sent them. He said they had disappeared like he was making the rest of the "waifs, street urchins, and unsightly scum" of the city. They congratulated him again on his endeavors and successes.

Alex burned with anger, and it took everything in him not to go after Viktor, right then and there. He probably would have, but someone had slipped him a note, saying to meet them on the edge of the forest and signed it, "Dahlia." They must be one from Foxgloves' network, given their code name.

He felt, rather than saw, Talia step next to him on the dirt street. Her unspoken question echoed in the silence. He filled her in on the night's excitement as best he could.

"I have a contact who claims to know where they are keeping them. I'm going after them. Come with me?" he asked.

She shook her head. "I can't just yet. Kor and I have to take care of a little matter here first. From what you said, it seems Viktor has been really busy lately. He's taken liberties with his authority. He sent the Navy to the Divina Iles to clear them out."

"He did what?" Alex clenched his fist. "That man needs to die, but it will have to wait."

"Alone?" she asked.

"What choice do I have?"

She frowned. "You don't know what you are up against... how many of them there are... the layout... I don't like it. Kor won't either, you know."

"But..." he started to defend his reasons, but she held up her hand.

"I don't like it, but I do understand. If our roles were reversed, and it was Kor in trouble, I'd tear down the mountains and drain the oceans to get to her."

"Thank you." He looked her in the eye. He hoped she saw the depth of his gratitude for her understanding.

She gave him a ghost of a smile. "Go save the world, Alex. Or at least our corner of it." She placed a hand on his shoulder and squeezed gently. "Here, you'll need this." She handed him the dagger she had taken from him in the warehouse.

Alex looked down at the dagger, then back up at her, but she had melded into the shadows as if she had never been there. Alex blinked and stared into the darkness for a moment.

"Ronin, I need you. Where are you?" he called in his mind. He knew he would not get an answer. He knew now that Ronin had been betrayed, set up, but now he knew where to look.

He reached the wall of the city a few minutes later. He was kicking himself for not stopping to borrow a horse. It would take all night to get to the bandits' camp on foot. He kicked a rock on the road, mad at his lack of foresight. He had been stupid, naive. He should have known better than to wait. He should have gone to the dungeon right then and not waited to free Ronin and the rest of the crew.

He just hadn't expected Viktor to pull what he did. He hadn't seen Viktor coming at all. Meddlesome, petty, despicable… How he thought selling information to the bandits on the people of Moradon who would be easy targets for kidnapping… He just… Alex was furious all over again.

Viktor was so smug about it, too. He thought he was helping rid Moradon of the weak and poor "burdening" the city. He thought he could pin it on the Phantom, on Ronin. Shipments had been going missing as well as people. How he found out Ronin was the Phantom was still beyond him. Viktor had sold all the prisoners to a group of bandits disguised as a troupe of dancers. Had been for months, possibly years.

He slowed his steps to catch his breath. It was dark out here in the overcast, moonless night. He was tempted to call his fire magic to light his way. Someone would probably think it was just a lantern or torch if he were seen, but no one was out tonight. Wait, he had an idea. The fire foal doesn't burn him, he remembered from the ice caves. Quickly, he called his little foal. "Do you think you can help me?" he asked, as if it were a real horse. He had already started thinking of it as if it were. It snorted and bobbed its head. "Alright, here goes nothing."

He held out his hand and concentrated. Something nudged his hand. A stallion made of pure fire stood before him, pawing the air. It bumped his hand with its amber and golden muzzle again and lipped his fingers. He could see the faintest outline of the foal blazing within the stallion. He hesitated for a moment longer, still not quite believing it. It worked.

He vaulted lightly up on its back and laced his fingers through its fiery mane as he pointed them toward the horizon. "Hold on, Ronin. I'm coming! I'm coming," he whispered as they broke into a gallop and streaked into the night.

✗✗✗

Alex neared the edge of the forest where Dahlia said to meet her and hesitated before urging his fire stallion to the trail between the trees. He didn't see anything or anyone moving in the flickering light. Wheel marks and footprints in the dirt appeared to be fresh. He followed the trail to a large clearing, but the remnants of campfires looked a couple of days old. Only one trail led into the clearing, but tracking had never been his strongest skill. If they had dispersed into the forest, he would more than likely have gotten lost before he happened upon someone. They were probably long gone anyway.

Gritting his teeth in frustration, he rested his forehead on the stallion's mane. He had been so close. He was so sure he would find Ronin and the rest of the *Oleander* crew here. He didn't know what to do or where to look. Before heading back to Moradon, he contemplated taking a nap. The thought of going back empty-handed made him sick. What other options did he have?

Quinn.

"Quinn! Ronin has been captured, and he isn't responding. I am pretty sure he was taken by the same people who have been kidnapping people from all over," Alex called with his mind. *"Quinn, I need you to hear me. Please respond. I need your help,"* he called desperately.

"*Alex, I know.*"

"*You do? How?*"

"*I don't have time to explain. How long will it take you to get to the edge of the dead lands?*"

That was halfway to Tayloridge and dangerously close to the battle lines. Why there? He thought for a moment. "*Just before dawn, I think.*"

"*Follow the dry riverbed to a natural stone arch. Just past it, you'll find a cave. Follow the right tunnel when it branches. I'll meet you just before dawn.*"

"*What are you doing there?*" He was met with silence. What other choice did he have? This was as good a lead as any. "*Okay, I'll see you then.*"

✕✕✕

Alex rode through the night, pushing his magical fire stallion as fast as he could go without falling off. The exertion of his magic on his already tired mind and body drained what he had left. He needed to rest, but he didn't have time. He knew it was dangerous to keep going when he was this tired, but kept pushing himself. Just a little more, just a little longer.

The sky was just beginning to lighten when he stumbled upon the old riverbed. He slid from his fire stallion's back. His knees almost gave way, but he held onto its mane to steady himself. The stallion bowed its neck and rested its forehead on Alex's chest, letting out a huff. Steam curled around them. Alex stroked its warm cheek, then it dispersed into a trail of sparks rising into the sky. He would have to traverse the rest on foot.

He was weary and tempted to rest, but it was getting lighter with each passing moment.

He found the arch and the cave without much trouble. The tunnels were dark. He had no idea how he would see, but as it turned out, he didn't need to be worried. Once he was out of sight of the cave entrance sconces burned at regular intervals. Quinn had said take the right tunnel, but when he came to the third set of branching tunnels, he wasn't sure if he should keep going right or choose another path. The left and center seemed more brightly lit. He was tempted to see where they led, but in the end, he kept going right.

The tunnel emptied into a natural ravine carved from barren stone. He shivered and looked around. Not a blade of grass or green anything grew in sight. He didn't see a way out of here. He had met a dead end. That couldn't be right, could it?

"Hey, I think you gave me the wrong directions. I met a dead end," he said to Quinn in his mind.

"No, you are right where I want you," a voice said behind him.

Alex wheeled around. Quinn stood in the mouth of the tunnel he had just exited. Relief flooded through him until he noticed a shadow lurking behind Quinn.

"Look out behind you!" Alex called to him, but Quinn just stood there watching him. The figure stepped up next to Quinn and looked at him. It was one of the minotaur Alex had seen him with in Osrealach before the Revealing ceremony. He was one of the guards?

Quinn nodded. Surprise and hurt lanced through Alex's chest as a net dropped on top of him, driving him to the ground. It was cold and heavy. With a jolt, Alex realized it was made of iron. He looked at Quinn, his feelings of betrayal etched deeply on his face. Four more minotaur watched from the bluff above him. He had walked right into their trap.

A sharp pain spiked on the back of his head, then everything went black.

CHAPTER 39

ALEX'S blindfold was removed suddenly. He was speechless. Quinn stood a couple of steps away, pretending like he had never laid eyes on Alex before. That was fine. Alex could pretend too. He wished he hadn't, that was for sure.

The sounds of battle rose all around him. Minotaur and fairies hurled javelins and shot arrows at the group of humans, dressed in outlandish costumes on the floor of an arena carved out of the old river bed. Pairs and groups faced off against each other with an assortment of weapons and shields.

One human, painted in gold and teal, brandished a net and a three-pointed fishing spear moved counter to another human painted in blood-red and bronze, wearing a lion pelt, wielding a short sword and crescent shield. They attacked and dodged in a deadly dance. It was mesmerizing. The ground shook. Overhead, the sky erupted as fire rained down on the combatants. Smoke billowed from pits dotted around the sandy arena floor. It was chaos, pure chaos.

Questions burned in Alex's mind demanding answers. Where had Quinn been this whole time? Here? How could he do this to his own people? Why? Was he working undercover, or was this who he really worked for? A thought struck Alex that made him stagger. He looked at Quinn questioningly. *"Why?"* he asked in his mind. No answer.

Alex's emotions stormed within him as he tried and failed to remain calm. Several figures were chained to the ground in the center of the arena, surrounded by mayhem. Through the dust, he thought he recognized Bronach. His fear gave way to anger and desperation. Bronach was smaller than Alex remembered. His skin showed months of abuse and neglect, with old and new scars and bruises covering his bare back and arms.

Quinn shoved Alex from behind and growled. "Keep moving. Don't gawk. Act like you've been here before, or you'll draw attention." He led Alex near a raised platform overlooking the arena. Several forms were seated in ornate chairs, watching the battle unfold below them. The individual seated in the middle focused on Alex. A sly, feral grin crept across her face.

She wore a gold embroidered turquoise toga belted at the waist with a golden cord. Golden bangles decorated her wrists and arms and golden paint swirled in intricate designs accenting her flawless ebony skin.

"Excellent, you are just in time. This is my favorite part!" she said, turning back to watch the fight.

Over the din of the battle, Alex heard a crowd roar. He gaped at the hundreds of masked people surrounding the arena, watching the fight. This was a sport to them. The woman stood and raised her hands. Immediately, the crowd quieted. Even the combatants paused their deadly performance and turned to face them. Alex felt the air around him grow tense with excited anticipation and dread.

Bronach looked up at him and met his gaze. His shock of recognition quickly transformed into a look of horror and disappointment. He shook his head and turned away. Alex begged in his mind for Bronach to look at him. He wasn't sure what he would do if he did. He wanted to say it wasn't what it looked like, and didn't know what was going on, and wanted no part of it. That he would get them out of this. But Bronach did not look up at him again.

Alex felt like the ground was falling out from underneath him. He wished it would swallow him. He valued Bronach's opinion more than anything. If only he could explain himself.

The woman's voice tore his attention away from Bronach. "Hello, my patrons! Are you having fun yet?" She exclaimed.

The crowd roared and cheered.

"I have a delicious new guest with me today!" she purred. "They have never experienced our hospitality before. Shall we show them a good time?"

The crowd cheered, wordlessly at first, but then one word emerged as the crowd chanted, "Box! Box! Box! Box!"

The combatants on the arena floor shifted nervously. Quinn stiffened next to Alex and inhaled sharply.

She quieted the crowd. "Oh! Well, I had thought to ease them into it." The crowd booed and she laughed. "But if you insist." The crowd's cheers were deafening.

She raised her hands, and again the crowd fell silent. "Oh, where are my manners? I seem to have forgotten to introduce myself. Won't you do it for me? Say my name!"

"Indra!" the crowd cheered in unison.

"Say my name!" she commanded.

"Indra!" the crowd yelled louder.

"SAY MY NAME!" she commanded again.

"INDRA!" the crowd chanted in perfect unison, then fell eerily silent.

She turned back to face Alex and spread her arms wide out to the side. "Hello, my name is Indra. Welcome to The Underground!" she grinned wickedly.

The crowd's cheers thundered wildly as they began chanting again. "Box! Box! Box! Box!"

She raised her hand and made a flicking motion. Alex watched as grates and gates in the floor and walls opened. The combatants in the arena scrambled through them, trampling whoever got in their way. Quinn led Alex down a tunnel, the sounds of the crowd fading into the background, giving way to an almost deafening silence only broken by their footfalls on the stone floor.

"What is the 'Box'?" Alex asked as they entered a tiny stone room furnished with a table and cot in the corner.

"The Box is an iron cage placed in the center of the arena. It is considered a great honor, and the best seat in the house. You get a… unique perspective of the entertainment," he trailed off, his eyes going distant. "But also potentially deadly. Which, for some, adds to the appeal of the experience." Quinn shuddered before schooling his features into stillness.

"Why?" Alex asked softly. His eyes pleaded with Quinn, but he refused to meet Alex's gaze.

"The thrill, I suppose." Quinn shrugged as he turned to leave.

"What about these?" Alex lifted his chained wrists.

Quinn looked at him, his face stony and unreadable. Alex raised his hand and placed one finger on his temple. He hoped Quinn would understand what he wanted. There were ears everywhere, so he couldn't risk being overheard. Quinn nodded and sighed, then unlocked Alex's chains.

"Yes?"

"Why? Why are you helping them? Why are you doing this? We have to free them, Quinn. I can't... I won't walk away. This isn't okay."

"I have orders."

"From who? From her? What does she have over you? Can I help? This isn't okay, and you know it!" Alex tried putting all his feelings into those words as he raged in his head.

"I KNOW. Don't you think I don't know that? Do you think I like watching her slaughter people–MY PEOPLE–for their entertainment?" Quinn yelled in his mind. Alex winced.

"Sorry," Quinn said out loud.

"Then WHY?!? What could possibly be more important than the lives of hundreds... thousands of people? Both fae and human."

"Alex... I can't. I have orders." Quinn looked tortured and defeated. He rubbed a hand down his face.

Alex was starting to piece things together, and the last piece clicked into place in his head. He reeled and staggered. "The council knows about this and hasn't stopped it?" He braced an arm against the wall to keep from falling.

Quinn looked at his feet. His shoulders slumped.

Alex continued, "Orders from the council? What is the purpose of having leaders and following orders if they don't have their people's best interest at heart? Why? What reasons could they possibly have?

I refuse to believe that anyone who knows this is going on and lets it continue could possibly want what is best for their people. I have to believe... I choose to believe that every person's life is just as valuable as the next. Regardless of their station, power, or birth. Each life is worth fighting for. Each person, fae and human alike, is worth *protecting. We each have value. We matter. Some are just more visible than others."*

Alex felt his words echo like they had been spoken in a much larger space, sending out vibrations that resounded through his entire being, seeming to grow, rather than fade. It was an odd sensation. *"I want to live in a world that understands that and embodies it at the core of its civilization,"* he said resolutely.

"That's not how it works." Quinn sounded mournful. He lifted a hand and inspected his palms as if they would give him answers to unspoken questions.

"But what if it could be?" Alex asked quietly. Silence stretched between them.

"Okay," Quinn breathed. He finally met Alex's eyes. *"What do you have in mind?"*

XXX

Quinn left Alex's assigned quarters a few hours later, having hammered out a decent plan. He was skeptical because it relied on far too many variables, but it was the best they could come up with on short notice. He had to resume his normal duties to remain inconspicuous.

Alex was to wait until nightfall and sneak into the cells and free Ronin. From there, they would work to free everyone while Quinn opened gates and redirected guards to provide them an escape route. If everything went according to plan, they would be long gone before anyone noticed something was amiss.

Alex's heart raced as he waited for the last of the sun's rays to sink behind the horizon. He wondered if Korynna and

Talia had found the cave entrance in the old riverbed and followed the little marks he had left for them. When Alex had asked about how no one had found the underground by accident, Quinn said it would be easy to get lost in the sprawling tunnel system even if someone wandered in.

The set of small iron keys weighed heavy in Alex's sweaty hand. He wiped his palms on his pants and rolled his shoulders to reduce the tension building. Any time now, the guard would finish their first rounds for the night, and Alex would sneak his way into the lower levels of the prison.

He went over the plan in his head. Find and free Ronin and Bronach. Free the rest of the prisoners, lead them through the tunnel to the south marked with a little sun, through the unlocked gates, and out into the forest. All before the second round of patrols. Simple and easy. Except, what if someone wasn't where they were supposed to be? What if they changed their patrols? What if they made too much noise? What if...?

Alex shook his head to clear it. *"What if's"* weren't helping. He needed to focus. He sat on the floor, closed his eyes, and tried to relax like Ronin had taught him all those months ago. Breathe in, hold, breathe out. Repeat. Breathe in, hold, breathe out. Repeat.

He set down the keys in front of him and held out his hand. Instantly, his fire foal appeared in his palm. It pranced and reared in his hand, then faced him. It seemed to say, "I'm with you. We've got this."

The pressure in his chest eased a fraction. The foal bobbed its head once before Alex let go of his fire magic. Next, he reached for his water magic. He felt the water in the air around him, the water in the small pitcher on the table next to his cot, and even the water in his breath. He drew the first two to him and held it suspended in front of him. Reaching out, he touched it, inviting it to flow across his palm and fingers.

A thought struck him, could he make temporary armor out of water with his magic? It would mean a great deal of concentration, at least at first, but he believed it could work. He needed to test it, but not now. He shaped the water like his friend Eirach and opened his mind to the colony.

"Little Defender missed," came the response from far away.

"Hello." He smiled as several sea dragons sent their greetings through feelings of concern, joy, and contentment. Some questioned him. Some he couldn't interpret what they were trying to convey. He sighed as he let them wash through his consciousness.

"Come?" Eirach asked. He was asking if Alex was going to join them anytime soon. Alex sent them pictures of what was going on, where he was, and everything he had seen. He felt the collective shudder and then felt a unified outrage.

"Where?" They wanted to know where he was. How to get to him. They wanted to help.

"Too far inland, I'm afraid," he replied back.

"Sky dragons." They wanted him to contact Saoirse and the dragons who could fly or walk to him. To call them to his aid.

"I can't. I don't have the guardian stone to talk to them," he replied. He had thought of that. He didn't know if they would respond, let alone come, but he had no way of talking to them.

"Then we will." Their unified voices were overwhelming. *"They will come. We will come."*

Alex sent all his feelings of gratitude to them and felt their acceptance of it, then bid them farewell. He directed the water back to his pitcher before releasing his water magic. It overflowed down onto the table, then dripped to the floor. He had drawn quite a bit of water from around him.

As soon as they were gone, he felt the absence of their presence. Feeling deeply alone and almost crippled with loneliness, he sat on the floor a moment longer before rising to his feet. His left leg prickled. It had fallen asleep as he sat on the cold stone floor. Once the sensation faded, he listened at the door for footsteps, then slipped from his room.

Quietly, he padded down the corridor, listening closely for anyone approaching, but he met no one. He found the door Quinn had indicated led to the cells below, unlocked, just as promised. Every little sound, every drip or scrape, set him on edge. He imagined guards around every turn, discovering him and locking him up before he could finish his goal.

His breathing sounded loud in his ears. He imagined it was loud enough to be heard all around him, when in reality, he was making almost no sound at all. Down a tight spiral staircase and through the last door, he found what he was looking for. He smelled it first. He covered his nose with the collar of his tunic.

The stench of unwashed bodies, waste, and sweat stung his eyes, making them water. How could anyone treat people like this? Even animals deserved better. Fury and rage bubbled just under his skin, begging to be unleashed.

It was pitch black, with no windows to let in light or fresh air. He kicked himself for not bringing a torch or lantern with him. He couldn't see in the dark like Ronin and Quinn, so against his better judgment, he called his fire magic to him. It came easily, fueled by his anger.

The silence was almost audible as soon as the foal sparked in his hand. He concentrated on making it bigger until it was life-sized. The air around him sizzled. Then the overpowering stench seemed to burn away, and fresh air flowed around him.

He released his collar and began peering into the cells as he passed. Humans and fae huddled in the corners of their cells; some covered their eyes with their hands or arms. Gasps and murmurs emanated from the cells. He didn't have time to release all of them just yet, but he didn't have to. Someone else could free them and lead them. He needed to find Ronin and Bronach.

One woman stepped toward him, eyes glowing in the firelight. She wore torn rags and leather and had bandages wrapped around her thigh. What stood out the most was, in spite of all this, she still stood like a warrior with defiant pride. Her.

He moved toward the iron bars of her cell door. His foal skittered behind him. He tried one of the keys. Not the right one. And the next and the next until he found the right one. The door groaned as it opened. As soon as the gap was wide enough, she slipped out. He pressed the key into her hand.

"Can you get them out of their cells? Any of them that can walk. Meet me by the far door as soon as you can. Quickly. Quietly. We don't have much time."

She held up the key in the firelight, then looked at him wide-eyed before nodding wordlessly. She moved to the next cell and opened it, gesturing to those inside. Alex kept moving, looking into each cell before moving on. He reached the end. Ronin wasn't here. He was a little disappointed.

"Who are you looking for?" a voice met him from the shadows.

He described Bronach and Ronin as best he could.

"Ah, the black warrior or 'Bacia' as some call him. He is kept isolated in the far cells. The blacksmith labors in the audition room when not in the arena."

"The audition room?"

"A sick joke of hers. She requires each prisoner to be auditioned to judge their skill level and placed in a fighting group. Those of us she deems 'worthy' she makes fight in pairs or single combat."

"That's horrible. Barbaric."

The voice snorted. "Don't the humans do much the same with their jousts and fighting tournaments?"

"How do you know I'm human?"

"I've seen you fight, Alexander of Creedon. I've even fought you once myself."

Shock rippled through him. He stepped closer to the voice to illuminate the shadows. Huddled in a corner, missing an arm, was Sayyid. He was one of the Keirwyn soldiers who had been a part of a special combat training exchange between Reyall and Keirwyn during the very brief period of peace between the two kingdoms.

"We'll get you out. I just need to find Ronin."

"It's too late for me, but I hope you accomplish what you set out to do. It's a pity I won't get to see it."

"What do you mean? We'll get you out soon." Then he noticed the growing dark pool all around Sayyid. "Oh. I'm so sorry."

Sayyid waved his hand at him in a shooing motion. "I don't have much time left. Don't waste yours on me."

As Alex turned to go, he heard Sayyid talking to himself. "I'm glad you let me see him one more time. I think he has what it takes, the poor soul. Watch over him and guide him." The door closed behind Alex, cutting off the rest of his words.

He repeated the same process through the next three rooms of cells, finding someone to unlock and lead them out, telling them where to meet him. He came to the last door and fit his last key into the lock. The door groaned on its hinges as it opened to a large cell with dozens of empty shackles lining the walls and floors. What was this place? What was it meant for?

In the center of the floor, a figure lay curled on their side. As his fire foal blazed in the darkness, it illuminated the countless chains attached to iron bands encircling their ankles, wrists, neck, arms, legs, and chest.

Ronin. He was completely covered in iron banding. Alex tried to fit the key into the first lock, but it didn't work. He didn't know what to do. He couldn't use his fire, or he might burn Ronin. He didn't have control of his air magic, so he couldn't simply unlock them.

He put his hands in his pockets as he paced, feverishly trying to come up with an idea of how to get Ronin out. Why hadn't Quinn given him this key? Did he have it? Did he know?

He felt a grain of something with his fingertips and pulled it out to inspect it. It was a seed. Hope flooded in him as an idea sparked. If he could grow the seed into the locks he could break or unlock them.

He knelt on the sandy floor and placed the tiny seed in front of him. He reached for his earth magic, and his fire foal snuffed out. Taking all the light with it. He willed the seed to sprout and grow, imagining small vines growing toward the locks and unlocking them. He released it and called his fire foal again to see what he had grown.

The seed had sprouted, but it was barely a shoot, nothing more. He growled in frustration and put his head in his hands. Why couldn't he do this one little thing? He slammed his fists down on the sandy floor and heard a crunch, like glass breaking. Two perfect glass imprints shaped like his hands rested in the sand.

He had another idea. Thoughts of Kynthelic drifted through his mind. If he couldn't make the seed grow, he could make keys out of sand. He scooped up the sand with his hands and poured it into the locks. Then he concentrated and directed his fire to make the sand solid. He poured more sand on top and willed it to shape like a handle enough for him to grasp and turn. It shattered. He tried again, making it thicker and sturdier this time. It worked. The lock fell open with a scrape and click.

He repeated the process on all the other locks and removed the chains. He pried open the first cuff and hissed at the little barbs lining the inside, meant to pierce the skin of its wearer. There was no doubt in his mind, these cuffs were made with fae in mind.

Ronin groaned and opened his eyes as soon as Alex had the last cuffs off him. "Alex?"

"Hey, Ro. How are you holding up? Sorry it took me so long to get here." Alex lifted Ronin's head and shoulders into his lap and brushed his hair out of his face.

"I'm good, just taking a nap in my plush quarters. I mean honestly, it felt like a vacation. You could have taken your time," he said sarcastically. His attempt at a grin was more like a grimace.

Alex couldn't help but chuckle. "Look, I grew a tree for you... or tried to."

Ronin tried to laugh, but it came out in gasps of pain.

"What did they do to you?" Alex asked as he inspected Ronin closely.

"When they took us, they were prepared. Iron from the start. It's like they knew."

"They do. The people running this barbaric slaughter are fae. They call it entertainment. Have you ever heard of someone by the name of Indra?"

Ronin shook his head. "No, but that doesn't surprise me. There are a lot of fae scattered throughout Reyall for various reasons." He groaned as he sat up. "I only remember bits and pieces since that night. I'm going to kill them all." His growl reverberated through the room making dust and sand fall on them from above.

Alex looked down at the sand, then back up at the ceiling. "Are we beneath the arena?"

Ronin shrugged and grimaced again. "They kept me pretty out of it once they realized I wouldn't fight in their mock battles. I overheard some of the guards say they had other plans for me. Sorry I'm not much help."

"No, you are fine. I'm just glad you are still alive. Do you think you can stand?"

"Give me a few minutes to clear my head and let my body heal without all the iron touching me. I'll be okay soon."

"Alright, I'll go check on everyone else and come back for you." Alex set Ronin gently on the floor and jogged to the door. He glanced back at Ronin before sprinting down the corridor, back the way he'd come. He found a group of prisoners huddled by the last door. Silently, they watched him approach with his fire foal at his side.

The four leaders he had assigned stepped out of the group and came to meet him. "What will you have us do now?" The warrior from the first group asked in a low voice.

"Through that door, a drainage tunnel marked with Fiera's symbol will lead you to the forest. Take your groups separately. Be as quiet as possible and do not draw attention. I'd like to avoid any more bloodshed if possible. We will regroup in the forest and decide what to do next. If no one else meets you by nightfall tomorrow, make your way to the coast to the east or west. I'll have someone meet you."

"Where will you be? This is your plan. What if something happens to you? Who will meet us?"

"I can't divulge their identity yet, but you will know them and they you when you get there. Let's hope we don't need them, though."

They nodded in agreement and moved to their assigned groups. Alex walked over to the main door and eased it open to look out. There was no one on the stairs. So far, Quinn had held up his end of the mission. Now, it was Alex's turn to uphold his.

Time to free them. He still needed to find Bronach, though. He crept up the stairs and peered around the edge.

Oh, no. There were dozens of guards stationed at regular intervals all along the halls. Was that normal? What were they doing there? Had he been down there longer than he'd thought?

This was the only door out of the prison cells. He pressed himself to the side wall of the staircase as he weighed their options. They could try to fight their way out, but without weapons and since most of them were injured, their odds were slim. They could try to make another exit. He could create a distraction. He sighed at an idea taking shape in his mind.

"Ronin?"

"It's good to hear your voice again."

"Same. There are too many guards to get out this way, but I have an idea."

"Why do I have a feeling I won't like this idea?"

"Do you feel strong enough to grow a tree?"

"A tree? I could probably manage if given enough time. Why?"

"I'm going to send everyone your way. I need you to grow that sprout into a tree, up through the arena floor."

"Uh, two problems. What about the guards? And how is being in the arena any better than being down here? We'll still be trapped."

"I need to find Bronach."

Ronin seemed to catch on to what Alex was thinking. *"No. Nope. No, we'll figure out a different way."*

"Ro, I have to."

"I was right. I don't like this idea. Not one bit. But I see your strategy in it. Is there really no other way? What about getting out of the arena?"

"Just grow the damn tree and get everyone up there. I'll handle the rest."

"I'd say be careful, but nothing about any of this qualifies..." Ronin trailed off. *"To the world in our dreams..."*

"...and this one here and now," Alex finished.

Alex tiptoed quietly back down the stairs and informed the group of their change in plans.

"Why should we follow the Bacia?"

"Quiet, we are all Bacia now."

"Bacia?" someone else asked.

Sully, one of Korynna's crew, answered, "Death bringer."

"Ronin will get you out."

"Where are you going?"

"To create a distraction for you. Follow him," Alex commanded, not waiting for them to agree as he turned on his heel and strode out. He leaned against the door and took a deep breath. In truth, he had no idea what he was going to do, but they were counting on him.

He stalked up the stairs and squared his shoulders. Releasing his fire magic, he stepped into view of the guards. Immediately, all eyes were on him.

"I wish to audition," he declared, leveling the nearest guards with his best intimidating glare.

"That's not how this works," the guard scoffed.

"Why would you want to audition?" another guard asked.

"This one here is crazy. Did you hear him? He wants to audition."

Quinn strode down the corridor like he owned the place. The guards saluted him. He ignored them and considered Alex skeptically. "If he wants to audition, let him audition." He shrugged. "Better chain him up first, though. Wouldn't want to make it too easy on him now, would we?"

Alex shot him a look as the guards approached him. *"What game are you playing at? That isn't helpful,"* he said to Quinn in his mind. Quinn ignored him.

CHAPTER 40

THE guards led Alex to a round, two-story stone building with vaulted ceilings. The afternoon sunlight streamed through windows down to the floor. Stone pillars supported the second-story balcony that overlooked the open center. They entered through one of four arching doorways spaced like the points on a compass.

Alex saw a courtyard and training grounds outside the arena through the doorway opposite him. To one side, outside the inner ring of pillars, Bronach hunched over a crude weapon. Alex guessed it was for the arena fighters. Chains ran from the base of a tiny forge to iron cuffs around his ankles, wrists, and neck. It pained Alex to see him this way. Gone was the kind, confident man of strength. This Bronach was barely a wraith full of defeat and resignation.

"This one wishes to audition. The captain ordered chains," the guard said by way of introduction. Indra sat with a couple of others along another wall. She didn't even look their way and simply waved her hand at them to continue.

They handed Alex a crude blade off the pile on the floor next to the forge. "Make it good, and you'll get better treatment. That's how it works. If you make it too clean, the crowd gets bored. Draw it out. No one likes a fight that ends too fast," the guard told him before stepping back.

Alex glanced at Indra, but she was only half paying attention to the ensuing fight. Alex danced back, away from his opponent. He eyed the mercs along the wall, watching with smug faces like this was entertaining for them. He heard the telltale jingle of coins being passed around. They were betting on this fight. Alex felt disgusted. There was nothing humane about forcing people to fight each other for sport. He spied Quinn leaning against one of the open doorways, arms crossed and frowning.

Alex's opponent wasn't incredibly skilled and had a very direct, hack-and-slash approach to fighting. Every once in a while, they tried to change it up. Alex tried to catch Quinn's eye. Too late, he realized his momentary distraction caused him to misjudge his opponent's feint. The tip of their dull blade scraped across his chest, just below his collarbone. He heard the chain around his neck give, followed by the distinct ring of metal on the stone floor.

Alex dodged and dove for his ring, but one of the mercenaries deftly snatched it up. He reached for it but was shoved back by several other mercs. They laughed and sneered at him. "That's not all you'll lose by the end of it."

Alex growled and lunged again, his "audition" forgotten. He felt the chains around his feet catch, yanking his legs out from under him. Something slammed into his temple, and kicked him in his gut. He gasped and tried to roll, staggering to his feet.

He raised his crude blade just in time to barely deflect a strike aimed at his head. His weapon was heavy and poorly weighted, and the iron cuffs around his wrists, connected by a long heavy chain, dragged heavily at his arms, making his movements slow and disjointed. The mercs cheered and yelled encouraging words to the brute before him.

His opponent hacked at him again. He dodged out of the way, only to realize they weren't aiming for him, but for his chains. They hooked the chains and twisted, wrenching his arms and sending his sword flying. Dropping their weapon, they grabbed his chains and yanked him toward them. He was a huge brute with scarred, corded muscles and fists the size of Alex's head. Alex saw the strike coming as if in slow motion and tried to move out of the way, but they held tight to his chains.

Alex felt the air leave him as their fist connected with his stomach. He doubled over as pain radiated through him. His vision swam as he felt, rather than saw, the other fist connect with his jaw. He hit the ground a moment later and felt a barrage of kicks to his back and head. Curling in on himself instinctively, he covered the back of his neck with his hands. He couldn't breathe. He heard a loud crack and felt his ribs break as he tried to roll away again. He was losing consciousness from the pain.

Laughs and jeers echoed around him. His whole body throbbed and his mind screamed for him to get up, to fight back, but his body wouldn't cooperate. His opponent yanked his chains, wrenching his arms again.

"Stop!" a voice yelled.

He saw a shadow looming over him through his blurry vision and felt a hand grasp the front of his tunic and lift his shoulders a little off the ground.

"Look at me!" the voice said, yanking him roughly.

Alex blinked and tried to focus on the figure in front of him. His vision blackened around the edges again, but he fought it. He knew if he passed out, he was as good as dead. The hand grasping his shirt shook him hard.

"This! What are you doing with this ring? How did you get it? Did you steal it?" Whispered comments from the other mercenaries informed him this one's name was Caspian.

"What's it to you?" Alex snapped.

"Tell me, or I'll end you here and now. It must mean something to you to wear it around your neck like a keepsake."

"Why should I tell you anything?" Alex spat. His words came out stronger than he felt.

"Answer me."

"My... mother gave it to me," he rasped. His split lip stung. His vision finally focused on his father's ring inches from his face.

"How did she get it?" he demanded.

"She said my father gave it to her," Alex gritted through his teeth.

Caspian snorted. "Your father? Did he steal it?"

"No. Maybe. I don't know. He was a mercenary like you."

"Why would he give this to her?"

"She said they were in love, but her father didn't approve. They were going to run away together, but he left and never came back, like the coward he was." Alex spat. Bitterness and resentment welled up in him. His nonexistent father was still a sore spot. "What is it to you?"

"Rose... was pregnant? But that would mean..." Caspian paused in shocked silence, "You're my son..."

"You? No." All the betrayal he had been stuffing down, the abandonment, the anger, rushed through him like a flood. This man, who captured people and made them fight each other for sport, couldn't be his father. What did that make him?

Alex lurched to his feet. His vision turned red, outrage overriding the pain in his body. "Don't you dare call me 'son'!"

he spat at Caspian, shoving him back and forcing him to let go of his hold on Alex's shirt.

"Where were you when she cried herself to sleep at the sight of this ring or the mere mention of you?" he demanded, his voice raw and raspy. "Where were you when the other children chased and tormented me every day because I wasn't like them... When the other knights and nobles scorned and scoffed at me, at her, for having me on her own? When they called her all manner of names and insults, where were you? Where were you when she needed you? When *I* needed you?" He pounded a fist to his chest. "No, sir, you do not get to call me that." Alex pointed to Bronach. "He was more of a father to me than you ever will." He seethed, his body shaking.

Caspian looked utterly shocked. Alex found Bronach watching the exchange and looked him in the eye. Bronach gazed back at him with tired eyes that shone, not with pity, but with pride. Alex clenched his fists at his sides. Blood dripped from his hair in front of his eyes. His chest heaved. Bronach nodded in affirmation and gave him a slight smile.

"Don't look at him, look at me." Caspian stepped between them.

Something in Alex broke. He let out a guttural yell as he took hold deep within himself to his magic... beyond himself, to Kynthelic, Chantara, and Vesuviius. As he reached out with his mind and will, he imagined a great river rushing to him from every direction. He drew the magic to himself, in spite of the iron cuffs on his wrists and ankles. His skin glowed as if covered in dragon scales. The iron shackles burned red, then orange, where they touched his skin, and melted off entirely.

Alex's eyes glowed white as he directed his attention to Bronach's restraints. Seconds later, they also melted and fell to the floor. Distantly, he heard shouting. Someone slashed Alex with a sword, but it melted on contact.

Heat radiated outward like a wall, repelling any assailants and pushing everyone back against the walls. The smell of burning hair filled the air. He walked out the nearest door and called to the wind. It whipped around him, lifting him off the ground and into the air. He was vaguely aware of Bronach yelling at him, but he couldn't hear over the raging inferno in his mind and gusting wind.

Enough. He'd had enough. No more. No longer would he take what others dealt him. No more would he let anyone else belittle him or his family. He could protect them now. He could protect everyone.

Alex focused on the iron grid work of the arena and every piece of iron he could feel. He sent it crashing down to the arena floor in pieces of twisted, molten metal. Next, he turned his attention to the guards and enforcers and clenched his fist, withdrawing the air from their lungs, causing them to collapse, grasping at their throats.

Waves of heat rolled off him, and thunderclouds gathered. He closed his eyes and screamed from his core, channeling all his frustration, fear, pain, anger, and defiance into it. Lightning streaked across the sky. It coursed through him down to the ground and spread out, reaching toward his captors. Raw power flowed through him, and time seemed to stand still. It was exhilarating. It struck him how frail life was, how easy it was to end it.

Slow, measured claps rang out over the wind in the courtyard below. *"You... are... magnificent! I can't believe it..."* Indra's voice cut through his mind, breathless, with a hint of pride and awe. *"We are the same, you and I."* That stopped him cold. *"No!"* he thought back. He surveyed the surrounding damage, the unmoving forms of the guards on the ground. Ice ran down his back in sheets. All his fight and fire snuffed out. He dropped to the ground and collapsed, utterly spent physically, mentally, and emotionally.

Heavy footsteps approached. Strong hands lifted him and slung his arm over their broad shoulders, supporting his weight and keeping him upright. "It'll be alright, lad. I've got ye," Bronach's deep voice rumbled in his ears and soothed his raw emotions like salve on a burn.

His body relaxed into Bronach's firm grip and his eyes closed as exhaustion pulled at him, gently at first, then more insistently. The prisoners! Did Ronin get them all out?

"Ronin!" he called frantically in his mind. But he was met with silence. *"Ronin?"* he called again, but the pull of sleep was overwhelming, so he gave himself over to the silence and wrapped himself in it like a comforting blanket.

His dreams were fraught with ever-shifting images of ships and dark tunnels, chains and blood, strange winged creatures, and a large golden tree, his tree.

CHAPTER 41

RONIN knelt on the ground to catch his breath, waiting for his body to knit itself back together, aided by his puka magic. His body trembled with exhaustion and lingering pain. Still, he knew he couldn't wait much longer before he needed to be ready for Alex to return.

"Ronin?"

"It's good to hear your voice again," he responded. He had felt Alex's absence these last days as the iron kept him from reaching out. He had almost believed he would never see him again.

"Same. There are too many guards to get out this way, but I have an idea."

Dread trickled down his spine and made the hair on his arms stand up. *"Why do I have a feeling I won't like this idea?"*

"Do you feel strong enough to grow a tree?"

"A tree?" What was Alex thinking? He looked at the little seedling next to him. *"I could probably manage if given enough time. Why?"*

"I'm going to send everyone your way. I need you to grow that sprout into a tree, up through the arena floor."

"Uh, two problems. What about the guards? And how is being in the arena any better than being down here? We'll still be trapped." His mind raced with possible solutions, but each time, it came back to they were stuck under the iron dome.

"I need to find Bronach."

"No. Nope," he protested. He was not going to lose Alex. Not like this. *"No, we'll figure out a different way."*

"Ro, I have to."

Frustration followed by a warm tightness surged in his chest at Alex's use of the nickname he'd given him back on the *Oleander*. It felt like just yesterday he had stormed onto the ship and held Korynna and Talia at knifepoint, yet a lifetime ago. He wanted to scream. *"I was right. I don't like this idea. Not one bit."* Ronin tried to think of another option besides Alex sacrificing himself to create a diversion. He wanted to tell him to just get himself out, to save himself.

He couldn't ask that of Alex anymore than Alex would of him. Alex would never do that, and Ronin couldn't ask it of him. He blew out a breath in frustration. *"I see your strategy in it. Is there really no other way? What about getting out of the arena? We'll still be trapped up there."*

"Just grow the damn tree and get everyone up there. I'll handle the rest."

Ronin hesitated. He trusted Alex. If he said he'd handle it, Ronin believed Alex would do everything he could to free them. *"I'd say be careful, but nothing about any of this qualifies,"* he trailed off. *"To the world in our dreams…"*

"…and this one here and now," Alex finished.

Ronin's heart felt lighter as he took a shaky breath and stilled his mind. He reached for the calm place within him. His magic felt faint, disconnected, distant. Almost out of reach, like a whisper on the wind.

He moved the iron aside, as far from the seedling as he could, then knelt next to it. Digging his fingers into the sandy floor, he buried his hands halfway up to his elbows. He let the familiar feel of sand glide against his hands as he imagined his magic spreading toward the delicate green shoot between his hands. He felt the faint vibration of life emanating from it. It was strong, but it wasn't meant to be a tree.

He matched its silent melody with his magic, asking if it was willing to change, to become more than it was designed to be. It responded to his magic and grew into a tall stalk of dune grass. Like it was meant to, but no further.

Despair seeped into his mind. He pushed as much magic into the grass as he could before collapsing. He heard a chorus of footfalls fast approaching. *"Alex, bad news. It didn't work. I grew grass, but I can't grow a tree out of a grass seed. Magic doesn't work like that. Any other bright ideas? Alex?"* He was met with silence.

He looked at the single stalk of grass beside him. He'd failed Alex. He'd failed them all. He scolded himself. There was no time for that. He needed to think of another way to get them up to the arena floor above, or Alex's sacrifice would be in vain.

Ronin took a deep breath and decided to try one more time. As he lay on his side, he placed one hand on the ground and the other around the base of the stalk. He reached for his already depleted magic and drew every last granule from within him to the palms of his hands, ready to release it into this grass, to instruct it to multiply and break through the barrier between it and the sunlight it so desperately craved.

Ronin hesitated for a moment more. He knew the consequences of draining the last of his magic. The cost would be his own life, but if Alex could sacrifice himself, so could he. He just hoped it was enough.

As he released his magic, begging it once more to grow tall, strong, and broad, a flood of magic surged from deep within the ground, from the heart of the earth itself. It melded and blended with his own in a harmony he felt, rather than heard. It coursed through and around him, as if seeking an unspoken summons. As it flowed through him, he felt his injuries heal, his tired body now imbued with more energy than he'd ever felt before. What was this?

The grass in his palm responded to this unknown flood of new magic. Its song changed as it began to change. He watched, not believing his own senses, as it thickened, growing bark and branches. Taller and taller, it rose toward the roof, this impossible tree. It pressed against the ceiling, pausing only a moment before it split the rocks easily. Sand and stone rained down on him as he was pushed aside by the ever-growing, twisting trunk. The ground shifted under him as its roots sunk down deep in the sand and into the stone floor beneath.

Suddenly, a shaft of sunlight illuminated the room as the tree broke through to the arena above. Ronin scrambled to stand and find his balance as he saw others shrink back from the now-open doorway a root had opened.

"Let's go!" Ronin yelled, half growling at the young, dirt-caked face that peeked through the doorway. There were several more people standing behind them. "We need to go now!" He motioned for them to join him at the base of the tree as it grew and expanded upward and outward.

They hesitated and drew back a moment before lifting their chin with a determined set to their shoulders as they ran forward. People streamed into the ever-shrinking room and began climbing the writhing, twisted roots toward freedom.

Ronin returned his attention to the tree and reached upward to find purchase for his hands to climb. A handhold formed just above where he was reaching, as if it knew what he needed. Just like before, he looked for his next handhold, and it formed where he needed it. He climbed as fast as he could, dodging newly grown branches in the process. He reached the arena floor and lept from the tree. His heart sank. The iron was still in place over the arena and all the exits.

Ronin desperately searched for a way out. Others had reached the arena as well. Some exclaimed in astonishment over never having seen a tree like this before, let alone grow this fast. Others asked the same question he was wondering, *How would they get out?* The tree kept growing, so Ronin climbed as high up as he could.

He heard several shouts below him. They were pointing to something rising into the air a little way off. Not something, someone.

"Alex," he breathed. Ronin watched in awe as Alex rose into the air in a cyclone of wind and turned to look at him. Almost as if he heard Ronin call his name. Alex reached out a hand as if reaching towards him. Ronin heard a wrenching sound above him as he felt the air around him heat. He watched as the metal glowed red hot, broke off in pieces, and fell to the ground.

"Look out! Take cover!" Ronin called below him. The others scrambled back under the tree as bits of hot metal rained around them.

Ronin looked up at Alex as he turned away and made a fist. Thunder clouds billowed and rolled in the sky, where moments before it had been clear. Lightning danced in a display of raw, intense power. Did Alex do this?

His breath caught when a bolt struck Alex and coursed through him to the ground. Ronin was too far away, but Alex seemed alright. He let out a breath of relief and admiration. *How was he doing this?* A moment later, his heart skipped a beat as Alex dropped from the sky out of view.

"Alex!" he called with his mind, panicked. He called out again, willing with every fiber of his being that Alex was alright. *"Alex! Answer me, please."* Silence echoed in his mind. He needed to get to Alex.

Ronin clung to the tree branches in stunned silence for a few moments as he tried to tell himself that Alex was fine. The tree had stopped growing at an accelerated rate. He tried to shift, but he was too spent. He had expended all of his magic. It would be a long time - days, weeks even, before he could shift, if ever again. Only time would tell.

He scrambled down the tree. When he reached the sandy floor, he found himself surrounded by a group of injured humans and fae looking to him for direction.

"Ronin!" His head whipped around toward the familiar voice. Through the crumbling remains of what used to be the arena's main entrance strode a short figure with fiery red hair, followed by a tall, dark-haired figure leading a group.

"K-" He stopped himself. What was he supposed to call her? Not sure what to say, he surveyed her group. It comprised citizens of Moradon, navy sailors, *Oleander* crew, soldiers, and even a few palace guards.

He blinked in surprise. How had she managed to bring all these people here? These people! Who, by every right, were potential enemies. Someone noticed a few of the minotaur, and suddenly there was shouting and weapons being drawn. The two groups faced each other, each intent on violence.

"Stop!" The words were out of his mouth before he realized he'd spoken. He stepped between the groups and held up his hands. The freed prisoners stopped, watching him with awe and reverence. They thought he did all this? He'd have to deal with that later. Right now, he needed to stop this.

Korynna's group seemed less inclined to listen. Some stopped, the ones who recognized him, but the others were too busy yelling about monsters needing slain.

"Halt," Korynna's voice cut through the din, and silence fell around them soon after. She stepped next to him and grasped his hand, and squeezed. "It's good to see you alive. It seems we missed all the fun." The corners of her mouth turned up in a half smile.

"I wouldn't say that. Seems you brought some of the fun with you. Have you seen Alex?"

"No, we have just arrived to see a tree growing out of the dry riverbed that hasn't had water for over one hundred years."

"Longer actually."

"What?"

"Nothing."

She tilted her head at him, but didn't challenge him. They turned to watch more people crawl up the tree and out into the arena. "What is this place? What happened here?"

"This is what some of the rich and powerful and shady of Reyall call 'The Underground.' As you are aware, they have been abducting people from all over. They dress them, us, up in different costumes and force us to fight for their entertainment. Quite often, to the death."

Korynna gasped. "I knew people could be brutal, but this… this is another level of horrible altogether."

Ronin nodded silently in agreement, resisting the urge to rub his wrists. He would not soon forget the horrors he had witnessed these last days. He shuddered to think of the others who had been here longer.

They were joined by some of the *Oleander* crew, who practically threw themselves at Korynna. They eyed some of the navy sailors warily, then turned their attention to Ronin.

"You saved us! Are we actually free? I had given up hope until that other one showed up."

"The other one?" Korynna inquired. Her eyebrow quirked up at Ronin.

"Yeah, the one with the flaming pony by his side. I thought I'd right gone mad and were seein' things until the doors opened and let us out."

"Flaming pony?" Her brows furrowed as if she didn't know whether to believe him or not.

"I'll explain later. Also, I didn't free you. I didn't even grow the tree, not really. I only helped it along a little. That was all Alex. Speaking of which, I need to find him. Can you handle things here for a bit?"

Korynna looked amused and slightly offended, but nodded.

Ronin hesitated for a moment, debating if he should run or fly. Could he even fly? Flying would be faster, but that would mean revealing himself and one of his abilities. Everyone had already seen some crazy things today. What's one more? He was going to try.

"Go. I can handle things here. Even those…" she pointed to the minotaur milling about or huddled in groups watching everything fearfully.

"It's not that," he said, then shrugged. He ran a couple of steps away, then jumped... and shifted seamlessly to his falcon. Gasps of surprise followed him into the air. A few others shifted as well and followed him. He circled overhead once, then shot out towards the rest of the compound.

His exhilaration of the shift and flight was overshadowed by his desperate need to get to Alex. He surveyed the ground below as he rose in the drafts of warm air. The others flew in formation behind him, waiting for his direction.

There were bodies everywhere. He couldn't tell from here if they were dead or just unconscious. None of them looked like Alex. Black, jagged lines in the sand spread out from a central point like tree roots. As he flew closer, he smelled singed hair and dirt.

This was from lightning? Did Alex do this? How? His thoughts whirred through his mind as he dove toward the prone form in the center. Alex.

"*NO!*" Was he too late? He couldn't be dead. "*Alex? Alex! Don't do this to me. Please be okay, Alex,*" he called with his mind, but was met with silence. He shifted as he landed and tucked into a roll. Bronach lifted Alex's limp body from the ground.

"It'll be alright, lad. I've got ye," Bronach said as Ronin raced up next to him.

"Is he...?"

"He's alive. Though I don't rightly know how. He shouldn't be, but he's breathing." Bronach repositioned his grip on Alex.

"I don't know where we can take him to let him rest."

"I do," Quinn said quietly.

Ronin hadn't even seen him in his mad dash to Alex's side.

"Lead the way," Bronach said, dipping his head toward him.

Quinn led them to a hatch in the ground, mostly disguised by sand and rocks. He pulled on a ring and revealed a set of stairs leading underground. The stairs led to a series of tunnels lined with torches.

"What is this place?" Ronin asked as he surveyed the small room. It had a cot against the wall, and a hole cut into the wall to let light in. It was too small for a person to fit through, but Ronin thought he could fit through in his falcon or otter forms if needed.

Ronin shook his head to clear the thoughts of needing escape routes. This place had changed him. Before, he would have scoped defensible positions, but now, small, dark spaces underground made his skin crawl. His chest tightened with anxiety. He forced down the desperate need to race back upstairs into the bright open space.

"Ye alright?" Bronach broke into Ronin's thoughts.

"What? Yes." Ronin realized his breathing was fast and erratic. He was quickly losing the battle to hold himself in this room. He wanted to stay with Alex. To help him, but he didn't know what he could do. The walls felt like they were closing in around him. He knew they weren't actually, but that didn't stop a cold sweat from breaking out on his skin.

Bronach smiled sadly at him. "Go. I'll stay with him."

Ronin was torn. He shivered in spite of the warm air coming in the window.

"C'mon. We can't do anything for him," Quinn said, uncharacteristically subdued.

Ronin followed him out into the tunnel and back up the stairs.

"They'll need someone to organize everyone. Supplies, healers, food, and the like..." Quinn trailed off, looking at him expectantly.

"And you think I should? Why can't you do it?" Ronin asked.

"Because too many people saw me as a part of the guards. They'll never follow me. But I suspect they'll follow you. They'd definitely follow him if he ever wakes up."

"When. When he wakes up."

"As you say. Either way, they need someone now, before fights break out over limited resources."

Ronin nodded. Quinn was right. Leading people made him uneasy at best. He couldn't help but see flashes of his old unit and comrades. He blinked them away and started making plans.

"Well, we should map out the tunnels if someone hasn't already, take stock of supplies, organize groups to search for any more prisoners or guards, designate sleeping arrangements, and watch rotations..." He ticked off things as they came to him.

Quinn's eyes blazed with something Ronin couldn't name. "I'll organize a team to map out the area and search for others." He turned without waiting for Ronin to respond and strode away.

Ronin went in search of Korynna to help organize everything else. He thought about what they should call this place. He didn't know if it had a name before, but the word "Maraithe" was stuck in his head.

Slaughter.

Everyone would know what had happened here. But, there would be no more bloodshed, not if he had anything to say about it. He pushed aside his racing thoughts and focused on the tasks at hand.

CHAPTER 42

ALEX awoke to the steady drip of water nearby. It exacerbated his pounding headache. It was dark in the room and his body ached all over. He must have groaned because he heard footsteps approaching.

"Ronin? Where's Ronin?" Alex rasped, his throat dry and gritty.

"He's fine. He and Korynna are seeing to the wounded and the rest of the rescued." Bronach helped him sit up and placed a cup in his hand.

Alex slumped with relief. It worked. He got everyone out. "Bronach, are you okay? I thought I was going to lose you. I can't even begin to process what you went through. How..."

Bronach's deep, soothing voice interrupted him. "It is ok, lad. What's done is done." He placed his large, warm hand on Alex's knee.

"I..."

"I'm not sure he wants to see you," a voice called from further away. From down a hallway, maybe?

"I need to speak with him!" Caspian's voice sounded desperate.

Two sets of footsteps approached. Alex took a deep, steadying breath and braced himself for confrontation.

"I didn't know," Caspian said earnestly. He grasped Alex's hand. Alex tried not to jerk away at the contact.

"You have to believe me. I didn't know. Her father and his men made me go. They said she would be better off without me. Said he would kill me if I came back. Said he would kill her before he'd let her be with the likes of me. I thought…" His words came out in pained gasps.

"I thought it was for the best. I have never stopped thinking about her. Many times I meant to go see her, see how she was, but I was… afraid… a coward. I thought it would be too painful to see her with someone else, having the life I wanted with her. I should've…" He trailed off and sighed. "I guess what I'm trying to say is, for what it's worth, I'm sorry."

Alex didn't have the energy to deal with this right now. He felt so tired. His head ached, his eyes burned, and his whole body trembled with the effort of just sitting up. He shook his head, then realized Caspian wouldn't be able to see that in the dark. "I… I just need more sleep." He set his empty cup on the floor and laid back down. Turned away from them and pulled his knees to his chest.

"But…" Caspian protested.

"Let the lad rest," Bronach interjected. "He's been through a lot. By all accounts, he shouldn't still be alive with what he did."

Alex sighed with relief as he heard footsteps fade in the distance, and he welcomed sleep as it claimed him again.

XXX

A warm breeze woke him as it caressed his face. He had no idea how long he had slept, but thankfully there had been no more dreams. When he opened his eyes, it was still dark out. He sat up. His head still ached and his eyes burned like he had gotten sand in them. He tried calling his fire foal to give him light, but nothing happened. He felt hollow where his magic had once been.

"Alex! Hey, he's awake!" Ronin exclaimed in the silence.

"Ronin! Something is wrong with my magic! It's not there. I feel... I feel empty. Is it normally like this when you use too much magic?"

The bed shifted with Ronin's added weight as he sat down. Despite his worries over his magic, the tension in Alex's chest loosened with Ronin's presence.

"I don't know, Alex." Ronin sighed. "No one has done what you did as far as anyone remembers."

"But it comes back, right?"

"I... I don't know."

Ronin rested his hand on Alex's arm. "I'll get you some food. Wait right there."

"Can you bring a torch or lantern with you or something?"

"Sure thing."

Ronin moved so quietly Alex never heard him leave or return.

"Here you go! All the lanterns are empty or currently being used, but I'll find something to grow a torch for you after you eat." He handed Alex a loaf of bread and sat shoulder-to-shoulder with him while they ate. "You gave us quite a scare. I'm glad you are okay," he murmured, his voice sounding relieved.

"How long did I sleep?"

"Seven days the first time, then another five this last time, so a fortnight, give or take."

Alex whistled. "That long? I'm surprised I'm not starving."

"Oh, we kept the nutrient poultices on you so your body could absorb what it needed while it was healing. They are not nearly as satisfying or delicious as eating, but they keep you alive when food is scarce," Ronin explained.

He finished his last bite and felt the familiar tug of sleep on his mind as he yawned. "Thank you, Ronin. That sounds interesting. I think I'd like to learn more about them later, but for now, I think I'm going to sleep a little more. Wake me in the morning?" He started to lie back down.

"Uh, Alex, it is morning. In fact, it's almost midday."

He froze. "What?! No. But how is it so dark?"

"Dark?" He took Alex's face in his hands and tilted his head up. "Oh Alex," he breathed.

Something in his voice made Alex panic. "Ronin, what do you mean? What's wrong?"

"You can't see me? It is a bright day with lots of light streaming in the window." He turned Alex's head to the left. "The sunlight is striking your face, and you are saying it is completely black?"

"I'm blind?" Something in him that had slowly been healing while he slept shattered. He pulled away from Ronin and felt his face with his hands. Nothing felt different. His head throbbed, sure, but that was normal. Wasn't it? His eyes felt like they had gotten too much saltwater in them. Pulling his knees up to his chest, he rested his chin on his knees. He felt numb. How? Why? He didn't understand.

He didn't hear anything else Ronin said, but was vaguely aware of when he left a while later. People came and went, but he shut them all out. Helplessness and devastation gnawed at him. Eventually, he gave in to the voices in his head: "Useless. Worthless. Helpless. A burden. Good for nothing. Unwanted."

He refused to eat and spent his time curled up on the bed, drifting in and out of consciousness.

XXX

"Lad, you need to get out of bed," Bronach's deep, rich voice broke into Alex's brooding. Bronach gripped his shoulder gently. "I'm headed back to Creedon with some of the survivors tomorrow. Fin's husband, Karl, has healed enough to travel. I had hoped ye would come with me."

"Why? So everyone can see me like this? So everyone can make fun of the poor boy who lost his sight and now can't even mend nets? So they can take pity on the poor, useless sot whose own father was responsible for the death of so many?" Alex snapped.

"That's not how it is at all."

"What do you know? Everything is easy for you."

"Alexander. Stop this." Bronach raised his voice.

Alex burned with shame. Bronach knew better than anyone what it was to be the outsider and unwanted. "I'm... sorry," he mumbled.

"I know this isn't easy for you, lad. Get out of bed and keep getting out of bed. Just focus on taking the next step." He patted Alex's shoulder. "You'll be alright. Let yourself heal."

"But what if it never comes back?" Alex voiced the question that had been plaguing him.

"Your sight or your magic?"

"Both?"

"Then you'll learn to live with it."

"I don't *want* to learn to live with it! I want back what I had," Alex growled and rolled to face away from Bronach so he wouldn't see the tears forming in his eyes. "Just go away and leave me alone."

Bronach sighed and placed his large hand on Alex's shoulder and squeezed. "Give it time, lad." He shuffled away. Alex heard him mutter something under his breath, but didn't catch what he said.

"You know he is worried about you," Ronin said as he sat on the edge of Alex's bed. Alex hadn't realized he was there.

"Would everyone just leave me alone? Don't you all get that? I want to be left alone. Go away, Ronin!" Alex yelled. He knew he was acting childish, but he couldn't find it in himself to care.

"You want to be alone? Fine," Ronin growled and stalked off.

✗✗✗

Ronin burst into the room, swearing up a storm. He was angry and hurt and worried. The floor vibrated as he walked.

Quinn looked up from his deep stretch pose. "What's eating you?" Quinn shifted positions to stretch his legs, taking controlled, measured breathing timed with his slow movements. Quinn seemed unfazed by Ronin's outburst.

Ronin paced the room in silent fury. He was tempted to ask Quinn to spar with him to blow off steam. Anything to get his mind off Alex.

"I don't know what to do," Ronin said finally.

"About?"

"Alex."

"Oh," Quinn sighed. "Alex isn't improving, I take it? Do you want me to talk to him?"

Ronin gave him a skeptical look. "He won't even listen to Bronach. He's withering away to nothing. He won't eat or drink. He just lays there. This isn't like him. It's like he's given up on living." Frustration roiled in his chest. The ground rumbled again. He was quickly losing control, and his magic was responding. He took deep breaths to calm himself and rein in his emotions and magic.

"I have an idea, but you might not like my methods."

"I'm willing to try anything at this point."

"Alright then." Quinn rose from his last stretch. "I need you to trust me and not interfere."

Ronin blew out a breath. "If it means I get my Alex back, I'll trust you."

Quinn held Ronin's gaze. "I know he means a lot to you."

"I sent for Mahkai. Don't give me that look. I didn't know what else to do. Maybe he knows something. You know how he is. He knows something about everything."

Quinn scowled at him. "Just keep him out of my way."

"That might be a bit difficult since I told him he could take notes in his books about whatever he wanted."

CHAPTER 43

ALEX felt the sharp sting of a slap to the face. "Hey!" he cried out.

"Get up!" Quinn commanded.

"Leave me alone." Alex huffed.

"No. Now get up," he commanded again.

Something heavy landed in Alex's lap. He ran his hands along it. It felt like a wooden staff. He pushed it off the bed onto the floor and turned over. "Go away, Quinn. What are you doing here anyway?" He flinched from a rap on his side.

"Get up, Alex," Quinn's tone of voice implied he wouldn't take no for an answer.

Alex felt another rap on his side. He winced, but didn't move. The soft scrape of wood on stone sounded nearby as Quinn picked the staff off the floor and dropped it next to him on the bed.

"So you are going to hide in here like a coward?" Quinn jabbed him in the leg. "It seems Corsen was right about you. The other knights were right about you too." Another jab.

Alex felt a flash of anger. Before he realized what he was doing, he was on his feet, striking out where he thought Quinn was. Wood cracked against wood as his staff hit Quinn's. He lunged again. All he could think was to teach him a lesson, to hurt him like he'd been hurt, to make him pay for what he did. How could he betray his own people? Why?

He dropped to his knees. "Why?"

"Why what?"

"Why are you here? Why did you betray your people? Why did you..."

"Why did I betray you? Is that what you mean to ask? Because I did. It happened. Move on. Get over it."

"Why do you care? Why are you here?" Alex could hear his own voice laced with bitterness and misery.

"I don't. Not about you, but I care about Ronin and what you are doing to him. We all have our backstories, Alex. Even you. So pull yourself together." Quinn's voice rumbled.

Alex slumped to the floor. His eyes burned. Hot tears rolled down his face. He couldn't do this. He couldn't be who Ronin wanted him to be, who the guardians wanted him to be. How was he supposed to defend anything, to save the world if he couldn't even save himself? He was useless.

He recognized the spiral he was heading down mentally. Ronin's voice echoed in his head, telling him to pull himself out of it. He heard the disappointment in everyone's voices. He could even picture their disappointed faces in his mind.

Not fae. Not human. Not royal. Not even a real knight. He was nothing.

"Are you done yet?" Quinn's deep baritone voice cut into his cyclone of thoughts.

Alex snarled. "No. Happy? Leave me alone. You've done enough."

"Oh, this again? Very well."

Alex heard the clatter of his staff hitting the ground in front of him. He reached for it, but heard it roll away, further out of his reach. He cocked his head and heard the faint swish of fabric indicating where Quinn was.

Alex felt the familiar tension of fury building in his chest. Quinn had kicked it away on purpose. Bastard. No, that was him. He was the bastard, the unwanted everything. All the fight drained out of him, and he slumped back against the wall.

"Again? Really, Alex. I had thought you better than this. Oh, come now. Is that all you've got? Pitiful," Quinn taunted.

Alex was angry, furious even. He climbed to his feet and swung the staff wildly, trying desperately to hit him.

"You're going to have to do better than that if you are going to hit me." Quinn chuckled as Alex swung and missed again.

Alex took a deep breath and centered his stance, letting his muscle memory guide his body. It knew what to do, even if he couldn't see. He would just have to use his other senses. He swung again. Crack. He heard the sound of wood striking wood.

"Not bad for a pathetic human," Quinn taunted him again.

They went at each other like that for a while. Quinn taunting him, Alex striking at him, trying to land blows, but mostly missing. The longer they fought, the better he started to feel, more like himself again.

Alex's body trembled with fatigue, so he waved a hand and sat down on the sandy floor of the training room. Quinn handed him a canteen. He drank his fill, then handed it back. He found himself smiling in spite of it all.

"What?" Quinn asked.

"Thank you."

Quinn snorted.

"No, really, thank you."

"We'll have none of that," Quinn said gruffly. "Now get up and go again."

"Hey! Why do you treat him so poorly?" a voice yelled from the entrance. "All you do is bully him! What are you even doing here anyway? You should be locked up with the other guards! You are one of them, after all!" They yelled louder as they ran into the room.

Alex heard and felt their footfalls speeding toward Quinn. He felt Quinn jump to his feet to face this new person.

"If they won't put you in chains, then I'll put you where you belong. In the ground," the voice declared.

"Stop!" Alex shouted. "Leave Quinn alone," he rose to his feet and shuffled toward the voice as quickly as he could. He attempted to put himself between the voice and Quinn. Quinn placed a hand on his chest and tried to move him out of the way, but Alex gripped his forearm instead.

He knew they could simply step around him if they really wanted to fight, but he wouldn't stand aside and let them attack Quinn. "Stop," he said again, more quietly. The room was silent except for their breathing.

"Now I see what you are doing," he said to Quinn.

"You can see again?" Quinn sounded uncharacteristically hopeful.

"No, no. Still completely dark, but I understand why you have been treating me the way you have."

"How can you defend him?" the voice demanded.

"Oh? And why is that?" Quinn's tone skeptical.

"You gave me someone to fight other than myself. You drew me out the only way you knew how, by getting under my skin. Conflict, competition, and strife, if used constructively, actually accelerate and become the catalyst for growth." He turned to the other person. "Without him, there would be no me. Without his actions and role these last few weeks, I would not be where I am today—who I am. I don't want you to kill him or chain him up. I want to thank him." Alex turned back to Quinn and walked as steadily as he could toward him. He reached out until he found Quinn's shoulder and squeezed.

"I appreciate everything you have done," Alex said, his voice thick with sudden emotions. "Thank you, brother."

XXX

Over the next week, Alex allowed Quinn to help him train. Quinn even started teaching him his stretching and breathing exercises to help him with his balance. Ronin and Mahkai came in occasionally to talk with him as he walked the corridors, learning to navigate with his other senses.

"Alex, there are some people to see you if you are up for it," Ronin said.

Alex nodded as he rose from the ground on unsteady legs. He wiped the sweat from his face with his sleeve and focused on steadying his breathing.

"How's he doing?" Ronin asked Quinn in a low voice as they moved away from Alex.

Suddenly, someone grasped his hands. "You saved us! How can I ever repay you?" a high-pitched voice asked as they clasped his hands and shook them up and down.

"I didn't..." Alex protested.

"I know! Can I get you anything? Where you go, I shall go! I will be your humble servant and do whatever it is you need. Are you hungry? I can bring you the best meal! Thirsty? I'll climb to the highest of mountains to find the sweetest spring and bring back the water to quench your thirst. I will…"

"Hold up, slow down," Alex interrupted their dramatic monologue. "I'm fine, really. You don't need to do all that."

They gasped. "You are most humble and modest! Only the best will do for the savior of Maraithe. Here, let me wipe the sweat off your brow with the shirt off my back. I insist. It is a great honor to serve you."

Alex protested, but that only seemed to encourage them further. He felt awkward and wished Ronin or Quinn would come back and rescue him from this over-eager admirer. He shuffled toward where he thought the door was and used his quarterstaff to feel the floor in front of him.

"Here." He felt them take his arm in theirs as they started guiding him. "It would be an honor to act as your eyes until the glorious day that you regain your sight and rise up to vanquish our foes."

Alex huffed at their dramatics. "No, really, I can manage on my own."

"No, no. I insist. Where would you like to go?" they continued. "To the Commander's Villa? Or perhaps you would like…"

"Actually, there is something you can do for me," Alex interjected.

"Oh, anything. Just name it." They sounded pleased.

"Can you draw water for me to bathe?"

"I will arrange it at once! Leave everything to me! It will be the most magnificent bath you have ever had," they said grandly before dashing off, leaving Alex alone.

"Finally," he sighed before continuing down the corridor. He heard someone laughing to his right.

"They can be a bit much," a familiar voice said. "We haven't been formally introduced. I'm Vithia. I am one of the people you gave keys to and instructed to free everyone in my cell block," she said by way of explanation.

He remembered her, though everything after that was still a bit hazy. He nodded anyway. "How can I help you?" he asked.

"I'd like to offer my assistance." Alex must have given her a look because she hurriedly continued, "Not that kind of assistance. I mean assistance with leading your army."

"My army? I don't have an army." Alex was confused.

"Oh, but you certainly do. Many of the fighters from the arena have left to go back to wherever they came from, but many of us either have nowhere and no one to go back to, or we are choosing not to. People like myself.

"Since I was a small sprite, I've been told what my value and destiny would be, but I always dreamed of something different, something more. Some of us heard about what you said about creating a better world. A world where everyone is equal. We want to be a part of a place like that. Will you help us create that? Will you lead us?" Vithia said with conviction.

"I can't. You have the wrong person. I don't have an army, and even if I did, I can't even see." He waved his hand in front of his face.

"Here, come with me. I need you to hear something," she said as she gently took his elbow and led him through the maze of tunnels.

Voices echoed throughout the tunnels as they approached what he was starting to recognize as the main eating hall. A hush fell over the room as they entered. Alex nervously played with his sleeve hem. These last weeks, he had avoided anyone besides Ronin, Quinn, and Mahkai. He worried about what everyone would say, so it had just been easier to avoid everyone altogether.

He heard the scrape of a chair on the stone floor in front of him, then a whole chorus of them. People whispered around the room, "The general! Did you know he was coming?"

"The general!"

"The general is here?"

"I heard he's been recuperating and training in a new combat discipline."

"The general!"

"He truly can't see? What a sacrifice."

The general? Are they talking about me? He wondered.

"We saw you fight for us, and what you did to the guards and the arena. We all saw even the sky respond to your call," Vithia said. The room called out their agreements.

"They are calling for you to lead us. You freed us and we are grateful, but we have nowhere else to go. Wherever you are going, whatever you are doing, please, let us come with you." She raised her voice for the entire room to hear.

"You said you envision a world where we can all be equals, no matter what we look like or whether or not we have magic. Where every person's life is valuable, regardless of their station, power, or birth. Where the leaders do what is best for their people. You said everyone is worth protecting and fighting for. That we have value. We matter. Let us help build that world. We choose you to lead us," she projected loudly.

The room called out their agreement and encouragement. "Hear, hear!", "Aye!"

I want that more than anything, Alex thought. "Humans and fae living alongside each other peacefully. But what if it's impossible?" He voiced the question all the negative voices in his head were saying.

"So what if it is?" Ronin came up beside him and placed a hand on his shoulder. "No one ever did the impossible without being put in an impossible situation."

"You're not alone; you'll have our support," Quinn said from behind him. "We'll do this together."

Alex took a deep breath. He was still uncertain, but nodded his head anyway. *You can't go back, only forward,* he thought, hearing Bronach's voice from many lessons when he was younger. He let out a sigh. "Alright. Let's do the impossible."

CHAPTER 44

"WE are almost there, my love," he said as the familiar stone markers came into view.

"Finally! I thought we would never get here," Alice sighed dramatically. "Wait! How does the story end? What happens next? What about Talia, Mahkai and Quinn and…"

He smiled affectionately. "That is a story for another time."

Laughter and music drifted toward them down the path. They emerged from the trail through the trees into a large clearing in the heart of the forest. The surface of the lake glittered in the afternoon sunlight. Alice danced and skipped excitedly beside him, the story all but forgotten.

"Alright, alright. Go on." He chuckled as she took off running. Her twin auburn braids bounced as her cloak billowed behind her. She squealed with delight as she found her friends. They embraced, then began a game of chase.

Two long stone tables stretched before him, soon to be laden with large baskets and platters of food for the feast tonight. He waved back to a group of ladies and nodded in turn to a pair as they strolled by. Several groups were already setting up for the festivities, and many more would join them by the day's end. Colorful streamers tied to branches fluttered in the gentle breeze. A little boy looked at him shyly from his cross-legged seat on the ground surrounded by flowers he was braiding into crowns.

"Ronin, it's good to see you!"

He turned toward the familiar voice. "And you, Zeit. You are looking well!" Ronin grasped his forearm in greeting.

Zeit smiled, the laugh lines around his eyes and his pure white hair the only evidence of his age. He nodded in Alice's direction. "She looks more and more like her mother each time I see her. Does she also have her cunning and strong will?"

Ronin grinned proudly. "She gets that from both of her parents."

"She will be a force to be reckoned with, I'd imagine," Zeit laughed. He leaned on his walking staff.

"She already is," Ronin agreed as he watched Alice outsmart the other children at their game.

"Well, I must continue on. Althenaea needs my advice about something or other." Zeit shook his head and chuckled. "I'll catch up with you a bit later, hmmm?" He patted Ronin's shoulder, then wandered off.

Ronin turned toward the edge of the clearing to set up their hammocks and stow their gear. After he finished, he sought out the solitary structure in the clearing. The large moss and ivy-covered stone archway rose well over his head, like a sentinel keeping watch over its companions.

"Oh, Ronin, good day. You simply must try my new blend of tea," Mahkai's familiar deep voice greeted him. Mahkai pulled out two cups from his bag and handed them to Ronin. He pulled a long cylindrical container from a different pouch and removed the lid. A faintly sweet, floral aroma greeted them as Mahkai poured a steaming golden liquid into both cups.

Ronin breathed deeply and handed Mahkai the second cup. "Mmm, thank you, Mahkai. This may be your best yet."

"You think so? Thank you. I added jasmine from Rose's garden. Oh, I wonder. Do you suppose…" Mahkai trailed off as he shuffled away.

Ronin watched him wander away for a moment, then sighed and turned back toward the arch. He rested his forehead on the left stone pillar and closed his eyes. Its cool, smooth surface grounded him as he shut out everything else around him. His fingers traced the familiar words carved into the rock face. He didn't need to see them to know what was inscribed.

To the world in our dreams and the one that made us,
And this one, here and now.

He set his cup beneath the arch and sat watching the steam swirl lazily through the empty stone doorway. The evening's golden sunlight bathed everything in a soft, warm glow. He lingered, unmoving a while longer, listening to the joy and vibrancy of life around him, letting it wash over him, through him. Taking a deep breath, he straightened, squaring his shoulders and lifting his chin.

The clearing had quieted somewhat. Ronin smiled fondly and wondered what mischief and mayhem his daughter might be up to. He rose from the ground and brushed a stray blade of grass off his tunic. Sighing, he turned his back to the monolith and went in search of Alice.

In the center of the glen, Alice stood atop a broad, flat rock, gesturing excitedly with grand, sweeping movements. She looked to be acting out an epic fight scene. She parried and twirled against an invisible enemy on her makeshift stage, slightly elevated above the other children seated in the grass. Pride and affection warmed Ronin's chest as he watched her captivate her audience. Finishing her performance, she sat on the rock with a fierce yet satisfied grin on her face.

"Tell us another!" they begged in chorus. "Please?"

"Alright," she agreed. "How about the legend of Sir Alexander and Bucephalus?" A hush fell on the group, and they leaned toward her, not wanting to miss a single word of her tale. Her eyes sparkled, and she leaned in conspiratorially.

"Once upon a time, because that's how the best stories begin..."

EPILOGUE

KREO closed the book with a sigh and stood from his seat on the large chaise lounge. He crossed the room and slid the book into its place on the shelf in the row of other similar-looking books. His fingers glided along the smooth leather spines, silently reading their gilded titles. *Osrealach, Guardian Stones, Peridios and Other Precious Materials, The Tale of Two Warriors, The Lighthouse Inn*… He paused, *The Oleander*.

Gently, almost reverently, he pulled the chosen book off the shelf and carried it to his seat. He gazed out at the nightscape through the open window beside his chair. The light of the full moon illuminated the large stone arch and the stump of an old tree in the center of his garden. A slight mist drifted through the arch on the jasmine scented breeze, reminding him of home.

Refilling his glass of water from the carafe on the tray next to him, he settled into his chair with a blanket on his lap and opened the book. Instantly, the words blurred on the page as he became immersed, transported to another world:

Waves lapped gently against the bow of the ship. The weather-worn, sun-bleached timbers creaked and groaned as the ship rocked gently in the sea. The salty breeze caressed his skin, teasing stray strands of hair across his vision as seagulls cried overhead. He took a deep breath, braced his feet, and drew his cutlass as enemy pirates streamed over the rails and onto the main deck. For a moment, he could feel his mind in both places at once, the library and the ship. He charged into the fray, a fierce grin on his face.

ACKNOWLEDGEMENTS

I want to take a moment to thank some of the key people who were instrumental in bringing about this book. This book wouldn't be possible without each of you and I am deeply grateful!

Allison Hamelin, my Caledonia, thank you for supporting me in a variety of capacities along the way; and for being one of the first to believe in my story way back when it was still just a ridiculous idea.

My alpha & beta readers: Alex, Brandon, Christyn, Kailin, Kristen, Lauren, Missy, and Vendy. You are my superheroes! I appreciate the hours you spent reading my stories and giving your thoughts and feedback. There were days your encouragement was the only thing that kept me going.

My parents. Thank you for letting me sit on your couch and spew nonsense for hours at a time until it was a bit less nonsense. And for all the other ways you have supported me throughout the years to get us here.

Amanda and her amazing team at Line by Lion publishing, Thank you for making my dream a reality and patiently answering all my questions!

And finally, to you my dear readers. Thank you for loving my world and characters and joining me on this crazy adventure.

Ingram Content Group UK Ltd.
Milton Keynes UK
UKHW021950270323
419267UK00016B/430/J